Michelle Smart's love af[...] she was a baby and she w[...] A voracious reader of all g[...] of romance established when she stumbled across her first Mills & Boon book at the age of twelve. She's been reading them—and writing them—ever since. Michelle lives in Northamptonshire, England, with her husband and two young Smarties.

Kate Walker was born in Nottingham, in the UK, but grew up in West Yorkshire. She met her husband at university in Wales and originally worked as a children's librarian. After the birth of her son she returned to her childhood love of writing. Her first book was published in 1984. She now lives in Lincolnshire with her husband—also a writer— and two cats who think they rule her life.

Discover more at millsandboon.co.uk

A BRIDE
AT HIS BIDDING

BY
MICHELLE SMART

A PROPOSAL
TO SECURE
HIS VENGEANCE

BY
KATE WALKER

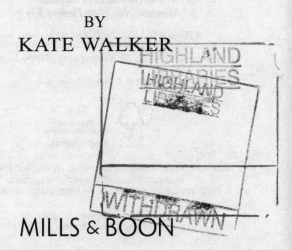

MILLS & BOON

First Published in Great Britain 2018
by Mills & Boon, an imprint of HarperCollins*Publishers*
1 London Bridge Street, London, SE1 9GF

A Bride at His Bidding © 2018 by Michelle Smart

A Proposal to Secure His Vengeance © 2018 by Kate Walker

ISBN: 978-0-263-93519-6

Printed and bound in Spain
by CPI, Barcelona

A BRIDE
AT HIS BIDDING

CHAPTER ONE

ANDREAS SAMARAS POKED his head into the adjoining office to his own. Having spent the day on a multinational conference call, he needed to check in with his PA.

'How is everything going?'

Debbie sighed. 'The world is going to hell in a hand-cart.'

'Quite.' His PA's theatrical tendencies were infamous throughout Samaras Fund Management. Andreas would find it wearing if she weren't the best business PA he'd ever had. 'Apart from that, is there anything I need to know? With regards to the business,' he hastened to add in case she started harping on about polar bears and Arctic ice melt again.

'Nothing important.'

'Good. How did the interviews go? Have you come up with a shortlist for me?' Rochelle, his domestic PA, had quit. The smitten fool was getting married and had decided that a job requiring a great deal of travel was not a good fit for domestic bliss. He'd offered to double her wages and increase her holidays but still she had said no. He'd dragged his heels for weeks about finding a replacement for her in the hope she would change her mind. She hadn't and finally he had accepted defeat.

Debbie held up a stack of papers. 'I've whittled the candidates down to five.'

Andreas stepped into the office. Debbie had been tasked with doing the preliminary interviews. She knew exactly what kind of person he was looking for to take on the role that basically entailed organising his domestic life. It was a live-in role that would see the successful candidate travel wherever he went, ensuring his domestic life ran as smoothly as his business. The person needed to be honest, loyal, unobtrusive and flexible, have impeccable references, a clean driving licence and no criminal record.

He took the papers from her hand and flipped through them. All had a square photograph of the candidate attached to the corner of their applications. It was a requirement he insisted on. Three candidates would make it to the shortlist and he liked to be familiar with their appearance before he met them for the final interview, which he would undertake personally.

By Debbie's computer was a stack of the applicants she'd already rejected. The top one caught his eye. There was something familiar about the direct gaze staring back…

'Why have you rejected this one?' he asked, picking up the form and studying it. Dark hazel eyes stared right back at him. Dark hazel eyes he knew instinctively that he'd seen before.

Debbie peered at it with a frown. 'Oh, her. Caroline Dunwoody. She interviewed well but there was something about her I didn't trust. I don't know what it was. A feeling, nothing more, but it made me check her references in more detail. One of them checks out okay but I'm suspicious of the other one. She says she worked as Head of Housekeeping at Hargate Manor for two years and has a letter in her file to that effect. I spoke to the gentleman who wrote the reference, the Manor's butler, and he verified everything.'

'Then what's the problem?'

'Hargate Manor doesn't exist.'

His eyebrows rose. 'Doesn't exist?'

'There is no Hargate Manor within fifty miles of this one's supposed location.'

If Debbie said it didn't exist then it didn't exist. She was the most thorough person Andreas knew.

He looked more closely at Caroline Dunwoody's photograph, racking his brain trying to remember where he could have met her. He usually had an excellent recall for faces but on this occasion he couldn't put a finger on it. She had dark chestnut hair that fell in a neat line to her shoulders and pretty if angular features, a short straight nose, a top lip slightly fuller than the bottom and a cute heart-shaped chin. Yes, a pretty face but not one familiar to him.

But he had seen those eyes before.

Just as he opened his mouth to order Debbie to do some more digging into this woman, it suddenly came to him.

Digging. Journalists did lots of digging.

Caroline. The extended version of Carrie.

Carrie Rivers. The journalist sister of his niece's old best friend.

The journalist for the *Daily Times* who had made a name for herself by exposing the illegal and often seedy practices of rich businessmen.

He doubted he would still remember their tenuous association were it not that her most recent undercover investigation into James Thomas, an old business acquaintance of his, had revealed James's business to be a cover for drugs, arms and people trafficking. A month ago, Carrie's meticulous work had seen James sentenced to fifteen years in prison. Andreas had read about the sentencing and silently cheered. He hoped he rotted in his cell.

With the feeling of a ball bearing pressing down on his guts, Andreas did an Internet search on his phone for her. There were no photographs of Carrie online. He supposed this wasn't surprising given the nature of her work.

But it was her. He was certain of it.

He'd only met Carrie once, three years ago. It had been such a fleeting moment that it was no surprise he'd struggled to remember. Three years ago, she had been blonde with rounded cheeks.

Her eyes were the only thing about her that hadn't changed. Their gazes had met as he'd left the headmistress's office of his niece's boarding school. Carrie and her sister Violet had been sat in the corridor waiting for their turn to be admitted. Violet had hung her head in shame when she'd seen him. Carrie should have hung her head too.

Neither had known it would be the last time they would be admitted into the headmistress's office. Violet was to be expelled with immediate effect.

Three years on and Carrie was applying for a domestic job with him under a different name and supplying fake references in the process. This did not bode well and his brain groped for reasons as to why she might now be targeting him. Andreas ran a clean business. He paid all his taxes, both personal and corporation, in all the relevant jurisdictions. He followed and exceeded local employment law. His romantic affairs over the years had been consensual and discreet, guilt and responsibility for his family overriding the urge to bed as many beautiful women as possible, something he intended to rectify now all the burdens had been lifted from his shoulders.

One thing Andreas had learned over his thirty-seven

years was that when problems cropped up, the only thing to do was keep a clear head and deal with them immediately, stopping the problems escalating into catastrophe.

A plan quickly formed in his mind. He inhaled deeply then smiled. 'Debbie, I want you to call Miss Dunwoody and invite her back for a second interview.'

Debbie looked at him as if he'd sprouted blossom from his head.

'Back it up with a letter. This is what I want you to say…'

Carrie sat in the spacious reception room of Samaras Fund Management's London headquarters and tried to get air into lungs that seemed to have forgotten how to breathe. Her heart was beating erratically, the thuds loud in her ears, and she had to keep wiping her clammy palms on her thighs.

She'd woken from fractured sleep with her stomach churning so hard she'd had to force her coffee down. Food had been unthinkable.

She had never known nerves like it, although calling this sensation nerves was like calling a river a small trickle of water. Soon she would be taken through to Andreas Samaras's office and she had to contain these mixed and virulent emotions that threatened to crush her.

She hadn't suffered any nerves while going undercover and investigating James Thomas. She'd been ice-cool and focussed as she'd systematically gathered the evidence needed to prove his heinous crimes and expose him, using the same mind-set she used on her regular investigations, her focus never swaying. The day James had been sentenced had been the brightest spot of the last three nightmarish years.

Andreas might not have fed her sister the drugs that had

destroyed her young fragile body but his contribution to Violet's descent into hell had been every bit as lethal as James's and far more personal, and now it was his turn for justice. Carrie could not allow her nerves or conscience to blow it for her…but this time it was different.

It had been common knowledge that James Thomas was a shady figure deserving of proper investigation. Getting permission and backing to go undercover in his workforce had been easy—the whole of the *Daily Times* had wanted that scumbag brought down.

Andreas Samaras, Greek billionaire investor and owner of Samaras Fund Management, was a different kettle of fish. There was nothing in his past or on the rumour mill to suggest he was anything other than clean. Only Carrie knew differently, and when she'd seen the advertisement for a Domestic PA mere days after James had been sentenced, she had known Andreas's time had come. She knew infiltrating his personal life carried a much greater risk than investigating him as an employee in his business life but it was a risk she was willing to take.

Three years ago she had written two names on a piece of paper. She had since struck James's name off. Now it was time to strike Andreas's off too.

To get her newspaper's backing to go undercover though, she'd had to tell a little white lie… A few surprised eyebrows had been raised but the go-ahead had been given. No one had disbelieved her.

As the clock ticked down to the moment she would be taken to see Andreas, the ramifications of her lie rang loudly in her head. If the truth that Carrie was undertaking a personal vendetta was revealed her career would be over. The *Daily Times* was no shady tabloid. It was a highbrow publication that had made it through the trials and tribulations all the British press had been through over the past decade with its reputation largely intact. It was a good employer too.

If they could print only a fraction of what was suspected about some of the world's most powerful people the public would need vodka spiked into the water system to help them get over the shock. The rich and powerful threw money into silencing the press and making problems disappear. They forced their staff to sign cast-iron non-disclosure agreements and were ruthless about enforcing them. Super-injunctions were *de rigueur*.

If Carrie got the job with Andreas she would be thrown directly into his personal world. She would be closer to her target than on any of her prior investigations. Who knew what she would find? When she'd first gone undercover with James in his accounts department she'd known he was a drug-abuser with a predilection for teenage girls but had had no idea of his involvement with people trafficking or arms. Andreas was that criminal's friend. Who knew what *he* was involved with?

She'd known the odds of getting the job with Andreas were slim, even with her rigged CV and falsified references. On paper, they'd made her the perfect candidate for the role but it had been a rushed job, hurried to meet the application deadline. She couldn't help worrying that there was a giant hole or two in it.

She hadn't thought the preliminary interview with his PA had gone well and had left the building certain she'd messed up. When she'd received the call inviting her to a second interview, she was so shocked a mere breeze would have knocked her over.

And now, as that ticking clock echoed louder in her ears, all she could see when she closed her eyes was the burning hatred Andreas had thrown her way the one time their eyes had met.

* * *

'Miss Dunwoody?'

Carrie blinked and looked up to find the superior young receptionist staring at her quizzically.

She'd gone under the name of Rivers for so long it had become a part of herself. Hearing her real name sounded foreign. She'd been known by the surname of Rivers since her mother had remarried when she'd been four and had thought it wise to continue using it when she embarked on her career in investigative journalism. There were a lot of sickos out there. In this instance, that decision had been fortuitous. She'd never legally changed her name. People in her world knew her as Carrie Rivers. Her birth certificate, driving licence and passport had her as Caroline Dunwoody. The advert for the job had explicitly stated it involved lots of travelling.

Falsifying references was one thing. Trying to fake a passport was a whole different ballpark.

'Mr Samaras is ready to see you now.'

He'd kept her waiting for an hour.

Swallowing back a sudden violent burst of nausea, Carrie tightly clutched the strap of her handbag and followed the receptionist down a wide corridor lined with modern artwork.

It had taken her ages to find the perfect outfit for this interview. She'd wanted to look professional but not as if she were applying for a job within Samaras Fund Management itself. She'd settled on a cream high-necked cashmere top with a dozen small buttons running the length, a pair of smart grey trousers and simple black heels that gave her a little extra height for confidence but which she could comfortably walk in. Now she felt as if she'd dressed in a smothering straightjacket, the heels a hindrance to her unsteady feet.

A door opened and Carrie was admitted into an office twice the size of the one she shared with the rest of the crime team and a hundred times plusher.

There, behind an enormous oak desk, working on one of three computers, sat Andreas Samaras.

Her heart slammed against her chest then thudded painfully and for one frightening moment Carrie thought she really was going to vomit.

He didn't look up from what he was doing.

'One minute please,' he said in the deep, quick, sharply staccato voice she remembered from their one telephone conversation instigated by Andreas five years ago.

Carrie's sister and Andreas's niece had been weekly boarders and roommates at school together. Their friendship had deepened and soon they had wanted to spend weekends and holidays together too. Andreas had phoned Carrie to agree on some ground rules. They had found much to agree on. It helped that they had both been in the same position, both of them the sole carers of their vulnerable teenage charges. After that one conversation, they would text message each other to confirm if Natalia was due at Carrie's for the weekend or if Violet was due at Andreas's. It had become a rhythm in Carrie's life, right until Andreas had engineered Violet's expulsion.

Finally, he looked up from his computer, pushed his chair back and got to his feet. The sheer size and power of the man was as starkly apparent as it had been when he had swept past her three years ago.

'It is a pleasure to meet you, Miss Dunwoody.'

She stared at the huge hand extending towards her and forced herself to lean forward and take it. Large, warm tapered fingers covered hers as he shook her hand briskly before letting go.

'Take a seat,' he commanded amicably, sitting back down and picking up a thin pile of papers from his desk.

The skin on her hand buzzed where he'd clasped it and she fought the urge to rub it against her thigh as she took the seat he'd directed her to, and expelled the tiniest sigh of relief.

There had been only a teeny ounce of doubt he wouldn't recognise her. Physically she'd changed a lot since that one fleeting glance three years ago outside the headmistress's office, when his light brown eyes had lasered her with such ferocity she had recoiled. Stress alone had made her lose three stone since then, which had altered her facial features as well as her body shape. She'd long stopped her quest for the perfect shade of blonde hair and reverted to her natural brown colour.

If Andreas had the slightest idea of who she really was, she would not be there. She wouldn't have got past the initial application.

It hadn't seemed feasible that he would recognise her or her name but she had learned through five years of her job to take nothing for granted.

Light brown thoughtful eyes studied her rather than the paperwork in his hand, which she guessed was a copy of her job application, and she fought hard against the flush of colour crawling over her skin. When she finally forced herself to meet his gaze, the raw masculinity staring back at her intensified the flush, enflaming her bones, taking her so unawares that for a moment her mind emptied of everything but the rapid tattoo of her heart reverberating in her ears.

Carrie swallowed, desperate for moisture in her parched throat, desperate to suck air into lungs that had closed in on themselves. Whatever kind of a man Andreas was, there was no denying that he was divine to look at. He had thick dark brown hair sun-kissed on the tips, barely tamed to flop onto a gently lined forehead, cheekbones you could ski down, a chiselled square jaw already dark with stubble and a sharp nose with a slight bend on the bridge. Deeply tanned and weather-beaten, he looked every one of his thirty-seven years.

He was the most overtly virile and handsome man she'd ever laid eyes on.

Then he gave her a crooked grin.

It was like being smiled at by the big bad wolf the moment before he ate Grandma.

'Congratulations on making it to the final shortlist,' he said in his impeccable English. Carrie knew, as she knew so much about this man, that he'd learned English at school in his Greek homeland and then perfected it at his American university. He spoke the language with true fluency, firing the words out so quickly his accent sounded like a musical cadence to her ears. 'I will be honest and tell you that you are my preferred candidate.'

She was taken aback. 'I am?'

His eyes sparkled. 'Before I go into more detail about my requirements, there are things I wish to know about you.'

She attempted to hide her fear with a smile that didn't want to form on her frozen cheeks.

Had he spotted the holes in her résumé?

After a moment of silence that seemed to echo between them she got her paper-dry throat to work. 'What do you want to know?'

'References and application forms only give a narrow perspective on a person. If I give you the job then we will spend a lot of time together. You will be my right hand in my domestic life. You will be privy to my most intimate secrets. So, Miss Dunwoody…may I call you Caroline?'

She nodded faintly. The only person who had ever called her Caroline had been her mother but she hadn't made her name sing as Andreas did. Even as it occurred to her, that struck Carrie as an odd thought to have.

'Caroline. If I give you the job I need to trust you and trust that we'll be able to work well together.' His relaxed frame, the musical staccato of his voice and the amusement enlivening his handsome features all worked together to reassure her that her ruse had worked but the scent of danger still lingered.

Her instincts were telling her to take her bag and coat and leave this office right now.

'Are you married or do you have a partner?' he continued. 'I ask because if you do, you should know you will be spending a lot of time apart from them. Your personal life must be conducted in your own time and you won't have much of that.'

'I have no significant other.' She never had and never would. Men could not be trusted. She'd learned that before she'd reached double digits.

'Children?'

She shook her head, immediately thinking of Violet, who she loved as much as if she'd given birth to her.

'Any other dependants? Dogs, cats, goldfish?'

'No.'

'Good. I make no apologies. I am a demanding employer and this job is a twenty-four-seven one. What did Debbie tell you about it in the preliminary interview?'

'That it entails the day-to-day running of your homes.'

His head tilted and his face grew thoughtful. 'That is how the job is advertised but you should know it is more about the day-to-day running of *me*. My domestic PA does oversee the running of my homes but they're not expected to do any of the manual chores themselves—I employ other domestic staff for that. I work long and demanding hours. When I am at home I like to live in comfort and I want all my needs and comforts met by someone who is capable of turning their hand to anything, without argument. I need someone on hand to tend to all my personal needs—pour my drinks, prepare my clothing for me, make sure a towel is on hand if I do any physical activity, that kind of thing.'

It wasn't a domestic PA the man wanted, Carrie thought in mute outrage as she listened to his seductive voice, it was a slave.

'In return, I offer a *very* generous salary.' He mentioned a figure that made her blink, it being four times what she earned at the newspaper.

She imagined that any genuine applicant would bite his hand off for it. It was an extortionate amount of money for what was essentially nothing more than being Andreas's dogsbody.

Now he put a forearm on his desk and leaned forward to stare at her with an intensity that made her stomach do a strange flip.

The more she looked into his eyes, the more startling she found them, the light brown having a translucent quality that still contained real depth.

If he gave her the job she would have to tread carefully for as long as she lived under his roof. This man was dangerous.

'Now, Caroline,' he said, the tempo of his speech finally slowing down a notch, 'I do have one more requirement from the person I give this role to.'

'Which is?'

'I require someone who has a cheerful disposition.'

She might as well leave, then. How could she be cheerful around the man who'd caused such damage?

'What I mean by that is that I get enough stress in my

work life. When I come home I like to be welcomed with a smile and not be bothered by petty gripes. *Can* you smile?'

He framed the question with such faux earnestness that Carrie found her facial muscles softening and the smile she'd been trying to produce since she'd stepped into his office breaking out of its own accord.

His eyes gleamed in response. 'Much better.' Then he sat back and folded his arms across his chest. The cuffs of his sleeves moved with the motion revealing a tantalising glimpse of fine dark hair.

He nodded slowly. 'Yes. I think you're going to suit me very well. The job is yours if you want it.'

She blinked her gaze away from his arms as his words sank in. 'It is?'

She hadn't expected it to be this easy...

Her heart started to thunder beneath her ribs.

This was *too* easy.

Andreas was one of the richest men in the world. He was highly intelligent—unverified reports placed his IQ in the world's top one per cent and he had the street smarts to match it. In short, he was no fool, and this job that he was giving her after less than fifteen minutes in his company would take her straight into the heart of his life.

'*Do* you want it?' he challenged, breaking the silence that had fallen.

'Yes.' She nodded for emphasis, trying to muster her enthusiasm, and forced another smile to her face. 'Yes, I do, definitely. Thank you.'

'Good.' His teeth flashed wolfishly. 'Did you bring your passport?'

'Yes.' The letter discussing the second interview had been specific about it. She assumed it was needed for him to photocopy as proof of her identity.

Andreas rose to his feet. 'Then let us go. We have a flight slot to fill.'

Carrie stared at him blankly. 'Go?'

'The letter you were sent clearly explained that the successful candidate for the job would start immediately.'

'It did…' But she hadn't thought immediately meant this immediately. 'Are we going abroad *now*?'

That gleam she was beginning to seriously distrust flashed in his eyes again. 'Yes. Right now. Do you have a problem with that?'

'No problem.' She hurried to stand. The job was hers and she wouldn't give him reason to change his mind. She would practise smiling as soon as she found a mirror. 'It's just that I have no change of clothes with me.'

'You will be provided with everything you need when we get there. Give Debbie your dress size as we leave.'

'Where are we going?'

'To one of my homes where it isn't raining.' And with that he opened his office door and ushered her through it.

CHAPTER TWO

ANDREAS SAT AT his desk on his private jet with his laptop open before him. Barely ten feet away, Carrie was at the dining table reading through the thick folder that contained the working details of all his properties. He had no doubt she would find it excruciatingly tedious to read through.

All his properties were listed except one—the one they were flying to.

'Which one should I concentrate on?' she'd asked when he'd given it to her, subtly letting him know he hadn't given her their final destination.

'All of them.' He'd smiled. 'I'll give you a test when we arrive.'

'Which will be when?'

He'd looked at his watch. 'In approximately eleven hours.'

Her eyes had flickered but she'd made no further comment. He'd seen her thoughts racing and had enjoyed watching her bite the questions back.

He'd enjoyed himself enormously throughout their meeting too, far more than he'd expected. The knowledge that he'd rumbled her before she'd even set foot in his office had bubbled away inside him, satisfying enough to smother the anger that had fought for an outlet.

Anger clouded logical thinking and he needed to keep his mind clear if he was to continue outwitting this viper.

He'd determined that getting her out of England and as far from her home and true employment as he could and as quickly as he could was the best way to proceed. Disorientate her. Put her at the disadvantage without her even realising it and then, when he had her in his private home, unable to escape or communicate with the outside world, he would demand answers. He wanted to know everything—why she was investigating him, what she expected to find and who had put her up to it. He'd made his own discreet enquiries amongst his media contacts but had come up blank. No one was aware of even a hint of a brewing scandal about him.

Instinct told him that Carrie's reasons for being here were at least partly personal. The coincidence was too great to be explained any other way.

He would discover her reasons in due course but rather than question her immediately, he decided he'd have some fun with her first. Let her suffer a little. It was the least she deserved.

Did Carrie really think him such a useless human being that he required someone to live by his side pouring his drinks and mopping his brow? Andreas liked his creature comforts but he was no man-child and he'd seen the flicker of surprise in her eyes when he'd outlined the duties expected of her, duties he'd made up on the spur of the moment just to see what her reaction would be.

For the next few days he would embrace the man-child role and make her wait on him hand and foot. She would hate every minute of it.

Excellent.

He would enjoy every minute of it.

He watched her put aside the notepad she'd been scribbling on as she'd read through the folder and remove her phone from her handbag. She angled her body away from him and switched it on. A few moments later her shoulders rose and she tugged at her hair.

Andreas grinned, enjoying her silent frustration to find it not working. He dealt with highly sensitive information. To get onto his jet's network required a password. He wondered how long it would be before she cracked and asked for it.

It took her three hours, an impressive length of time he thought, before she lifted her head, cleared her throat, and said, 'Would it be possible for me to have the Wi-Fi password?'

'I didn't think you had anybody to check in with,' he commented idly, enjoying the flush of colour that crawled up her slender neck.

'I don't,' she said with only the smallest of hesitation. 'I just wanted to check my emails.'

'Expecting anything important?'

She shook her head, her whole neck now aflame. 'Don't worry about it. I'll check them later.'

Carrie Rivers, Caroline Dunwoody, whatever her real name was, had a beautiful neck. He'd seen by her photograph that she was pretty but in the flesh she was so much more, her features softer, her skin dewy and golden. She was beautiful.

He thought back to the slightly plump woman he'd caught that momentary glimpse of three years back. Her eyes had been striking enough for him to remember but at the time he'd been too angry to think properly let alone remember any other detail about her. He'd been angrier than he'd ever been. The previous evening, he'd come home early from a rare evening out to find his niece and her best friend off their heads on drink and drugs. What had followed later that night had been almost as bad.

Taking guardianship of an orphaned teenage girl had

never been easy but that weekend had been the hardest of his life, harder even than the night he'd received the call telling him his sister and brother-in-law had been found dead or the day he'd learned his parents faced financial ruin.

Where was the manual that gave step-by-step guidance on how to handle the discovery that your niece, your responsibility, was creeping towards drug addiction, or how to handle waking to find your niece's sixteen-year-old best friend naked in your bedroom intent on seducing you? Where had Violet learned that kind of behaviour? From her older sister? Was the seemingly prim and proper woman sitting just feet away from him as wanton and reckless as her sister had been?

Despite his best attempts, he'd been unable to discover anything significant about Carrie. Her page on the *Daily Times* website listed her awards and achievements but nothing of a personal nature. He only knew her age because of their old personal links. Twenty-six. An incredibly young age to have achieved so much in her career. That took real commitment and dedication, something he would have admired had those traits not now been aimed at him. But unlike the men—and they had *all* been men—she'd brought down before him, Andreas had nothing to hide. His business was clean. So why had she set her sights on him? Why was the award-winning investigative journalist Carrie Rivers after him? *Was* this personal?

Whatever the reasons, he would learn them and nip whatever trouble was brewing in the bud. The old maxim of keep your friends close but your enemies closer stood the test of time.

Until he learned the truth, he would keep Carrie *very* close to him and then…

And then, unless he could think of a better plan than the

one formulating in his head, Carrie would be kept close by his side for the foreseeable future.

It was dark when they landed. The early spring storms London had been dealing with were but a distant memory as Carrie disembarked Andreas's jet and found herself engulfed in a heat the like of which she had only ever read about. She removed her jacket and looked up to find a cloudless black sky glittering with stars.

'Where are we?' She'd diligently read the folder Andreas had given her, pored over the location of all his homes and, as time had extended on their flight, convinced herself they were going to Tokyo.

'The Seychelles.' Andreas stood beside her. 'Welcome to Mahe, the largest island of the Seychelles Granitic Archipelago.'

Her mind turned frantically. How could she have missed a home in the Seychelles? She'd read his property folder from cover to cover three times, and there had been nothing about a home there in any of her prior investigations into him.

'It's the most private of my properties,' he said in a low voice close to her ear. The tangy freshness of his expensive cologne swirled around her.

Carrie casually sidestepped away from him and swallowed the sudden rush of moisture filling her mouth. 'What time is it?'

'One in the morning. We have a short flight on my helicopter before we reach my home.'

They were whisked through security and within twenty minutes of landing were climbing into a sparkling helicopter.

'Have you been in a helicopter before?' Andreas asked as he strapped himself in beside her.

There were six seats to choose from and he had to sit right next to her?

Carrie shook her head and determinedly did not look at the thigh resting so close to her own she could feel its warmth on her skin.

'It's an enjoyable experience and the quickest way to my island.'

'*Your* island?'

He pulled a thoughtful face. 'It's more of a peninsular off another island but the peninsular belongs in its entirety to me.'

Carrie silently swore as, under the heavy noise of the rotors twirling, the helicopter lifted off the ground.

She hadn't had an inkling about any of this. What else had she missed in her research on him?

Whose name had this property and accompanying land been bought in? Was it a secret shell company? She would get digging into it as soon as she had some privacy and a decent Internet signal. She needed to check in with her editor and let him know where she was too. But after she'd had a shower and, hopefully, some sleep. She'd been in the same clothes for almost a whole day, not having dreamt when she dressed that morning that she would end the day in the famed wedding and honeymoon spot of the Seychelles.

By contrast, Andreas had showered an hour before landing and changed from his suit into a fresh, crisp white shirt and light grey tailored trousers.

She dragged her attention away from the powerful body brushing so close against her own and the tangy scent playing under her nose by envisaging the shower she would have when they reached his home. She wouldn't have the temperature scalding as she usually did. To rid herself of the stickiness clinging to her pores she would lather herself under refreshingly cool water.

Her thoughts dissolved as a particularly sharp movement from the pilot caused Andreas's thigh and arm to compact against hers. An immediate shock of awareness crashed through her, so acute and so sudden and so totally unexpected that she froze.

It felt as if she'd been tasered.

For long moments she couldn't breathe.

A large hand covered hers and squeezed.

'It's nothing to worry about,' he murmured. 'Just a little turbulence.'

Carrie swallowed and forced a nod, trying desperately to get a coherent thought into her scrambled brain, her lungs finally opening back up again when he let go of her hand.

She was just tired, she assured herself, digging her nails into her palms.

Better he think she'd been frightened by the sudden turbulence they'd flown into than know of the turbulence that had exploded inside her at the feel of him pressed so tightly against her.

She looked out of the window and made an effort to relax her frame.

Come on, Carrie. You've always wanted to fly in a helicopter. At least try *and enjoy it.*

Violet had always wanted to fly in a helicopter too. She remembered how excited her sister would get during sunny days when their mother was still alive and they would go out for walks and spot helicopters zooming overhead. Her chubby little arms would wave frantically and she was always convinced the pilots waved back.

What was Violet doing at that moment? Her sister had been in California for three months now, her recovery from addiction and all her other issues a slow, fragile process.

Carrie had called her a couple of days ago, their weekly conversation as stilted and awkward as they had been since Violet had woken from her coma and it was spelled out how close to death she had come. Whenever she spoke to her sister now it was like talking to a stranger. The little girl whose first word had been 'Cawwie,' and who had followed Carrie like a shadow from the moment she could crawl was gone. In truth, she'd been gone for a long time and it tore at Carrie's heart to remember the sweetness that had once been there.

Blinking away hot tears at all that had been lost, Carrie continued to gaze out of the window. The moon was bright, allowing her to see the small landmass they were approaching in the middle of the Indian Ocean. Soon they flew directly over a beach gleaming white under the moonlight, the form of a large house emerging from the shadows as the pilot brought the helicopter down.

Andreas got out first then held out his hand to assist her, his eyes holding hers with a look that made her stomach knot in on itself.

Knowing she didn't have any choice, she took the hand. His fingers tightened as they wrapped around hers, solid and warm, keeping her steady as her feet reached for the ground.

'Thank you,' she muttered, glad the darkness cloaked her flaming cheeks from his probing gaze.

'My pleasure.' His fingertips swept gently over hers as he released his hold and then he climbed back inside to speak to his pilot.

Alone for a moment, Carrie inhaled deeply and found her senses filled with the heady scent of unseen flowers. The breeze of the ocean had cleared the humidity away, a fresh warmth brushing over her skin. It was all she could do not to close her eyes and savour the feeling.

Savouring the feeling would have to wait as suddenly lights came on and Andreas's house—villa—mansion—which the pilot had landed in the back garden of, was revealed.

It was breathtaking.

Only two storeys high, what it lacked in height it made up for in width, looking like a white stonewashed Buddhist temple surrounded by a deep red wraparound veranda. Matching deep red roof tiles gave what could easily have been an imposing building a welcoming air.

Andreas had rejoined her. She could feel his eyes on her and knew he was looking for a reaction.

What kind of reaction would a true employee give?

She opted for a truthful one.

'It's lovely.'

'Isn't it?' he agreed. 'Wait until you see it in the daylight. I fell in love with it from a photograph. I was looking for a holiday home and here I've found the perfect place. I can get away from the world but there's people and nightlife only a short flight or boat ride away.'

'This is your holiday home?'

'Of course,' he said with mild surprise. 'Who would want to conduct business on a paradise like this?'

'How long will we be here?'

'Why? Is there somewhere you have to be?'

'No, it's just...' She felt herself getting flustered.

'Relax. I'm teasing you. I know you have no commitment you have to rush back for or you would have disclosed it on your application form. We'll stay here for a while. I haven't had a proper holiday in some time and need to recharge my batteries.'

She hadn't had a holiday in some time either. At least a decade, two or three years before her mother had died.

But this wasn't a holiday for her. She was here to work.

Her job was to ensure the smooth running of this beautiful mansion and take care of the whims of its owner while secretly undertaking her own work of discovering its owner's darkest secrets. What kind of secrets she would find in Andreas's holiday home was anyone's guess. Chances were she would have to wait until they moved on to one of his other homes where he actually conducted business before she discovered anything useful.

Expecting a member of his staff to greet them—all his homes had at least three permanent live-in employees—Carrie was a little disconcerted to step inside and find the house shrouded in silence. Yes, it was the middle of the night, but surely the staff wouldn't retire for the night before their boss's arrival?

'I'll give you a quick tour before I show you to our bedrooms,' Andreas said, leading the way. He headed through an arched doorway without a door and said, 'Here's the living area.'

Her misgivings were put to one side as she slowly took in the beauty of Andreas's house, a home that managed to be both luxurious and yet welcoming. High ceilings and white walls were given colour by an intricate tiled mosaic that covered the floor wherever they stepped, including the large, airy dining room dominated by a large, highly polished mahogany table.

The kitchen was the size of an entire floor of her home.

'This is Brendan's domain,' he informed her.

'Brendan's your chef?'

'Yes. If you're hungry I can call him and he'll make something for you.'

'I'm fine, thank you.' Regular meals, which she'd had to force down into her cramped stomach, had been provided throughout the flight by Andreas's cabin crew.

He shrugged. 'If you need anything before morning I'm

sure you won't have any trouble finding it. I assume the kitchen functions as a normal kitchen.'

'You assume?'

He pulled a face. 'I employ staff so I don't have to do these chores for myself.'

'When was the last time you used a kitchen?' she asked before she could stop herself. Somehow, she doubted Andreas welcomed his domestic employees questioning him.

Her doubt proved wrong.

'In my university days in America—I studied at MIT—I discovered I was a terrible cook so I got a job working as a waiter in an Italian restaurant where they were always happy to feed me. I've not cooked for myself since.'

'An *Italian* restaurant?'

'There were no decent Greek restaurants where I lived then. There was a tapas bar but they didn't do breakfast so I opted for the Italian one.'

His long legs powered on gracefully up the cantilevered stairs to the first floor. Carrie hurried behind him, smothering a yawn. All the travelling on top of minimal sleep had exhausted her.

'My room.' Andreas pushed open a door to reveal a bedroom equal in size to the kitchen, containing everything a spoiled billionaire could need. Carrie hung back, reluctant to enter until he beckoned her inside with the crook of his finger and the hint of a gleam in his piercing light brown eyes. 'Don't be shy, Caroline. You need to become familiar with my room.'

Familiar with it? All she could see was the enormous carved bed heaped with pillows, and her imagination immediately stripped Andreas bare and pictured him sliding with that masculine grace she'd never seen on another man between the navy satin sheets.

She clenched her teeth together, trying to blink the

image away and pretend the rush of blood she could feel pumping around her was not connected to it.

She'd never imagined a man naked before and it disturbed her that she should have such unwelcome thoughts about this particular man.

There was such a sensuous potency about him. It was there in his every move, his every breath, his every word, and all it did was add to her growing sense of danger.

Sheesh, she really, *really* needed some sleep.

'What other staff work here?' she asked. Once she knew where everyone was she would stop feeling as if she'd been trapped in a gilded cage that only Andreas had the key to.

Everything had happened so quickly and smoothly that day that there hadn't been time for her misgivings to do more than squeak at her but now, here, standing in Andreas's bedroom in his secret home in the middle of the night, those misgivings were shouting loudly.

'I inherited most of the staff from the previous owners. The grounds are managed by Enrique and his eldest son. Enrique's wife Sheryl and a couple of her friends take care of all the cleaning. Between them they know everything there is to know about the house and the peninsular and the Seychelles itself.'

'Where are the staff quarters?'

'There aren't any. Brendan and his assistant live in a cottage on the grounds but the others all live on the main island.'

Another chime of alarm rang in her ears. 'So who actually lives in the house?'

Surely she had misunderstood something. Surely she wouldn't be the only person living under this roof with him while they were there?

'We do. You and me.'

'*Just* you and me?'

'Yes.' His eyes seemed to do more than merely sparkle. They *smouldered*. His nostrils flared as he added, 'While we're on this beautiful spot of paradise, the night time belongs to you and me alone.'

CHAPTER THREE

ANDREAS ENJOYED CARRIE'S attempt to hide her horror at this clearly unwelcome revelation.

'I bought this place as a getaway from the world so it's run in a more relaxed way than my other homes,' he said. 'As long as I have someone close at hand to take care of my needs, I don't need much else and that, *matia mou*, is why you are here. Consider it an easy breaking-in for you. The house runs itself so you can dedicate your time here to me and we can get to know each other properly in the process.'

The colour drained from her face, her hazel eyes widening.

Understandable, he thought lazily. Carrie wouldn't want him delving into her life with probing questions that would put her on the spot. She wouldn't want to trip herself up with easily forgotten lies.

He admired that, through the tumult of emotions flickering through her eyes, her composure didn't waver. If he were ignorant of her true identity he doubted he would have noticed anything amiss. If he didn't know the truth he would assume she was a naturally quiet, self-contained woman.

He looked forward to seeing how far he could push her before she cracked and the real Carrie emerged.

'Now for your room. You will find it adequately appointed.' But not as adequately as Rochelle's had been. She was being put in a much different room from the one his former Domestic PA had enjoyed. Rochelle's room had been located at the other end of the house so she could have her privacy.

He didn't intend for Carrie, this cuckoo in his nest, this spy, to have any privacy during her interlude in his life. Her duties would be of the kind he would never dream of imposing on a proper employee.

Andreas turned the handle of a door in the middle of the left-hand wall of his room. It opened into a much smaller, adjoining room.

He spread a hand out. 'See? You have everything you need. A bed, a dressing table, wardrobe and your own bathroom.' But no television or other form of entertainment. Andreas intended to be Carrie's only source of entertainment while she was here.

The colour that stained her cheeks this time was definitely of the angry variety but she kept it in check to ask with only the slightest tremor, 'My room adjoins yours?'

'How would you take care of my needs if you were on the other side of the house? The previous owners used this room as a nursery. I admit it's rather small—it was designed for a small child before they went into a proper room of their own—but I can assure you it's perfectly adequate.' Adequate for a baby or toddler. Barely adequate for a fully grown woman, even one as slender as Carrie. He'd intended to turn it into another dressing room and was glad he hadn't got around to organising it.

'Where's the lock?'

'There isn't one so it will be nice and easy for you to come and go between our rooms.' He winked. 'But do not worry. I am a gentleman and only enter a lady's bedroom when invited.'

And should she be tempted to enter his room without invitation, which she undoubtedly would seeing as her whole purpose for being here was to snoop, then the microscopic cameras he'd had installed in his bedroom and throughout the house would monitor her every movement.

He'd intended to bug her room too with voice-activated cameras but had talked himself out of it. There was a line a person should never cross and bugging a lady's bedroom, even a journalistic spy like this one, was firmly on the wrong side of it. Now that he'd spent the day in such close confines to her, he was doubly glad he hadn't crossed that line.

Carrie had an allure about her that played to his senses like a finely tuned violin.

She also had eyes that looked bruised from exhaustion.

'I can see you're tired. Is there anything you wanted to ask before we retire for the night?'

She shook her head, those soft, plump lips drawing in together. The situation had clearly overwhelmed her. He could sympathise. When she had walked into his offices in the heart of London's financial district that morning she could not have guessed she'd finish the day cut off from everything she was familiar with in the paradise that was the Seychelles. No doubt she was feeling vulnerable.

Good.

He *could* sympathise but he would not. Carrie was a vulture. A beautiful vulture for sure, but a vulture nonetheless.

She deserved nothing less than what was coming for her.

'In that case, I bid you goodnight. The clothes I promised you were flown in while we were travelling. Sheryl has put them away for you. You will find them imminently suitable. And remember…'

A pretty brow rose cautiously. 'Remember?'

He winked. 'I like to be welcomed with a smile.'

As he closed the interconnecting door he smiled himself to imagine her reaction to the clothing selected for her.

His fun with Carrie was only just beginning.

Carrie threw the entire contents of her new wardrobe onto the narrow excuse of a bed and rifled through them with increasing anxiety.

She'd expected to be given outfits akin to what chambermaids in hotels wore, not clothing like this.

Her wardrobe and dresser had been filled with soft, floaty summer dresses, vest tops, shorts that put the meaning into the word 'short', bikinis and sarongs. There was underwear too, all of the black, lacy variety.

Every item had a designer label.

Her skin had never felt so heated as when she'd picked up a pair of knickers and wondered if Andreas had chosen them personally.

But how could he have done? She hadn't left his side since she'd stepped into his office. It must have been his PA, Debbie, who she'd been certain hadn't liked her in the initial interview and who she'd had to give her vital statistics to as Andreas had whisked her out of his building.

Carrie tugged at her hair with a mixture of consternation and fear.

Whoever had chosen the items, which included beach paraphernalia along with all the clothing, this was not right, not by any stretch of the imagination. To make matters worse there was no Internet she could connect to and her phone signal seemed to be non-existent. The text message she'd written to her editor forty minutes ago was still trying to send.

Who knew she was here? Andreas and his PA Debbie, his flight crew and his Seychellois domestic staff. No one from her own life knew she was in the Seychelles, only people employed by Andreas.

Rubbing her eyes, she told herself she was probably worrying over nothing. It had been an incredibly long day and she was sleep deprived. Sleep deprivation did funny things to the brain.

The letter inviting her to the second interview *had* stated the successful applicant would be expected to start the job immediately. It was her own fault that she hadn't taken the letter literally enough.

She was exactly where she wanted to be, with greater access to the man than in her wildest dreams.

But he also had access to her, and she eyed the adjoining unlocked door with nerves fluttering in her chest.

There was no way she would trust his word that he wouldn't enter her room uninvited.

The way he looked at her… Did he look at all his employees with that same intensity? Did he leave the rest of his employees feeling that he was stripping them bare with a glance?

Or was it just her guilty conscience playing at her and making her see things that weren't there?

Movement from the adjoining room made her catch her breath.

Andreas was still awake. They were connected to each other's rooms and she couldn't even lock herself away from him.

She forced herself to breathe.

She needed to take a shower but had been holding it off until she could be reasonably sure he'd gone to sleep. An hour after he'd left her in this tiny bedroom, there was nothing to suggest he was ready to turn in.

What was he going to do? she chided herself. Walk in on her while she showered?

Sexual foibles were the easiest secrets to uncover. Andreas Samaras might be many things but a sex pest was not something that had been flagged up about him, not even on the secret grapevine from which she and other journalists like her got so many of their stories. He rarely dated and when he did it was discreetly. If there was anything along those lines she had to worry about she would already know about them.

She was being over-cautious when she didn't need to be.

Carefully putting the expensive clothing back into its rightful place, she realised what her real problem with it was. These were the sort of clothes a man bestowed on his lover for a holiday, not his employee.

Carrie awoke in the unfamiliar tiny room minutes before the digital alarm clock on her bedside table went off. It had been set for her by some faceless person that she would no doubt meet shortly, a person with whom she would have to pretend to be someone she was not.

Lying on an investigation had never bothered her before. The few she had done before, though, had been office-based. Offices were places where *everyone* wore a mask. She'd fitted in without any problems and without any guilt, knowing she was working for a good cause.

This was different. This was Andreas's home. She had told herself over and over that this was an opportunity that had been gift-wrapped for her but she still felt as if she'd breached an invisible line.

He deserves it, she told herself grimly, focussing her mind on Violet's scarred, emaciated body and its root cause. *He deserves everything he gets.*

She checked her phone and sighed to see the message to her editor still pending. Her room must be in a black spot.

After a quick shower under the disappointing trickle of water in her private bathroom, only mitigated by the expensive, wonderfully scented toiletries provided for her, it was time to select an outfit to wear.

After rifling through her new clothing for the dozenth time she chose a dark blue dress covered in tiny white dots. It was made of the sheerest material, had the thinnest of spaghetti straps and fell to mid-thigh but at least it covered her cleavage. And, she had to admit, it *was* pretty.

Scrabbling through her handbag, she found a hairband wedged in the bottom and tied her hair into a loose bun at the nape of her neck. She had no make-up with her. Usually that didn't matter as she rarely wore it but today she felt she could do with some camouflage.

Dressed and feeling much more alert, she pulled the floor-length curtains open and gasped.

The sight that greeted her could have come from a postcard.

If she'd peeked through the curtains during the night she would have seen her room had its own private balcony. She stepped out onto it now, heart thumping, the sun kissing her skin good morning.

She closed her eyes to savour the feeling then opened them again, hand on her throat, staring in stunned awe at the deep blue sky unmarred by so much as a solitary cloud and at the stunning azure ocean that lapped gently onto the finest white sand imaginable, the cove's shore lined with palm trees. A short distance ahead sat an isolated green landmass that looked, from her dazed estimation, close enough that she might tread through water to it. An artist couldn't have painted a more perfect scene.

'Good morning, Caroline.'

The deep, cheerful voice startled her and she gripped the balustrade before turning her head.

So mind-blown had she been by the view before her, she hadn't noticed her balcony was far too wide to be hers alone.

Hair damp and wearing nothing but a pair of low-slung black shorts, Andreas strolled to stand beside her and grinned. 'What did I tell you about the view in daylight—takes the breath away, doesn't it?'

Her grip on the balustrade tightening, she stared back out at the view and nodded. 'It's stunning.'

But it was the view standing feet away from her that had truly stolen her breath and, though she tried her hardest to keep her attention on what lay in front of her, her senses were leaping to what stood beside her.

His body was even better than her imagination had allowed her to believe. Broad shouldered, muscular without being overdone and deeply tanned, this was a body kept fit by plenty of swimming and enjoyment of the outside life, not by lifting weights or working on a treadmill. This wasn't a body that had been sculptured out of vanity.

'Sleep well?' he murmured, resting his arms on the balustrade.

She inhaled and gave a sharp nod, intensely aware of his penetrative gaze on her.

So much for sleep curing her inexplicable awareness of him.

'Fine, thank you.'

'Good. Ready to start work?'

She nodded again.

'Then let's introduce you to the others and get some breakfast. I don't know about you but I'm starving.'

'Okay.' She turned to go back into her room.

'Caroline?'

She met his sparkling gaze. 'Yes?'

'Have you forgotten my most basic requirement?'

She furrowed her brow as she tried to clear her mind of his semi-nakedness enough to think, pretended her insides hadn't just clenched and heated to see the fine dark hair that lightly covered his chest snaked down and over his hard abdomen to where his shorts rested low...

He shook his head in amusement. 'Where is my smile?'

'Still waking up,' she replied without thinking.

His grin was wide enough to eclipse the rising sun. 'Ah, you *do* have a sense of humour. I did wonder. Now let's get some breakfast.'

And with that, he strolled back into his room.

Carrie was on the brink of laughter for reasons she couldn't begin to understand, although she suspected it would have a hysterical quality to it if it came out, when clarity suddenly came to her.

She was *here*.

She'd got the job.

Everything was in place to allow her to do what she'd spent the last three years dreaming of doing. The last thing she wanted was to blow the opportunity by not performing as required and getting sacked before she'd properly started.

Whatever strange reactions Andreas provoked inside her, she had to ignore them and do her job.

He'd made his requirements crystal clear. She was to be good humoured and cater to all his whims. Well, she would do just that. She would do everything he required of her *and* she would make darned sure to keep a smile on her face while she did it. She would inveigle her way into his confidence and uncover the secrets Andreas Samaras kept hidden from the world.

And then she would expose them.

And then, finally, she would find some peace of mind. Violet would have been avenged and both the men who'd destroyed her life would, in a much different way, be destroyed too.

With that happy thought in her head, she hurried to join him.

Breakfast had been laid out on the sunny veranda, an array of breads, pastries, fruits, condiments and yogurt.

'I take my coffee black without sugar,' Andreas said as he took his seat.

He'd introduced Carrie to his staff but had kept it quick. He'd taken Enrique and Sheryl into his confidence and they'd been outraged to discover an investigative journalist was trying to infiltrate his life. They were honest, upstanding people who he knew would struggle to hide their true feelings towards her for any length of time.

He liked to think he was an honest man too, but dealing with the shysters and scumbags that littered the financial world he inhabited like the dregs of a pot of coffee had taught him how to play the game that the people he employed on this island could never understand.

Carrie, still standing, poured his coffee for him. She even poured it with a smile.

'I will have honeydew melon and yogurt,' he told her.

She took a bowl and, with another smile, spooned chunks of melon into it. 'Tell me when to stop.'

Her disposition since he'd startled her on the balcony had changed considerably, and very much for the better. He would bet her new, cheerful disposition was external only.

He waited until the bowl was full before raising a hand. He noticed her own hand was incredibly slim, the nails long and nicely shaped. If Carrie were to look at the hands of any of his domestic staff she would see none of them had nails as well maintained as hers. She would see her nails were a dead giveaway that her life had not been spent undertaking domestic work.

'Four spoonfuls of yogurt,' he commanded amiably.

Again, she obeyed. 'Can I get you anything else to go with it?'

Tempted though he was to ask her to spoon it into his mouth, just to see if the smile fixed on her face cracked, he resisted. 'That will do for the moment. I will let you know when I want anything else.'

She nodded and folded her hands together over her belly.

Andreas put a spoonful into his mouth and took the opportunity to cast his eyes over her again in an appreciative open manner he would never dream of doing with an ordinary employee.

She was a little smaller than the average woman, the modest dress she'd selected showcasing the lithe legs of a model and breasts he would never have guessed could be so full on so slight a person. The morning sunlight beamed on her face highlighting the soft dewiness of her skin, reflecting off her complexion in glimmering waves.

Carrie didn't need make-up. She was stunning exactly as she was.

It was fortuitous that she wasn't a proper employee of his, he thought, as a thick heaviness pooled in his loins. Boss-employee relationships were disasters waiting to happen and he steered well clear of them, just as he avoided anything that could harm his business and personal reputation. In today's climate, where sexual harassment charges were a mere compliment about a pretty outfit away, he was too conscious of his position and power to risk his reputation.

Carrie would be a challenge to his self-imposed ideals. If he had to work with her in a close environment for real he knew he would find it a challenge to keep their relationship on a professional footing, a notion he found faintly disturbing.

Here and under these unique circumstances, his personal ethics could be safely pushed aside. She wasn't his employee. She was a snake. A beautiful, beguiling, incredibly sexy snake who wanted to destroy him.

'Are you not going to sit down?' he asked once he'd swallowed his mouthful.

Her hazel eyes flickered, her brow furrowed slightly, but the smile stayed in place.

'Are you not intending to eat?'

Now the furrow in her brow deepened.

'I dislike eating alone, *matia mou*. While we're here it is my wish that you dine with me, so, please, sit. Pour yourself a drink and eat something.'

As she complied with his request, he couldn't resist adding, 'Also, if you dine with me, it makes it easier for you to wait on me.'

'Whatever makes your life easier,' she said demurely and with only a hint of teeth being ground together. 'I am here to serve you.'

'That you are,' he agreed. 'And you look beautiful doing it. Are you happy with the clothes selected for you?'

Her spoon, which had been adding a little yogurt into the bowl she'd taken for herself, hovered in her hand. 'Yes. Thank you. Although… I thought I would be given more… practical clothing.'

Poor Carrie. How disconcerting it must have been for her to open her wardrobe and find there was no uniform to hide behind, no means to slip unobtrusively into the shadows of his life.

'Practical clothing has no place in such a beautiful setting.'

'Well, it's very generous of you. I'm amazed you were able to get it all here before we arrived,' she said lightly.

'It's a bespoke Internet service my niece uses. She holidayed here during her Christmas break but flew over on a commercial flight and lost her luggage. Twelve hours later she had a whole new designer wardrobe delivered.' He gave a rueful laugh. 'I did wonder if Natalia lost her suitcase deliberately just so I could buy her new clothing.'

Carrie's face pinched in on itself as he spoke his niece's name but only briefly. If he hadn't been watching her so closely he would have missed it.

It was good to know she was squirming inside.

'Anyway, with all this talk of clothes, I should tell you that you will need to change after we've eaten,' he said.

'Why?'

'The current on my beach is too strong to swim in at this time of year but there's a cove on Tortue Island that's perfect. We will take my boat out there and swim and get to know each other better. Doesn't that sound good?'

Her throat moved before she nodded and smiled. 'I can't think of anything I'd like more.'

CHAPTER FOUR

IF THE WIND CHANGED, Carrie was quite sure her face would freeze with this pathetic smile stuck on it for ever. Her cheeks ached with the effort of it and all she wanted was for the slave-driving Greek egomaniac to let her go to bed and get away from him for some respite.

She'd thought the day before had been long... It had *nothing* on the day she'd just endured, which, despite being late evening, showed no sign of ending soon.

Tortue Island had been the tiny green island paradise she'd spotted from her balcony, a mere five-minute hop on Andreas's speedboat. He'd taken her to a secluded cove surrounded by enormous palm trees and drenched in sunlight. That was where paradise had ended.

Violet as a toddler had been easier to take care of than this overgrown infant. Practically the only thing she hadn't had to do for Andreas was towel him dry after his frequent swims. She'd kept him supplied with constant refreshments, opened his bottles of water, peeled his fruit, fanned him when he'd decided he was too hot, even read news articles off his tablet for him, which had been financial articles and as exciting to read as it was to watch paint dry.

And she'd had to do it all with a cheerful demeanour!

The only thing that had kept her cheerful was imagining his smug face when he discovered her true identity. He'd mentioned that they would be flying back to London before heading on to Frankfurt and she couldn't *wait* to get going. Both of those homes had proper offices set up for him to work from—he was so lazy she was surprised he bothered having offices outside his homes—and she just knew it wouldn't take her long to discover his illegal secrets.

She couldn't get over how spoilt and lazy he was. If someone had told her the rugged Andreas Samaras liked to have his grapes peeled for him as if he were a Roman emperor, she would never have believed it, and she had applied for a job with him with the lowest expectations of the man. It just didn't fit with what she thought she knew of him. But, no, he clearly adored being waited on, a wolfish smile near enough constantly playing on his lips.

Once he'd grown bored of Tortue Island, they'd returned to his peninsular where Carrie had waited on him some more while he'd sunbathed by his swimming pool.

She had never imagined a man like Andreas could do so much sunbathing!

Her duties at the pool had consisted mostly of sitting by his side with a handheld fan aimed at his face in between runs to his fully stocked poolside bar for ever more refreshments for him. Then it had been time to prepare his clothing for dinner and take a super-quick shower herself before they went to sit out on his veranda for their evening meal. Other than her shower, she hadn't had a minute to herself, had only been able to check for a phone signal as she'd chucked a clean dress on after her super-quick shower. No magical signal had been found; her text message still sat pending.

The meal cooked for them by Brendan had been possibly the best food she'd ever tasted, fat succulent tiger prawn salad—Andreas had got her to shell his prawns for him—followed by a creamy coconut curry, but she'd been unable to appreciate it as Andreas had had her running back and forth to the kitchen like a yo-yo.

She hadn't done so much exercise in years.

'Caroline?'

She suddenly realised that while she'd been silently fuming about his lazy, slave-driving ways, he'd been speaking to her.

She fixed the wide smile back on her face.

What do you want this time? Another bowl of water set at the optimum temperature to dip your fingers into? Another napkin to dry them with or to wipe your mouth to go with the five I've already had to get for you?

'Sorry, I missed what you said.'

He drained his white wine and set the glass on the table. 'I'm ready to go in…'

About time.

'…so I need you to run me a bath and turn my bed down.'

'Turn your bed down?' she answered blankly, not having the faintest idea what he was talking about.

His forehead creased and he tilted his head. 'You've never turned a bed down before?'

Sensing danger, she hid her apprehension with a smile. 'It's not something that's been asked of me before. Maybe I know it by another name?'

'I thought it was a universal term.' A suggestive gleam sparkled in his eyes. 'It just means preparing my bed so it's ready for me—turning the sheets over so I can slide into them.'

'Oh, *that*,' she said with feigned brightness. Yes, this was exactly the sort of thing this spoilt man would demand. She would bet that in colder climates he would demand his domestic PA personally warm his bed for him. 'Of course. Yes. Anything else?'

'I'll let you know if anything comes to mind while you're running my bath.'

I just bet you will.

She got to her feet. 'I'll run it for you now. What temperature do you like it?' Scalding or ice-cold? she prevented herself from asking.

He waited a beat before answering, a smile tugging on his lips. 'Why don't you run it to the temperature *you* like?'

Andreas watched Carrie walk into the house to run him a bath with amusement fizzing in his veins.

He couldn't remember the last time he'd enjoyed himself as much as he had that day.

She waited on him as if she'd been born to serve his whims. Her determination to act the role he'd set for her and act it well had been exquisite to watch.

The little tells that had betrayed her real feelings had been equally exquisite. When this was all over he'd have to arrange for her to be given an acting award because he was quite certain he would never have seen those betraying signs if he hadn't been looking for them.

When this was all over...

That was a thought to knock the smile from his face.

He would have to put Carrie out of her misery sooner rather than later, however enjoyable it was to play the role of spoilt playboy, a role that, despite his riches, he'd never had the time or inclination to play before. With Carrie being the one to act the role of slave, the spoilt playboy role had been one to relish. What a shame he would have to put a stop to it so soon.

Debbie had messaged him earlier with news that made it clear he needed to return to London and start on damage limitation. Whatever Carrie's reasons for being here, she'd prodded a hornets' nest.

He poured himself another glass of wine. Other than shave, it was the first thing he'd done for himself all day. He took a sip, leaned back and closed his eyes.

His graduation from university had coincided with his parents' world falling apart. Since then, his life had been one long conveyor belt of obligations. Family, work, responsibility, with Andreas the one holding everyone and everything together. Then, as he'd seen light at the end of the long dark tunnel, his sister and brother-in-law had died and he'd suddenly found himself guardian to his teenage niece. Natalia had been raised in London and was already a weekly boarder at her school in the English capital when her parents died. Andreas hadn't wanted to uproot her life any further so had uprooted himself instead, moving his life and business from Manhattan to London. Natalia had become his priority.

He had never begrudged anything he'd done for his family. It was what families did—they loved and took care of each other. But it was only when Natalia had left for university and he'd felt the burden of responsibility lifting from his shoulders that he'd realised what a weight it had been on him. That weight had been there most of his adult life.

Now Natalia was approaching the end of her first year at university, that flicker of light beckoning his freedom he'd seen before her parents had died was flickering again, brighter than it ever had before. Technically Natalia was now an adult. She still needed him but not in the way she had before. Nowadays she only needed his money and his London home to 'crash' in, as she put it, when she went out partying with friends in the city. She was young, working hard and enjoying her life, exactly as she should be.

He'd promised himself that once she'd completed her first year he would start living his life for himself. He no longer had to worry about being a good influence or role model. He could enjoy the wealth he had created and experience what life had to offer but which responsibility had denied him for so long.

He never wanted to have any form of responsibility in his personal life ever again.

His business, though, was a different matter entirely and it was this he vowed to protect from Carrie Rivers's poisonous pen.

He drank some more of his wine and reflected that it was fortuitous that Carrie had set her sights on him when he had the freedom to do whatever was needed to stop her. Whisking her to the Seychelles would have been unthinkable a year ago when he'd still planned every minute of his life around Natalia's schedule.

Setting his empty glass on the table, he got to his feet, rolled his neck and stretched.

He would hit Carrie with the truth in the morning. Until then, he intended to extract his last few hours of fun from her.

Carrie marched into Andreas's bathroom, switched the light on and stopped short.

Soft lighting revealed a space that wasn't a bathroom but a marble palace. The walk-in shower alone was bigger than her bathroom.

But it was the deep, sunken bath she approached, as opulent as anything Roman emperors had bathed in. Half a dozen people could fit in it with room to spare.

It took her a few moments to work out where the plug was. Then she turned the taps on. A surge of water gushed out, not just from the taps but from tiny round holes the entire circumference, all pouring quicker than she had ever known water to pour before.

She found bath foam in a cabinet and added a liberal dollop, which immediately filled the room with a delicious warm spicy scent, then adjusted the water temperature some more, resisting the urge to set it on cold. When the bath was run and filled with thick foam, she dried her hands and went back into his bedroom.

Her bravado almost deserted her as she approached his bed.

She'd been in his room a number of times that day but this was the first time she'd had to go near his bed.

She took a deep breath before carefully untucking the sheet. She pulled it back to form a triangle, then smoothed it, trying not to think that only the night before these sheets had covered his naked body.

Because he did sleep naked. She knew that on an instinctive level she couldn't begin to understand and the mere thought made her lower abdomen clench tightly.

You've had too much sun, she told herself grimly, lifting his pillow to plump and immediately releasing Andreas's scent trapped in the Egyptian cotton. She hurriedly put the pillow back down as the scent entered her bloodstream and, for a moment, her pulses soared with such strength she felt dizzy.

She blinked hard to regain her focus and stared at the pillow as if it could bite her.

'Is my bath ready?'

She jumped.

Andreas stood at the threshold of his bedroom, a wry smile playing on his lips.

How long had he been there, watching her…?

'Yes. There's fresh towels on the rail. Everything's ready for you.' How she managed to get the words out with her heart thrashing so wildly and leaping in her throat she didn't know.

'Good.' He stepped into the room, eyes on her as he removed a cufflink from the sleeve of his shirt.

Suddenly terrified that he was going to strip in front of her, she forced her legs to move towards the door to her own room, sidestepping around his huge figure, which somehow seemed even taller and broader than it did in daylight hours.

'I could do with some water,' he said as her hand touched the door handle. 'Can you bring a glass up for me please?'

A please? That was a first.

Carrie nodded tightly and hurried out of his room, down the stairs and to the kitchen, resolutely telling herself over and over that she'd had far too much sun that day and that was why her veins were fizzing so. The young kitchen assistant was just finishing for the night, a reminder that very soon the house would be empty of everyone but her and Andreas...

All she could hope was that this was her last duty of the evening.

Her heart still hammered frantically as she walked back up the stairs with his glass of water.

His bedroom door was ajar. She knocked lightly on it. When there was no response she stepped tentatively inside. His room was empty, the bathroom door wide open.

'I have your water,' she called. 'Shall I leave it on the table for you?'

His reply was muffled by the thick walls. 'I'll have it in here.'

Hoping she'd misheard him, she confirmed, 'What, in the bathroom?'

'Seeing as that's where I am, yes.'

Taking a deep, fortifying breath, Carrie trod slowly to the open door, praying he hadn't removed all his clothes yet.

It was a futile hope.

Andreas was in the huge bath, leaning back, the top of his chest right in her eyeline, facing the door. Facing her.

Knowing her face had gone the colour of sun-ripened tomatoes, she looked everywhere but him, searching for a decent spot to put the glass on.

'Bring it to me,' he commanded casually.

She couldn't get her feet to work.

Water sloshed as he sat up and extended an arm. 'Don't be shy, *matia mou*. I only bite if invited to.'

Flames engulfing her, resisting the urge to throw the water right in his face, she finally put one foot in front of the other, her eyes darting everywhere but at him.

She *couldn't* look at him, not directly. As long as she looked at the beautiful cream tiling around his head she would be fine.

When she reached his side she extended her own arm to put the glass in his waiting hand, careful not to allow their fingers to brush, then quickly stepped back.

'I'll leave you to enjoy your bath,' she said.

'You're not going to stay and keep me company?'

Without her meaning them to, her eyes found his and her heart leapt then twisted.

A breathless, suspended moment passed between them, the only movement the growing ache in her most feminine place and the colour she could feel creeping up her neck.

And no wonder she couldn't breathe. The look in his eyes... The gleam...

This beautiful, ruggedly handsome man was staring at her as if she were a delicacy he wanted to feast on.

Heat rose in her that she was quite sure had nothing to do with the steamy vapours coming from the bath.

Suddenly her imagination ran riot, a feast of its own, racing into places she had never been before of naked limbs and soft sighs…

She'd spent the whole day with this man's semi-naked body within touching distance and had successfully kept him fully clothed in her mind, just as if she'd been a subject in *The Emperor's New Clothes*. Blocking out his near-nakedness had been as hard as keeping that stupid smile on her face but she had done it. Now the veil she'd put over her eyes had been ripped away and she saw *him*, darkly tanned, a homage to rugged masculinity, and the base feminine part of herself responded to it.

And then she saw something else in his eyes, something darker even than the desire that swirled and pulsed, and it was this something, this dark danger, that pulled her out of the hypnotic spell he'd cast over her and snapped her back to herself.

She forced herself to breathe and dragged her lips into a smile.

'You're a big boy,' she said in as light a tone as she could muster. 'I'm sure you can cope with your own company for a while.'

There was a moment of utter stillness before his firm lips curved into an all too knowing smile. 'I didn't think you'd looked.'

Looked…?

Suddenly his meaning became clear and her eyes, with a will of their own, gazed down at the water, at the long, muscular legs laid out, covered in foam but not covered enough that she couldn't see the dark hair between his thighs or his…

Shocked rigid, she quickly blinked and turned away.

But she couldn't blink enough to rid herself of what she'd seen.

She'd never seen a fully naked man before, not in the flesh, and, even with the bath water and foam distorting the image, she didn't need to be experienced in matters of the flesh to know that he was in proportion *everywhere*.

'I'll be in my room if you need me,' she mumbled, hurrying to escape from this seductive atmosphere and all the danger lacing it.

She closed the bathroom door with the sound of his low laughter ringing in her ears.

Alone in her bedroom she sat on her bed and clutched her still-flaming cheeks, breathing heavily.

She despised Andreas, had hated him from that moment outside the headmistress's office when he had stared at her as if she were something dirty he had trodden in.

He had destroyed her sister! How could she feel such attraction to him? How was it possible that her first real flush of desire should be for her enemy?

And how was it possible that he could be so aware of it? She'd seen it in those seductive eyes...

She flopped onto her pillow face-first and gave a muffled scream.

How could she be thinking these thoughts?

Too much sun.

Of *course*. That was the answer.

She'd had more sun in one day than she'd had for at least three years. It had addled her brain in much the same way sleep deprivation had addled it yesterday.

Feeling calmer, she stretched herself out on the narrow bed, closed her eyes and concentrated on inhaling and exhaling in long, regular breaths, the way she had long ago trained herself to fall asleep when her terrified fears for her sister had threatened to stop her ever falling into oblivion.

* * *

A loud rapping woke Carrie from the light slumber she had fallen into.

The digital bedside clock showed it had just turned midnight. She'd been in her room for less than an hour.

The rapping vibrated through the door again. 'Caroline?'

'I'm awake.' She staggered off the bed and took the one step needed to reach the door, straightening her dress, which she'd fallen asleep in.

She braced herself before opening the door only to find her senses hit immediately with the tangy scent of Andreas's cologne and the faint spice of his bath foam.

He was standing in a pair of faded jeans, his torso bare, a smile playing on his lips.

'Were you sleeping?' he asked with one eyebrow raised.

'Dozing.' *I forgot that working for you meant only sleeping when you gave the order.*

'Good. I'm in the mood for a nightcap.'

Of course you are.

'You want me to get it for you?'

He pulled a face that said very clearly that that was what he employed her for.

'Give me a second to put something on my feet,' she added hastily.

'Bring me a tumbler of Scotch—any single malt will do—three fingers, two cubes of ice, and one for yourself. I'll be on the veranda.' Then he winked, turned and headed off.

Taking a deep breath while internally cursing him to the heavens, Carrie slipped her toes into the gold designer flip-flops she'd been given and trudged down the stairs to his den, where he kept his indoor bar.

How could any normal self-respecting employee put up

with this? she wondered. No salary, however large, could compensate for being at Andreas's permanent beck and call.

She fixed his Scotch exactly as demanded and poured herself some lemonade. As tempting as the vast array of liquors and spirits was, she didn't want any alcohol in her bloodstream when dealing with this tricky man. She'd refused wine with her dinner for the same reason.

She carried the glasses outside, where a fresh breeze whispered over her skin, and found him back at the outside table reading something on his phone.

She still didn't have a signal.

His teeth glimmered white in the moonlight as she put the drinks on the table. 'Before you sit down, go to my dressing room and get me a pair of swim-shorts. I might want a swim later.'

Later? It was already the middle of the night. Did the man not plan on getting *any* sleep?

Was *she* not allowed to get any sleep?

Then she caught something in his eyes, an amusement that immediately aroused her suspicions…

Was he…?

Could he be…?

Was Andreas playing a *game*?

He stared right back at her, the amusement no longer just in his eyes but quirking on his lips, as if he were biting back laughter. But something darker lurked in those light brown eyes too, something that sent fresh alarm bells ringing inside her.

She backed away slowly, suddenly wary of taking her eyes off him.

Her job had taught her the importance of listening to her instincts and her instincts were telling her loud and clear that something was off and that some unseen danger awaited her.

Climbing back up the stairs, she realised that she'd had this instinctual feeling of something being amiss since her interview with him but Andreas had kept her so busy running around after him that she'd had no time to listen.

She paused at the threshold of his bedroom and gazed around with narrowed eyes. She'd resisted looking too deeply before as there had always been someone around and she hadn't wanted to seem as if she were doing anything other than what Andreas was supposedly paying her for. The newest members of staff in any organisation always attracted curious glances, whether the work was in a business or domestic environment. It was human nature to watch strangers more closely than people you were familiar with. She'd thought it wise to hold off before she started any snooping.

Slowly she took all the expensive furnishings in, unsure what, if anything, she was looking for.

It was just a bedroom. A masculine, richly opulent bedroom for sure, but still, just a bedroom…

What the heck was *that*?

Right at the end of the curtain pole that covered his French doors, a tiny round object winked at her.

Carrie had been an undercover journalist long enough to know exactly what she was looking at but it still took a few moments before it really sank in.

The tiny round object was a camera. And it was filming her.

CHAPTER FIVE

ANDREAS SIPPED HIS Scotch as he watched Carrie on his phone.

He'd seen the suspicion in her eyes in the moments before she'd gone back inside to cater to his latest whim. Instinct had made him switch his phone over to the live feed coming from his bedroom.

Judging by the stillness in her frame as she stared around his bedroom, he suspected her own instincts had kicked in too.

After a couple of minutes of nothing, her expression suddenly changed, sharpening, her head tilting, brow furrowing as she walked trance-like towards the French door.

And then she was looking right at him…

Her pretty lips formed a perfect O as he watched realisation hit her.

Suddenly she was on the move, her face set, lips now pressed tightly together. She dragged a chair to the curtains and climbed onto it and yanked the camera out. The picture disappeared and he had to wait a few seconds for one of the others to kick in in its place. By then she'd found another, hidden in plain sight on the television. Her face now twisted with rage, she mouthed a curse at him before yanking that one out too.

She made her way systematically around the room until

she'd removed all four hidden cameras and there were no more feeds left.

Andreas sipped more Scotch and prepared himself for the storm that was surely going to follow, breathing deeply to abate the weighty beats of his heart.

This was it, a few hours sooner than anticipated. Time for the truth to be revealed.

He didn't have to wait long.

The patio doors slammed open and Carrie appeared, marching straight towards him. When she reached the table, she snatched the glass from his hands and dropped the four tiny cameras into the Scotch.

He looked her up and down as she faced him, hands clenched in fists at her sides, chest heaving, her furious face pinched, looking ready to punch his lights out.

'Why don't you sit down?' he suggested coolly.

In many respects, it was better for the truth to come out now, when it was just the two of them and no witnesses.

Her lips parted and her jaw moved, clearly struggling to get any words out. When they finally came they were barely audible. 'You know, don't you?'

'That you're the undercover journalist Carrie Rivers?' He hooked an ankle on his thigh. 'Yes, *matia mou*, I know exactly who you are. I've always known.'

'So…this has all been a game?'

He allowed himself a smile. 'And what a game it has been. You have played it exquisitely. You make an excellent skivvy.'

She moved so quickly she was a blur, grabbing her glass and throwing the lemonade in his face.

Carrie, her heart a heavy burr, her stomach a mass of knots, fought for breath, feeling not the slightest bit of satisfaction to see the cold liquid soaking his face and hair.

He hadn't even flinched.

Of all the things she hated about him, at that moment the greatest thing to loathe was that he was sitting there, as cool as a cucumber with lemonade dripping off him while she couldn't even control her own breathing.

But then his eyes clashed with hers and she realised he wasn't as cool as he appeared. His jaw was taut and his eyes as dark as she'd ever seen them, filled to the brim with the danger she had always sensed but had stupidly chosen to ignore.

He'd known who she was all along. Right from the beginning.

Her brain burned just to recall it all. She'd *known* there was something wrong with the way he'd got her waiting on him hand and foot, had been too focussed on the prize at the end to allow herself to think about it. She'd also, she had to admit with painful humiliation, been too busy fighting her reactions to him to pay attention to all the dangers and warnings.

She'd ignored everything her instincts had been telling her.

It had all been a game and she had fallen for it.

She had infiltrated his life to bring him down but he had turned the tables on her and played her like a toy.

Slowly and deliberately, he wiped his sodden face with his hands and shook the liquid away, his piercing eyes never leaving her face.

'I believe it is time for you to tell me why you are really here, *Carrie Rivers*.'

His tone cut through her along with the words he used.

'But before you start, tell me your real name. Are you Carrie or Caroline? Or would you prefer I address you as Lying Snake?'

'I'm not the snake here.' Why did her voice have to

tremble so much? 'How many cameras have you had spying on me?'

'Enough to have monitored your every move if the need had arisen.'

'You spied on me while I slept? While I...?' She shuddered, unable to voice her thoughts.

He must have read them though for he frowned. 'There were no cameras in your bedroom or any of the bathrooms. Unlike you, I have boundaries.'

'Boundaries?' she shouted. 'You had me bring you a drink while you were in the bath!'

'And didn't you enjoy looking at me?' he mocked. 'Now answer my question. Your real name.'

Cheeks burning, she glared at him, willing him to feel the hate vibrating out of her and to be scorched by it. Then she straightened her spine and spoke steadily. 'My legal name is Caroline Fiona Dunwoody, exactly as it says on my passport. I have been known as Caroline Rivers since my mother remarried when I was four but my name was never legally changed. I have always been called Carrie.'

'So, Caroline Dunwoody Rivers, why are you investigating me?'

She put her hands on her hips and glared at him. 'I'm not answering that.'

'You are,' he contradicted amiably. 'I promise that by the time the sun comes up you will have told me everything I wish to know.' He leaned forward. 'You are an award-winning journalist. You specialise in exposing the illegal practices of rich businessmen. You went to a lot of effort to infiltrate my life. You supplied false references. Debbie spoke to the people you stated were your referees. I assume these were your colleagues and that this sting has been carefully orchestrated by you and your newspaper. Investigations are not started on a whim. I want to know what started this whole ball rolling. I want to know *everything*.'

She listened to his words, delivered in such a reasonable tone but with steel lacing the staccato, with mounting fury at herself.

Why had she not listened to her instincts when she'd walked into his office and every nerve in her body had told her to turn on her heels and run?

And how was she supposed to answer any of his questions without dragging herself deeper into the hole she'd stupidly and unwittingly allowed herself to fall into?

When she remained tight-lipped, he sighed. 'Caroline…'

'Carrie.'

His broad shoulders raised nonchalantly. 'I don't care. What I *do* care about is the truth and we're not going anywhere until you give me answers. You've lied and lied and now you owe me the truth.'

She put her hands on the table and glared at him. 'I don't owe you a damned thing and you lied too. You didn't have to go along with the pretence. You could have confronted me in the interview.'

'And have you run straight back to your newsroom and out of my reach?'

'But why have me skivvy after you? What was the point in that?'

'You really need to ask?' Amusement flared in the darkness of his eyes. 'You wanted to destroy me. The least I could do was let you suffer a little humiliation in return. I haven't enjoyed myself so much in years.' The amusement dropped. 'Someone is out to destroy me. It is either a business rival or a disgruntled ex-employee, or you are on a personal vendetta…because you and I have history, don't we, Carrie Rivers, sister of Violet?'

It was the way Carrie's face contorted at the mention of her sister's name that was the clincher for Andreas.

His intuition had been right all along. For Carrie, this was personal.

He got to his feet. 'Stay here. I'm going to get us a drink.'

'I don't want anything.'

'*I* do. And when I get back you will sit down and you will tell me everything because I promise you this—you won't be leaving the Seychelles until you do.'

He left her standing there, white-faced in her fury, and strode inside to his bar. He looked through the rows of bottles and plumped for a bottle of whisky, a brand with the spicy bite he needed right then.

Grabbing two crystal tumblers, he headed back to the veranda, part of him expecting Carrie to still be stubbornly standing where he'd left her but she'd sat down, legs crossed and arms folded across her chest, giving him what he could only describe as a death stare.

He took his seat opposite her, unscrewed the lid and poured them both a hefty measure. He pushed one of the tumblers to her. 'You're welcome to throw this in my face or smash the glass but it won't change anything.'

She picked it up with a scowl and sniffed it. 'It smells disgusting.'

'Don't drink it, then.'

She took a sip and pulled a face. 'It tastes worse than it smells.' That didn't stop her taking another sip.

He settled back and stared at her. She met his gaze, the hazel of her eyes reflecting fire at him. The effect gave her beauty a majesty.

Whatever had motivated Carrie to set out to destroy him, she thought she had right on her side. She was set for a humiliating disappointment.

'Okay, let us establish some facts to begin with. The paper you work for has a reputation for excellent journalism and I include you in that. When it splashes on a big story the rest of the media follows. It is rarely sued for libel and when it is it rarely loses—namely, it backs up its stories. It is a serious, weighty newspaper. It doesn't print spurious gossip. It stands to reason that there was evidence for your editor or whoever is in charge of signing investigations off to think it worth their time and expense sending you to investigate me. What was that evidence?'

She dropped her gaze from his and took another sip of the whisky she professed to hate.

'The evidence?' he repeated, his patience waning.

'There were rumours.'

He drummed his fingers on the table. 'Rumours? About what?'

Her chin lifted. 'That you were embezzling your clients' funds.'

'What a pile of rubbish. Where did these rumours come from? Because I can assure you they are lies. Markets go up and down but I invest my clients' money with the same care I would if it were my own. I defy you to find a single investor who would say otherwise.'

Something flickered on her face, a shamed, guilty expression she tried to cover by taking a bigger sip of her whisky.

But it was too late. He'd seen it. Seen her guilt.

'The rumours came from you, didn't they? What did you do? Go to your editor and say you had a credible tip-off about me that was worth investigating?'

She lifted her head to look at him, her lips drawn tightly together. The truth was right there in her eyes.

He breathed deeply, trying to contain the anger swirling like a maelstrom in him. 'Come on, Carrie. It is just you and me. There is no one to hear what we say. We have both been playing games and now it is time for them to stop. Be honest and admit the truth. You went to your editor with a pack of lies about me, didn't you?'

Carrie's chest had compacted so tightly that she couldn't draw breath.

They'd both been playing games?

This had *never* been a game for her. This had been her sister's life, which Andreas had destroyed.

Everything she had done, the risks she had taken, the lies she had told, had all been for Violet and now she had to face that it had all been for nothing.

He'd rumbled her before she'd even set foot in his office and any secrets he had would remain secret.

She would never be able to expose him. Violet would never see justice.

Pulling air into her cramped lungs, she looked him square in the eyes. 'Yes.'

'Yes?'

'Yes. It was a pack of lies. I told my editor that I'd had a tip-off from a credible source that you were embezzling funds and, yes, he believed me.'

'He authorised your investigation into me on nothing more than your word?'

She leaned forward, willing him to feel every atom of her hate for him. 'I have spent three years dreaming about bringing you down and when the time came, there was no way I was going to let it slip through my fingers. Believe me, I was *very* convincing.'

'You have been plotting this for three years?' He shook his head slowly. 'I assume this has something to do with your screwed-up sister?'

His words cut through her like an arsenic-laced blade. 'Do not speak of Violet like that.'

Now he was the one to lean forward, close enough for her to see the stubble breaking out on his jaw. 'I have no idea what kind of a woman she's grown into but do not delude yourself as to what she was like three years ago. She was a mess.'

Carrie's rage consumed her so totally that it took what felt an age before she could speak. When she finally managed to get the words out, they tumbled from her, three years of pent-up heartbreak and anger spilling out in a torrent.

'Yes, Violet was a screwed-up mess. And do you know why? It was because *you* let your drug-peddling friend seduce her under your own roof. Between you and your bastard friend, you ruined her life, so yes, the reason I'm here *is* for Violet. I knew all I had to do was find a way into your life and I would find the evidence I needed to expose you as the monster you are and kill the squeaky-clean image you've fooled the world into believing.'

'What the *hell* are you talking about?'

Andreas had listened to the venom pouring from Carrie's tongue with growing incredulity and outrage. He'd suspected her motives were personal, that she had a grudge linked back to her sister's expulsion, but had assumed she had seized the opportunity to investigate and potentially expose him when the opportunity had come.

While he could take some relief that there was no business rival trying to blacken his name or anything nefarious going on within his company he was unaware of, it felt like ice in his veins to know he'd spent the past three years unaware he had such a dangerous enemy patiently biding her time and working against him.

'As if you don't know!' Putting her hands on the table, she rose to her feet like a phoenix emerging from the ashes, her face more animated and alive with colour than he could have believed. 'James Thomas. Violet met him when she was staying in your home, under your care. He groomed her—what teenager wouldn't be thrilled to have a rich, handsome man showering her with expensive gifts and attention? He bedded her for the first time on her sixteenth birthday, the clever, underhand bastard. He was *thirty-six*! They had a six-month affair and in that time he introduced her to drugs and all manner of perversions, and then he dumped her.

'When she refused to go quietly, he threatened to destroy her—five days later and drugs were found in her school bedside table and she was expelled, her life destroyed exactly as he'd promised. *You* instigated the search of her bedroom, *you*, his friend, and don't you dare deny it—the headmistress told me that you had informed her Violet and Natalia had been taking drugs and urged her to search their room. What an amazing coincidence that drugs were only found in Violet's possessions and only Violet was expelled. Your niece got off scot-free.'

Andreas took a deep breath, veering from rage to horror and back again, furious at the accusations being levelled at him but also revolted that Carrie—that anyone—could think him capable of covering up such depravity.

'Let me make one thing very clear,' he said levelly. 'James Thomas is no friend of mine and never has been. I knew nothing of this.'

'You would say that,' she scorned.

He downed his whisky before looking her in the eye. 'Be very careful, *matia mou*. I can see you are emotional right now but you have made many slanderous accusations against me and I *will* defend myself. James Thomas came to my home once, years ago, with a number of other potential investors for a business dinner. That is the only time I met him because I disliked him on sight and refused to take his business. I don't remember Violet being there that weekend but accept she could have been. I knew nothing of any affair between them.'

'If you weren't in cahoots with him—and I congratulate you on keeping your association with him out of the public eye—then why did you get Violet expelled?'

'Because I came home early from an evening out and discovered Violet and Natalia off their heads on drugs and alcohol. It was the weekend before her expulsion. Do you remember? Because I sure as hell do. That is a weekend I will never forget.'

The rage had turned to bewilderment. 'You caught them taking drugs?'

'Yes.'

'And you didn't think to tell me?'

'I would have called you in the morning but events took a turn that changed everything. After letting them know how disgusted I was with their behaviour, I sent them to bed to sleep it off and sober up. An hour later Violet came into my bedroom naked.'

'Liar.'

'I do not lie. In her intoxicated state she thought I was going to call the headmistress to warn her of what I had found. She thought seducing me would soften my anger and stop me reporting them. Violet had left cannabis and cocaine in her bedside table at school and knew it would be found if their room was searched and that she would be expelled. She was already on a final warning for disruptive behaviour as you know perfectly well.'

Carrie looked as if she were going to be sick.

She would look worse if he relayed how Violet had tried to climb into his bed and the filthy language she had used. He dreaded to think what kind of films she'd watched to imagine he would find such language a turn-on.

'I will spare you the details but Violet became hysterical when I rejected her. The noise woke Natalia. She tried to calm her and got a smack in the face from Violet for her trouble. If Violet hadn't been only sixteen I would have kicked her out onto the street. As it was, I waited until morning and sent her home in a cab.

'You are correct that I influenced Violet's expulsion. I make no apologies for it. Natalia confessed in the morning that Violet had been running wild and using drugs for months. Natalia was being drawn into a world she didn't know how to escape. That is what prompted me to call the school—I was protecting my niece. I am not in cahoots with James Thomas. I despise the man.'

As he'd been relating the sordid details, Carrie's face had turned ashen. She paced a few steps then spun around. 'Why didn't you tell me? If Violet tried to seduce you... If *any* of this is true...' Her eyes found his, censure merging with the bewilderment.

'I left it to the school to fill you in on what your sister had been up to.'

'The school...?' Fresh fury wiped the ashen complexion from her face. 'The headmistress didn't give us even two minutes of her time. All she told us was that drugs had been found in Violet's personal effects and that she was expelled. She kicked her out just like that.' She snapped her fingers for emphasis. 'You should have called me as soon as you found them. I was her guardian. I should have been told.'

Andreas hardened himself to the guilty feeling pooling in his stomach and rose to his feet, walking over to look her in the eye. 'After the stunt Violet pulled I wanted nothing more to do with either of you. If I am being honest I assumed she had learned her tricks from you...'

Almost too late he saw the hand come flying towards him and only just managed to snatch hold of the wrist before the fingers connected with his face.

CHAPTER SIX

HOLDING HER STRUGGLING wrist up in the air, Andreas stared into the furious hazel eyes. 'Let me finish. At the time I made the assumption she had learned to seduce a man through watching you, her older sister. That was my mistake and I apologise for it—I was angrier than I have ever been and incredibly worried for my niece, who told me the next morning that Violet had been in and out of different boys' beds for months. What would you have done in my position? What would you have done if it had been Natalia running wild and dragging Violet down with her?'

She'd stopped her struggle against his hold. For a moment the anger disappeared to be replaced with sadness. 'If it had been the other way round I would have told you. Violet needed help not condemnation. If I had been told then…' She sighed, seeming to deflate with the motion. 'It probably wouldn't have made any difference. The damage had already been done. Violet *had* been sleeping around— the naïve fool thought it would make James jealous. She was desperate for him to take her back, totally unable to accept they were over, and she had no one to talk to about it. He'd made her keep it a secret and I think that screwed with her head as much as anything but she'd been completely under his spell. I only discovered the truth after the expulsion.'

And now, as she recalled the horror and despair she'd felt when Violet had made her confession, she felt the same guilt that she'd been so unaware that her darling baby sister had had an affair with a rich man old enough to be her father and who had fed her all the drugs she could consume.

Slowly it penetrated that Andreas's hold on her wrist had loosened and slid down to cover her hand. She shook it off and stepped back. She didn't want his sympathy.

Even with all the anger and hate that had flown between them there had still lived in Carrie a basic toxic awareness of him that her brain had no control over. Her hand zinged from his hold, causing a thrashing in her chest that echoed loudly in her ears.

She forced out a long breath and fought to think clearly.

She mustn't let his touch affect her thoughts.

But he didn't even need to touch her to make her react.

Moments ago she'd been inches from hitting him. She'd never hit anyone before, never even come close, and the violence she felt towards him terrified her as much as anything else.

When she next spoke, she did everything she could to keep her tone more moderate. 'Why did Violet say you set her up if it wasn't true? She was adamant about it. I took her home after that awful meeting with that condescending witch of a headmistress and she swore you had planted the drugs. That's when it all came out about James.'

'Revenge?' he suggested with a deep sigh. 'For rejecting her? For informing the school? For telling her she wasn't welcome in my home any more? For telling her to keep away from Natalia?'

'I suppose that makes sense,' she admitted heavily. 'She hates you as much as she hates him.'

Andreas inhaled. As much as he felt for the screwed-up Violet and the atrocious, immoral way she had been used by that monster, he couldn't rid himself of the anger that Carrie had thought of him in the same light, had been willing to think him corrupt and immoral too, had used her position as a journalist to get vengeance for something in which he was innocent.

'You know, it would have saved a lot of grief if you had confronted me with Violet's allegations when she made them.'

'Truth or lie, you would have denied it,' she answered flatly. 'I wouldn't have trusted your answer.'

'Natalia would have confirmed it if you had asked.'

'Natalia hero-worshipped you. She would have said anything you told her to.'

'Are you saying you still don't believe me?' he asked with incredulity.

'I don't know what I believe.' Suddenly, she laughed, the sound startling, cutting through the heavy sadness that had brewed between them. But it contained no humour. 'You've led me on an un-merry dance for two days. I would have to be mad to trust you, of all people, and quite frankly I don't trust anyone, especially not rich, powerful men who are used to bending people to their will and stamping on anyone who gets in their way and think the laws of the land are for lesser mortals to obey. And you're one of the richest and most powerful of the lot.'

She turned her back on him and stepped over to the lawn, walking to the stone wall that separated his immaculate garden from the rocks and sand that led to his beach, and put her hands on it, tilting her face to look up at the stars. The moonlight cast her silhouette in an ethereal glow. Seeing her like that sent a strange ache through him.

He wanted to touch that effervescent skin. He wanted to grab those shoulders and shake the truth into her.

Her reached her in four long strides.

'You know damn well I speak the truth,' he said, standing behind her and placing a hand on her shoulder. 'I saw it in your eyes. Your sister lied to you about me. You know it and I know it.'

She went rigid under his touch. When she spoke, there was a breathless quality to her words. 'I'm a journalist. I deal with proof.'

'You lied to infiltrate my life,' he reminded her. 'Where was your proof then?'

'I infiltrated you in the hope of finding it but it doesn't matter any more, does it? You're safe. You rumbled me. Any dirt or skeletons in your closet will stay hidden. You'll get on with your life and I'll return to London and try to forget this whole mess ever happened. At least I can take comfort that I managed to get James put down for his crimes. Now take your hand off me.'

Although Carrie stood with her back to him, she was painfully aware of his stare burning into her just as his touch was doing.

He removed his hand as she asked but before she could exhale he leaned into her, his warm breath breezing through her hair as he spoke into her ear.

She squeezed her eyes shut and held her breath.

'Ah, *matia mou*, you think this is the end of it and I'm going to let you leave? Just like that?'

Closing her eyes was no barrier, she realised with silent desperation. The heat emanating from him seeped into her, the warmth of his breath playing through the strands of her hair and tickling her earlobes, sending tiny shivers dancing over her skin and into her bloodstream.

How could she *still* react like this to him? Whether or not he spoke the truth about his acquaintance with James and his role in Violet's expulsion—and if she believed that then she would have to believe Violet had lied to her—he'd played her like his own personal puppet.

She clenched her hands into fists and turned to look him in the eye. 'You said I couldn't leave here until I'd told you the truth. Well, you've had the truth and now I can go.'

He gave a sound that was like the antithesis of a laugh and stepped back but not far enough for her to dare move. He was still too close. She could still breathe in his scent and feel his warmth.

His eyes bore into hers, mesmerising her with the depth of their strength.

'I said you couldn't leave until I'd had the truth, that is correct,' he mused thoughtfully, his voice as hypnotising as his stare. 'But I never said you would be leaving without me. I foiled your attempt to infiltrate my life and my business but now I have the staff of your paper, some of the most respected journalists in the world, thinking about me and wondering what kind of man I really am. There are already whispers in the media circulating about me. You have set something in motion, *matia mou*. Suspicions have been roused.'

Carrie's heart was beating so hard she had to fight to speak through its heavy echo in her throat. 'I will tell them I made a mistake.'

'Enough of the lies,' he whispered. 'You still think I am corrupt. Even if I believed you would say you had made a mistake and was able to say it convincingly, it wouldn't be enough. The doubts will linger. Every time a journalist sees my name the kernels of doubt will start again. My business will come under much closer scrutiny.'

'If you have nothing to hide then you have nothing to worry about.'

'If only it were that simple.' He grimaced and finally stepped away from her and walked back to the table.

Carrie rubbed her arms, the sudden removal of his warmth producing chills on her skin.

'All it takes is a few enquiring words in the wrong ears and the seeds of doubt are sown,' he said, picking up the whisky bottle. 'My clients invest their money with me because they trust me. They trust my ethics. It is a reputation I have cultivated with great care—it is the reason I refused James's business; I didn't trust him or his ethics. Once that trust is cast into doubt the repercussions can be disastrous, something I know from my parents' bitter experience. I am not prepared to take any risks with my business's health or with my reputation.'

He poured himself another drink, shaking his head with such faux regret that Carrie's internal danger signals fired back into red alert.

Raising his glass, he said, 'There is only one thing that will kill your colleagues' suspicions and the suspicions of anyone else who knows you've been investigating me. You will have to marry me.'

She stared at him, her brain freezing, her vocal cords stunned into silence.

He had to be playing more games…

'It is the only thing that will work,' he said with a decisive nod. 'You are a respected journalist. You have a reputation for fearlessness. You fight the underdog's corner. You fight for justice. If you marry me any lingering doubt about Samaras Fund Management will be killed stone dead.'

The idea of marrying her had first occurred to Andreas on the flight over, a plan he had sincerely hoped he would never have to enact. Embezzlement, though, was too serious an accusation to let slide. He had to nullify the rumours before they gained traction.

'It's the most stupid thing I've ever heard,' she whispered, her voice barely discernible in the breeze.

He took a drink and welcomed the spicy burn. 'Either you marry me or I send a copy of your confession to the proprietor of your newspaper, to my lawyer and to the police. I don't know how many laws you've broken but you've certainly broken all the ethics you're supposed to aspire to. Marry me or you're finished. Your career will be over, you might even go to prison.'

'What confession?' Her voice had strengthened. 'I haven't signed anything.'

With slow deliberation, he pulled his phone out of his top pocket where he'd put it since she discovered the hidden cameras.

'No,' she breathed.

'Yes.' He smiled grimly. 'I recorded every word.' To prove his point, he pressed play. Interference crackled loudly through the stillness of the night, then:

'You know, don't you?'

'That you're the undercover journalist Carrie Rivers?'

'You hateful bastard!' She stormed so quickly over to him she appeared to fly, until she was before him, her entire body trembling and her shaking hand held out to him. 'Give me that phone.'

'I think not.' He stopped the recording and tucked it back in his pocket. 'If you're thinking of stealing it from me, it's backed up automatically. But you're welcome to try.' He stood still and raised his hands in the air as if in supplication.

The look on her beautiful face could freeze lava. 'I can't believe you would be so underhand and deceitful.'

He lowered his hands and shrugged, unmoved. 'You're the journalist. Deceit is second nature to you as you have already proved. You were attempting to destroy me. I reserve the right to protect myself with whatever means I deem necessary. Under the circumstances, I would say I'm being generous. I am giving you the chance to save your career, your freedom and your privacy. And let us not forget your newspaper's fine reputation. Oh, and your sister.'

'Violet?' Her eyes widened alarmingly. 'You leave her out of this.'

'How can I when this is all about her? She is on the transcript. Everything we discussed is recorded. I don't imagine that everyone who hears it will be discreet—how long do you think before the tabloids get hold of it? Loose lips, *matia mou*…

'All you have to do is marry me for…let us say six months. Yes, that is a decent amount of time. Give me six months of marriage and then I will destroy the recording and all back-ups.'

'You can't expect me to give up six months of my life for you!'

He gazed at her pityingly. 'You should have thought of that before you began your vendetta against me. I am a good man. I am loyal to my family and my friends. I do not cheat in life or in love. But I am not a man to cross and you, *matia mou*, have crossed me and now you must accept the consequences.'

Her shoulders rose and then sagged as if in defeat, and she took the steps back to her seat and slumped onto it.

'Drink?' he asked, sliding into the seat next to hers and stretching his legs out.

She shook her head blankly before looking at him. 'You can't want to marry me.'

'I have no wish to marry at all, least of all to a poison-ous viper like you.'

'Then *don't*.'

'I will do whatever is necessary to protect my business and my reputation.' He rolled his shoulders and looked at her. 'I've been waiting more than fifteen years for the freedom to do whatever the hell I want; I can wait another six months for it. And, you know, I think a marriage to you could be fun.'

'It will be hell. I'll make sure of it.'

He laughed. 'I'm sure you will, *matia mou*, but you *are* going to marry me. My cousin is marrying a week on Saturday. You will come as my guest and we will announce our engagement then.'

'*What?*'

Ignoring her outrage, he continued. 'We will marry by the end of the month. The sooner we do it, the sooner we can separate and get back to our real lives.'

'No one will believe it.' Hysteria crept into her voice. 'I don't want to marry, especially not a rich man, and everyone I work with knows that.'

'You have made your feelings about rich men very clear,' he said drily. 'One could accuse you of having a prejudice against us.'

'I *do*.'

'Then you will have to act to the very best of your ability to convince people that you've fallen in love and changed your mind, won't you?' He reached out a hand and fingered her hair.

She slapped it away. 'There is no way I can pretend to have fallen in love with you; I hate everything about you.'

'That is good because I hate everything about you too. Won't that make everything much more fun?'

'Fun?' she practically shrieked. 'You're mad!'

'Not mad,' he corrected. 'Practical. I could look at your beautiful face and allow myself to be furious with you for your vendetta against me and the potential it has to destroy everything I've spent a lifetime working for, or I can flip it around and enjoy the fact that the woman who would have done me such harm is locked to my side. You can behave exactly as you want behind closed doors but you can and will make the world believe you have fallen madly and passionately in love with me, because if anyone doubts it the deal is off and I expose your underhand, illegal dealings to the world and your sister's name will be dragged into it. Do it my way and we both keep our reputations and Violet gets to stay under whatever rock she is currently hiding under.'

She breathed deeply through her nose, the baleful glare she was casting him developing an air of resignation. 'How do I know I can trust you to destroy the recording?'

'It is a gamble you're going to have to take but I *am* a man of my word and if you stick to your part of the arrangement I will stick to mine.' He cupped her cheek and brushed his fingers over the satin skin and felt the tiniest hitch of her breath before her hand rose to slap his away again. He caught it and pulled it to his chest.

'Don't pretend you don't welcome my touch, *matia mou*,' he murmured. 'We've finally been honest about everything else so why pretend? There is an attraction between us, a desire. You know it and I know it. We are going to live together for many months so why deny it?'

Her eyes held his for the longest time, a dozen emotions flickering through them, her lips pulled in tightly. Then they parted, the hazel eyes flashed and she tilted her head. 'You are suffering from what I like to call Rich Man's Delusion.'

He brought her hand to his lips and razed a kiss over her fingertips. 'Oh, yes? And what is that?'

'It's a syndrome only found in the ridiculously wealthy

man.' Her voice had dropped, become breathy. Seductive. It whispered through his skin and seeped into his loins. 'It makes him think he's irresistible. I quite understand why a man like you would suffer from it—your wealth acts as a magnet to many women, I appreciate that, but sufferers, in their arrogance, then think *every* woman is attracted to him. It's beyond your concept that a woman can look at you and not want to drop her knickers.'

Rising from her seat, she gently removed her hand from his hold and palmed his cheek so she stood over him, the tip of her nose almost touching his.

Her pretty fingers caressed his cheek and, *Theos*, his skin revelled in the sensation, little sparks firing through the rest of him, heating him like a gently firing furnace.

She moved her hand to thread through his hair. 'I don't desire you,' she whispered, her lips so close to his that if he made a sudden movement they would fuse together, her sweet breath warm on him. 'I don't want you. If I did, I wouldn't be able to do this…'

The plump lips he'd stared at for hours imagining their feel and taste brushed against his in the whisper of a kiss.

For a moment Andreas did nothing but close his eyes and savour what might possibly be the most erotic moment of his life.

Her lips pressed a little more to his, still not fused, tentative but breathing him in, sweet yet sensuous, his loins, already charged, responding as his blood thickened and all his senses sprang to life.

Right at the moment he sensed her nerve failing her, he hooked an arm around her waist and jerked her to him. As he pulled her onto his lap she gave a tiny gasp and he took ruthless advantage of it, sweeping his tongue into her mouth and holding her tightly, primal lust surging through him. Her lips were softer than a pillow and moulded to his perfectly as he deepened the kiss, savouring her taste and the shape of her body pressed so compactly to his, the furnace heating his blood fired to a roar.

Her hands clasped at his skull, her fingers massaging into him, her mouth moving with his own as if they had fused into one entity.

She fitted perfectly into him, he thought dimly, sweeping a hand over her back and then round to stroke her stomach, which pulled in with a spasm at his touch, a moan so faint it could have been the breeze vibrating from her. He slid his hand up and rubbed his thumb on the underside of her breast, felt its softness through the fabric of her dress, but before he could touch any more she jolted and dragged her mouth from his.

Her fingers still clasping his skull, her breathing erratic, kiss-bruised lips parted, she gazed at him with confused heavy-lidded eyes before whipping her hands away and scrambling off his lap.

Looking anywhere but at him, she ran her hands through her hair and straightened her dress.

Andreas swallowed and took in air, the aching weight in his groin making it hard to think let alone speak. Only the heaviness of their breaths and the beats of his thundering heart cut through the stillness of the night.

When she looked at him again some semblance of composure had returned that would have fooled him if her voice didn't sound so breathy when she said, 'See? If I desired you I wouldn't be able to walk away from that.'

Then she turned and walked away from him to the French doors, her head high, her back magnificently straight. Only the tiny missteps she took showed she was as affected by what they had just shared as he.

'Next time, *matia mou*,' he called after her, his own voice hoarse, 'you will not be able to walk away.'

She didn't look back. 'There won't be a next time.'
'Do you want to put money on that?'
She didn't answer.
A moment later she had disappeared into his house.

CHAPTER SEVEN

CARRIE LAY FULLY dressed and wide awake under the covers of the narrow bed, kicking herself for not finding another room to sleep in, one far away from Andreas. If she weren't so afraid of bumping into him on the landing she would move to another room now. She didn't need to stay in this one any more. He was hardly going to fire her.

She laughed into her pillow, a maniacal sound that she immediately smothered.

If she'd heard that noise from anyone else she would assume they were mad.

Was she mad? Had all the glorious sun that had shone on her these past two days infected her mind and driven her out of it?

It was as good an explanation as anything, she supposed, to justify her behaviour.

Twenty minutes after crawling under the bedsheets and she still couldn't get her head around what had possessed her to play with fire like that.

She'd wanted to prove a point to him and wipe that smug grin off his face but it had gone too far. *She* had gone too far.

His touch…it had scorched her. She could still feel the imprint of his lips on hers and had to stop herself from rubbing her fingers over them. And she could still feel the contours of his body pressed against her. Her blood still felt fizzy, an ache in her loins she'd never known before.

Her brain burned just to remember it. It burned to remember the effort it had taken to walk away. They had been the hardest steps she'd ever taken, fighting her own yearning body.

Her first kiss.

She gritted her teeth and wished she were in a place where she could scream her frustration. She shouldn't be reliving their kiss, she should be trying to think of ways to get out of marrying him.

Marriage! To him!

And he was deadly serious about it too.

Violet was his trump card. If it were only Carrie's future at stake she would tell him to stuff it and take her chances. She'd been prepared to lose her job and her freedom before she'd embarked on investigating him, but that recording had changed everything. Andreas was too well known and her professional name too renown for that recording not to be dynamite to the tabloid press. Andreas would probably deliver a copy of it to them himself or upload it onto social media if she refused to go ahead with his plan, and then the whole world would hear him talk of how her sister had tried to seduce him and her affair with James and all those other awful things.

She screwed her eyes tight shut, fighting the fresh panic clawing at her chest.

That recording must never find its way into the public domain. Violet's recovery was too fragile and nebulous to cope with that. She didn't want her sister to have an excuse to dive back into the horrid, seedy world that had almost killed her.

A sliver of hazy light filtered the gap in the heavy curtains. Night was fading, the sun was rising and Andreas still hadn't come to bed.

Rubbing her hand over her forehead, she rolled over so her back was to the door.

What was the point in moving rooms? she thought as hot tears prickled her eyes. She would be sharing a roof with him for the next six months.

She was trapped.

Andreas stepped onto the veranda and breathed in the hot salty air, trying to clear the last of his lethargy away.

Going to bed after the sun had risen had not been conducive for a decent sleep but he'd thought it safer to wait until he could comfortably walk before putting himself an unlocked door's distance from Carrie.

He'd dreamed of her, hot lusty dreams as disturbing as they had been erotic, waking to the taste of her kisses on his tongue. He hardly ever remembered his dreams but these were still vivid, playing like a reel in his mind.

The real kisses they'd shared were still vivid in his mind too. He smiled to remember the little stumble she'd made when she'd walked away from him, her nonchalant charade not fooling either of them.

She wanted him. It had been there in the heat of her kisses and the heat from her flesh.

She really thought she could resist the attraction for the six months they would be married?

He'd known her for mere days but knew, as he knew his own name, that Carrie would resist until her stubborn little feet got sore.

It was more than mere stubbornness. When she set herself on a path it needed a bulldozer to steer her off it. Look at her work, the powerful men she had exposed, the focus and dedication it had taken to infiltrate their organisations and find the evidence needed to expose them.

And then there was her unflinching support for her sister and her stubborn refusal to accept the truth about what had happened those years ago when she knew—and he was certain that deep down she did know—that he spoke the truth.

She'd believed him to be the friend of a monster, a thought that darkened his mood. Carrie had believed him capable of setting up a teenage girl with drugs. She believed him to be the same as the men she'd described who didn't think twice about stamping on lesser mortals if they got in their way.

There were many men in his circles who did behave like that, men who believed their wealth and position in society gave them free rein to do exactly as they pleased and generally they were right. Society turned a blind eye unless irrefutable evidence of the kind that tenacious journalists like Carrie produced meant action had to be taken.

She believed he was just like them. She believed he'd become seduced by the trappings of his wealth and lost his soul.

He inhaled even more deeply and closed his eyes, letting the burst of anger flow into his lungs and then expelling it out of his body.

His father had held onto his anger at the business rivals who had used such cruel tactics to destroy his business and it had put him in hospital with a failing heart. Deal with the root cause of the anger, punish those that needed it and move on—that was Andreas's way.

Carrie had held onto her hatred towards him for three years. She'd bided her time, taken out James first and then had decided the time was right to strike at him.

He took much satisfaction in knowing he'd cut her off

at the head and foiled her plans. Marrying her ensured his business and reputation would be safe. And what were six months? As he'd told Carrie, he'd already waited fifteen years for his freedom so a few extra weeks were nothing.

At least those months would be eventful, something he'd not had the luxury of allowing his life to be since he'd left his Greek Island of Gaios for the adventure that was America. He'd planned out his whole life: work hard and play hard at university then work hard and play hard as he built a financial business for himself and then, and only after he'd enjoyed everything life had to offer, find someone to settle down with.

Of those three goals only the first had been achieved and he looked back on his university days with nostalgia.

No sooner had he graduated than he'd discovered the dire mess his parents were in.

Movement behind him made him turn. A member of his staff had brought him a tray of food, a light mezze to sustain him, the time being closer to lunch than breakfast and the sun already burning hot.

'Have you seen Carrie?' he asked. He'd knocked on her door before leaving his bedroom and, when there had been no answer, had taken a quick look and found her room empty, her bed neatly made.

A shake of the head. 'Do you want me to look for her?'

'Don't worry about it. Let me know when she turns up.'

She couldn't have gone far, he assured himself. He kept just one car here, in an outhouse and for emergency purposes only, and there was only one road off the peninsular. It would be impossible to take his car or his speedboat without someone seeing or hearing.

Pouring his coffee first, he was helping himself to melon and yogurt when he caught a glimpse of a figure walking along the beach in his direction.

The tightness he hadn't noticed in his chest loosened.

He watched her while he ate as, step by step, she came into clearer focus, the memory of their kiss playing in his mind all over again.

'Good morning, *matia mou*,' he said when she reached the table. 'Have you eaten?'

She shook her head, her eyes hidden behind the designer shades he'd bought her. They were the only things he could see that she was wearing that he'd provided her with. Today, in temperatures already in the high-twenties and guaranteed to rise much higher, Carrie wore the outfit he'd interviewed her in, her cashmere jumper and grey trousers, which she'd rolled up to lay mid-calf. Her feet were bare.

'Coffee?' he asked, reaching for the pot.

There was a tiny hesitation before she nodded and sat down in the seat furthest from him. 'I didn't think you knew how to pour coffee.'

'Now that my minion has been upgraded to fiancée I thought I should reacquaint myself with the simple tasks I have always done for myself. And for the record, I have never expected a proper employee to perform the slavish chores I got you to do. I'm no man-child.'

He poured the coffee, added a splash of milk and one spoonful of sugar, and pushed the cup over to her.

'Thank you.' A tiny smile played on her lips. 'I didn't realise you'd paid attention to how I take my coffee.'

'I pay attention to everything, *matia mou*, especially with you.'

She tilted her head to look up at the sky then gathered her hair together and tied it into a knot without using any kind of device to hold it in place.

'Feeling hot, are you?' he asked drily. 'Maybe you should consider changing into clothing more suited to the weather.'

She took her cup and cradled it in both hands. 'Now I'm no longer your minion I can wear what I like, and what I like to wear are clothes that don't expose all my flesh.'

'Afraid you will drive me wild with desire?'

'You're putting words in my mouth,' she said stiffly.

'I have managed to keep my hands to myself since we arrived here and you have had plenty of flesh on display.' As he spoke he helped himself to a fresh bread roll and cut into it. A delicious yeasty aroma was released, a smell almost as good as Carrie's scent, and he inhaled it greedily. 'After all, you were the one to kiss *me, matia mou.* Do you need to cloak yourself to resist me?'

The knuckles holding her cup had turned white. 'I kissed you to prove a point. It meant nothing to me.'

'And you proved it very well. If I'd had any doubt that you desire me, your kiss dispelled it.'

'The fact I walked away proves I felt nothing.'

Digging his knife into a pot, he slathered jam over his roll. 'It proves that you have mastered the art of walking. For the avoidance of doubt, I am prepared to be used by you whenever you want to prove that you don't desire me. Any time at all. Day or night.' Then he bit into his roll.

Carrie fought hands that wanted to shake and put the cup to her mouth to drink her coffee, closing her mind to the vivid images playing in her mind of being in his arms and the hunger of his mouth on hers.

After three hours of sleep she'd woken from dreams already fading into haziness but which her body ached to recapture. Then everything that had passed between them had come back to her in one huge rush, all the words, their kiss...

She'd jumped out of bed, dug her own clothes, which had been laundered by Andreas's staff, out of the wardrobe and put them on as a form of armour. Then she had escaped to walk on the beach, desperate to exercise the ache deep inside out of her system and clear her mind. It had all been pointless. She could cover herself from head to toe in sackcloth and she would still feel naked before him. She could walk a thousand miles and her stomach would still flip over when she looked into those piercing light brown eyes.

And he seemed to know it.

Putting the cup back on the table, she strove to compose herself, a difficult task when she felt as if she were sitting in a sauna, the heat from the sun and her body's reaction to merely sitting and talking to Andreas combining together to be almost unendurable. But endure she would. He had the upper hand over her life now but she wouldn't allow him to have the upper hand over her emotions and feelings too. 'I don't need to prove anything to you.'

He swallowed his food. 'You have six months to convince yourself of that. For now, you should eat something. We will be leaving soon.'

'Where are we going?'

'Back to London.'

Thank God for that.

It would get better when they were back there, she assured herself, when cold drizzle and concrete greeted her rather than brilliant blue skies and palm trees.

London was her home. Her territory. It was where she belonged.

She hid her relief to ask, 'What happened to your holiday?'

'We have wheels to set in motion, *matia mou*…a wedding to prepare.'

'You said we wouldn't announce our engagement until your cousin's wedding.'

'We still need to arrange our own and you need to return to work and inform your colleagues that the tip-off you had been given about me is completely unfounded and that you are so convinced of my innocence that you have fallen madly in love with me.'

She scoffed.

He laughed loudly. 'I'm sure faking mad, passionate love will not be a problem for such an accomplished actress as yourself.' Getting to his feet, he stretched his back. 'I'm going to have a swim in the pool before we leave. Can I tempt you to strip off those clothes that are making you so uncomfortable to join me?'

'I can't think of anything less tempting.'

He shrugged and whipped off his T-shirt, the movement sending a wave of his cologne into her senses. The sun shone down on his bare torso, his toned and oh-so-masculine physique seeming to shimmer under it.

Tiny pulses set off low inside her as she remembered just how good it had felt to be held so tightly against that body...

Moisture filled her mouth and she fisted her hands against her thighs while striving to keep her features neutral, fighting the fresh hunger uncoiling itself inside her.

For a long moment he stared at her. A smile played on the lips that had kissed her so thoroughly, before he placed his T-shirt on the back of his chair. 'Are you sure you're not tempted?'

'Very sure.' But she wished her voice sounded more convincing and that she was the only one to have heard the husky rasp that had come into it.

His eyes gleaming, he hunched over to whisper into her ear, 'Your mouth says one thing, *matia mou*, but your eyes say another. I know which I believe.'

The sensation of his warm breath against her skin was

all too fleeting for no sooner had he spoken than he was striding away from her.

'You've only just eaten so try not to get a stitch while you're swimming,' she called out, forcing strength into her voice. 'It would be dreadful if you were to drown before we marry.'

He turned but didn't stop walking, surefooted even as he trod backwards. 'But it would mean you having to give me the kiss of life so it would be an excellent way to meet my maker.'

Then he winked and hardly broke stride to turn around again.

Carrie put a hand to her chest, her heart thumping hard against it, watching the long, muscular legs walk away from her.

Once he was out of sight, she took some deep breaths and closed her eyes.

It would all feel different when she was back on home soil.

It had to.

CHAPTER EIGHT

THE ELEGANT FIGURE stepped out of the revolving doors with an older woman a pace behind her, the two women chatting between themselves.

The older woman was the first to spot him standing against a black Bentley watching them. She nudged Carrie and nodded in his direction.

He raised a hand in greeting.

Carrie's eyes found his. Even with the distance separating them Andreas could see the high colour slashing her cheeks as she mimicked his greeting, then used the same hand to smooth a loose strand of hair that had fallen from the knot it had been tied into off her face, then to smooth her long cream overcoat. Her movements were rapid but her colleague noticed, a smile spreading on her face as she watched Carrie subconsciously groom herself.

After a beat, Carrie said something to her colleague, then walked steadily to him, chin aloft, her right hand clutching the strap of her handbag to her chest.

'This is a pleasant surprise,' she said when she reached him, speaking in a voice loud enough that those of her nearby colleagues, all hurrying to the nearby underground station in their eagerness to get home, would be able to hear. The inflection of surprise she put in it was a masterstroke.

Andreas had been waiting by his car for twenty minutes. He estimated a dozen of the people who had come out of the building that housed the *Daily Times* had done a double take at his presence outside their offices.

He gave a slow smile, feasting his eyes on the face that had consumed his thoughts all day. The wind picked up the strand of hair she'd only just smoothed down and he reached out to tuck it behind her delicate ear.

Her already coloured cheeks went a few shades darker, and her throat moved.

'I have been thinking of you all day,' he murmured for her ears only, delighting at the way her eyes pulsed at his words.

He'd dreamed about her again. She'd been the first thing on his mind when his eyes had opened that morning. By lunchtime he'd taken to checking his watch every few minutes, the time ticking down until their prearranged meeting outside her work offices slowing to a lethargic snail's pace. He assured himself this restlessness, this yearning to see her again was due to his impatience to get the ball rolling in the fake relationship they were about to establish. He desired Carrie but more than anything his desire was to protect his business from the lies she had told her zealous colleagues about him.

In a clearer tone that anyone passing would hear he added, 'I know it must sound crazy but I was hoping you would let me take you out for dinner.'

She swallowed, her eyes pulsing again before she blinked it away. 'That sounds totally crazy but...that would be lovely.'

'Excellent. Can I give you a lift home?'

'If it's not out of your way.'

'I wouldn't care if it was.' He grinned then opened the back door for her and followed her in.

The moment the door closed them in, her demeanour changed. Carrie perched herself rigidly beside him, knees tucked tightly together, hands clasped on her lap.

Once they were moving in the heavy London traffic, she said in a clipped voice, 'That must have been difficult for you, having to ask politely rather than just bark orders at me.'

'It was a nightmare. I'm used to people asking how high when I tell them to jump,' he replied drolly. 'How did it go today?'

She rested her head back on the leather seat and closed her eyes. 'We had a meeting about you. I said my tip-off had been wrong and that the person who gave it to me is refusing to answer my calls.'

'And that sounds plausible?'

'I've made it sound like my source is avoiding me. I'll give it a few days and say I met up with him and that he confessed he'd made it up for money.'

'And does *that* sound plausible?' He watched her response closely, looking for signs of an untruth or the bending of facts.

'It's not uncommon. We do pay for tips that are verified and lead to a story being printed, but it doesn't happen much. Most of the people who give us tip-offs do it because it's the right thing to do—we're not a tabloid, we deal with weighty stories that are often in the national interest.'

'Will they want to check with your source?'

'Our sources are sacrosanct. We never reveal them without the source's permission, not even to each other.' Carrie rolled her shoulders, trying to ease the tension in them. Her colleagues had seemingly taken her story at face value—Andreas's instincts had been proven right in that regard—but the cramped feeling of guilt had spread its way inside her and through to her muscles.

It nauseated her to think of all the barefaced lies she had told her colleagues in recent weeks. When she'd embarked on the single-minded task of bringing Andreas down, she'd been so certain of his guilt and so filled with anger at what he'd done to her sister that she had smothered her own screaming conscience. Now she was lying to her supportive colleagues for a second time but what else could she do? If she didn't go ahead with Andreas's plan then her sister's name would be dragged into the world's consciousness and whatever recovery she'd made would be destroyed. Violet would be back on the drugs quicker than a wannabe vegetarian lion passing by a wounded gazelle; unable to resist.

'How did you explain my learning your true identity?' Andreas asked.

She could happily scream. She'd had almost a whole day away from him but he'd been breaking into her thoughts the whole time. She might as well have taken him to work with her. Her morning had been devoted to talking about him in the staff meeting, her afternoon fielding female colleagues' whispered questions about what he was *really* like, if he was as handsome in the flesh as in pictures...

Every time she'd been asked her cheeks had flushed. It had been excruciating. Half the office thought she had a crush on him without her having to say a word.

Andreas would be delighted if she told him, which of course she would not.

Instead, she told him in as cool a voice as she could muster—anything to counteract the skipping warmth being back with him was inducing, 'I said your PA had learned my references didn't check out after all—at least that wasn't a lie—and that by the time this was discovered, I was already convinced of your innocence. Exactly as we agreed.'

She felt him relax beside her, pressing his own head back against the seat and facing her. She kept her eyes facing forward, not looking at him.

He inched his face a little closer to her. 'You didn't like lying to your colleagues, did you?'

How could he read her so damn *well*? He barely knew her.

Her throat caught. 'I hate it,' she muttered. 'Lying on an investigation is never real because I always know I'm getting the facts needed to expose corrupt and illegal practices. This is very different.' She turned her head to meet his gaze. 'You know I'm only going along with this to protect Violet, don't you? If it was just my own future at stake I would let you throw me to the wolves.'

He brushed his thumb over her cheekbone lazily but there was an intensity in his stare. 'She is lucky to inspire such devotion.'

Carrie grabbed his hand, intending to push it off her face but instead wrapped her fingers around it tightly and stared back with matching concentration to his. 'Do we have to do this…this marriage thing?' she asked on impulse. 'My colleagues all believe I made a mistake. I've convinced them there's nothing worth investigating about you.'

His light brown eyes continued to ring into hers for a long time before he answered. There was none of the usual staccato beat to his voice, his tone slow and thoughtful. 'A good reputation takes years to build but can be knocked down in minutes by nothing more than careless words. Do you know what happened to my parents' business?'

She shook her head.

'They owned their own water taxi company. Do you know what that is?'

'Like a regular taxi firm but on water?'

He nodded. His face had inched so close to hers she could feel his warm breath on her skin.

A voice in her head warned her to shift away from him, not allow him to get any closer.

Carefully she released her hold on his hand but his eyes...

This was why she tried to avoid looking into them.

It was as if he were hypnotising her.

'They took tourists and locals island hopping or from one side of the island to another. They also had a handful of larger boats they chartered out for daytrips through the holiday companies. It was a good living for them.' His lips tightened, the mesmerising eyes darkening. 'When I was in my final year at university a rival company set itself up. These rivals were predators. They sabotaged my parents' fleet. One of the charter boats sank; it's a miracle none of the passengers were killed. Then rumours were spread that they knowingly employed paedophiles—can you imagine the impact that had on an island built for families? People stopped using their taxis, the holiday companies cancelled their contracts...in months the business they had spent their whole marriage building was in ruins.'

Chills raced up Carrie's spine. 'That's...horrific. What did your parents do?'

He grimaced and rolled his face away from hers. 'They tried to fight but did not have the resources. They had used all their savings to get me through university. I went on a scholarship but they paid for all my accommodation, flights back home for holidays... I thought they could afford it. If I had known they were putting themselves in such a precarious financial situation I would have worked more hours to support myself...' He cut himself off and shook his head before straightening in his seat.

His gaze fixed on the screen separating them from his

driver, he continued, 'It is done. I cannot change what they did or what I did. I didn't go home at all in that last year. There was too much going on in my life. Studying. Girls. Parties. Too busy to call home and only listening with one ear when we did speak. I didn't have a clue what was happening with them. They didn't want to worry me and made my sister promise not to tell me. I learned the truth when I graduated.'

'Would you have been able to do anything if you had known?'

His jaw clenched before he answered. 'If they had told me when it first started I might have been able to scare their rivals off. I could have at least shared the burden with them. Once I did know, I helped as much as I could. Their financial situation was an incentive for me to work all hours so I could support them through it and pay for lawyers who were able to take the case to court. To prove the allegations wrong and prove that their rivals deliberately sabotaged their business. It took four years to get there but they went to prison for it.'

'Good,' she stated vehemently.

He turned his face to look at her. A faint smile appeared on his lips. 'I should have guessed that what happened to my parents would make you angry. You are a one-woman crusader against injustice.'

'I'm surprised I didn't already know about it.' She swallowed before giving a small, apologetic smile. 'I did a *lot* of research on you.'

His low laugh showed his lack of surprise at her confession. 'The press coverage was minimal and all in Greek. My name wouldn't have been in any of the reports—it all happened before I became well known.'

'How are your parents now?'

'In a good place, thank God, but it took them a long

time to recover. The whole thing did not just affect their finances but everything else too. Their reputations and health were ruined. Friends, neighbours, people who knew them well, all shunned them. By the time it went to court what mattered most to them was having their reputations restored. It was a bitter thing for them to accept, that people believed them capable of knowingly employing child abusers. My mother has since fought two different forms of cancer and my father has had a quadruple heart bypass. Losing Tanya almost finished them off.'

'I'm sorry.' Her heart twisted for this couple she had never met who had been through so much pain and heartache.

And Andreas had lost his sister.

Carrie knew what the pain of loss felt like. Her mother had been dead for seven years now but there were still times when grief caught her; a song playing on the radio, seeing her shampoo on a supermarket shelf, little things that could poleaxe her.

She felt her heart wrench to imagine all the little things that could poleaxe Andreas with grief too.

When he reached for her hand and brought it to his lips she didn't snatch it away.

'It does not take a lot to destroy a reputation and a business,' he said sombrely as he brushed his lips over her fingertips. 'I will not take the risk of assuming the damage can be prevented with some carefully chosen words. Even a *whisper* of embezzlement could cause irreparable harm to my name and then who can say what the repercussions would be? Marrying you, the woman who started the whispers, is the best way to kill it.'

Her hand tingled, her fingers itching to open up and explore his face and touch all the hard, masculine features her eyes could not help but drink in…

'We are here.'

Blood roared so hard in her ears his softly delivered words sounded distant. 'What?'

'Your home. We have arrived. Are you going to invite me in?'

Coming to her senses with a jolt, Carrie snatched her hand from his and jerked back, then fumbled with the door handle, her sudden desperation for air that wasn't filled with his scent making her all fingers and thumbs. Before she could break the handle off, the driver appeared and opened it for her.

She practically threw herself out of the car. The cold drizzle was a welcome relief on her flushed skin.

'Carrie?'

She dragged the fresh air into her lungs before looking back at him. 'Yes?'

His eyes were alive with amusement, as if he knew exactly what had got her so flustered.

He probably did know. He seemed to be able to read her like a book.

'Tomorrow, we book our wedding.'

She shrugged, pretending a nonchalance she absolutely did not feel.

'And you need to book leave from your work.'

'I can hardly marry you if I'm in the office.'

He grinned. 'I meant for my cousin's wedding. It's being held in Agon, an island near Crete. We'll fly over at the weekend.'

'But the wedding's not for a fortnight.'

'We can spend the week before it there. I'm already bored of the English rain.'

'I can't just take a week off at this short notice.' She'd thought they would spend the weeks leading up to their marriage in London, in her home territory, where she was safe…

She hadn't been safe in the back of his car.

The cold English drizzle had proved no barrier to her ever-growing awareness of him.

'Tell them I've agreed to an exclusive interview with you.' His lively eyes carried steel in them, clearly saying, *You will do exactly as you are told or our deal is off.*

He had her exactly where he wanted her and he knew it.

'Fine. But you'll have to actually give me an exclusive interview in exchange.'

Now his eyes gleamed with more than mere amusement. 'There are many exclusive things I can give you, *matia mou*. An interview is just one of them.'

The gleam deepened, his suggestive words hanging in the air between them for what felt like a whole epoch before she got her vocal cords to work, her cheeks flaming like a bonfire. 'I'll book the time off.'

A knowing smile played on his lips. 'I will pick you up in two hours.'

'What for?'

'I am taking you out to dinner, *matia mou*.' The smile turned into the wickedest of grins. 'Unless you wish to invite me into your home and cook for me?'

'Hell will freeze over before I lift a finger for you again.'

He gave an ironic shake of his head at her defensiveness. 'It is funny how your mouth tells me one thing but your eyes and body the other.'

It was with great delight that she slammed the car door in his face.

When her front door was closed and locked for good measure she stood with her back against it, trying to breathe properly.

Being on home soil hadn't changed a thing.

* * *

The knock on the front door Carrie had been anticipating for the past ten minutes still made her jump and set her already skittish heart thrumming maniacally.

She took one last look in the mirror and smoothed her hair, then breathed deeply as she walked down the stairs. Her shoes were ready by the front door and she slid her feet into them and removed her coat from the hook before she opened it.

After a mere five days in London it was time to get her passport out again.

Andreas stood at the threshold, dressed in a sharp navy suit with an open-necked white shirt, that wicked, wolfish grin on his face. 'Good morning, *matia mou*. You look as beautiful as ever.'

She rolled her eyes. 'Cut the cheesy lines, there's no one to hear you.'

Over the past five days they'd been on four 'dates', all in restaurants where the paparazzi liked to camp out. As he was a man who had always kept his private life discreet, the paparazzi responded to Andreas's presence as if he were Father Christmas bearing early gifts.

The lengths she had gone to in the past to keep her face hidden from public view, like all journalists who worked undercover, had been for nothing. That the Greek billionaire Andreas Samaras was dating the respected journalist Carrie Rivers had generated more excitement than even she had expected.

Her name would be linked to his for ever.

'It cannot be a line when it is the truth.' The pulse in his eyes shot straight through her flesh and into her bloodstream. 'You *are* beautiful.'

Heat rose inside her, a now familiar throbbing ache.

When they dined out together he would stare at her with

that same look, his eyes holding hers as he probed her with questions about her job and her interests, drawing her into conversation as any other dating couple behaved.

She'd been surprised at how...*easy* it had all been. She'd expected there to be awkwardness between them but Andreas had carried all the conversations with an easy-going wit, always keeping talk in safe territory, displaying a droll humour that often made her laugh without her having to fake it for the paparazzi lenses.

There had been moments when she had forgotten why they were there, forgotten that she hated him. Forgotten *why* she hated him; struggled to reconcile him with the man she'd spent three years dreaming of destroying.

And underlying everything lay the strange chemical cocktail that snaked between them. Always she refused to drink wine with their meals; his intoxicating presence enough for her to fight against without adding alcohol to the mix. She had to keep her defences up as much as she could, not blithely allow herself to lower them.

'Are you packed?' he asked.

She blinked sharply to clear her head—it seemed she was always having to clear it when with him—and nodded. 'My case is in the kitchen. Give me a...'

'I'll get it for you,' he interrupted with a wink, then swept past her and into the house. 'I have some papers for you to read through before we leave.'

Carrie couldn't help the laugh that burst out of her.

Until that moment, she had continued to refuse him admittance into her home. This was her territory, her sanctuary away from him, the one place she felt safe from all the turbulence that her life had become and the wild emotions he continually evoked in her.

She sighed and rolled her eyes. She had only been delaying the inevitable and, frankly, she was surprised she'd been able to keep him out of her home for this long. Andreas had proved himself to be a steamroller when it came to getting what he wanted done. Even at the registry office the other day when they'd gone to book their wedding, the date he'd wanted had been fully booked and yet somehow the registrar had been able to accommodate him for that particular date and for the exact time he wanted.

Carrie followed him down the long hallway behind the trail of his tangy cologne.

Breathing in his scent drove away her momentary amusement and replaced it with the tell-tale flutters of panic and with it a certainty that she would never be able to walk down this hallway again without thinking of him...

How could she know that?

Stop being so melodramatic, she chided herself grimly.

'This is nice,' he commented as he stepped into the airy high-ceilinged kitchen. 'It's much bigger than it looks from the outside.'

'Yes, it's a regular Tardis.'

'It's a good location too. It must have cost a lot of money to buy.'

'I guess so. It costs a fortune to maintain and heat.' The front looked out over Hyde Park but as a child the monetary value of such a prime location had meant nothing to her. She remembered sunny days there, going for picnics, curling up on her mother's lap under a tree as she read her stories, remembered teaching Violet how to do cartwheels and walk on her hands. Remembered dropping her ice cream and trying so hard to be grown up and not cry about it and Violet, chubby legged and her hair in pigtails, toddling over to her.

'You eat mine too, Cawwie...'

She blinked the bittersweet memories away before they could lance her heart any more.

She'd spoken to Violet only the day before, another stilted conversation but this time it had been stilted on both sides, the question Carrie most wanted to ask she'd found herself incapable of saying: *Did you lie about Andreas setting you up?*

She hadn't asked because she was afraid of the answer. She was afraid that even if Violet's answer was negative, she might not believe it.

'I've lived here since I was four,' she explained, speaking over the fresh roil of nausea that was induced whenever she allowed those doubts to gain too much space in her head. 'My stepdad bought it when he married my mum. She got it when they divorced.' And Carrie and Violet had inherited it when she'd later died. 'What were the papers you wanted me to look at?'

He pulled a thick envelope out of his inside pocket and held it out. 'It's a draft of our pre-nuptial agreement.'

'What pre—?' She caught herself and shook her head. 'Of course. You're protecting yourself.'

'Anyone in my position would protect himself but you will see I have made more than adequate provisions for you.'

'Unless that document says we both walk away with nothing from each other I don't want to read it. I don't want your money.'

Andreas stared at her beautiful set face.

Had there ever been a more stubborn person in the history of the earth?

He thought of the thousands of pounds' worth of designer goods she'd left behind in the Seychelles, giving them to one of Sheryl's young daughters who was the same dress size. He only knew this because an anxious Sheryl had called him to make sure it was okay for her daughter to have them.

That Carrie had done this shouldn't have surprised him when he considered she'd spent their last day there sweltering in her own clothes rather than changing into any of the items he'd bought for her. It had still stung though, just as her refusal to take the envelope from his hand and read it also stung. She would much rather overheat than wear something paid for by him. She would rather struggle to pay her heating bill than accept a cash sum from him that would keep her comfortable for life.

If she were starving she would still refuse his money.

And he'd thought they'd been making progress.

She still believed him to be corrupt.

'Carrie,' he said, making sure to keep his tone moderate although he wanted to snarl his words at her, 'I'm only giving you what a court would award you on our divorce.'

'I don't want it. I earn my own money.'

He shook his head, incredulity and anger merging like a toxin inside him. 'You are unbelievable.'

'Why? Because I won't play the money roulette game? I'm only marrying you to protect my sister. I don't want your money. The only thing you could give me that I would want is a time machine that can fast forward the next six months.'

He held the envelope up. 'You are sure about this? You are certain you want to give up a small fortune?'

'Yes,' she answered without any hesitation.

'I'll get a new one done, then, that spells out you receive *nothing*.' He ripped the envelope in half and let the pieces fall to the floor. Then he stepped over them to the large old-fashioned suitcase by the kitchen table. 'And now that that is settled, we can go. Maybe some sunshine will make you more agreeable although I doubt anything could.'

CHAPTER NINE

CARRIE OPENED THE French doors of the living room of the lavish Mykonian-style villa she had been given for her stay on Agon and looked out over its beautiful garden. Fruit trees had come into blossom, filling the air with the most wonderful spring scent. She breathed it in deeply, letting it calm her ragged nerves.

The island itself was dazzling, mountainous and overlooked by blue skies, but that was where the similarity with the Seychelles ended. Andreas's peninsular had been remote, his and the chef's cottage the only homes for miles and miles. Agon was filled with pristine white homes, its beaches golden where the Seychelles sand was white. There was a different feel to it too, different smells and a much different vibe. This was a rich island and a growing financial powerhouse. Carrie's villa would befit royalty and if she were in a different frame of mind she would be delighting to find herself staying in such a beautiful place for the next week.

She didn't know if the villa was hers alone or if Andreas was sharing it with her. She hadn't seen him since his driver had dropped her off and brought their cases in while Andreas waited in the car. His only words as she'd got out of the vehicle had been, 'I'll be back by seven to take you out for dinner.'

Since they had left her London home that morning he had hardly exchanged three sentences with her. His cases were still by the front door. If he were planning to stay here they would have been taken to whichever of the six bedrooms had been appointed as his.

A housekeeper and a general handyman had been in the villa to greet her and show her to her room, the handyman carrying her case up the marble stairs for her.

Her bedroom had taken her breath away; it was the complete opposite of the box room she'd been given in the Seychelles. She'd then been given a tour of the rest of the place and given the phone number for the staff house, where a small army of workers lived, all available twenty-four-seven for whatever she needed.

She'd been alone now for three hours and time was dragging insufferably. She'd had a bath in her en-suite bathroom, feeling decadent in the freestanding roll-top bath, and then had changed into a pretty summer top in a light peach colour with spaghetti straps and a full matching skirt that fell to mid-calf. The top half of it especially was very similar to the summer dresses Andreas had bought for her but…this didn't feel as good. The clothing he'd bought for her had caressed her skin in a way she hadn't realised until she'd put her own, much cheaper clothing back on.

She'd paced from room to room ever since, checking her watch every few minutes.

She checked it again and bit her lip.

It was almost seven.

Nerves were accumulating in her belly at an ever-increasing rate, far more violent nerves than she'd become used to when waiting for him to pick her up for their dates in London.

She'd angered him and while it was a thought that should make her glad, it made her stomach feel all coiled and acid-filled. In all that had passed between them in the past week she'd forgotten what it felt like to be on the receiving end of his anger, as she had been three years ago when he'd lasered her with his stare outside the headmistress's office.

He'd been angry the night when the truth had been revealed between them but that had felt different. They'd both been angry—furious—with each other. Since then he'd been all charm and geniality and she didn't think it was an act. He was that way with everyone, treated even underpaid and always undervalued waiting staff in restaurants as if their opinions on the dish of the day truly mattered, made a point of learning their names and *remembering* them.

She couldn't help thinking that her refusal to open his envelope had wounded him in some way, which she knew was a ridiculous notion...

Footsteps treading on the marble floor sounded out behind her and she spun round to find him standing there holding an enormous bunch of red roses.

Their eyes met and held, and her heart made the most enormous thud against her ribs, the motion knocking all the air from her lungs.

There was no humour in his eyes, no knowing gleam, not even any anger, just a steadfast openness that made the thuds in her heart morph into a racing thrum.

He'd changed into fresh clothes, tailored dark grey trousers and a black shirt, since he'd dropped her at the villa. But there was something unkempt about him, his hair a little messier than he usually wore it, his jaw thick with stubble when he'd always been freshly shaved on their dates.

He held the flowers out to her. 'Peace offering.'

She paused for only a moment before taking them from him.

'Thank you,' she whispered.

She'd never been given flowers before.

Keeping her eyes on his, she rubbed her nose against the delicate petals. They smelt wonderful.

'You look beautiful,' he said simply.

Her heart now racing so hard she could imagine it bursting out of her ribs, she attempted a smile but found one impossible to form.

'I'll find a vase to put these in.' Forcing her feet to uproot themselves from the floor, she walked past him and headed to the vast kitchen on the other side of the villa.

Andreas kept step beside her. 'Have you settled in all right?'

'Yes, thank you.' She hadn't found it this awkward to talk to him since the interview in his office. Back then, her tongue had been tied with the fear of being discovered. Her fear now was of a completely different hue. 'Have you had a good afternoon?'

'It has been productive.'

'Oh?' They'd reached the vast kitchen.

Carrie put the flowers on a worktop and immediately busied herself opening cupboards and drawers, ostensibly to find a vase but more to keep her attention diverted from him and the terrifying things happening inside her.

'I had a meeting.' He opened a high cupboard and took down a crystal vase. 'Is this what you're looking for?'

She took it from him with a small smile of thanks and almost dropped it when their fingers brushed.

A shock of electricity skipped over her skin and danced into her veins, and she hurriedly turned her back to him as she muttered her thanks.

Just breathe.

First she filled the vase with water and added the sachet of feed to it.

Breathe.

She'd spotted scissors earlier when she'd made herself coffee, and she grabbed them out of the drawer and cut the pretty cellophane wrapping around the roses, then took the first rose—thankfully the thorns had been removed—and cut an inch of the base off and put it in the vase. She grabbed another, certain she remembered her mother doing something else when she was given roses but her brain was overloaded, trying to focus on the task at hand while tuning out the huge figure standing so close to her.

She could feel his eyes on her.

As she reached for another rose, a warm hand pressed into her lower back while another wrapped around her reaching wrist.

She couldn't move. She couldn't breathe. Her blood had thickened to a sludge that pulsed through every crevice in her body.

Andreas felt the pulse in Carrie's wrist beat madly against his thumb, the only movement on her still frame.

Theos, he wanted her so badly it had become a constant ache he carried everywhere with him.

He'd been so damned *angry* with her and her stubborn refusal to take her blinkers off when it came to him.

When he'd dropped her at the villa he'd had half a mind to check himself into a hotel for the night but then he'd left his meeting hours later and a woman in a soft-top convertible had driven past him, roof down. She'd had chestnut hair almost identical in colour to Carrie's. His chest had contracted so tightly in that moment he'd had to fight for breath.

Why should he care what Carrie thought of him? he'd told himself as he'd dragged air into his lungs. She was only going to be in his life for a short period. All that mattered was that she marry him and kill the rumours before they properly started.

But even as he was thinking all that he'd found himself walking into a florist and asking for their largest bunch of roses.

He'd never bought flowers for a woman before.

It had been the look in Carrie's eyes as he'd passed the flowers to her that had driven the last of his anger out. There had been a vulnerability in those eyes he'd never seen in her before.

He leaned forward to breathe in her cloud of hair, the silky strands tickling his nose, and heard a jagged inhalation.

His need for her, the compulsion to touch her, the yearn to taste her... He had never wanted a woman more.

He breathed the fragrant scent of her hair in again then cupped her cheeks in his hands, his body almost touching hers, close enough to feel the tiny quivers vibrating through her.

Stark, frozen hazel eyes stared into his, her trembling lips parted but no sound coming out.

'I'm going to kiss you,' he said huskily. 'I'm going to kiss you until you tell me to stop.' Then, caressing her cheeks with his fingers, he pressed his lips to hers...

At first she remained stock still, not even breathing, her body like soft concrete. Slipping his hands round to spear her hair and cradle her head in much the same way she had cradled his what now felt like a lifetime ago, he moulded his mouth a little more firmly to hers, gently coaxing her into a response he knew she was fighting with everything she had.

Stubbornly, she continued to resist, her body still rigid, her soft plump lips refusing to move with his. But she didn't push him away or tell him to stop.

Emboldened, he gently moved his mouth over hers and ran a hand down the length of her back.

He felt her give the tiniest of shivers.

Then she took the tiniest of breaths.

And she still didn't push him away or tell him to stop.

He pressed himself a little closer, trapping her against the worktop.

She gasped into his mouth then quickly closed her own again but made no effort to break away from his kiss.

And still she didn't push him away or tell him to stop.

His mouth still covering hers, Andreas brushed his hands lightly down her sides and clasped her hips, then in one movement broke the kiss to lift her onto the worktop. Her hands sprang to life and grabbed his arms as if to steady herself.

Her eyes fluttered open.

For a moment that passed like an age, they stared into each other's eyes, Carrie's hooded gaze pulsing dazed desire at him. The hands holding his biceps like a vice loosened but she didn't let go.

Suddenly desperate to feel the softness of her lips against his again, he crushed his mouth to hers and gently pushed her thighs apart through the fabric of her skirt and stepped into the space he'd just created so the unmistakable feel of his arousal pressed against her pelvis, obvious even with all the layers of thin clothing separating them.

Her breaths were now coming in sharp ragged motions, her sweet yet coffee-laced scent whispering over his mouth and seeping into his pores, but still she made no effort to kiss him back.

And nor did she push him away or tell him to stop.

And nor did she push him away or tell him to stop when he found the hem of her top and slipped his hand under it.

The texture of her skin was silkier and softer than he remembered, as if some benevolent creator had wrapped her in satin.

Needing to kiss more than just her mouth, he dragged his lips over her cheeks and jaw then made a trail down her neck, the scent of her flesh firing into senses already fit to burst.

He was fit to burst. Never—*never*—had he felt sensation and heat like this and it was everywhere in him, from his heart that battered against his ribs to his loins that weren't aching, they were burning.

And never had he felt he would give all his worldly goods to receive just one kiss.

Carrie was letting him kiss her. She was letting him touch her. But she was giving nothing back. She was clinging onto that last ounce of stubborn denial for dear life.

But still she didn't push him away or tell him to stop.

He brushed his lips over her mouth again and nuzzled his nose against hers. His hands swept over her back then moved to her belly, which quivered under his touch as it had when she had kissed him on his veranda. She jolted again when his fingers brushed the underside of her breast, her own fingers tightening reflexively on his arm, but this time she made no attempt to escape.

For a moment he thought fevered wishful thinking had imagined her rubbing her pelvis tighter to his until he heard her swallow between the shallow breaths and her fingers tighten on him again.

Cradling her head in his hand, he tilted her back a little to stare deep into her eyes.

She stared back mutely, everything those stubborn, beautiful lips wanted to say, everything she was feeling reflecting back at him.

Wordlessly he brought his other hand up to her throat then slowly dragged it down, over the breasts he longed to touch without a barrier, feeling the heavy beats of her heart through it, skipping over her quivering belly, down her thighs until he could reach no further and he gathered the material of her skirt into his fist. Then, working slowly, he brought it up to her knee before letting the skirt go so it covered his hand, which now rested on her bare thigh.

Her left hand still gripped his biceps, her right hand...

Her right hand was now splayed on his abdomen, the heat from her touch penetrating through his shirt.

Andreas gritted his teeth. He wanted nothing more than to escape the straightjacket his clothes had become but instinct told him to wait just a little longer...and Carrie pressed her pelvis into his again, her body making spasmodic movements, her lips parting as if readying herself for his kiss again...

He obliged, covering her mouth with his. He felt the lightest of movement beneath it before she clamped her lips back together and turned her head to rub her soft cheek against his. Her fingers on his abdomen had slipped around to splay across his back in short grabbing motions.

He traced his fingers further up her thigh until he found the heat he was seeking and brushed his thumb against the damp, burning cotton.

She jerked against him, the hand holding his lapel moving up and gripping his neck. When he slid his hand under the cotton and found the damp, downy hair that covered her most intimate secret, she jerked again and pressed her cheek even tighter against his.

He slid his fingers lower and discovered her in full bloom, the feminine complement to the painful constriction in his underwear.

Closing his eyes to everything but this moment, he breathed her in as he continued to touch her, finding a rhythm with his fingers that had her grinding against him, her breaths so shallow and rapid he couldn't distinguish where one breath started and another began until she flung herself tightly against him and buried her face in his neck, crying out. Shudders rocked through her frame as she clung to him, her breaths rapid and hot in his neck.

Andreas, his cheek pressed into her hair, now had both arms wrapped around her, stroking her back.

And she held him tightly too.

'Don't say it.' Her words were spoken into his neck but then she shifted and loosened her hold on him, disentangling herself to cup *his* face with *her* hands. Dark, ringing hazel eyes beseeched him. 'Please, don't say it.'

He gave a short, sharp shake of his head. Blood roared in his ears, his chest the tightest he had ever known it.

Even if she hadn't asked, he couldn't look at her and smugly say, *See, I knew you wanted me.*

That had been the most erotic, mind-blowing and... *touching* moment of his life, and he would never diminish it.

Her eyes still gazing into his, she swallowed then slowly brought her face closer and covered his lips with her own.

It was the sweetest, most tender kiss of his life.

And then her lips parted, her tongue danced into his mouth, her arms locked around his neck and he was kissing her back with all the passion his soul possessed.

Carrie shut off the part of her brain shouting at her in increasingly terrified shrill tones to stop this madness *now*.

She shut it down completely.

She had never felt so alive, had never known her body capable of such intense, concentrated pleasure.

He had done this to her. Andreas. His touch, his scent... him. It was as if every part of her body had been tuned to a frequency only he had the dial to.

She had fought her desire with everything she had and it hadn't been enough. He'd broken through her resistance completely. And now she wanted the rest of it and she wanted him to have the pleasure he had just bestowed on her too.

He tasted so darkly masculine, she thought headily, as she drank in his kisses and razed her fingers up and down the nape of his neck. Why fight something that felt so right? Just what was she scared *of*?

But she had to shut her mind off again when the shrill voice tried to break back through to tell her exactly what she was scared of.

She was giving her body to Andreas, nothing more. Nothing more…

For the first time in her life she was going to let her body guide her. Consequences only happened when people allowed foolish dreams to overtake their reality.

Dimly she was aware of him gathering her tightly to him and lifting her off the worktop.

Later, she would have no concrete memory of them getting to a bedroom, just floating images of being carried in his arms and them falling onto the nearest bed in a tangle of limbs.

Their eyes locked.

Carrie lifted her top up and over her head, discarding it without thought.

His throat moved before he held out a hand.

With fingers that fumbled with inexperience, she undid his shirt buttons. As soon as she had the first three opened she put her lips to his chest and breathed in his clean musky scent, a pulse rippling through to her core when he groaned. His skin felt so smooth yet so different from her own, hard where she was soft and so very warm. Brushing her lips all over his chest, rubbing her cheek against the fine hair covering much of it, feeling his raging heartbeat thrum through his skin, she worked the rest of the buttons until the shirt was undone and Andreas shrugged it off, then his arms wrapped around her waist to undo her bra. He flung it away and sat back to stare at her naked breasts for the first time.

His eyes dilated, a moan dragged from his throat. He raised a hand that belied the faintest tremor and cupped her.

A bolt of need pulsed through her, so pure and so shockingly strong that she snapped her eyes shut and struggled for air.

Breasts that had always just…been there, a part of her like her arms and legs, suddenly felt heavy and swollen and needy. He massaged them gently then replaced his hand with his mouth.

She gasped and clenched her hands into fists.

All those wonderful feelings he had brought about in her such a short time ago were building up again but this time they felt so much more, the need being evoked no longer concentrated but *everywhere*, every part of her aching for his touch and yearning for his kiss.

As if he could sense her need, Andreas stripped off the rest of her clothes, trailing hot moist kisses all over her flesh, increasing her hunger.

Her skirt was unbuttoned and pulled off, thrown to the floor, the plain cotton knickers quickly following and then she was naked, lying fully exposed to a man's gaze for the first time in her life.

Andreas stared down at her, his eyes a colour she had never seen before, dark and molten. He'd removed his trousers—how, *when*?—and now all that was left to remove was his underwear.

Not taking her eyes from his, Carrie sat up to kneel before him and placed her hands on his heavily breathing chest. She dragged her fingers slowly down, over the hard muscles of his abdomen, to the band of his snug-fitting grey boxers.

Swallowing the moisture that had filled her mouth, she gripped the band between her fingers and tugged them down over his hips.

Released from its tight confines, his erection sprang free.

She swallowed again, unable to hide her shock.

The glimpse she had seen when he'd been in the bath… that had been nothing to seeing it loud and proud in the flesh. She'd already gauged that he was well endowed but had been unprepared, not only for his size but also the unexpected beauty of it.

She looked back into his eyes and drank him in, a languid, floaty feeling seeping through her. *How could it have been anything but beautiful when it belonged to the most beautiful man in the world?*

The molten eyes seemed to drink her right in too. He took her hand and brought it to his lips, then gently lowered it down to his erection, holding her loosely enough that she could snatch her hand away if she wanted.

She did not want to snatch it away, she thought dreamily. She *wanted* to touch it. Tonight, she wanted everything.

Letting him guide her, she took it into her hand and felt it throb beneath her fingers.

He moaned, his throat moving.

With his hand covering hers, showing her without words how he liked to be touched, she followed his lead. Thrills raced through her to hear his tortured groans and see the ragged movements of his chest. She could feel the heat bubbling inside her, every bit as turned on with what she was doing and the effect it was having on him as she had been when he'd been touching her.

She didn't hide her disappointment when he suddenly pulled her hand away.

He speared her hair and brought his face to hers to growl, 'I want to come inside *you*.' And then he kissed her, a kiss so deep and passionate she felt her bones turn to heated liquid.

The kiss was over all too soon as he pulled away from her and climbed off the bed. Stepping out of his boxers, he grabbed his trousers and pulled out his wallet. From it, he removed a small box of condoms.

He flashed her a tortured grin. 'I have been living in hope, *matia mou*.'

He was back by her side on the bed before she could blink.

He dropped the box on the pillow and pinned her down beneath him, kissing her again, her mouth, her cheeks, her neck, his hands roaming her body, muttering words she didn't understand into her ear but which added to the sensations already consuming her. The weight of his erection lay heavy on her thigh and she made to touch it again but he grabbed her wrist to stop her.

'Later,' he whispered hoarsely. 'You can do whatever you want to me later but right now I need to be inside you.'

She kissed him, sweeping her tongue into his mouth, letting him know with her body how badly she needed him inside her too.

It didn't matter that this was something she had never done before. She hadn't done *any* of this before, had spent her adult life denying herself something so beautiful and... *necessary*. Not any more.

Keeping his body so deliciously flush on hers, he groped for the packet and quickly extracted a square foil from it, which he ripped open with his teeth. Then he shifted slightly onto his side and deftly sheathed himself.

His mouth found hers again as he twisted back to lie on top of her, using his thighs to nudge her legs a little further apart so his erection was right there...

He entered her with one driving thrust, plunging her straight into a world where heaven and hell collided.

Hell; the sharp pain she hadn't expected and that made her suck in a shocked breath...and which Andreas either felt or sensed because he stilled.

'Carrie?' He lifted his head a little to look at her, confusion appearing in the molten depths of his eyes.

But already her body was adjusting to the feel of him inside her, the pain already diminished.

She smiled and tilted her chin to press her mouth to his. For long moments they simply touched lips together and breathed each other in. Then she closed her eyes as he began to move, and then...

Then she found herself in heaven.

He made love to her slowly, his thrusts tempered. His hands held hers tightly as he ground his groin against hers, stimulating her as he filled her.

Yes, she had found heaven.

Then he raised himself onto his elbows to lock eyes with her, causing the stimulation to deepen in rhythm with his deepening thrusts. Sensation pulsed like bolts of lightning in her core, a burning need growing and intensifying.

Wrapping her arms tightly around him, she ran her hands down his back exulting in the feel of his muscles and sweat-slicked skin beneath her fingers, then closed her eyes to everything but the sensations taking control, submitting to them, submitting to the pleasure and magic of everything they were creating together until the lightning exploded.

Pleasure shattered through her like a tsunami, bolts tearing down her spine and into her every crevice with an intensity that sent white light flickering behind her eyes and a cry from her mouth that sounded distant with the drumming in her ears.

Electricity danced on her and through her, almost stunning her. She held onto Andreas as if he were an anchor in this world, a dim acceptance that this was all because of him and only him, that there could never be another...

His lips crashed onto hers as he gave a roar that seemed to have been dredged from his very soul and drove into her for one last powerful thrust that made him shudder with the force of his own release.

Shocked eyes fell on hers before he gave one last groan and lowered himself onto her with his full weight, and buried his face in her hair.

Carrie tightened her hold on him, sighing to feel his breath tickling her scalp.

The sensation that had erupted through her with such violence was now a gentle ripple and she closed her eyes, wishing with all her heart that she could bottle this moment for eternity.

CHAPTER TEN

ANDREAS AWOKE ON his side to find Carrie's face pressed against his chest, an arm and thigh slung around him.

He also awoke to find himself fully aroused.

He took a deep breath and rolled onto his back, careful not to disturb her sleep. She rolled with him, her face now buried in his side, her hand drifting to rest on his abdomen.

The room was shrouded in such darkness he knew without having to look that he'd slept for many hours. He smiled ruefully to know he'd done that most male of male things and fallen asleep almost immediately after sex.

Yes, a most male of male things but not something he had ever done before. But then, he had never known sex to be like that before, an experience so intense that climaxing had felt as if his brains might explode from his head. He'd made it to the bathroom to dispose of the condom then fallen back into bed, scooped Carrie into his arms to cuddle against her, and fallen straight into blissful sleep. The evening had still been light outside.

He'd never done that before either: fallen asleep with his arms wrapped so tightly around someone.

He had good reason to believe Carrie had never done any of this before.

The little spot of blood he'd seen on the sheets when

he'd climbed back into bed had only consolidated what his body had told him when he'd first entered her.

Carrie had been a virgin.

He hadn't bedded a virgin since he'd lost his own virginity. Then, they had both been seventeen and full of raging hormones. He'd promised faithfully to marry her if she slept with him, a blatant lie told by horny teenage boys the world over. They'd given each other their virginity and afterwards he'd ridden off on his scooter, cigarette dangling from his mouth, feeling like a king.

He smiled at the memory. He hadn't thought of Athena for years. She'd dumped him for one of his friends a few weeks later, which he was sure had broken his heart for at least five minutes. As far as he knew, Athena and Stavros were still married with an army of children running them ragged.

He was quite sure she was the last virgin he'd been with. The irony of him actually marrying the second virgin he slept with after promising to do that faithfully with the first did not escape him.

He ran a hand gently over Carrie's hair, smoothing it, enjoying the silky feel of it on his skin.

What had made her wait so long?

To have missed out on those heady teenage years where hormones dictated every part of your life? No office romances either? He kept a strict hands-off rule with his staff but he didn't expect them to keep their hands off each other. So long as it didn't interfere with their work he couldn't care less what the consenting adults he employed got up to.

Had Carrie been waiting for someone special?

He brushed his finger along her cheek, his chest tightening to imagine the myriad reasons why she had chosen to remain a virgin and what the implications for them were.

She stirred against him and nuzzled into his chest. Her movements were enough to tighten the other, much baser part of him that had already been wide awake and aroused and when her fingers began to drift lightly down his abdomen…

Minutes later and he was inside her again.

Carrie was awake for a long time before she dared move. She was pretty sure she had the huge bed to herself. The heat that had enveloped her throughout the night had gone.

Eventually she plucked up the courage to slowly roll over and confirm what her instincts were telling her.

Andreas had left the room.

She stared at the indentation on his pillow and was horrified to find tears filling her eyes.

Quickly she averted her gaze to the ceiling and breathed raggedly through her mouth, a hand on her chest, blinking frantically as she fought the tears back.

What had she done?

Oh, dear God, what had she *done*?

She had slept with him. Not once, but three times.

She had become someone new in his arms. She'd felt like a beautiful butterfly that had emerged from its cocoon for the very first time and found its wings.

Andreas had taken her to paradise but now, with the early morning light streaming through the shutters, paradise seemed as distant as the moon. Now she wanted to find her old cocoon and crawl back inside it.

What was the protocol for dealing with this? *Was* there a protocol lovers kept to when seeing each other for the first time after making love?

Lovers?

Heat suffused her everywhere and she covered her face with both hands, fighting back the sobs desperate to break out.

She didn't want to be Andreas's lover. She didn't want to be anything to him, not his fake fiancée, not his fake wife, not anything…

The door opened.

As quick as lightning, she turned back onto her side and squeezed her eyes shut.

If she pretended to be asleep maybe he would leave her alone.

Footsteps padded over the floor tiles. New scents filled the room. Coffee. Fresh bread.

She heard another door slide open and cool air filled the room.

A minute later the bed dipped. A hand brushed against her hair.

She couldn't stop her shoulders moving in reflex at his touch.

Holding her breath as tightly as she held the sheets around her, she rolled onto her back.

Andreas was sitting on the edge of the bed wearing nothing but a pair of jeans.

His eyes were on her, a wariness underlying the intensity of his stare. 'Good morning,' he said quietly.

She managed the semblance of a smile but couldn't get her throat, echoing with the vibrations of her hammering heart, to move enough to speak.

'I've got breakfast for us,' he said after an impossibly long period of silence between them during which they did nothing but stare at each other. 'It's on the balcony.'

She hadn't known this room had a balcony.

She didn't even know what room they were in. It certainly wasn't the one she'd been given.

'Give me a minute to get changed and I'll join you out there,' she whispered.

His eyes narrowed slightly before he nodded and got to his feet.

She watched him step out onto the balcony, sliding the glass door shut behind him. Only when he was out of her eyeline did she slide out of the bed and snatch her discarded clothes from the floor. She found the en-suite and locked the door behind her.

Barely twelve hours ago she had felt not a modicum of shyness in showing her naked body to him. He had kissed and touched every single part of her and she had thrilled at the sensual pleasure of it, a pleasure she had never imagined; seductive and addictive.

She had been drunk with it all. Drunk on Andreas.

Now she wished for nothing but to hide back in her protective cocoon and forget it had happened.

Throwing her clothes on, she splashed her face with water and smoothed her hair as best she could with her fingers, trying not to look too hard at her reflection in the mirror so she couldn't see the bruised look of her lips or the glow on her skin that had never been there before.

Andreas was eating a Greek breakfast pastry when she joined him on the balcony.

'Coffee?' he asked amiably.

'Yes please.' She sat opposite him and looked at the huge spread laid out between them. 'Did you do all this?'

'Of course not. I called the chefs in and got them to make it.' The mockingly outraged face he pulled as he said this, that *How dare you even suggest I soil my hands by preparing my own food?* expression, tickled her and she found herself fighting back a grin.

But then she met his eye and the smile formed of its own accord. Not a full grin, but her lips loosened enough to curve a touch.

His features relaxed to see it. He pushed her cup of

coffee to her then leaned back. 'Eat something. You must be starving.'

That reminded her of their missed dinner. And his roses...

'What's wrong?' Andreas asked, seeing her brow suddenly furrow.

'Those poor roses. I never...' She dropped her gaze from his and snatched a bread roll, opening it with her fingers.

He knew exactly what had caused her face to look as if she'd been dipped in tomato juice and his loins twitched to remember lifting her onto the worktop, the roses abandoned, and all that had followed.

And what had followed had been one of the best nights of his life. Maybe the best. He couldn't think of a better one.

'The housekeeper has revived them,' he assured her, remembering the way Carrie had rubbed her nose against the petals when she'd taken them from him.

She'd rubbed her nose over his stomach in the exact same way...

The twitch in his loins turned into a throb, the memory of her nails digging into his back as she'd orgasmed strong enough that he could feel the indentations on his skin as fresh as if she were making them still.

'That's good,' she said, nodding a little too vigorously. She stretched for the jar of honey with a hand that trembled and said in a voice so low he had to strain to hear her, fresh colour smothering her entire face, 'Does she know I, err, we, slept in the wrong room?'

'It doesn't matter, *matia mou*.'

'She needs to know.' She struggled to remove the lid. 'When we're gone someone else will stay here. The sheets...'

'Carrie.'

She stopped talking and reluctantly met his gaze, eyes shining with what looked suspiciously like unshed tears, her chin wobbling.

She'd been a virgin.

Until twelve hours ago she had reached the age of twenty-six untouched.

He could not shake that thought from his mind.

'Let me open that for you,' he said gently, nodding at the honey jar clasped so tightly in her hand.

She pushed it across the table to him, her shoulders slumping.

He twisted the lid off and pushed it back to her, resisting the urge to force her to take it from his hand.

She had been a virgin.

She had never made love before.

She had never faced a man the morning after before.

The vulnerability he had seen in her when he'd given her the flowers was even more starkly apparent now and it tugged at his heart to see it and with it came a compression in his chest, an overwhelming punch of emotion he couldn't begin to comprehend but which set alarm bells ringing inside him, a warning that he was steering into dangerous territory and it was time to back away.

'There is no wrong or right room here because the villa is mine,' he said in as even a tone as he could manage.

She darted a little glance of gratitude at him before dipping a teaspoon into the honey jar. 'What do you mean?'

'I signed the paperwork for it yesterday. That's where I went after I dropped you here, to meet with the previous owner.'

'You bought it? But why?'

He shrugged. 'I was looking for a villa to rent for the week. I didn't see anything I liked so I looked at villas for sale and this was available.'

'You bought a villa on a whim? Without even looking at it?' She spread the honey on her roll.

'I saw the pictures. I know the island pretty well—I've had an eye on buying something here for a while. I knew it was in a good location with plenty of privacy. Why not?'

'You already have a holiday home.'

'This will not be a holiday home for me, not like my property in the Seychelles. I can work from here. Agon is a prosperous, independent country with a growing economy. It has many residents looking to invest their cash. It is close enough to fly or speedboat to Athens. It has staff familiar with the house and I get to speak my native tongue for a change. It ticks all the boxes and best of all it has year-round sunshine.'

'Why do you run your business from London?' she asked. 'You clearly hate the city.'

'I don't hate it. In the summertime it is beautiful but the rest of the year it is so grey and dreary. I grew up with the sun on my back. But to answer your question, London was never my first choice to run my business from. When I was younger I wanted to live in America. That's why I went to university there. I had many ideas in my head about what America was like and assumed it had year-round sunshine like my home in Gaios.' He grinned, remembering his youthful naivety and lack of geography skills.

Her lips twitched with humour as she took a bite of her honey-slathered roll.

The tension in her frame was loosening.

'The winters in Massachusetts came as quite a shock, I can tell you,' he continued. 'When I graduated from MIT I was offered a job with an investment firm in Manhattan who were offering an obscene amount of money for a graduate. As you know, that's when my parents were on their knees, financially speaking, so I took the job, worked hard and built many contacts so I could strike out on my own, and tried not to freeze to death in the dire winters. When I started Samaras Fund Management, my intention had been to build the American side up then set up European headquarters in Athens. London and the other European capitals would have been subsidiaries. I'd reached the point where I was earning serious money, my parents were in reasonable health and settled in their new home...'

'Did you buy it for them?' she interrupted, eyes alive with curiosity.

'As soon as I could afford it. They didn't want to stay in Gaios any more, which I could not blame them for after the way they had been treated by the people there, so I brought them a house on Paros. We all thought the worst of what life could throw at us was over and then my sister and brother-in-law died.'

Carrie sucked a breath in.

Andreas said it so matter-of-factly that if she hadn't seen the flash of pain in his eyes she could believe his sister's death had meant nothing to him.

'It was carbon monoxide poisoning, wasn't it?' she asked softly.

He nodded, his jaw clenching. 'They were on holiday celebrating their wedding anniversary. The apartment they were staying in had a faulty boiler.'

She remembered reading the inquest report and wanting to cry for Natalia, their orphaned daughter, a girl Carrie had welcomed into her home and loved fiercely. Violet hadn't been the only one hurt when Natalia stopped staying at their home. Carrie had missed her too, missed the sunshine the girl had brought to their home.

In the year before the expulsion it had been rare for Violet to be at home without Natalia. Had that been why Carrie had failed to see how badly off the rails Violet was falling, because Natalia's cheerfulness and sweet nature had masked it?

But hadn't Carrie herself noticed the sunniness in her demeanour wilting those last few months before Violet's expulsion? A strain in both girls' eyes she had put down to teenage hormones.

Natalia had been so comfortable in their home. She would make herself drinks if she was thirsty, help herself to cereal if hungry…

Natalia would never have dropped Violet like a stone if something major hadn't occurred. If she'd wanted to keep seeing Violet she would have done; not even a strict uncle could have kept her from making contact if that had been what she wanted.

But she hadn't wanted to contact Violet because Andreas had been speaking the truth.

Violet had tried to seduce him, had punched Natalia in the face and blamed Andreas for her expulsion in revenge and, Carrie deduced, her mind ticking frantically, ice plunging into her veins, because she hadn't wanted to admit to the one person in the world who loved her that she had bought the drugs herself, and admit what she was becoming. An addict.

Violet had lied to save face and for misplaced revenge against the man who'd rejected her advances. Her vengeance was misplaced because the man she'd truly wanted to get back at, namely the vile specimen who had taken her virginity on her sixteenth birthday, had become unreachable. In Violet's mind at that moment, Andreas had been interchangeable with James; two rich, handsome men of a similar age. The expulsion, her desperate, wanton behaviour in the months leading to her expulsion…

Caught in her reckless heartache, Violet had managed to discredit herself without even trying. No one in their right mind would believe her story about the fabulously rich, media-friendly James Thomas grooming and seducing her. No one other than her big sister.

The ice in her veins had moved like freezing sludge to her brain.

Carrie had never followed a story without some initial proof. Violet had produced plenty of proof against James; blurry photos on her phone taken slyly when he hadn't been looking and screenshot messages—he'd been clever enough to insist on using apps where messages deleted themselves after being read but not clever enough to guess a lovestruck teenager would still find a way to save them.

There had been no proof against Andreas. Not a shred.

Carrie had gone after him on nothing but her damaged sister's word and that word had been a lie.

'Carrie?'

She blinked and looked into the eyes of the man she had tried to ruin.

'Are you okay? You are very pale.'

How could he even bear to *look* at her, never mind with concern?

She could still feel his touch on her skin, his kisses on her lips. He had made love to her as if she were the only woman in the world.

He should hate her.

He probably *did* hate her.

She hated herself.

What she had done…

Her chest had tightened so much it hurt to draw breath.

She needed to speak to Violet, she thought, as fresh panic clawed at her chest. There was still the chance Carrie might be wrong. She couldn't condemn her sister without giving her the chance to defend herself.

'I'm fine,' she managed to say. 'I was just thinking of Natalia.'

And I was thinking that you are not the monster I've been telling myself you are for the past three years.

This conversation they were having…

Andreas had started it to calm her down.

He knew she'd been a virgin. He'd known it the moment he entered her. He could have chosen to embarrass her about it and demand to know why she, a seemingly confident twenty-six-year-old woman, had spent her adult life as a singleton.

Instead he had given her a way to face being with him without making her burn with humiliation.

'Did you move to London for her?' she added.

He gave her another narrow-eyed unconvinced look before nodding. 'My sister used to read all those wizarding books to her. Natalia thought all boarding schools were like that and asked if she could go.' He smiled though his eyes saddened at the memory. 'I could afford it so I offered to pay the fees for any school my sister thought suitable. They chose London. I bought Tanya and Georgios a house close to the school so Natalia could spend weekends with them. When they died I moved to London and kept Natalia at her school. I couldn't put her through any more disruption.'

So he had uprooted his own life instead and moved to a city he didn't particularly like with a climate he hated.

'Is that what you meant when you said you'd spent fifteen years waiting for your freedom and that another six months wouldn't make any difference? Because you'd had to make your parents your priority and then your niece?'

'Natalia is at university, my parents are happy and settled and have all the home help they need… Now I want to spend as many of my days as I can where the sun shines and live my life as I please.' The wolfish grin she'd once so hated but now tugged at her heart curved on his lips, the gleam returning to his eyes. 'And if delaying my freedom for another six months means I get to see your beautiful face every day then it will make the delay a little sweeter.'

She swallowed. 'How can it be sweet when I tried to destroy you?'

'Because living with me is the price you have to pay to put it right. When it is over we will be even.'

'And last night?' The question was out before she could take it back.

He gazed into her eyes a long time before answering. 'Last night was nothing to do with you putting things right. I make no apologies for desiring you and you should make no apologies for desiring me. Attraction is bound by no rational thought. I have wanted you from the minute you stepped into my office and my bedroom door will always be open to you. If you enter is up to you.'

The meaning in his eyes was clear.

Andreas would make no further move on her.

If their marriage was to be more than a piece of paper she would have to be the one to instigate it.

It was a thought that should make her feel safe but didn't. Not in the least.

One thing Carrie did know for certain, required no proof or corroborating evidence for, was that with Andreas her feelings were like kindling.

One touch and she turned into fire.

CHAPTER ELEVEN

ANDREAS'S NEWEST STAFF were true professionals. He'd taken Carrie out shopping in an exclusive enclave in Agon's capital, where an arcade of designer boutiques and chic cafés resided, tiny compared to London and Paris's exclusive areas but with staff who could smile without looking as if their bottoms were being sucked out of their cheeks and who treated their clientele as if it were a pleasure to serve rather than a chore.

When they'd returned to his newest acquisition late afternoon he'd found the garden transformed exactly as he'd asked before they'd left and the scent of charcoal filling the air.

'I thought you said you couldn't cook,' Carrie said accusingly when he'd added the two juicy steaks onto the newly built brick barbecue.

She was sitting at the garden table, lithe legs stretched out, wearing a strapless mint-green summer dress and a cream wrap around her shoulders to stave off the evening chill.

His senses told him she wore no bra under that dress.

'I can burn meat as well as any caveman,' he replied with a grin. 'Why don't you make yourself useful and get a bottle of wine from the fridge?'

'Because I'm not your skivvy any more?' she suggested.

'Do you not feel guilty that I'm doing all the work while you are sitting there doing nothing?'

'Nope.' She looked pointedly at the bowls of salads and rice that had been prepared for them by his new chefs and laid on the beautifully presented table.

The staff had all gone now.

'Please?' he asked pointedly.

She pretended to consider then got to her feet. 'Okay, then. Which wine do you want?'

'There's only one variety in the fridge.'

She bounded off into the villa, a spring in her step he'd never seen before.

It occurred to him that her jest about not being his skivvy any more had been the first time she'd alluded to those few days when he'd had her at his beck and call.

They had been on Agon for only three days and the change in her had been incredible. Yesterday they had explored Agon together, admiring the island's rich heritage and what Andreas considered to be the most beautiful palace in the world. They'd eaten out, their conversation light and non-confrontational but the wariness he'd been greeted with at breakfast had still vibrated from her rigid frame. She avoided his gaze. The few times their eyes had met colour had suffused her face and her top lip would pull in. When they'd returned to the villa she had mumbled a goodnight before disappearing—fleeing—to her bedroom.

He hadn't touched her once and he hadn't flirted with her either.

He wanted to make love to her again. He hadn't thought it would be possible to want it more than he had before but that was how it was, a constant ache, a constant fizz in his blood, a constant awareness of her every movement but her virginity had changed everything.

If they were to make love again Carrie had to make the

first move. He needed to know that what they were sharing came from her head as well as her body.

Today, she had greeted him at breakfast with a smile that had been undoubtedly genuine.

That smile had pierced into his chest.

When he had taken her shopping for a dress to wear for his cousin's wedding, he'd prepared himself for a fight. When he'd explained, keeping his tone even, that she was only attending the wedding because of him and therefore it was only right he pay for her dress she had taken him by surprise by actually agreeing.

She hadn't let him buy her anything else though, and he hadn't argued the point. Carrie had a fierce independent streak he admired even if he did find it infuriating. He no longer found it insulting. There was a reason for it and sooner or later he would discover what that was.

She reappeared with the wine at the exact moment he judged the steaks to be cooked.

At the table he put the steaks on their respective plates and sat down, reaching for the wine.

She surprised him again by allowing him to pour her a glass. The only alcohol she had shared with him had been his Scotch the night the truth had come out.

He held his glass out. 'Yamas.' At her blank expression, he said, 'It means good health.'

She chinked her glass to his and took a sip of her wine. Her eyes widened a touch. 'I'm not a big fan of white wine but this is nice.'

'I should hope so for the price I paid for it,' he said drily. 'I have it imported directly to all my homes. This crate arrived while we were shopping.'

She had another sip. 'This really is lovely. And you have it imported to *all* your homes?'

He shook his head self-mockingly. 'I don't take drugs,

I no longer smoke…good quality wine and Scotch are my only vices.'

'You used to smoke?'

'Something else your investigations into me didn't reveal?'

As he finished the question with a wink, Carrie couldn't help but smile.

She could hardly believe they'd reached a place where they could *joke* about her attempts to investigate him. Both of them.

It was all down to Andreas. He'd rumbled her, had his fun while he punished her, then insisted she marry him to put things right but he wasn't holding a grudge. He wasn't one to hold a grudge but that, she suspected, was because he didn't need to. If a problem arose he fixed it straight away with whatever means he thought necessary.

He was no angel but by no means was he a monster like most of the rich men she'd dealt with through the years. When he wanted something done he expected it to be done immediately, patience was not his strong point, but he wasn't spoilt. Considering the wealth he'd accrued he was surprisingly grounded.

'I smoked when I was a teenager. I was obsessed with everything American and old seventies movies where the cool heroes always smoked and rode motorcycles. I wanted to be Steve McQueen.' He burst into laughter. 'The closest I could afford to a motorcycle was a beaten-up old scooter but cigarettes were easy to come by. I thought I was the coolest kid in Gaios, driving around on that pile of junk without a helmet and a cigarette hanging from my mouth. I turned my poor mother's hair white.'

His self-mockery and evident amusement were infectious and Carrie found herself laughing at the image he'd painted.

When she had set out on this endeavour she hadn't suspected for a minute that Andreas could be such good company. Their one conversation on the phone all those years ago had been short and to the point, his tone what you would expect if speaking to a bank manager. That one time she had seen him outside the headmistress's office he'd oozed menacing power. He'd frightened her.

Yes, Andreas had a dark side but she had come to realise that it only came out when people he loved were threatened.

What would it be like to be loved by this man…?

She would not allow her thoughts to go down that road.

Andreas was rich and powerful. He had charm and looks. He was everything she hated, everything she feared.

But he'd been honest about everything. He wanted his freedom. What they were sharing here, now, was pure circumstance. What she felt for him was a result of the forced proximity she'd been thrown into. When this was all over she would walk away. She wouldn't give this strange chemistry another thought. He would be out of sight and out of mind.

But right here and now he was in her sight and completely filling her mind.

Putting her knife and fork together, she pushed her plate away, put her elbow on the table and rested her chin on her hand. She'd eaten half of the steak he'd cremated for her but had no recollection of it, too caught up in listening to Andreas's staccato voice. 'You sound like you were a right tearaway as a child.'

'I was the bane of my parents' life,' he admitted unrepentantly, 'but also the apple of their eye so I got away with murder.'

'I was a good girl.'

'Really?' He topped their glasses up with more wine.

'Do you have to sound so surprised?'

He studied her as he sipped his wine, his own plate pushed aside too. 'No. I am not surprised.'

'Because I was a virgin?'

There. It had been said. The elephant that had parked itself between them had been acknowledged and the knot in her stomach loosened because of it.

The knot had become like a noose.

'It doesn't suggest a wild past,' he said slowly, his gaze on hers as he put his glass to his lips.

'I never had the chance to be wild,' she admitted. 'My mum was diagnosed with cancer when I was thirteen. I had Violet to look after—she's seven years younger than me—so I guess I supressed any teenage hormones that might have been primed to unleash. I comfort ate a lot. I never felt comfortable in my skin. It's funny because my mum was *beautiful*. Honestly, she was stunning. She'd be hooked up with drips and machines all around her and the doctors would flirt with her. Mind you, she flirted with them too. Men loved her.'

'Were you jealous of her?'

'No.' She shook her head as she thought about it. 'No, I felt sorry for her. She was married twice and had a string of boyfriends. None of them treated her well.'

'And you thought all men were like that?'

'No. I just thought she had terrible taste in men.'

Andreas laughed into his wine but his eyes read something other than amusement. There was compassion there, and something baser, the same something that had been there from the very start.

Carrie hadn't spoken about her mother for a long time and it felt good to do so now, brought her memory alive. Her darling mother had been a princess in Carrie's eyes, a woman who adored her two daughters and never shied from showing her love for them.

'There are some good men out there,' she said softly, staring into the hypnotic gaze that no longer frightened her. The meaning she read in it…it was nothing that she too didn't feel. She wanted Andreas, with a burning yen that had seeped into her soul. 'My grandfather was a good man. He was poor. Humble. Not flashy like the men my mother went for. She was like a magpie, always wanting the shiny pretty things. She could pick a rich man at ten paces and have him eating out of her hand with the flutter of her eyelashes.'

'So your father is a rich man?'

'Actually, he was the only poor one. He didn't even have a job—they were at school when they got together. Mum gave birth to me when she was seventeen.'

'You were an accident?'

'My mum always said I was the best accident in the world.' She would say it while planting kisses all over Carrie's face and tickling her ribs until they were both crying with laughter.

Andreas listened to Carrie open up about her life, watched those plump lips talking, feeling as if he had a fist pushed against his chest, pressing against his heart. Her hazel eyes shone in a way he had never seen before, her love for her mother shining through, dazzling him.

What would it be like to have those eyes shining with love for you…?

'They married when they discovered she was pregnant but split up not long after I was born,' she continued in that same, slow cadence, those shining eyes fixed on him, an openness in them he had never seen before. 'My dad moved away after they split up so I've never seen much of him but he's always remembered my birthday and makes a point of visiting a few times a year. I've always known he loves me.' A look of mischief flittered over her face. 'He's head gardener at the real Hargate Manor.'

He burst into great rumbles of laughter at this unexpected twist. 'It is a real place?'

Her lips puckered with sheepish amusement. 'I've been there a couple of times. It's a beautiful estate.'

Andreas drank some more wine and continued to stare at her. She mesmerised him. She'd mesmerised him from the moment she'd stepped into his office.

'*You're* beautiful,' he said throatily.

She tilted her head and smiled, a smile that stole his breath and made a man feel he could fly to the moon. 'You make me feel beautiful.'

A long, breathless moment passed between them as he gazed into eyes that shone with a hundred emotions.

Then she straightened, put her hands on the table and pushed her chair back.

She stood up, the wrap that had covered her shoulders sliding off and falling into a puddle at her feet. She didn't notice, a whole range of emotions flittering in hazel eyes that burned into him.

Slowly she trod towards him.

The air between them thickened in those few small movements and by the time she stood before him it crackled.

Andreas could no longer breathe.

Two elegant hands cradled his cheeks, delicate fingers rubbing against his skin. She leaned forward and pressed the tip of her nose to his.

Her eyelids closed and she breathed him in then her lips brushed his.

'You make me feel beautiful,' she repeated in a murmur into his mouth. The sweetness of the wine mingled with the sweetness of her breath and seeped right into his airways and through his veins.

Carrie had a taste that had been designed for him.

And it was *all* for him, he thought, the thickening in his loins a weighty ache. No other man had tasted her sweetness. And no other man would...

'You make me feel like a woman,' she whispered before her lips closed around his and she was kissing him, deep scorching kisses, her fingers sliding to cradle his head, everything a mimic of the night she had kissed him in the Seychelles but everything new.

This time there was no restraint. No pretence, no holding back, no hate, no anger.

Just two people with an unquenchable thirst for each other.

In one motion, he gathered her to him, pulling her onto his lap just as he had what seemed a lifetime ago and as he felt her bottom press into his lap, raw hunger slammed into him.

In a flurry of ravenous kisses her soft, pillowy breasts crushed against his chest, Carrie's fingers raked over his neck, over his shoulders, her nails scraping over his shirt, her hot tongue trailing over his cheeks and jaw, tasting him, her teeth biting into his skin, delicious jets of pleasure igniting everywhere.

And he touched her back with equal fervour, roaming his hands over the hot flesh that quivered and burrowed closer into him at his every touch, as if she were trying to burn their clothing off through willpower alone.

Somehow, with her chest crushed so tightly to his, she found the buttons on his shirt and opened them enough to burrow beneath the material to find his bare skin. Her fingers splayed all over his chest, nails raking his skin, scorching a trail of burning heat over him with her touch alone, her mouth devouring his again, her breaths shortening.

His mouth found her neck and he inhaled her earthy yet delicate scent, that erotic, womanly smell that was Carrie's alone.

When she found the waistband of his trousers, she didn't hesitate to tug at the button but when she couldn't undo it, cupped her hand over the tightly compressed erection and squeezed over the material.

He groaned into her neck at the constrained pleasure her touch there unleashed, then licked all the way up to her chin and her mouth.

Her eyes were open yet hooded. If a look ever had the power to make him come without a touch, the look ringing from her eyes would be it.

Holding her tightly, he lifted her in one motion and sat her on the table so he was standing between her parted thighs.

She stared at him, desire vibrating from her, then tugged the top of her dress down to her waist.

She wore no bra.

Her plump golden breasts shone under the rising moon. Spearing her hair as he cradled her head to support her, he lowered her back then dipped his head to take one of the pebbled nipples into his mouth.

The gasp that flew from her mouth turned into a moan as he slavered her with his attention, kissing, nipping, licking.

Her legs hooked around his waist, gyrating herself closer to him, her ankles digging into his buttocks as her back arched, her need for him as beautifully obvious as the emerging stars above them.

When he ran a hand over one of her clinging thighs and slid higher to her buttocks, he was the one to moan when he found her hot and damp. She jerked against him, trying to find whatever relief she could get.

Abandoning her breasts, he kissed her hard on her mouth and she matched it, a violent fever spreading between them as he pinched the sides of her knickers with his fingers and she raised her bottom to allow him to pull them down to her hips.

With one final clash of mouth and tongue, he then tugged her knickers down her legs and past her pretty feet, threw them onto the floor and removed his wallet from his back pocket. As he took the square foil out, Carrie returned to undoing his trousers, this time unbuttoning it with one flick of her fingers and tugging the zip down.

As he took the condom out of its wrapping she tugged his trousers down his hips, freeing his erection.

There was not a moment of hesitation.

Andreas slipped the condom on in one deft movement, hooked an arm around her waist to pull her to him, and thrust himself inside her.

Tight and hot, she welcomed him, pulling him deeper inside her, the look in her eyes as he stared into them sinking him deeper into her spell.

She slipped a hand around his waist and up his shirt, her nails biting into his skin, urging him on, their lovemaking hot and frenzied, tender and hard all at the same time, and then she was grabbing his buttocks to drive him even harder into her, mumbled, sensual words flying incoherently from her lips until her head tilted back. A ragged cry escaped her mouth and then she was thickening around him, clinging to him and Andreas found himself slamming headlong into the ecstasy of his own release, brighter, sharper and more intense than anything he had ever known before.

As he held her protectively, waiting for the shudders vibrating through both their bodies to lessen and the heavy beats of their echoing hearts to subside, a fierce possessiveness grabbed at his chest, words floating in his head he couldn't shake.

Carrie was his.

CHAPTER TWELVE

CARRIE APPLIED HER mascara for the third time and willed her hand to stop shaking and poking the wand in her eye.

The nerves she was feeling were almost as bad as when she'd waited in the reception room to be taken in to Andreas for the first time.

His cousin was getting married in three hours. Andreas had gone to collect his parents and niece from the airport and drop them at the hotel where the evening reception would be held. The whole family was staying at the hotel, Carrie and Andreas included. Apparently it was a Samaras tradition for the bride and groom to have their first breakfast as a married couple with their family all looking at them and knowing exactly what they'd been getting up to in the marital bed.

Thank goodness she and Andreas were marrying in a Chelsea registry office. It would be just them and a couple of witnesses.

She was terrified of meeting his parents but even more scared of seeing Natalia again. It scared her even more than having to pretend to everyone that she and Andreas were in the throes of a whirlwind love affair.

A whirlwind lust affair she could easily fake, mainly because that wouldn't involve any fakery.

She could hardly keep her hands off him.

She didn't know exactly when the shift in her thinking had occurred, just knew that as she'd changed for dinner after their shopping trip, she'd looked in her mirror and asked herself what she was so afraid of. Why fight something so pleasurable? Why deny them both? She'd slipped her dress on and closed her eyes, remembering his touch on her skin.

Carrie had discovered the joys of sex. Twenty-six years of a dormant libido had been unleashed and now her body was making up for lost time on all it had missed out on.

She told herself that on an hourly basis.

The good news was that she had a full six months to get all this making up out of her system because she couldn't quite quell the fear that her body only reacted this way because of Andreas. *For* Andreas.

But as she also continually told herself, if it was only him she reacted this way to, then so what? It was still only sex, glorious, blissful sex.

Ta da. Her make-up was done. Third time lucky.

Her phone rang.

She grinned to remember how Andreas had deliberately kept her incommunicado when she had first infiltrated his life. It was one of the reasons he'd chosen to take her to the Seychelles, because the signal on his peninsular was so dire.

Her grin dropped when she saw her sister's name flash up.

Carrie had left three messages for her in the past week. She'd bitten back the hurt to find herself being ignored again. Violet had always been good at ignoring her if she didn't want to speak.

Taking a deep breath, she answered it. 'Hi, Vee. How are you?'

Silence.

'Are you there?'

'Is it true?'

Carrie's heart sank. 'Is what true?'

'That you're seeing Andreas Samaras.'

She took another deep breath. 'Yes. It's true.'

And it's all because of you and the lies you told.

'You know what he did to me, right?' After only three months in California her sister had picked up an American twang.

'Violet… Are you still seeing the counsellor?'

'Answer my question.'

'I will when you answer mine. Please, tell me you're still seeing him.'

'Her. My counsellor's a her.'

'I'm sorry. I thought you were seeing a man.'

'I was.' The stiff angry tone suddenly changed. Became softer. 'We decided I would find it easier to talk to a woman.'

'And are you finding it easier?'

'Yes.' She sounded surprised. 'I am. She's really nice and non-judgemental.'

Carrie tried not to take that as a dig against herself. 'I'm glad.'

'Now you answer my question. You know what that man did to me?'

'He didn't do anything to you, did he, Vee?' she said gently, her heart thumping, mouth dry. 'He didn't do what you accused him of. He didn't set you up. The drugs were yours. Vee, it doesn't change how I feel about you. I still love you.'

All that played in her ear was silence but she knew her sister was still there.

'I'm sorry you felt you couldn't trust me enough to tell me the truth but please, I beg you, admit the truth to yourself. Talk it through with your counsellor. You were treated terribly by James but Andreas isn't James. He is nothing like him.

'Violet… I love you. I forgive you. Now, please, find a way to forgive yourself.'

This time the silence on the other end was the silence of a disconnected line.

Violet had hung up on her.

'Was that your sister?'

Carrie jumped and spun around.

She hadn't heard Andreas come in. Normally she was very attuned to his movements around the villa but she had been so engrossed with her one-sided conversation with Violet that she hadn't heard him return.

He was standing in the doorway, his black tuxedo on minus the jacket, a sombre expression on his handsome face.

She nodded.

'What you said…you believe me.'

She nodded again.

'Since when?'

'Since you told me,' she whispered before hanging her head in shame. 'I just couldn't admit it. Violet is my Achilles heel. She always has been.'

He paused before asking, 'Why is she seeing a counsellor?'

'Because she's a drug addict.'

Suddenly she could hold it in no longer. She slumped onto her dressing room chair and burst into tears.

The tightness Andreas had experienced when he'd listened to Carrie say she believed him, to hear her defending him, became a tight ball to see her dissolve before his eyes.

These weren't tears, these were racking sobs, each one tearing his soul.

In three strides he was before her, crouching on his haunches to cradle her head on his shoulder, stroking her back, her tears soaking through his shirt.

It was a long time before the sobs lessened and she removed her face from his shoulder and wiped it with her hands.

Red-rimmed hazel eyes fixed on him and she inhaled deeply. 'My sister is a drug addict. She is in recovery in America, living with her father because one of her drug dealers beat her into a coma when she couldn't pay her tab.' The tears filled her eyes again, spilling over to race down her cheeks, shoulders shaking. 'She nearly died. My baby sister nearly died.'

Stunned at this revelation, Andreas took a moment to process it.

'That bastard didn't just seduce her. He fed her drugs. He gave an innocent girl a drug addiction.' She covered her mouth then dropped her hand as she gave a long, ragged exhalation. 'I must have been blind. I had no idea how bad her addiction was until a few months after her expulsion.' Her lips made a little grimace of distaste. 'I found her in bed with a much older man. There were drugs on the floor…she denied it but I knew she'd had sex with him in exchange for the drugs. She had no other money. Her father had cut her allowance off when she got expelled; she'd been able to afford her own until then. I was only a recent graduate and not earning very much. She had no money and absolutely refused to get a job.'

He got to his feet and ran a hand through his hair, kneading his scalp. 'Why wasn't she at school?'

'Because she'd been expelled,' she reminded him.

'I know but she could have gone to another school after she'd taken her exams.'

'She wasn't allowed to take them.'

Anger coiled in his gut. 'The headmistress promised me Violet could sit them.' He had insisted on it.

'Then she lied to you. Violet wasn't allowed to set foot in that school again. I tried to arrange for her to sit the exams somewhere else but she refused. She gave up on life. She'd stay out all hours and never let me know where she was, then turn up steaming drunk and high as a kite, often cut or bruised from fights she'd got into and I'd patch her up and pray it was the last time I had to put ice on her face or sleep on her floor because I was terrified she'd choke on her own vomit, but it never was. She was arrested God knows how many times, hospitalised, had her stomach pumped... I honestly thought she was going to kill herself.'

Andreas sat heavily on the bed facing her, his heart pounding.

Carrie's beautiful golden skin had paled as she'd relayed this tale of horror that no one should ever have to live through, and to think his beautiful Carrie had been the one to live it made his guts coil again in fresh anger and self-loathing at the part he had unwittingly played in it.

After a few moments of silence, her eyes found his and she continued in a voice so low he strained to hear.

'I watched her try and kill herself for three years and there was nothing I could do to save her, and I tried *everything*. I locked her in her room; she smashed the window and jumped out. I staged numerous interventions with professionals; she just laughed in our faces. I even flushed a bagful of her cocaine down the toilet and got a punch in the face for it.' She gave a shaky laugh. 'Natalia has my sympathy. I know what a mean right hook Violet has.'

'Carrie...'

'No, please, whatever you want to say, just let me say this first. I believed Violet's lies that you set her up and I listened to her drunken ranting about you in the same way she would drunkenly rage about James and not once did I question them. As a journalist, you would think I would have had the sense to verify it all first, and I want you to know I am sorry for believing that about you and for all the lies I told in some stupid, futile, *dangerous* attempt at revenge. I could have caused your business and reputation untold damage and I am truly ashamed of myself. I think... I think I lost my mind.'

It was all true, Carrie realised bleakly as she spoke her confession.

She didn't need to verify Andreas's version of events. She knew the truth in her heart.

'What you have had to deal with these last three years would cause anyone to lose their mind,' he said quietly.

'It wouldn't cause you to lose yours,' she said with certainty. 'I don't think anything would ever cause you to lose your mind.'

'I came close when my sister and brother-in-law died,' he admitted. 'I couldn't fix that. All the other stuff my family and I had had to deal with before then, it was all fixable, even my parents' health issues. However bad things got, there was always hope. Tanya and Georgios's death... what hope was to be found there? But then you know all about that with your own mother.'

She nodded. 'Death is the one thing that can't be fixed, isn't it?'

'It's the finality,' he agreed. 'One minute they are there the next they are gone and all that's left are the memories. But I had Natalia to care for just as you had Violet after your mother died and...

'Why is Violet living with her father now?' he interrupted himself. 'Why wasn't she living with him before? I always assumed she was an orphan.'

'She might as well have been an orphan for the time

he gave her. Raymond, Violet's father, divorced our mum and moved to America years before Mum died. When she did die he didn't want Violet—he had a nice new nubile wife and was living the childless dream. We agreed that he would continue paying for Violet's education—did I tell you he was also rich?—and that she would become a weekly boarder so I could concentrate on my studies, but that she would live with me at weekends and holidays. He gave us both an allowance for it to work.' Her smile was bitter. 'When it came to money, his generosity was limitless.'

'And that's when you became Violet's guardian?'

'Yes. He handed his twelve-year-old daughter's welfare into my nineteen-year-old hands and washed his own hands of the pair of us.'

'Theos.' He gave a low whistle. That was the same age Natalia was now. He'd been a grown man of thirty-one when he'd become Natalia's guardian. 'I didn't realise you were so young when you became her guardian. And her father didn't want her? No wonder she went off the rails.' He shook his head, unable to comprehend how a man could turn his back on his own child. Natalia wasn't even his and he knew he would lay down his life to protect her. 'Why is she with him now when he didn't want her before?'

'I blackmailed him.'

He found himself smiling. 'Really?'

She met his eye and matched the smile. There was no joy in either of their curved mouths. 'I'd been begging him for years for help and he kept fobbing me off and fobbing me off. She almost died from that beating, Andreas. She was in a coma for three days. Something in me went ping. I didn't even think about what I was going to say, I just phoned him and said if he didn't fly over and see his daughter and finally take responsibility for her then I would publish a photo of Violet's battered body on the Internet and tell the world he'd refused to help her.'

'And that worked?'

'He arrived the next day. A week later he flew her back to America with him. I don't know why I hadn't threatened it before but I'd spent so long just getting through each day, caring for Violet, plotting my revenge on you and James...' She winced. 'Sorry.'

'It is okay.' He slid off the bed and knelt before her. Taking her hand in his, he kissed the palm. 'No more apologies. I'm the one who is sorry. I should have told you, not the school...'

'You did the right thing.' Carrie squeezed the hand holding hers so tenderly. 'You were protecting Natalia. Violet would have been expelled sooner or later. She was using drugs on school property. They would have noticed eventually.' She shrugged then took a deep breath. '*I* should have noticed. I should have seen what was happening to her—I *did* see—but I didn't know what I was seeing. Does that make sense?'

'Carrie...' He raised himself up and put a hand to her neck and pressed his forehead to hers. 'You must not blame yourself. None of what happened to her is your fault. You have put your life on hold to raise her and to save her. She is nineteen now, yes? The same age you were when you became her guardian. You have given her all the support and help you can, you have avenged her against the monster who first steered her on this awful path. You can do no more. I heard you say to Violet that she has to forgive herself. You must do the same and forgive yourself too.' Kissing her forehead, he moved back and rubbed his thumbs under her eyes.

The motion made her remember the make-up she must

have ruined with all her tears and she let out a cry. 'Your cousin's wedding!'

'It doesn't matter.'

'It does. We need to go.'

His brow furrowed and he stared intently into her eyes. 'Do you feel able to? I can make an excuse if you would rather stay.'

'No. They are expecting us.' She blew a long breath out and gave a wobbly smile. 'We have a wedding announcement of our own to make. You would look very strange doing it without your fiancée by your side.'

'Are you sure?'

How could she be anything but sure? She would do whatever was needed to kill the whispers against Andreas's business and his reputation. That was a mess of *her* making, no one else's.

Andreas was a good man who had put his life on hold for his family, just as she had for her family. A good, generous man who didn't deserve to have his reputation smeared by rumours and innuendoes. He deserved to spend the rest of his life living it with the freedom he'd had denied him for so long, and in six months he would be able to do just that. He could hop from country to country as he pleased, for work and pleasure, however he saw fit. He could drink Scotch in a palm-lined bar until the sun came up, he could bed all the women he wanted without worrying about being a bad influence on an impressionable teenager...

A hot red pain pulsed in the centre of her brain at this thought and she slammed her palm to her forehead.

'Are you okay?'

She heard the concern in his voice and quickly forced a smile.

Where had that pain come from?

'Yes, I'm fine. Just imagining how badly my face needs repairing from all those ugly tears.'

He stroked her cheek. 'Your tears are not ugly and your face just needs a clean.'

'Give me five minutes.'

He nodded and got to his feet before helping her to her own. Then he took her head in his hands and kissed her. It was gentle and fleeting but with so much tenderness in it that for one awful moment she thought she might cry again.

CHAPTER THIRTEEN

ANDREAS'S DRIVER JOINED the procession of cars lining up to enter the church's car park. There seemed to be some issue with one of the cars—an engine failure if Andreas was to guess correctly—and nothing was moving.

He could see his parents and niece standing at the front, chatting happily with the dozens of other guests. Both his parents had many siblings so family weddings were always large, noisy affairs.

Carrie was looking out of the window at the exuberant greetings taking place too. 'Why did you buy a holiday home in the Seychelles rather than closer to your family?' she asked, turning to face him with a wrinkle in her forehead. 'The way you speak of them—you clearly adore them.'

He looked down at their entwined fingers then back to her face. She'd cleaned herself up and put on only a little make-up. Her eyes were still a little red but he doubted anyone else would notice. She still looked ravishing in her long, off-the-shoulder cream silk dress with subtle blue leaf prints.

'I wanted a bolt-hole away from them all,' he admitted. 'My parents only like to travel short distances. The Seychelles is too far for them.'

And he'd thought he was done with family.

Not *done* done, just his time for some distance whenever he wanted to escape but…

'I was preparing myself for my freedom. I have been planning it for two years now, since Natalia told me she was going to medical school and I could see my freedom from responsibility waving a flag at me.'

His heart-rate began to accelerate, blood racing to his head, staring from Carrie to his family, his family to Carrie, Carrie to his family.

His father had just whispered something in his mother's ear, lovingly squeezing her seventy-four-year-old waist.

Andreas thought of the longevity of their marriage, and all they had been through, all the ups and downs, all the highs and lows.

Why had he thought having the freedom to see and do whatever he liked was better than having someone he loved to share all the experiences with?

He had a sudden vision of him and Carrie, forty years from now, surrounded by their own grown-up children…

Children?

He had long stopped wanting children. He'd raised a teenager he loved as if she were his own and had been so certain, so damned *adamant* he didn't want to go through it again…

'I can't do it,' he said suddenly.

'Do what?'

'Introduce you to my family as my fiancée when we don't mean it. I cannot marry you knowing it isn't true. I cannot make false vows.' And as he said the words aloud, he knew them to be true, and a weight he hadn't felt on his shoulders lifted.

Somewhere, somehow, he had fallen for his poisonous viper of a journalist.

He could laugh at his old notions about her.

There was nothing poisonous about Carrie. Prise off the shell she carried herself in and there was a kind, loving, independent, fiercely protective woman. When Carrie loved someone, it was with everything she had. She loved with her whole heart.

And he loved her with the whole of his.

'Oh.' She had gone very still beside him.

He tugged the hand he was holding to his mouth and pressed his lips to the knuckles. 'Marry me for real.'

'*What?*'

'I am serious. Marry me. For real. Not for six months.'

'No.'

'Carrie…'

'The answer is no.' She pulled her hand from his and shifted away so her back was to the door, staring at him warily as if he were a dangerous dog that could bite. 'I agreed to six months. You can't change the terms now.'

'I am not changing the terms. I am telling you I cannot go through with the terms we agreed on. It would not feel right.'

'Why not? Is it because I was a virgin so you feel honour-bound to keep me for ever?' She spoke slowly, not taking her eyes from his face.

'It has nothing to do with you being a virgin. I admit, I like knowing I'm the only man you have been with…'

She gave the briefest of smiles, one that did not reach her wary, watchful eyes. 'Your sexist undertones are coming out.'

'I am being honest with you and I say *this* with all honesty too—you could have slept with a hundred men and I would still be asking you to marry me for real.'

In the few, intense weeks they had been together they had seen the worst in each other and the best. She had slipped so effortlessly into his life it was as if she had always been there.

'Okay.' She dragged the last syllable out then nodded her head. 'Well, I am telling *you*, with all honesty, that I will not commit to anything longer than six months.'

'Why not?' he challenged.

'You have to ask? The whole reason I am here is to put right the awful wrong I did to you but that shouldn't mean I have to give up my whole life…'

'Do you not feel anything for me other than a debt you need to pay?' he asked, forcing his voice to stay even, not wanting to jump to conclusions. They had done that enough already…

But if they hadn't jumped to their prior conclusions about each other they wouldn't be sitting there now…

And he wouldn't be feeling as if he'd started swimming only to find the water had turned into treacle. The shell he had so carefully prised open was reforming around her. He could virtually see the seams knitting themselves together.

'Are you telling me I have imagined everything that has happened between us?'

'No, I'm not saying any of those things.' There was an air of desperation in her voice. 'You can't just throw something like this at me and expect me to fall in line with it.'

'I don't want you to fall in line.' He took a deep breath and pinched the bridge of his nose. 'How long do you want to have?'

'Six months.'

'I mean how long do you want to think about it?' he asked through gritted teeth.

'I don't need to think about it.' She pulled her knees up to her chest and hugged them tightly. 'We marry for six months and then we divorce and I move back into my London house and you live the life you've been dreaming of.'

'I don't want that life any more. Being with you…it has…not changed me but made me see I want someone to share it all with.'

'Oh, so you want a constant companion while you live the high life and I'm here and available and you've got to marry me anyway so I'll do? How am I supposed to do that around work? Or am I expected to give up my job?'

'Did I say *any* of that?' he demanded, the anger clawing in his guts finally finding a vent.

He wouldn't say he'd expected her to agree to his proposal on a whim but he'd thought—in as much as he'd thought about it, which he hadn't really considering he'd only just accepted his own feelings for her—she would at least be receptive to the idea.

He acknowledged his own lie to himself.

His feelings for Carrie had been like a runaway train from the minute she'd stepped into his office. He'd thought it had been the same for her.

Had he *really* got it so wrong?

Had the closeness they'd developed really just been a figment of his imagination?

'Six months of marriage where we live in London then you can relocate your headquarters to Athens and I stay put. That's what we agreed,' she said obstinately.

'What if I were to offer to live permanently in London with you? For ever.' He laid his challenge down.

'The answer is still no. I do not want to marry you. Don't you get that? I will pay my debt. I will do six months. And then I will leave.'

'How can you be so cold?' he asked in disbelief. 'I am offering to give everything up for you and you…'

'Cold?' she interrupted. Suddenly she leapt from her perch on the seat and pushed him back so she was on top of him, pinning him down, her little hands holding his wrists above his head, her snarling face above his.

She'd moved so quickly he'd had no time for defence. If the situation were more humorous and less of a feeling that everything was fraying at the seams, he would have admired her ninja skills.

'Don't you call me cold!' she shouted. 'Don't you dare! I have spent my life caring for the people that I love and losing them. I nursed my mother for six years and then she was gone. I have loved and cared for Violet her entire life and what good did that do? She's gone too! She is lost to me. I would give my entire life to have them back so don't you dare call me cold and don't you dare ask me to commit the rest of my life to a man who's been yearning for his freedom and would only break my heart. Yes, Andreas, *you*,' she spat. 'If our marriage was for real you would bore of me in months; that yearning for freedom would still be in you getting stronger and stronger and then what would happen? You'd get your chequebook out and pay me off like all rich men do when something nicer and newer grabs their attention.'

Andreas stared into her spitting eyes and felt the very coldness he'd accused her of creep into his veins.

Everything made sudden gut-aching sense.

He twisted his wrists easily from her hold and snatched her hands, pulling them together to hold her wrists in one hand while he levered himself up with his free hand.

Then they were staring at each other, enough hate and poison swirling between them to choke on.

He had been wrong about her. Prise her shell off and she was still just a poisonous viper of a journalist.

'Oh. I get it,' he said slowly. 'You still think I'm just a rich bastard who is pre-programmed to cheat and treat women like dirt.'

Her eyes widened. Suddenly the fury went from them and she blinked rapidly, shaking her head. 'No. No, sorry, I didn't mean it like that. I know you're not like other...'

'You have said enough,' he cut in icily, then he dropped her wrists and banged on the dividing window. 'I'll get out here. Take Miss Rivers back to the villa to collect her belongings and then take her to the airport.'

He turned back to stare at her now pale face for the last time. 'I will arrange for my jet to take you back to London. Your debt to me is over.'

Then, without a word of goodbye, he got out of the car and strode through the other idle cars to his family.

Carrie watched him walk away, her heart in her mouth, loud drumbeats banging in her head. The scratchy panic that had torn her insides into pieces as Andreas had spoken of marriage had gone and all that was left was a numbness, as if she had been anaesthetised.

She rubbed her wrists, the look in his eyes as he'd let go of them, discarding them as if they were trash, right there in her mind.

Andreas had looked at her as if she were a toxin.

He merged into the merry crowd outside the pretty white church without once looking back.

A separate merry crowd had gathered together to push the broken-down car away. She watched them as if through a filter, seeing but not seeing, Andreas's hateful look the only thing she could picture with clarity, as she sat there too numb to take anything else in.

He had never looked at her like that before. Not even when the truth had first unravelled itself.

She was barely aware of her own car moving until the driver made a slow U-turn in the space that had opened up before them and crunched away from the happy wedding party, just as Andreas had made a U-turn on their plans...

Their plans?

There were no plans now, she realised, her heart hammering more painfully than it had ever done.

Their relationship, such as it was, was over.

They were over.

She was still too numb to do more than swallow back a huge lump that had formed in her throat.

Andreas sipped at his single malt as he read through the emails Debbie had decided were worthy of his attention, keeping one eye on the time. An old friend from his Manhattan days, when he'd been a mere employee, was due any minute. As was their tradition, they'd agreed to meet in their old 'watering hole', as Frank still liked to call it.

'Can I get you another drink, sir?'

He looked up from the screen at the young, pretty waitress who had been paying him extra attention since he'd arrived at the bar and settled himself in an empty corner booth. It was still early but tonight was the opening game of the baseball season and this bar was a firm favourite for Yankee fans. He estimated that he and Frank would have an hour of catching up before the place filled up.

'I'm good for the moment, thank you,' he answered with a quick grin. 'I'll let you know if I need anything else.'

She winked before sashaying away. 'Be sure that you do.'

Focussing his attention back on his smartphone, he rubbed the back of his neck and chided himself for wasting an opportunity for a little flirtation.

This pretty waitress was a perfect example of what he'd been looking forward to all these years: grabbing opportunities for fun when they came along. Andreas was now free to do what he liked with whom he liked when he liked. Natalia had announced at his cousin's wedding that she was moving in with her boyfriend. A boyfriend she had conveniently forgotten to mention to her protective uncle until she was certain things would work out between them.

He'd wished her luck and even managed to inject sincerity in his voice.

Who knew, he thought cynically, taking another sip of his Scotch, maybe it would work for them? And if it didn't he would be there to pick up the pieces. He'd come to accept that when it came to Natalia, he would always be there.

The main thing, he had told himself numerous times, was that his freedom had officially arrived. He didn't even have a fake fiancée to worry about.

Lord knew what he would do if the rumours about him gained traction. It had been six days since he'd shut the door on the viper and their relationship. He'd ordered Debbie to check in frequently with their media contacts and inform him immediately if the rumours started up again. So far, all was quiet.

Maybe their brief relationship had been enough on its own to quell the rumours.

The waitress caught his eye again. She really was incredibly pretty, a true all-American girl with a toothy smile and perfectly blonde hair.

Carrie's hair had been blonde the first time he'd met her, their first oh-so-fleeting glance...

He took a deep breath and downed his Scotch.

Do not think of her. Not by name.

It was easier to depersonalise her. Depersonalise her and forget about her.

Less than a minute after he'd slammed his empty glass on the table, the waitress brought him another over.

'Where are you from?' she asked, lingering at the table.

'Greece.' He returned the smile and willed himself to feel something.

Anything.

'Greece, huh? I've always wanted to go there.'

She'd moved close enough for him to smell her perfume. It was nice. Floral.

It did nothing for him.

Carrie's scent had been evocative. It had hit him in the loins.

His mind suddenly loosened, memories he'd shut tightly away springing free. The heat of her kisses, the movement of her lips when she spoke, the way she smiled sleepily when she looked at him after waking…

The way she had cried on his shoulder, her desolation over her sister, the way she had clung to him, as if he were the lifeline she'd needed when her emotions had thrown her out to sea…

Carrie…

Carrie…

Carrie!

Her name rang loudly in his ears.

'What's your name?'

'Carrie.'

'Sorry?'

He blinked and saw the waitress looking at him with puzzlement.

He'd said her name aloud.

Carrie.

Scared, terrified Carrie who'd spent her life watching her mother and sister being used and sometimes abused by rich men.

Her kisses didn't lie. Her lovemaking didn't lie.

Her scared brain did.

'Her name is Carrie,' he said more clearly. 'The woman I love. She's called Carrie.'

He hadn't told her he loved her. He'd held that back as the strength and vehemence of her rejection had accelerated, protecting his ego.

Why had he not recognised the fear in her eyes for what it was rather than just listened to what she'd said? Why had he not laid his heart truly on the line for her?

The reason for that was simple. As this pretty waitress would no doubt say, the reason was because he was a shmuck.

He got to his feet, pulling a couple of twenty-dollar bills from his wallet, and thrust them into the waitress's hand. 'If a tall bald man called Frank asks for Andreas, tell him I remembered I had to be somewhere else.'

Hurrying out of the bar, he hailed the first cab that came his way and instructed the driver to take him to the airport.

CHAPTER FOURTEEN

CARRIE CLOSED HER laptop after her video chat with her sister feeling slightly lighter.

They had just shared their first real, meaningful conversation since Violet had confessed to her affair with James.

Violet had done as Carrie had beseeched and confessed her lies about Andreas to her counsellor. It had been at the counsellor's behest that Violet had arranged the video chat.

Seeing her sister's face on the screen, in real time, had been almost as good as the conversation itself. She'd put on weight, no longer the gaunt stick-thin figure who could still fit in children's clothes. Her complexion was clearer too, although the effect of that was to highlight the scars that had accumulated on her face over the years. Raymond had promised that he would pay for treatment for the scars once she had been clean for a year.

The man who'd been such a scummy, negligent father had finally come into his own and was doing the right thing by his daughter. He'd even come to the computer and waved at Carrie, which she'd conceded was a big deal for him considering the last time they'd spoken she'd been blackmailing him.

In all, things were looking good. Much more positive.

The only dark cloud had come when Violet had asked how things were going for Carrie with Andreas. When

Carrie had responded with a prepared airy, 'It fizzled out,' Violet had been crestfallen.

'I thought you'd be pleased,' Carrie had said, trying her hardest to keep things light.

Violet had bitten her lips in the exact same way their mother had done. 'I just want you to be happy,' she'd blurted out.

'I *am* happy,' Carrie had promised, her stomach wrenching.

Violet had not looked convinced.

All week Carrie had kept her airy face on, telling curious colleagues that yes, she and Andreas had had a brief romance but that they had decided it wouldn't work between them long term.

Her only real gulp-inducing moment had been when the features editor had asked when she would have the exclusive interview written up. She'd forgotten all about that.

She opened her laptop back up and decided to write the feature now. She had no transcripts of any of their conversations but she knew if she started, they would come back to her.

She would write it, email it to Andreas for his approval—after all, everything they had discussed had been between the two of them and not for public consumption—and if he agreed, she would send it to the features editor. If he refused she would say he'd pulled out. She would take the blame for it. Happily. She would not have his name tarnished.

Even if he did hate her.

She caught sight of the time and saw it was almost one in the morning.

It was Saturday.

This was supposed to be their wedding day.

She took a long breath and opened a new document to write on.

The time didn't matter. She'd hardly slept more than a couple of hours a night since her return to London.

The nights had become her enemy, a time when her brain did nothing but try to think of Andreas.

And now it was time to slay his ghost. Finally allow herself to think about him properly, write the feature and then spend the rest of her life forgetting about him.

Oh, but the pain in her chest. It *hurt*. Really hurt. It was as if someone had punched her right in her heart.

So she started writing.

She soon discovered she didn't need transcripts.

Every minute of their time together had lodged in her brain.

Every shared conversation had committed to memory.

Andreas Samaras's fortune came about almost by accident, she wrote, her fingers almost flying off the keys as she wrote about the terrible time when his parents' business had gone under and how it had been the spur he'd needed to work as hard as he could to save them from financial ruin.

The more she wrote, the clearer it became, the clearer he became, emerging from a picture in her mind so he might as well be standing right there, in front of her. If she stretched out a hand she'd be able to touch him.

His life. His selflessness.

Everything he'd done had been for his family. His great wealth couldn't insulate them from tragedy but it ensured his parents never had to worry and his niece could train as a doctor without the usual student encumbrances. His extended family had benefitted too, aunts, uncles, cousins, all either having their mortgages paid off or new homes bought for them.

No member of the Samaras family would ever struggle financially while Andreas was alive.

Five hours later, her hands cramped, hot pains shooting up her arms, she stopped, exhausted, and burst into tears.

For the first time she admitted to herself what she had thrown away.

She hadn't meant to cast him in the same torrid light as those other rich men who had abused their power. She had been long past that, had long accepted Andreas was nothing like those men.

His proposal, his idea they should marry for keeps, hadn't just taken her by surprise but terrified her. She'd already been feeling raw after spilling her soul to him and had panicked.

He'd never said that one word she'd longed to hear from his lips, the same word that also would probably have made her dive out of the window.

At no point had he mentioned love.

But she had never given him the chance. She had said no without even having to think.

No, I will not marry you properly. No, I will not take the chance of us finding happiness together because I'm a big scared, distrustful baby who requires proof.

What proof could he give her that their marriage would last and that he would never cheat or break her heart? None, because that proof didn't exist! He had no crystal ball or time portal.

And neither did she.

All she could do was trust her instincts and her heart, and both were telling her—*screaming* at her—that she had made the biggest mistake of her life.

Andreas had offered her his world but she'd been too scared to take it from him.

And now it was too late.

Shoving her laptop so hard it fell off her desk, Carrie buried her face in her hands and wept.

It was too late.

Too, too late.

Andreas banged hard on the blue front door for the third time.

Still no response.

Pushing the letterbox open, he crouched down. 'Carrie? Please. Open the door. Please.'

'She's gone out.'

He spun round to find an elderly woman walking a small dog up the neighbouring front path.

'Did she say where she was going?'

The woman shook her head as she rummaged in her pocket for her keys. 'She went out when Trixie and I went for our walk. Half an hour ago or so.'

'Did she say when she was coming back?'

'No. She was all dressed up so I wouldn't think she'll be back soon.' The woman opened her door then looked at him one last time. 'If you're thinking of robbing her place, I'd be very careful. She has a very noisy burglar alarm.'

Despite the situation, he couldn't help but grin. 'Noted.'

The door slammed shut.

With a heavy, defeated sigh, he slumped down onto Carrie's front door step and cradled his head in his hands.

He would just have to wait until she came back from wherever she'd gone *all dressed up*.

Carrie rarely dressed up. She was always, always elegant, but never noticeably dressed up. The only occasion she had properly dressed up for had been his cousin's wedding, the day everything had imploded between them.

That had been a week ago.

He looked at his watch. Half past one. Their wedding was supposed to take place in half an hour...

His brain began to tick.

Had Carrie cancelled the registry office? Because he hadn't…

And just like that, he was on his feet, racing past his idling driver, pounding the ground to the nearest Tube station, racing down the stairs, yanking his bank card out and waving it at the turnstile, pausing only to check which line he needed to take before racing to the platform.

People of all shapes and sizes were clambering onto a train and he joined the throng.

He hadn't used the Tube in years but this was one occasion where speed trumped luxury. He hardly noticed the people jostling into him. He certainly didn't care.

Four minutes later and he was in Chelsea, following his nose to the registry office, checking his watch constantly until, with five minutes to spare, he was there and racing up the stairs to the waiting room outside the room he'd booked for their service.

The waiting room was empty.

He doubled over, partly from exertion but mostly from grief.

The cramp in his stomach spread to his chest and clenched around his heart.

The pain was indescribable.

What a fool he was.

He'd allowed hope to override common sense. What on earth had he been thinking?

Why would Carrie have come here? She'd made her feelings perfectly clear but he, egotistical fool that he was, had been unable to accept the truth and had…

'Andreas?'

He froze.

Slowly he straightened before turning around.

The door to the officiating room had opened. Standing

at the threshold, clearly on her way out, stood Carrie, the registrar hovering behind her.

She stared at him as if she'd seen a ghost.

The neighbour had been right that she'd been dressed up. She wore a knee-length summery cream dress and a soft cream leather jacket. On her feet were cream heels.

The only colour on her were her eyes. They were red raw.

'What are you doing here?' she whispered.

'What are you doing here?' he countered, not trusting what his eyes were telling him.

Silence hung over them as they gazed at each other, Carrie drinking in the tall figure she had resigned herself to never seeing again.

She'd told herself she was running a fool's errand but that hadn't stopped her rifling through her wardrobe for the most bridal-type clothing she could find.

She'd fallen into bed, utterly exhausted, at six in the morning and after three hours' fitful sleep had woken with a cast-iron certainty that she had to get herself to the registry office.

Even now, with what looked and sounded like Andreas standing in front of her, she couldn't say where this certainty had come from. It had been a compulsion that had taken over her.

She'd made it to the registry office well before the appointed time and had watched one happy couple and two dozen happy guests pile into the room, then pile out twenty minutes later.

During those twenty minutes she had waited on her own.

When the last guest had gone and her reality had come crashing back down on her, she had burst into fresh tears. The registrar had been sympathy itself, taking her into the room and making her a cup of tea, giving her the time she needed to gather herself together in privacy rather than have her humiliated should anyone come into the waiting room while she was wailing.

And now, as she looked at the ghost before her, a scent played under her nose, a fresh, tangy cologne that had her bruised heart battering against her ribs.

She gazed into the light brown eyes she loved so much, saw them narrow with the same disbelief that must have been ringing in hers then saw the truth hit him at the exact same moment it hit her.

In seconds, he'd hauled her into his arms and was kissing her fiercely as she clung to him, inhaling his scent, more tears spilling from her eyes and splashing onto his face.

It was *him*! Andreas was there! He had come.

'I'm sorry, I'm sorry, I'm sorry,' she cried, raining kisses all over his face, hungrily inhaling more of his scent, tasting his skin…

It really was *him*.

Eventually he disentangled their clinging bodies to take her face in his hands and stare at her.

There was a wonder in his face. 'You are here. Oh, *matia mou*, you are *here*. I didn't dare believe…'

'I'm so sorry,' she said, tears falling over the fingers cradling her face with such tenderness.

'No, my love, it is I who is sorry. My pride—my ego—never let me say what was in my heart.' His words came in a rush. 'I want to marry you for ever because my heart will not accept anything less. I love you. You are the bravest, most loyal and loving woman I have ever met. You are stubborn and sexy and I love everything about you. The only freedom I want is the freedom to wake next to your face every day for the rest of my life, so please, I beg you, marry me. I love you. I can't be without you.'

Carrie covered his hands with her own feeling as if her heart could burst. If it did, glitter and starlight would explode over them.

'I love *you*, Andreas, and I'm so sorry for…' she raised her shoulders helplessly '…*everything*. You are the best person I know. You're sexy and funny…the way you have taken care of your family… I should never have… I was scared.'

'I know.' He covered her mouth with his. 'I need to learn patience. You know what I'm like. I want something and I want it *now*. You need to think things through. I have to accept our brains work differently.'

She laughed softly into his lips. 'I'll teach you patience if you'll teach me spontaneity.'

'It's a deal.'

Their kiss to seal their deal was broken by a loud cough.

They broke apart to find the registrar looking at his watch, a faint smile on his lips. 'If we're going to marry you we will have to do it now, I'm afraid. We have another wedding party due any minute and my colleagues who are supposed to be acting as your witnesses have other duties to attend to.'

Andreas looked at Carrie. 'Well? Do you want to do it?'

She kissed him. 'I'm here, aren't I?'

The brightest, most dazzling grin she had ever seen broke out on his handsome face. 'Then let's do it.'

So they did.

And neither of them ever regretted it.

EPILOGUE

'YOUR VEIL IS falling off!' Natalia screeched as Carrie attempted to get out of the limousine.

'I don't know why I agreed to wear the stupid thing,' she said in a mock grumble.

'Because you want to make an old woman happy… Violet, can you hold your side still for me?'

Between them, Carrie's two bridesmaids fixed her veil then both inspected her face one last time before the door swung open and her father was there to help them all out, bemused to be wearing a fitted tuxedo, a beaming smile on his craggy, weather-beaten face, delighted to be there, as proud as punch of his only child.

As soon as they were all standing, Agon's glorious spring sun shining on them, the girls fussed with her dress, making sure there were no wrinkles around her protruding bump.

Carrie was six months pregnant. It was a year to the day since she and Andreas had exchanged their vows in the Chelsea registry office with two strangers acting as their witnesses.

When they had gone to visit his parents to share their happy news, his mother had promptly burst into tears. Those tears were only pacified when Andreas had promised they would do it all over again, properly. And by properly he meant a full church wedding with his entire family in attendance, everyone congregating to the same hotel afterwards and everyone then meeting the happy couple for breakfast.

As Carrie had taken an instant shine to both of his parents she had been happy to go along with the plans for them but then, as the date neared, found herself excited for hers and Andreas's own sake.

A big white wedding, surrounded by friends and family, the people who loved them, everyone wishing them well...

It had been a strange experience, being embraced into the bosom of the Samaras family, especially as her own was so small. She hadn't properly appreciated what a close-knit family they all were, not until she and Andreas had moved to Agon permanently a few months ago and found their villa under constant siege from aunts, uncles and cousins all inviting themselves round for a holiday. Anyone would think they weren't all scattered on varying Greek islands with their own beautiful beaches a short walk away. Andreas had since bought the neighbouring villa for his family to use so they could have some privacy. Their only real houseguests now were his parents, Violet and Natalia.

Her sister and his niece were tentatively rekindling their old friendship. Both were doing well. Violet had decided to stay in California permanently. She was still clean. Every day was still a battle but, she had assured Carrie, it was a battle that was getting easier. She *wanted* to stay clean. She wanted to live a long, healthy life. Her words were music to Carrie's ears.

As for Carrie, she'd handed her notice in when they moved to Agon. She had come to love their home there, loved the life, the sunshine, everything about it. Somewhere along the way she had lost her drive for investigative journalism and, anyway, it wasn't as if she could go undercover any more when she was half of a famous couple. Her exclusive feature on Andreas—he had *loved* it—had been a huge hit and the features editor had offered her freelance work, interviewing business leaders and politicians. With Andreas's encouragement, Carrie had been delighted to accept.

The church doors swung open, the organ started to play and, her arm securely in her father's hold, her free hand resting on her kicking baby, she began the slow walk to her husband to repeat the vows they had made in private to the rest of the world.

Andreas stood at the top of the aisle next to his father, who was acting as his best man. The two Samaras men had identical beaming grins.

Her heart skipped to see him.

Her heart *always* skipped to see him.

She had never believed heaven existed.

With Andreas she had found it.

* * * * *

A PROPOSAL
TO SECURE
HIS VENGEANCE

For dear Kathy W, one of the special friends
I've gained from Writers' Holiday—
even if you only come there in July!

CHAPTER ONE

THE WALK DOWN the aisle on your wedding day was supposed to be the longest walk in the world, and today it certainly felt as if that would be the case.

Imogen shivered at the way the words whirled in her head as she contemplated the stone-flagged aisle of the small village church, making her admit to the state of mind she'd been trying so hard to hide—even from herself—for the past few weeks.

A feeling that had grown so much worse as the date of her wedding had come closer, so that now it was just a couple of days away and she still wasn't ready at all.

She doubted if she would ever be ready.

It could all have been so much worse. She could have had no one to turn to, no one who could help her and her family out of the morass of disaster they had fallen into, and with it the loss of the stud that had been in the family for over a century. Even perhaps the prospect of a prison sentence for her father.

No one to push her into a marriage she didn't want but saw as the only way she and her family could possibly go forward.

Imogen pushed her hands through the tumble of black hair that fell onto her shoulders, exerting extra pressure with her fingers as if she could erase the chaos of her thoughts.

It was the only way, she told herself silently. Adnan at least was a friend; they liked each other—always had—and they both had so much to lose if this didn't go ahead.

Besides, there was another possible advantage, she hoped, that perhaps, after her marriage, the scandal press would let go of the hateful nickname they used whenever she or her sister Ciara were mentioned. If this redeemed Ciara's reputation too, left her free to go forward in life and put her own shadows behind her, then that was another reason it would be worth it.

She'd always loved this little village church. The church where her parents had married, where she'd been christened, and her sister after her. She had so loved being an older sister, until their mother had run away with a new, much younger lover, taking Ciara with her. At least the preparations for this wedding had brought Ciara back to the family home where she belonged and now, hopefully, could actually stay.

After a lifetime apart, she had only discovered the whereabouts of her sister a couple of years ago, but the two of them hadn't had any real time to get to know each other properly. Ciara since then had been living and working in Australia, and Imogen's whole attention had had to be focused on fighting to save the reputation and financial position of the stud. But she'd adored Ciara from the moment they'd met again and if she could do anything to help make up for the loss of happiness and family life that Ciara had endured, then she'd do her damnedest to make sure that happened.

She owed Adnan so much. After all, it could have

been someone else she was so deeply indebted to, some-one else she was having to marry.

Someone like Raoul Cardini, a wicked, tormenting little voice whispered into her subconscious.

'No!'

Involuntarily she started away from the pew beside which she had been standing, the surge of memories taking the strength from her legs. She was so distracted that she didn't hear the heavy wooden door open behind her, the soft footsteps on the floor that marked the ar-rival of someone else into the church.

He hadn't expected to see her here, Raoul reflected as he stood just inside the open porch, staring down the aisle at the tall, slender figure who stood with her back to him, one hand on the polished edge of the pew beside her. Just seeing her like this, so unexpectedly, brought all the bitterness, the cold fury that he'd been fighting to hold in check bubbling up inside him.

The original idea had been to wait until the pre-wed-ding dinner tonight to implement his plan for revenge. He had been looking forward to seeing the sudden rush of shock in her eyes, the way her expression would change. Yes, he was sure she would fight to keep con-trol, do everything she could not to show how she was feeling. She was good at that, he recalled, remembering the cool control he had seen her exhibit at times during the two weeks they had spent almost every moment in each other's company.

She certainly hadn't shown any emotion when she had left him, two years before, her face tight and con-trolled. He hadn't begun to suspect the secrets that lay behind that expression, the truth she had hidden from him without a qualm. She'd never even revealed a hint of that life-changing secret until it was gone, the tiny beginnings of what might have been his son or daughter thrown away with the help of the expensive clinic she'd taken herself to. He'd never seen her composure break.

Except for the night she and her sister had been caught by the paparazzi emerging from the casino arm in arm, he recalled, his hands clenching into fists at his side. Neither of them had seemed in the least bit steady on the towering heels they'd worn.

The Scandalous O'Sullivan Sisters! the headline above the photo had shrieked, and it had been in that moment that Raoul had put Imogen and Ciara together, realising that the surname of the nanny who had threatened to ruin his sister's marriage was shared by the woman who had destroyed his chances of being a father. He had recognised her in a moment, but had been stunned to see both of them out of control in a way he had never seen the older O'Sullivan girl before.

Except in bed.

Raoul felt a curse echo inside his thoughts as he fought the rush of heat through his body. He'd thought he'd wiped that particular memory from his mind but it seemed that all it needed was her presence, just metres away from where he stood, and every cell was inflamed. He couldn't afford to let that distract him from his purpose.

She looked a little different, but he knew inside she would be the same. Still tall and elegant, but now with a glossy mane of black hair tumbling down her back. It was longer than before. He remembered the crisp, silky feel of the sharp pixie cut she'd sported back then, the smooth strands catching the gleam of the sun. She was dressed differently too, in a plain white tee-shirt and tight-fitting jeans, simpler and more subdued than the bright skirts and sundresses she'd worn on the beaches at Calvi or Bonifacio. She'd grown thinner too, the tight-fitting denim clinging to shapely hips and long, slender legs, the occasional stylish rip in the material exposing the pale cream of her beautiful skin. She didn't look like a woman who had carried a child. But then, of course, she had never let her baby live long enough to change the shape of her body, had she? It had barely existed before it was gone.

It was shocking how even that dark knowledge didn't stop his more basic male urges responding to the feminine appeal of her.

No! She would not remember Raoul!

Imogen shook her head sharply, desperate to drive away the last lingering threads of memories that bruised her soul; memories she had never wanted to recall. But it seemed that just dredging up that once-loved name from the silt in which she'd hoped to have buried it brought everything rushing back.

'The longest walk in the world.'

The voice spoke suddenly from behind her, its rich, husky accent obvious on the words. An accent that sounded alien in this small Irish village. But not un-known. She knew that voice only too well…but how she wished she didn't.

'Is that not what they say?'

'I— No…'

She whirled around to face the newcomer, spinning so hard that she went over on one ankle, needing to reach out and grab a nearby pew for support. But it wasn't the worn, polished wood that her fingers closed over. Instead she felt the warmth of skin, the strength of muscle and bone under her grasp, and there was the scent of lemon and bergamot in her nostrils, blended with a sensual trace of clean, musky male skin.

It was a scent that jolted her sharply out of the present and right back to a holiday in Corsica two years before. A starlit night, still warm after the burning heat of the day. The slide of soft sand under her feet, the sound of waves breaking in her ear and the hard, warm palm of the man who had just become her very first lover tight against her own as they walked along the beach.

The man who, just six days later, had broken her heart.

'No?'

That shockingly familiar voice was back, softly questioning in her ear, and she blinked hard against the red mist that had hazed her eyes.

This had to be a mistake; a crazy, mindless fantasy. Her unwanted memories had created a mirage in her mind, conjuring up an image of the man she had weakly let into her thoughts for a moment but now wanted so desperately to forget.

'R-Raoul...'

The name stumbled from her lips as she forced herself to focus and found it only made matters worse. That tall, lean frame was a powerful, dark force in the silent atmosphere of the little church.

'*Ma chère* Imogen.'

It was soft, almost gentle. But that gentleness was a lie, she knew. There was no tenderness in this man, as she should have realised from the start. If she had, she might have escaped with her body and her heart intact. Her baby might never have been conceived—or was that actually the worst thing that could have happened? To have known Raoul's child growing inside her for even the shortest time had brought her such joy, such happiness, that she could never have wished it hadn't happened. Even if it had ended so cruelly.

'I'm not your *chère* anything!' she retorted, pulling away from him with a force that rammed her hip into the wooden side of the pew. 'Not now—not ever! And I never wanted to be.'

'Of course not.' His tone made a mockery of her declaration.

He moved slightly, stepping out of the direct light and into a spot where the multi-coloured gleam of the sun burning through the stained-glass windows turned his face into a mosaic of blues and reds, a tiny touch of gold gilding the hard slash of carved cheekbones. The skin was drawn rather more tightly across those bones than it had been before and there were a few more lines around his eyes than she recalled but, if anything, those tiny signs of the passing of years only added to the devastating appeal of his stunning features. The colours from the window played like a kaleidoscope over the white shirt he wore, sleeves rolled up over long, muscular forearms. The shadowy interior of the church hid the burnished glow of golden skin, softly hazed with crisp black hair, but Imogen didn't need to see to remember.

She knew what those arms looked like when gilded by the Corsican sun; knew only too well the feel of them curled around her waist, pressed close up against her skin where it was exposed by the vivid blue bikini she'd felt brave enough to wear in the heat of the sun. And in the heat of his appreciative eyes. She knew what it felt like to lie with her cheek resting on the strength and solidity of his bones, the power of his muscles, the scent of his skin in her nostrils as the beat of her heart slowly ebbed and she slipped into sleep, exhausted after a night of love-making.

She knew too well—and she didn't want to remember.

'You'll forgive me if I don't believe that,' he drawled now.

'Believe it! It's the truth.'

The burn in her veins chilled as she watched his beautiful mouth twist in a cynical response.

'That wasn't what you said at the time.'

It sounded almost gentle, but the ice in his golden-eyed stare warned her she'd be a fool to believe there was anything kind in him at all.

'What I said at the time didn't mean a thing.'

Imogen drew in her breath in a rush, fighting for control. She felt she was being dragged backwards into her past, swallowed up by a dangerous quicksand, suffocating slowly and painfully. Head over heels and crazy in love, all she'd done was to say that she didn't want their sun-filled idyll to end, that she wanted to stay with him. She'd never expected he would turn on her, accuse her of being a greedy gold-digger and dismiss her—for good, he had declared.

'Those were the foolish, thoughtless declarations of a naïve adolescent. I'd had too much sun, too much wine...or something.'

Too much of Raoul Cardini, certainly. But she'd never been drunk when she was with him—she'd never needed to be. He was intoxicating enough to make her mind swim in heated abandon. She'd never had a head for wine anyway, or the taste for it. Except for that one crazy evening she'd spent with Ciara just after they'd rediscovered each other. They'd both been struggling with the darkness that had fallen over their lives, and as a result the joy of the evening together had gone to their heads faster than the most potent alcohol.

'None of it was true—none of it was real.'

'And none of it is relevant now.'

Cold and cutting, it made her feel as if the ground beneath her had shifted disturbingly. She'd known two years ago that he could turn away from her without a second's thought, dismissing all she'd believed they'd been to each other in between one breath and another. But she'd never heard him state it in words of pure ice that he tossed in her face without a blink. And once she knew just how impossible she had found it to forget him, that realisation slashed deep into her soul.

She wished she could find the strength to turn and walk right out of here. Brush straight past him and head for the door. The trouble was that she didn't think 'brush' would be the word to describe the way she would encounter Raoul on the way. Even whispering past the tall, forceful body of the man before her would be like thudding straight into a brick wall.

'Nothing between us is *relevant* at all. So, if you'd just let me past...'

An elegant wave of his hand indicated the fact that there was plenty of space for her to walk by him.

'Be my guest.'

She was nearly past him when he stirred slightly and she could hear the hateful smile in his voice as it drifted after her.

'I'll see you back at the house.'

It stopped her dead, her head ringing as if his words had been a blow.

'I think not!'

It was only now she realised, shockingly and disturbingly, that there was a question she had never asked. One that should have been right at the forefront of her mind from the moment he had first spoken to her but she'd been too stunned even to consider. She'd never thought fate could be so unkind. It was bad enough that he should be here, now, so close to her wedding day, but to think that this was not just an appalling error of chance…

'You're not coming back to the house!'

'Oh, but I am.'

That brought her spinning round, needing to see his face. The deadly smile was still there in his voice but there wasn't a trace of it in his expression.

'No way. I mean…why are you here at all?'

There it was. The question she should have asked from the start. The one that, she now realised, she hadn't dared to ask because she'd feared the answer.

Now the smile was not just in his eyes but very definitely curling the edges of that obscenely sexy mouth. At least, it was obscene for Imogen to consider *anything* about this man sexy. That was what had caught her in the first place, trapping her in the coils of his dark sensuality, taking her life out of her hands and putting it into his, to torment and break as he wished.

'Your father invited me, of course.'

The deadly nonchalance with which he tossed the words at her made her stomach tighten.

'Dad? You're kidding!'

That was just too much. She actually laughed in a blend of shock and relief, at the realisation that this simply could not be true. How could he ever be here for the wedding? How could he have been invited when no one but her knew him well enough to offer him an invitation? She sure as hell had never let anyone know that for a brief space of time he had once been such an important part of her life. Her short-lived summer love affair and its bitter consequences would neither have concerned nor interested her father.

'Do I look as if I'm joking?'

He looked supremely confident, totally at ease, and with not a trace of amusement on his carved features.

'My father would never invite you here. And definitely not for this wedding.'

'Why not?'

There was the flash of challenge in those golden eyes now, clashing with the disbelief in her own stare.

'Not good enough, is that it? You think, *ma belle*, your father would not want to invite a simple olive farmer to his daughter's wedding of the year?'

'Oh, come on!'

She had to cover up her reaction to that casual *'ma belle'*, needing to hide the way it had the bite of acid. Once she had loved to hear him call her that, had gloried in a new-found sense of feeling beautiful in his eyes. But now the bitter memory of how quickly she had gone from being *ma belle* to a mere nothing, a plaything tossed aside and abandoned on the beach where they had first met, curdled in her stomach.

'We both know you're no simple olive farmer and you never were.'

That had been the pretence he had hidden behind when they'd met. He'd let her believe he was a hard-working farmer who was delighted to meet this young Englishwoman on holiday and spend time with her. His friend Rosalie had been the one to warn her that there was more to Raoul Cardini than that. But even she had never revealed the full story. It was only when Imogen had got home and, still nursing the hurt in her heart, had been unable to resist looking up the beautiful island of Corsica on the Internet that she had found the truth that had rubbed salt deep into the wounds his rejection had inflicted on her.

'I don't think the Cardini olive oil empire could ever be described as just farming!'

What had she said? It was only the truth, after all, but it was as if she had flung some vile insult into his face so that his head went back, bronze eyes narrowing, beautiful mouth clamping tight, turning his lips into a hard, thin line.

'Not just the olive oil empire,' he said. 'At least get your facts right.'

'Of course there's more, isn't there? More you didn't trouble to tell me. Did you think it wasn't worth me bothering my head about?'

She flicked her eyes at him, there and away again fast, wanting him to see that she really couldn't give a damn about anything else he hadn't revealed to her. At one time, discovering the fact that, like her family, he was a dedicated breeder of fine horses might have brought them together. But the time to care about the lies he had told, the secrets he had kept from her, was long gone. The memory of the one secret *she* had kept from him burned in her soul, threatening to destroy her if she let it free.

'Your father thinks it is. That's why he agreed to a deal I proposed. And he wanted to mix business with pleasure.'

Could he make that last word sound any more toxic? She knew something was very wrong—it had to be. How could her father have agreed to a business deal when there was nothing left of the family business? If there had been any other possibility then she wouldn't be here, living through her last days of freedom before she walked down this aisle with Adnan Al Makthabi. The marriage was supposed to save the Blacklands Stud from complete ruin. It was supposed to ensure they didn't have to sell off the few remaining horses, including the magnificent stallion Blackjack.

The cost of the stallion had crippled their already overly strained finances, the loan her father had insisted on taking out to pay for him depleting further an already empty bank account and adding thousands to the interest repayments. But at least Adnan and his family wanted Blackjack—perhaps more than they wanted Imogen herself.

'He suggested I come now and share in the celebrations. And he offered me a room in Blackland House for the week so we could discuss the deal at the same time.'

He made it sound perfectly reasonable, natural even, but the nasty twisting sensation in Imogen's stomach told her it couldn't possibly be that way. Her father couldn't discuss any sort of 'deal'—he had nothing to offer! From the date of her wedding, he wouldn't even own the stud—or Blackjack.

'So tell me—what did you use to buy my father's interest?'

She'd gone too far with that. Dangerously so. She could see it in the way a muscle ticked in his cheek, the glare that had turned the warm colour of his eyes to ice in the space of a heartbeat.

'I don't buy my business partners. Ask your father. *You* might not want me here but, believe me, your father does. He invited me to stay and be a guest at your wedding—so, naturally I said yes. I wanted be here to watch you plight your troth to your perfect bridegroom.'

Raoul spat the words at her before he spun on his heel and marched away, down the aisle and out of the church. The staccato sound of his angry footsteps echoed through the silent interior of the church until the heavy wooden door slammed loudly behind him.

CHAPTER TWO

THE SUN WAS burning away the fine dawn mist that had clouded the distant hillsides as Imogen turned the bay mare and reluctantly headed back to the stud. The long, solitary gallop on her favourite horse had been a welcome time of peace and quiet in the bustle of the weekend. Time to reflect and draw breath before considering what her next move might be where Raoul Cardini was concerned.

Because of course Raoul was the real problem she had. The preparations for the wedding were well in hand, everything would have been fine if it hadn't been for Raoul's unexpected arrival and the crazy scheme that her father had embarked on to bring him here.

'Oh, why now!' she exclaimed aloud, making the mare's ears prick in response to the sound as they trotted down the path that led to the stables.

But she knew why. Adnan had revealed last night at the pre-wedding dinner that her father had mentioned Raoul's approach, his interest in the stud services and the stallion Blackjack in particular. But they had agreed to wait until the wedding was over, he said. Or that had been the original plan.

It was obviously not what Raoul believed, Imogen reflected now, slowing the mare to a walk as her hooves rang on the cobbled stones of the stable yard. Last night she'd finally managed to get the truth out of her father, discovering to her horror that things were as bad as she'd thought. Her father had planned to get the deal for stud services for Blackjack signed and sealed before the magnificent horse became the property of the Al Makthabi stud—which he would on the day of her marriage. Adnan had agreed to clear her father's debts, save Blacklands from destruction and restore it to something of its former glory, but only on condition that Blackjack became his as part of the deal.

If she couldn't get her father to cancel the whole thing then the wedding would be off. And even if she could she would still have to worry that Raoul would reveal everything to Adnan.

If that was everything. The mare danced sideways and whickered a protest at the way Imogen's grip had suddenly tightened on the reins.

'Sorry, Angel!'

She gave the sleek bay neck a reassuring pat as she struggled with the bleakness of her thoughts. Just remembering how Raoul had appeared at the dinner last night, dark and sleek in immaculate evening dress, made her throat close up. This was the man she had once thought of as her future, only to have that hope thrown back in her face. She couldn't believe he was here only to discuss a business deal with her father, so she was forced to wonder just what other wicked schemes were brewing behind that cold-blooded, heartless facade of his.

Last night she had thought all she had to do was speak to her father, demand that he break off this ridiculous deal with Raoul. It was only later, when she had had time to think about things, she'd realised how that might not solve matters. Instead, it might be like knocking down the first domino in a carefully planned and balanced arrangement, sending them all tumbling in a wild cascade. One that had the potential to destroy everything she and Adnan had worked and planned for.

'Almost there.'

The memory of the words Adnan had directed at her, the smile that had accompanied his statement, swirled in her mind as it had done all through the night.

She knew he had meant it as a reassuring smile. The trouble was that it had done nothing to soothe the jittery pins and needles that had been running through her veins ever since she had got back from the church.

Last night should have marked the moment when she and Adnan perhaps could have started to relax. They were, as Adnan had said, almost there. Last night's dinner marked the final stage in the preparations for the wedding. The day after tomorrow would be the main event and then after that, as man and wife, they could start to put back together all the pieces of the two families, the two studs, that had broken apart.

Instead, she now felt as if she was deeper into the mire of trouble than ever before—and it was all because of this one man.

'*Bonjour*, Mademoiselle O'Sullivan!'

The voice hailed Imogen as she dismounted from her horse and she bit back a groan of despair. This early in the day, she had hoped to have the fields and the stables all to herself, but of course she should have remembered that Raoul too was an early riser. So often when in Corsica he had stirred before dawn broke and was out before the heat of the day could start to build up. She had deluded herself at the time that as a farmer he had needed to tend to his land, never suspecting that he was up and out to deal with major business decisions so that he could return to the quiet hotel to share breakfast and then the rest of the day with her.

'Good morning, Monsieur Cardini,' she forced herself to respond, finding it hard to make it sound casual and relaxed, and failing miserably on both counts. 'I trust you slept well.'

'I was perfectly comfortable,' Raoul told her, crossing the yard to smooth a hand down the mare's soft nose. He watched the way Imogen's crystal-blue gaze flicked up once towards his face, then away again as soon as her eyes collided with his. 'But I should be no concern of yours. It was your father who invited me.'

'You are one of my wedding guests.'

That cool control was back, at least on the surface, but there was a tremor in her voice that pleased him.

'And I thought you would want to be at breakfast by now.'

'You know me.' Raoul watched her face as he spoke. He knew she was struggling to make polite conversation, but he had no intention of offering her any sort of lifeline. 'A cup of coffee is all I need to set me up for the day.'

She had once been inclined to chide him about that, he remembered, taking him out to one of the bustling little cafés in Ajaccio where she would attempt to entice him to eat something more.

'You work on the land,' she'd reproved. 'You need to eat.'

He recalled that she'd been almost addicted to the local bread made with chestnut flour and pine nuts, her appetite much better then than it seemed to be these days.

He'd watched her at dinner last night and if she had

eaten any of the meal in front of her then he was a complete fool, Raoul told himself. She had stirred her food around, occasionally lifting her fork towards her mouth in a way that might convince anyone else, but not him. So totally aware of her as he was, there was no way he could have missed the fact that her fork had nothing on it.

Her sister was not much better, he acknowledged, having noted how Ciara O'Sullivan's eyes had barely left her sister and her fiancé, her own plate totally abandoned after one or two mouthfuls.

'I need to give Angel a brush down,' Imogen said, turning to lead the horse into her stall. It was obvious she wished he'd leave her alone, but Raoul had no trouble ignoring the blatant hint, strolling along beside her, one hand on the mare's flank.

He was seeing yet another side of Imogen O'Sullivan this morning. One which couldn't be more different from the elegant creature at dinner last night. Today she was dressed for riding, the simple white shirt and skin-tight jodhpurs clinging to her slender frame, her feet pushed into muddy black boots. Last night she had looked stunning and sleek as he had never seen her before, her burgundy silk gown glowing richly against the creamy pallor of her skin. The dress had had a deep, plunging neckline but one where her modesty was carefully preserved by the panel of delicate lace that had covered the lush curves of her breasts.

He couldn't see them, but he could remember. For a moment Raoul was totally distracted by the memory of the time he had undone Imogen's bikini top to expose the pure whiteness of her flesh where she had been protected from the sun, in contrast to the lightly tanned colour of the rest of her skin. Her breasts had been smaller then, each one just fitting into the curve of his palm. He had loved to smooth and caress them, tease the soft pink of her nipples into thrusting life. But just the thought of what might have made her breasts become larger had him biting down hard on his tongue to hold back the curse of rage that almost escaped him.

'So how are you liking your first time in Ireland?'

Imogen had obviously accepted that he wasn't going to leave her and had turned again to making polite, if rather forced, conversation.

'This is not my first visit here.'

There was an odd note in the reply, she recognised. One that warned of unexpected darkness at the bottom of what was just a simple statement.

'It's not? Was that recently?'

Her training at boarding school, the strict discipline of the nuns and their determination to turn out 'young ladies', stood her in good stead. She found that the disciplined part of her personality was working on auto-pilot while all the time, hidden inside, a far less controlled version of Imogen was stirring, uncurling, as if awakening from a long sleep and demanding a new sort of attention.

It reminded her of how it had once felt to be young and carefree, lost on the dangerous seas of her first sexually passionate relationship, the recognition of just how it could be between a man and a woman.

She still felt that way; even last night, with Adnan beside her and his ring on her finger. Adnan was the only man who could stand next to Raoul and match him, inch for inch in height, in the lean strength of his body, the force of his personality. Both were black-haired and brilliant-eyed—but, where Raoul's eyes were that gleaming, golden bronze, Adnan's were a cool, clear blue.

Adnan was stunning—hadn't the reaction of her own sister, when Ciara had first met her fiancé, left no room for doubts on that score? But it was Raoul who had knocked Imogen for six from the start, and now apparently had only to reappear in her life to make her feel as if the world had rocked dangerously and couldn't be righted again.

Raoul was nodding in response to her question.

'I was last here just over a year ago.' There was a dark note in his voice that tugged on already raw nerves. 'That was what first sparked my interest in your father's stud.'

It was only when Angel pushed an impatient nose into the small of her back, urging her forward, that Imogen realised she had stood stock still in confusion at the thought. Raoul had been here a year ago—when she and Adnan had just been starting to discuss the possibility of their marriage, of uniting the two families…

'And of course the magnificent Blackjack.'

Was that comment as loaded as he made it sound? The truth she knew about the stallion, and the way it made her father's deal with Raoul null and void, sat like a lump of lead in Imogen's stomach, forcing her to fight against a twisting rush of nausea.

Raoul reached forward and took Angel's reins from her limp hands, leading the mare into the open stall. The movement meant that their fingers touched just for a moment, something like electricity fizzing between them, so that Imogen couldn't stop herself from snatching her hand away as if she'd been burned. Angel didn't like the unexpected movement and shifted restlessly with a whinny of protest.

'Sorry, sweetheart...' she soothed, and the softness of her tone caught on an image in Raoul's mind, pouring acid onto an already bitter memory.

She had once spoken to him like that, in the darkness of the night, turning the sound of his name into a caress. The change that the spontaneous smile brought to her face was almost magical. Her eyes lit from within for a moment and her skin glowed. He cursed inwardly as the clutch of physical hunger grabbed at him right between his legs so that he shifted uncomfortably where he stood. Wanting to hide the betraying response, he bent to unfasten the girth and ease the saddle from the mare's back. He had never expected still to have this primitive and instantaneous response to her. Not after all he now knew about her. But it seemed that he could hate and hunger in the same heartbeat.

'Everyone's interested in Blackjack,' Imogen said and, although her eyes were on the bridle she was removing from Angel's head, he could tell that the words were not the throwaway remark she wanted them to sound like.

She wore no make-up, and the pallor of her porcelain skin was emphasised by the brush of dark shadow under those sapphire eyes, making them look faintly bruised and disturbingly wounded. She was thinner than when he had known her before, he thought again. He knew that brides were traditionally said to lose their appetites before the wedding, but she looked more like someone who was going to face execution rather than marry the man of her dreams.

But, of course, he wasn't the man of her dreams. Just the thought twisted harshly in his guts. If he'd even suspected that she really cared for Adnan Al Makthabi, then there was no way he would be here. But it was obvious this was a union arranged because of the financial benefits it brought—to the O'Sullivan family at least.

Once again, the cold-blooded gold-digger who had aimed to win herself part of his fortune was setting her sights on someone who had the money she sought. Someone who, it seemed, was more easily persuaded. Or so he'd believed. But, now that he'd met Adnan Al Makthabi, he wouldn't have put the other man down as the sort to be so easily fooled. He'd also been startled to find that he actually liked him.

But then yesterday he had discovered more about this proposed marriage than either she or her lying father had been prepared to acknowledge.

'Look, about…' Imogen began, then hesitated, broke off and, when she began again, Raoul was sure that she had not taken up where she'd left off but had veered onto another topic altogether.

'Where did you get to last night?'

She tossed the question at Raoul, trying so very hard to make it sound casual and relaxed, and failing miserably on both counts.

'Nowhere.'

'But I saw you leave…'

The words faded awkwardly and he raised a dark, cynical eyebrow as he saw the moment she realised she had given herself away. She should have been occupied with her guests, her family and friends, but she hadn't missed the fact that he had left the dinner early, with no explanation.

'I needed some air.'

He had been suffocating in the atmosphere in the room. Three O'Sullivans—because of course the father had been there, knocking back the vintage champagne as if it were water—was more than enough for anyone to take. Not caring if anyone noticed, he'd slid his plate away from him, pushed back his chair and stood up.

The huge patio doors had been open to the garden, voile curtains wafting in the gentle breeze. He'd slipped out into the cool of the evening air, the silence of the night. Over to the left were the stables and the exercise yard, the occasional sound of the thoroughbred horses shifting in their stalls and whickering softly to each other reaching him across the stillness.

He could fall in love with this place, he'd admitted to himself as he'd strolled to the edge of the huge patio. The soft green hills and lush fields of this country were so unlike the rougher, drier terrain of his homeland. Here, the climate was closer to the one in the mountains—and of course there was always so much rain. It had been drizzling just a little and he'd held his face up to the moisture while drawing in deep breaths of the clear night air, filling his lungs with it and wishing he could fill his mind in the same way, to wipe away the anger and disgust he felt at finding himself amongst the members of this corrupt, immoral family.

He had almost left then, headed straight for the airport, onto a plane and away. Only the thought that if he went then the O'Sullivan family—the weak, corrupt father and those scandalous O'Sullivan sisters—would all get away with what they'd done and go on their way so carelessly had stopped him. He'd come here to make sure that didn't happen, and he was not going to back out now.

'I had hoped that you might show me around,' he said now, lifting the saddle and carrying it out of the stall to place it with all the other tack at the end of the stables. 'I'd like to see more of the stud.'

'I'm afraid I'm much too busy.'

Imogen flashed a cold, tight smile in Raoul's direction. She certainly didn't want to spend any time with him if she could possibly help it, and luckily the preparations for the wedding gave her the perfect excuse. He didn't need to know that there was nothing she had to prepare; that Geraldine Al Makthabi had everything in hand and that her future mother-in-law was enjoying every minute of the time she spent making sure everything was perfect.

'I have things to do. I am getting married…'

She flung the words at him like a dart. His presence might put her totally on edge, as if she was balancing on a very high, very tight rope with savage, bone-shattering rocks beneath, but she wanted him to understand that she was not alone and defenceless. She was in her family home, with her father and her sister—her fiancé just ten minutes away.

No…the instant curdling in her stomach at that thought brought a wave of nausea up into her throat. Adnan might be her friend, and currently her family's saviour, but he was also a proud and powerful man. His bloodline was saturated with the ferocious strength and arrogance of his Bedouin ancestors. She knew Adnan could be a hard man, a difficult man if his temper was roused. She'd heard stories of his reputation with women, and as a shrewd businessman, but she'd never had that side of him shown to her, and she never wanted to either.

He might have agreed to this marriage of convenience, but if it turned out to be anything else or, heaven help her, became *inconvenient*, then she had little doubt he would call the whole thing off without even blinking.

'I'm aware of that.'

Raoul's wickedly knowing smile left her only too

aware of the fact that her attempt at attack had simply bounced off the cold steel of his armoured heart—if it really was a heart that beat inside that powerful chest.

'That is why I'm here.'

That—and what else? The words were on the tip of her tongue, but at that moment the door opened and Ciara wandered into the stables. Her red-gold hair tumbled round her shoulders, her green-and-white floral sun dress with its thin straps and flirty short skirt looking cool and comfortable in the already growing heat of the day.

'Hello, honey!'

Imogen's smile of welcome was blended with a rush of relief at the thought that she was no longer alone with Raoul. The verbal fencing, neither of them coming right out and saying anything real, had stretched her nerves to breaking point. So much so that her heart was racing, her breathing shallow at the ordeal of just being in his company.

She was no longer the wide-eyed innocent who had first met Raoul Cardini on a warm summer evening on a beautiful Corsican beach. Met and fallen in love in the time between the sun burning directly overhead in the middle of the day, and the moment when that fiery ball had slipped below the horizon. She'd found herself in the warm darkness with her heart no longer inside her body but handed over to the care of the devastating man she had secretly nicknamed the Corsican Bandit.

If she had only known how appropriate that nickname would come to be, she would have turned and run, as far and as fast as she possibly could. But now she was two years older, she'd been tested by life, been down some long, dark tunnels and had reached the other side. Perhaps she was still bruised and bloody, with scars barely healing over deep wounds she'd endured, but she *was* standing, and she wasn't going to let anyone knock her down again.

But there was a huge difference between feeling that and actually challenging someone like Raoul Cardini to come right out and say exactly what his plans were. Especially when she didn't know how much danger her whole family was in.

She was aware of the way Ciara had reacted last night when she'd learned that Raoul was their guest, staying at Blacklands for the days leading up to the wedding. She had been subdued all through the evening and this morning; something was clearly upsetting her sister. She looked distracted and unusually unsure of herself, her eyes slightly puffy from lack of sleep in a way that concerned Imogen.

'*Bonjour*, Mademoiselle O'Sullivan,' Raoul inserted smoothly, strolling out of the tack room with lazy grace. Ciara shot a swift, strangely nervous glance in his direction.

'Morning,' she muttered almost inaudibly, her hazel eyes focused on Imogen's face. 'So, what do we have left to do today, Immi?'

'Perhaps you can give me a guided tour of the stud that Imogen is apparently too busy to manage today,' Raoul put in, something in his lazy drawl scraping uncomfortably over nerves that were far too close to the surface of Imogen's skin. And Ciara's too, it seemed.

It was definitely an appeal for help that Ciara turned on her now—a plea to be rescued from heaven knew what—but it obviously had something to do with Raoul Cardini. Just what had frightened her sister so badly? Could it be that Raoul had come here not just for the business deal he had described, but perhaps for something to do with Ciara's past? Perhaps to do with the reason her job as a nanny had ended so rapidly, which her sister had refused to reveal to her? Imogen wished she'd had more time to get to know Ciara properly before the threat of total ruin had brought this wedding on them.

'There's plenty still to do,' she managed over-breezily. 'We have to sort out that hemline on your bridesmaid's dress...'

Imogen had made the right move. Immediately some of the tension left her sister's face and she almost smiled.

'And you promised Geraldine you'd help her with the name cards for the table.'

Raoul would never know just what a fiction that one was. Adnan's mother was totally in charge of every preparation for the reception and she would give anyone who tried to intervene very short shrift indeed. But the glance of gratitude from Ciara made the lie worthwhile. Her sister was already turning towards the door, looking like a rabbit that had just been released from a trap,

'I hope you have a good day, Mr Cardini,' Imogen tossed in his direction, not quite having the nerve to meet his stony glare, though she hoped her rather breathless tone could be taken for airy and unconcerned. 'I'll ask one of the grooms to give you the tour, if you like.'

The tour of the part of the business they'd be happy to show him, and not the one he'd obviously been angling for. The one that wouldn't let him pry into secrets that were none of his business. So far they'd managed to hide just how bad things were; she didn't want Raoul finding out more.

'Oh, don't bother.'

That lazy voice was back but she could catch the

thread of steel that ran through it like a warning rumble of thunder before a storm broke.

'I'm sure I can manage on my own. You can find out the things you most want to know that way.'

It was meant to sound casual, indifferent, but there was so much more in his voice. The growing storm was coming nearer, dangerously so. She would have to find out just what was happening with Ciara and figure out how she could proceed from there. And she'd have to make sure that, whatever Raoul had in mind, he didn't get a chance to put it into action.

This sleek, elegant man with the closely cropped black hair, the burning golden eyes above lean, bronzed cheeks and the arrogant tilt to his proud head was so very different from the man she had met on that magical holiday. The young, carefree, raw and sexy Raoul with the suntanned skin, bare feet and over-long hair was the man she had fallen in love with. The man who had broken her heart. Then his friend Rosalie had warned her that Raoul was not all he seemed, but she'd been so deep in love she'd ignored it. Or at least hadn't listened to it properly. So she'd been stunned to find that her own teasing nickname for him was the very one that was used in the international business world to describe his ruthless, cold-blooded determination to make a profit.

The Corsican Bandit was the man she was dealing with now. Because of that, she was going to have to tread carefully. And her sister's arrival had reminded her that there was more than her own future at stake.

'Enjoy your day!' she said over-brightly, praying it didn't sound as fake to him as it did to her own ears. 'Come on, Ciara, we have lots to do!'

Moving to the open doorway, Raoul stood, eyes narrowed, feet firmly planted wide apart, as he watched the two women walk away across the lush green field towards Blacklands House. He wouldn't have known the two women were sisters if he hadn't been told, he reflected. Ciara was shorter, with more rounded curves, and her hair was a glorious red-gold. Just Pierre's type, damn him.

'She's so young, Raoul, and so lovely.' Marina's words echoed in his head. 'And twenty years younger than me—it's no wonder he's entranced. I wish I'd never given her the job as nanny!'

Deep in his pockets, his hands clenched into tight, aggressive fists. The image of Imogen and her sister walking so close together, arms linked without a care in the world, it seemed, brought back a bitter remembrance of that photograph in the papers.

The Scandalous O'Sullivan Sisters. His breath hissed in between clenched teeth.

Yesterday had been just the start. A preliminary survey to get the lie of the land. Tomorrow he would put his plan into operation and he would set himself to bring down the O'Sullivan family, one by one.

Starting with Imogen.

CHAPTER THREE

IT WAS FAR worse than she had thought. Imogen had tried to imagine all sorts of things that Raoul might have against her sister, but never this. Her blood ran cold. It was bad enough to think that Raoul Cardini had appeared out of her past, to be the spectre at her wedding feast, but to realise that her younger sister too was caught up in the dark shadows he had brought with him made her nerves knot in her stomach.

'Why didn't you tell me before now?'

'I couldn't,' Ciara admitted, and Imogen was shocked to see how white she looked. 'I didn't really know you when all this happened.'

That was her mother's fault, Imogen reflected, feeling the raw scrape of bitterness on her soul. Lizzie O'Sullivan had abandoned her marriage when she'd run off with her much younger, much more glamorous lover. Arturo had never wanted children, but Lizzie had persuaded him to take her toddler daughter with them. She had always struggled to get close to Imogen whose bookish, studious nature was nothing like her mother's. Besides, the elder girl had inherited her father's love for horses and the stud that provided their livelihood, while her mother loathed and feared the great, enormous beasts. Determined to break off all ties with the family she had left behind in Ireland, Lizzie had never even told Ciara that she had a sister—and to hide it she had adopted Arturo's name for the family.

The memory of the long years not knowing anything about her little sister still had the power to hurt Imogen. When Lizzie had finally resurfaced, abandoned by her lover and left without the financial support she had looked to him for, it was to demand her right to one half of the O'Sullivan 'fortune'. A fortune that had dwindled dangerously while their father Joe had taken his hands off the reins and let the stud run down desperately. Her mother's demands had threatened to bring bankruptcy crashing down on their heads, but Joe had been determined to pay her off to get her out of his life, even though it had taken every last penny and put the stud even further into debt. That was why Imogen had finally agreed to Adnan's businesslike suggestion of a marriage of convenience between them.

The one good thing that had come out of her mother's reappearance was that it had brought the sisters back in touch with each other. Only then had Imogen discovered that Ciara and her mother had been estranged for some time and that her sister had been working as a nanny in Australia, but the job had come to an end and she was now living in London.

At last, Imogen had finally made contact with her again and they had arranged to meet up. It had only been in the time she'd spent away from Blacklands and the stresses of her father's gambling addiction that she'd noticed her period was late. A pregnancy test had confirmed her fears.

Imogen nodded sadly. 'We might be sisters, but we were complete strangers at the start.'

'And we didn't have enough time to get to know

each other when I was heading for that new job in Melbourne.'

A brief visit to the stud before she'd left was all they'd managed to fit in. That was why she'd had such high hopes when Ciara had come to the wedding. Perhaps now they could build real bridges and finally erase the separation of the past.

'Then you were so ill…'

This time Imogen had to bite down hard on her lower lip to hold back the pain that almost escaped her.

'I don't think I'd have got through losing my baby without you.'

Ciara had held her tight when Imogen had endured the agony of an ectopic pregnancy, losing the baby she had conceived during those magical two weeks on the island of Corsica. It had meant so much to have another female to hold her and murmur soothing words. She had endured so many long years without a mother's comfort, so a sister's love had been a wonderful solace when she most needed it. She had never been able to share anything of her sadness with her father. He had been busy driving himself down the path to destruction, turning to the bottle for solace, and had never even picked up on her unhappiness.

She only wished she could have brought her sister home to see the stud as it had been, if not in its glory days, at least in some degree of stability and success. But Ciara had only been in London temporarily. She'd been looking forward to creating a new life in Australia.

Ciara had never shared just what was troubling her when she had returned home. Did that mean Imogen hadn't really been there when her sister had needed her? Had her own misery blinded her to the way Ciara was feeling when she had lost her job—and the circumstances in which she'd lost it?

Imogen had never suspected that Raoul Cardini was the brother-in-law of Pierre Moreau, the man who had caused her sister so many problems, dragged her name through the mud and ultimately sacked her in disgrace. Now that she did know, it seemed obvious that Raoul would delight in making Ciara pay for what he saw as the insult to his family, his sister and her children. The tension that had been dragging at her insides just knowing Raoul was here, bringing with him those dark shadows of the past they had once shared, twisted into tight, painful knots. What did Raoul plan to tell Adnan? Because he did mean to expose someone and something, that much was certain.

Imogen was determined to make sure Raoul did nothing to hurt Ciara. It was the way she could make up for not realising just how low her sister had been at that first meeting.

She'd been trying to find Raoul ever since she'd made her way back to the stud but there hadn't been a trace of the damn man. In the end, she'd had to take the chance that he still had the same number as the one she'd been weak enough to keep on her own phone in a last attempt to reach him.

What would Adnan do if Raoul revealed all he knew about her own past, and her sister's? Would he go through with the wedding? Or would he decide that even their friendship, and the prospect of keeping his promise to his grandfather to provide him with an heir, cost too much at the price of tying himself to her scandalous family? He was a friend, but was he that much of a friend?

Raoul's phone beeped again, for perhaps the tenth time that afternoon, and a twitch of a smile curled the corners of his mouth as he saw Imogen's name as the sender of the incoming text.

We need to talk.

'Answer it,' the man with him said easily.

Raoul shook his head, his shoulders lifting in a shrug of indifference.

'It's not important—it can wait.'

'No, answer it. I'll make us another drink.'

As his companion got out of his seat and strolled out of the room, Raoul reached lazily for the phone that was still buzzing annoyingly.

We have things we need to talk about.

His thumb flew over the keyboard, casually creating his reply.

I'm busy.

He waited a nicely calculated moment, then added:

I'm talking to Al Makthabi right now.

After that he deliberately switched off the phone and dropped it into his jacket pocket.

Just how long could Raoul be talking to Adnan—and about what? Imogen stared out of her bedroom window and down onto the winding drive that led to the main house, her fingers drumming against the window pane.

Her phone calls had gone straight to voicemail, her texts unanswered after that final declaration that he was with her fiancé, and she had heard nothing, seen nothing of him, for the rest of the day.

With a sigh, she rested her aching head on the hand that rested on the window pane—a hand that had been carefully manicured, the nails painted a delicate pink, ready for the moment when Adnan would place a gold ring on it and make her his wife. Behind her, the beautiful white silk dress hung outside the wardrobe, protected by a cotton covering. Imogen hadn't been able to bring herself even to look at it since the dressmaker had delivered it. She had always had contradictory feelings about it, knowing it was part of a wedding of convenience, not a true, romantic marriage of love. But now she felt the nerves tightening in her throat and stomach as her eyes blurred after too long spent watching to see when Raoul would appear.

'I think I need an early night, to be fresh for tomorrow,' she'd told her father, knowing there was no chance at all she would sleep.

Even if Raoul returned soon, Ciara was still out somewhere in the dark, wet night, the sudden storm and driving rain taking all trace of summer from the atmosphere. She would never be able to settle until she knew her sister was safe.

The glare of headlights drew her attention, warning her that a car was arriving. Squinting through the rain, she saw the sleek, dark vehicle draw to a halt at the door and three male figures get out, heads bent as they dashed through the rain and up the steps.

'At last!'

Now, surely, she would have a chance to try to get the truth out of Raoul, to find out just what fiendish scheme was in his mind. Would he let the wedding go ahead tomorrow or did he plan to spoil it somehow?

The shudder that ran through her was as if the window had suddenly blown wide open, letting the rain in. She had changed into her nightwear when she'd come up to the room, but now the strappy nightie felt too cold, too little protection against the chill of the night, so she turned from the window, reaching for her robe as an extra layer of warmth. Adnan had been one of the men who'd arrived; she recognised the distinctive leather jacket he wore. Her father had been another. How could she manage this without being seen by these two men? She couldn't bear to wait until everyone was asleep. The burn of apprehension and fear was bad enough already.

Her question was answered by her father's voice down in the hall declaring that he had a fine whisky to share.

'We could have a nightcap…?' he offered jovially.

'Not for me, thanks. I'm going to turn in.' That was Raoul; the sexy accent made it clear.

As heavy male footsteps came up the stairs, the sound of the library door swinging shut behind the other two men made Imogen sag against the wall in relief. At last she was free to make her way to Raoul's room, and she wasn't going to leave without some much-needed answers.

But she couldn't head for Raoul's bedroom openly—across the main landing, straight to his door. That would be just asking for trouble.

Luckily, Blacklands House was old enough to have many secrets, amongst which were the hidden passages that linked one room to another by a series of stone steps. Much of her childhood had been spent running along these passages, learning how to get into them from every room and where each one came out.

The fake wall beside the bookcase was easy to open

if you pressed one of the plaster roses that decorated it. Slipping inside, she made her way along the passage in darkness, bare feet making no sound. It was as she pushed slightly open the secret entry door into Raoul's room that she heard the main door open again down in the hall. At last, Ciara was home. Now she needed to make sure that her sister's fears—and her own—could be put behind them. Somehow, she had to convince Raoul not to ruin the wedding, or to drag Ciara's name any further through the mud than it had been already.

The roar of the elderly shower from the bathroom hid the sound of the door sliding closed behind her as she crept into the room.

Raoul reached up and switched off the shower with a violent snap of his wrist. It had taken an age for the damn thing to run even close to warm, never mind hot, and he was far from feeling the relaxation he had hoped for.

Grabbing a towel, he rubbed it roughly over his soaking hair, thankful that the short, cropped cut retained little of the water. It was so damn cold in this ramshackle place; no hint of warmth in the old-fashioned bathroom.

'Nom de Dieu!' he swore explosively, tossing the damp towel aside and reaching for another, slinging it around his hips and fastening it tight. It was supposed to be summer!

But it wasn't just the weather that was turning his mood sour, he knew. It was being here at all that was the problem. Being here, surrounded by the beauty of the countryside, the magnificence of the spectacular animals that grazed in the field, and knowing that the whole enterprise was rotten to the core; that there was no money to support the business and everything was in hock to the bank. Even the magnificent stallion Blackjack… Knowing that he had been conned into paying stud fees for a horse that didn't actually belong to Joe O'Sullivan burned like acid in his gut.

Rubbing the back of his hand across his face to wipe away the moisture, he padded across the tiled floor, wrenching the handle to yank the door open. The financial situation couldn't be any worse, so Imogen had clearly turned to the oldest trick in the book—marrying the nearest really wealthy man in order to help clear her family's debts. The same trick that she'd tried to pull on him when she'd discovered that he was not the simple olive farmer he'd claimed to be. Obviously, the financial problems had already begun to bite back then.

'Damn her to hell!'

He had known this—most of this—before he'd arrived. It was the reason he was here, after all. But it had all seemed so much simpler before he'd left Corsica. The woman who had tried to get her hands on his fortune had now found someone else equally wealthy to marry. Someone else whose child, it seemed, she was prepared to have when the truth was that she had already got rid of her first baby—his child. Tossed it aside because its wealthy father wasn't going to fall into the trap she'd laid for him.

But now, she'd found someone who would do just as she wanted. Someone who would marry her, pour money into this downtrodden estate and pay off the bills.

He had come here to stop that wedding.

But things had got so much more complicated since he'd arrived. He'd seen Imogen and her sister. He'd met the man Imogen was going to marry, and—damn it to hell—he liked Adnan Al Makthabi. Respected him.

Adnan was the type of man he'd like as a friend—if he had such a thing.

'Raoul…'

A voice, soft, uncertain and shockingly familiar, broke into his thoughts, bringing his head up. Dashing any last trace of water from his eyes, he swung round sharply to face her.

It was as if his heated sexual memories of their time together, the ones that had made the inadequate temperature of the shower a positive bonus, had brought her out of the past, conjured her up as a real person here in his room.

But how the devil had she got in here? He was between her and the exit and he knew he'd turned the key in the bedroom door when he'd gone into the bathroom. Yet there she was, tall and slender in a deep crimson robe wrapped tightly around her, tied at the waist. She was standing against the wall, half-hidden by the heavy, embroidered drape of the curtains around one of the carved posters of the bed.

'What the hell are you doing here?'

He saw the way her breasts rose and fell under the delicate silk of her robe with every sharp, uneven breath she took. The wide, wide eyes were clear and sapphire blue even in the dusky shadows, and her mouth was partly open, as if to speak—*or to kiss*, his rebellious thoughts whispered to him. She'd always been beautiful. Hell, she was still beautiful—more so than before, if that were possible.

She had once worn a scarlet dress that had been little more than the nightgown she had on under the robe, but it had been short and sweet with a flippy sort of hem that had shown off her long legs. He had revelled in watching the pale, Celtic skin slowly tan to a subtle,

sexy golden brown after days in the sun. The kick of
lust at his groin was unwelcome and ill-timed—and
appallingly distracting. The white towel suddenly felt
like no covering at all and he shifted uncomfortably,
pulling it tighter at the waist, tucking the edge in again.

'I said, what the hell are you doing here?' he demanded, his voice rougher than before as he fought
with the temptation his memories were throwing at him.

He saw her flinch, blink hard, but then she drew herself up to face him defiantly, blue eyes clashing with his.

'I came to talk to you.'

'About what, exactly?'

She had spent all yesterday trying to ignore him.
Today had been the reverse of that, bombarding him
with text messages and demands that they meet. It was
obvious she was on edge, even if she was trying to look
down her pretty little nose at him.

'About…?'

The rap at the door was loud and staccato, and it came
in the same moment as her response, so that he could
barely hear the word. Imogen broke off abruptly, eyes
going to the big wooden door behind her, a faint questioning frown creasing the space between her brows.

'Monsieur Cardini? Are you in there?

'Ciara!'

Her sister's name was a sound of pure shock and
Imogen looked around frantically, clearly hunting for
somewhere to hide.

'I need to talk to you.'

'Another one,' Raoul drawled, one black eyebrow
drifting upwards cynically. 'My, but I am popular tonight.'

'Not *popular*!' Imogen's outburst was a hiss of fury,
like that of an angry cat.

'Open the door—please. Let me in. I need to talk to you.'

'She mustn't know I'm here!'

'Monsieur Cardini...' Ciara begged. 'We can't let things go on like this.'

'Un moment...'

He was about to suggest to Imogen that she hide, but she had taken action herself, stepping further back, closer to the wall, pressing herself flat up against it. She reached out and caught hold of the embroidered drapes, tugging at them and pulling them closer around her until she was totally concealed.

'Please...' Her sister was clearly getting anxious on the other side of the door.

'All right.' Not sparing another glance at the spot where Imogen stood hidden, he turned the key in the lock and pulled open the door.

Ciara must have been right up against the wood because, as he opened it, she almost tumbled into the room. Her red-gold hair was wet from the rain and was flattened against her skull, and her face still had traces of damp along her brow and cheekbones, the waft of cool evening air coming into the room with her.

'What the devil is this?'

He'd had enough of intruders in his room, enough of the O'Sullivan sisters invading his life, rocking the balance of his thoughts.

'I need to talk to you—to try and sort things out so that you don't spoil my sister's wedding, and— Oh!'

The small cry of shock was because she had only just registered his half-naked state, the towel hitched around his hips. The rush of pink into her cheeks was unlike the response of her sister, who had merely regarded him with the sort of cool control that had set his teeth on edge. But the knowledge that that sister was behind him, hidden behind the heavy curtains, only aggravated his already irritated mood. He brought his hand down in a slashing sort of movement, wanting to cut short the hesitation and get to the point.

'Mademoiselle O'Sullivan—say what you have to say and then leave me in peace.'

Did she hear the noise behind her, the footsteps on the stairs? If she didn't, he certainly did, and the sounds destroyed any last grip on his patience.

'Speak!'

Behind the concealing curtain, Imogen winced instinctively as she heard that cold bite of anger in Raoul's voice. She'd heard that once before, when she had tried to persuade him to continue their relationship beyond the weeks he had prescribed. It meant trouble—ice-cold, ruthless trouble.

Silently she willed Ciara to say her piece and *go*.

'I'm here to beg you not to do anything. Not to say anything.'

The quaver in her sister's voice told Imogen that Ciara had recognised the danger in Raoul's tone, even if she didn't know the full story behind it. But she had never seen the tall, dark Corsican's eyes blaze with golden fire, the way his nostrils flared, his mouth clamping tight over the anger burning inside, turning it into savage ice with the force of his control.

Imogen prayed her sister would never have to experience the way it felt to be on the receiving end of that sizzling glare and feel it burn her almost to ashes.

'About what?'

'About me... Don't tell anyone about my—my past. Because I need you not to spoil things for Imogen and Adnan. Don't ruin her marriage...please.'

'And you think that what her silly little sister got up to would ruin Imogen's chance of marriage? Why would that be?'

Imogen shivered to hear the coldness in Raoul's voice. Ciara was too young, too sweet, too innocent to contend with a sophisticated monster like Raoul Cardini. Wasn't that why she had got herself entangled with that hateful womaniser Pierre Moreau? She had emerged from that encounter bruised and battered, and only now was just beginning to put her life back together again.

'I couldn't bear it if you said anything. Imogen's been through enough already. My father doesn't know, nor does Adnan, and...'

'But Imogen does?'

Now Imogen could see where his cold, dark, vengeful thoughts were going. He had always seen her as nothing but a gold-digger, worth no more than a brief holiday fling and some hot summer sex before tossing her aside. He'd been happy to walk away without a single backward glance, but then he'd obviously discovered that her family wasn't out of his life after all, that her sister was the nanny who had been accused of almost breaking up his sister's marriage—the source of the *Nookie with the Nanny* headlines that had called open season on Pierre Moreau and his wife Marina.

And the proud Corsican was not going to stand for that.

'Monsieur Cardini—please—I'll do anything if you'll just let Imogen and Adnan...'

But that was more than Imogen could take. She couldn't stay here in hiding and listen to the break in her sister's voice, the savage ice in Raoul's. She couldn't let Ciara fight for her sister's future, for what she thought was Imogen's happiness, by taking the blame on her own slender shoulders.

Particularly not when the marriage Ciara was fighting to save was not the love match she obviously believed it to be. Now she regretted letting her sister believe in the delusion that this was a true romance.

'Ciara—no!'

Imogen was rushing forward as she spoke, pushing her way out from behind the heavy curtains, struggling to get free.

She stumbled out into the room, blinking at the light after being hidden in the darkness. In the haste of her movements, her robe came adrift and was tugged backwards, pulling the sides apart, the belt open. Her hair had been dragged loose as well, tumbling round her shoulders, falling across her face, but she couldn't care.

'No—don't say any more. I'm dealing with everything. Raoul and I...'

Her voice trailed off, dropping into silence as she blundered into the hard, solid form of Raoul Cardini standing right in the middle of the room.

'Imogen!' he exclaimed, his voice a bark of reproof.

'Are you sure about that whisky, Cardini...?'

To her horror, that question came from her father, overly cheerful and still some way down the corridor, looking for someone to share his nightcap.

'Oh, Immi!' Ciara's voice clashed with his but hers was a sound of shock and consternation.

Even as she caught her sister's stunned exclamation, Imogen heard her father's voice again, closer now. Desperately she struggled to brush back her tangled hair, sweep it out of her eyes and focus on the scene that was before her.

'Imogen?'

That was her father who was inside the door now, one hand on Ciara's arm, the other reaching up to cover his mouth as if to hold back further expressions of total disbelief.

It was bad enough being caught by her father and sister like this, on the night before her wedding in another man's bedroom, in her nightclothes with her hair in disarray… But as her thoughts reeled, and she wondered how to explain the situation without making it any worse, her eyes cleared and she saw that it already was far worse. The worst.

It was not just her father who had come into the room. Someone else had been drawn by Ciara's voice. Someone else was out in the corridor, his tall frame blending into the shadows, his battered leather jacket giving him away at once.

'*Imogen!* What the hell is going on?' thundered a voice that could only belong to a savagely shocked and furious Adnan Al Makthabi.

CHAPTER FOUR

'F-FATHER…'

It was all Imogen could manage, even that one word being almost beyond her. What was impossible was actually looking into the corridor, after that one brief, horrified glance that had met with the blazing glare of the man who was supposed to be her bridegroom tomorrow.

Or was that today? The clock out in the hallway at the bottom of the stairs was already beginning to strike midnight, the deep, booming notes reverberating up the stairwell towards them.

'Don't you know it's bad luck for the groom to see his bride before the actual wedding…?' Raoul drawled cynically.

Which wasn't very far from the mark. Her brain was whirling in a lethal combination of shock and disbelief, thought processes shattered. Her eyes wouldn't focus either so she couldn't actually see Adnan's face, only her sister's white, stunned expression and her father's features drawn in appalled disbelief.

'What wedding?' Adnan tossed at her, hard enough to cut through the air in the room and making it difficult to breathe.

'Our—' She swallowed audibly. 'Obviously *our* wedding…'

'Nothing obvious about that from where I'm standing.'
'But Adnan…'

Everyone else had frozen into silent figures in the room. But then just as she tried to move forward, past Raoul, she found that she was grabbed, her arm gripped in a punishing hold that pulled her back against a warm, powerful, masculine form.

It was the feel of the heat of his skin against her now exposed back, the thud of his heart underneath the hard frame of his ribcage that shocked her into silence. She had forgotten—how could she have forgotten?—that, while she was wearing only the half-on, half-off night-dress with her robe falling down her back, Raoul was *half-naked*, barely covered by the white towel knotted at his narrow waist. Pressed up against him like this, the scent of his clean skin overlaid with the tang of lemon from his shampoo curled around her from behind, en-closing her in a sensual haze, scrambling her thoughts even further.

'Adnan…' she tried again, but the burning image of what he must be seeing dried her throat so that no fur-ther words would come out.

She was grateful for the blurring of her vision so she couldn't see the anger, the betrayal, in his face. The wedding might not have been any sort of love match, but Adnan was her friend. He had also offered to help her out of the hard place in which her father had dropped her and the rest of her family. He deserved better than this.

'This isn't what it seems,' she managed miserably, then, forcing a new strength into her voice, 'Tell them, Raoul.'

Tell them, Raoul. The man who held her registered that. It had come out like a command. She might as well have accompanied it with a snap of her fingers. Obviously, she expected him to obey.

Equally obviously, that was the last thing he planned right now.

For one thing, he had never jumped to any woman's command and he didn't intend to start now. For another, one which was starting to become much more important, the feel of her pressed up against him like this was scrambling his thoughts. He had forgotten how it felt to be this close to her. To feel the soft, warm silk of her skin against his. The black fall of her hair slithered over his shoulders, his chest, delicate strands of it catching against the evening's growth of beard and tangling in the stubble. And her neat behind was pressed close up against him, his erection against the cleft between her buttocks.

The effect on him would be obvious if she moved. And that would clearly only make things so much worse. Not that he gave a damn if it ruined Imogen's chances. Wasn't that what he had come here for in the first place?

'No need for it to be explained,' he drawled, pulling Imogen back against him as she tried to move away towards her fiancé.

If Al Makthabi was still her fiancé after this. Surely the other man would thank him for freeing him from marriage to a woman who was only after him for his money?

'This is exactly what it seems.'

He spoke over Imogen's gasp of outraged indignation, tightening his grip warningly on the arms she tried to pull away from him. He caught her tiny murmur of discomfort and immediately loosened his grip just a touch. Not enough to let her break away, but enough not to bruise that soft white skin that was making it hellishly difficult to concentrate on what he was saying.

What he really wanted was to tell them all to get to hell out of here, to press his mouth against the fine line of her exposed neck, kiss it, let his tongue slip out to taste it, press nibbling little bites...

Hell, no!

Brutally, he dragged his mind back from the wanton path it seemed determined to follow, the shockingly sensual little wriggle that Imogen gave against him revealing without words that she was aware of the effect she was having on him. The battle he was fighting to control his most basic feelings roughened his voice so it sounded harsher than he had intended.

'Imogen came to see me—we knew each other before, didn't we, *chérie*?'

'*No!*'

Imogen couldn't believe what was happening, what he was saying. How could he possibly be calling her *darling* when it was so far from any sort of truth? Particularly when it was hissed in her ear like the voice of the serpent in the Garden of Eden.

'*Oui, ma chère.*'

Long fingers stroked down her arm, making her writhe in uncontrolled response. A tiny, abandoned moan escaped her, sliding out before she could bite down hard on her lower lip to hold it back. How could this be happening?

But she couldn't suppress the red alert flaring in all her senses; couldn't bring that yearning memory under control. Behind her, Raoul's strength supported her, his heat surrounded her, his mouth drifted across her neck at the point where her pulse throbbed in desperate, uncontrolled response. Even now, with no trace of privacy in the room. With her father, her sister… Oh, dear heaven—*Adnan!*

To her horror, she found herself closing her eyes in response then frantically forcing them open. And wishing she'd never done that when she caught the raw savage rage in Adnan's eyes, the snarl of fury that twisted his mouth.

'You were lovers.'

It was thrown straight into her face and there was no way she could avoid it. It was as if the ground had opened up beneath her, throwing her down, deep down into hell, and she couldn't possibly escape. She couldn't deny it either. To do so would be to lie to Adnan and she couldn't do that. She owed him the truth if nothing else.

Rough and raw, she dragged in a painful breath to give her the strength to speak. At the same time, unexpectedly, she felt the change in Raoul's grip, the new way he was holding her. Still tight, but somehow stronger, supporting rather than restraining her.

'Yes…' she sighed, sad and low. 'Yes, we were.'

Raoul hadn't expected that. She sensed it from a new tension in the long body against which hers was pressed. He clearly hadn't expected her to speak the truth. But what else could she do? She had valued Adnan's friendship for so long. She couldn't wrong him now.

The words fell into icy silence. The only sound in the room was her own heart thudding heavily in her ears, the blood pulsing along her veins. There was the tiniest sensation of Raoul's breath, warm and soft on her neck, and shockingly it felt like a touch of comfort in a world where everything had turned black.

'But…' She tried to start again but her voice had no

strength and no one could hear her whisper because of the snarl of icy fury from Adnan that covered it.

'You're welcome to her.'

The words were tossed into the room, cold, stark, totally indifferent. And they were directed at Raoul, flying past her as if she no longer existed.

She didn't exist any more—not for Adnan. She had no doubt about that. If she needed any further proof, it was there in the way he turned on his heel and strode away, angry footsteps echoing down the corridor.

She tried to tug herself away from Raoul's hold.

'Let me go!' she cried, turning her head to direct it at his cheek.

But that was a terrible mistake. It brought her face so close to his that the scent of his skin warmed her senses; and, when she cried out her rage, her lips actually grazed the stubble covering the rich, olive skin of his jaw. She could taste him against her tongue and the rush of memory almost took her legs from under her. She would have sagged against him if it weren't for the sudden tightening of his grip, the strength of his muscles supporting her.

'Let me go!'

'Not if you're going after him.'

'Going after him? Don't be stupid! Did you hear what he said? Do you think he'd want me now?'

She twisted round in Raoul's arms, needing to face him, then immediately wished she hadn't. The movement brought her hard up against him, her pelvis crushed against his so she couldn't be unaware of the swollen evidence of his arousal beneath the inadequate concealment of the towel. The heat of it, the burning sensation, froze her in total shock.

'Let me... I'll go after him...'

It was Ciara who spoke, turning and running out the door, following where Adnan had marched away just moments before. Imogen heard her dashing along the corridor, down the stairs, and then her steps faded into silence.

'No point,' she tried to respond, but no one was listening. Outside, there was the roar of the powerful engine of Adnan's car and the spurt of gravel under the wheels as he sped away.

'Immi…'

She had forgotten her father was there.

Joe O'Sullivan's stunned expression was just too much for her battered and bruised mind to take in. Her senses were assailed by the strength of Raoul's arms around her, the rise and fall of his powerful ribcage as he breathed, the dark glint of watchful golden eyes. If she inhaled, she took in his scent; if she moved her head, she felt the scrape of his bristled chin. And all the time there was that hot, hard, demanding pressure into the cradle of her hips, reminding her of wilder times, dangerous days when she had lost herself in the strength and fire of this man's passion.

'Oh, Immi…'

The sound of her name from her father again barely reached her through the whirling confusion in her thoughts. It also had a fraying edge on the word, one sadly she knew all too well. Joe O'Sullivan had been celebrating his daughter's upcoming wedding—and his own prospective freedom from fear and debt—just a little too well. As she blinked away the sense of apprehension in her own eyes, she saw Raoul look down at her, dark and intent, his focus fixed on her and nowhere else.

'Get out,' he said, cold and stark.

For a moment, Imogen thought his words were addressed to her and she lifted her head to try to look around. Then immediately wished she hadn't. The movement brought her eyes round to the mirrored door in the huge, old-fashioned wardrobe that stood against the far wall, with her image reflected in it. And the sight of that reflection brought the heat rushing up her body, scorching through every cell.

Was that what Adnan had seen? If it was then it was no wonder he had walked out without a single glance back, their arrangement, their friendship shattered in a moment. He must have seen that wanton-looking woman in another man's arms, her hair tossed and tangled down her back, the make-up she had forgotten to take off in her haste to talk with Raoul smudged under her eyes. The robe had been dragged apart and hung halfway off one shoulder, the thin strap of her nightgown following it to drape partway down her arm.

No wonder Adnan had stalked away. No wonder he had turned his back on her—and the future they had hoped to secure for Blacklands. Guilt tore at her conscience and blended fiercely with fury at the way Raoul had behaved, the way he'd trapped her here like this with her father.

'Dad…please,' she begged, unable to turn and look at him, unable once again to drag her gaze away from Raoul's burning eyes. The hypnotic hold he had on her was far stronger than the muscular grip that held her so close. 'Go now.'

'But Immi—what about the wedding? What—?'

'Go.' It was Raoul's voice, flat and emphatic, no room for argument. 'Go now.'

'Dad—please do as he says.'

If she could hear the pleading note in her father's

voice, then surely Raoul could too. Or was that just because she knew what was behind it? How much had depended on her wedding, and how much would be ruined now that Adnan would never go through with the event.

'Go!' Raoul repeated, his tone darkening dangerously.

Imogen didn't have to look back over her shoulder to see her father's expression. She could sense it in the quality of his silence. The bristling defiance was combined with an underlying fear and the need to protect himself from the consequences of his own irresponsible actions. It had been there in his face, in his tone, when she had told him that she was going to marry Adnan. He'd known he shouldn't be asking this of her, but he hadn't been able to hold back the relief at the thought that there was a chance of being rescued from the desperate situation he had found himself in. It was no wonder he was in this mess; he was fine with the horses he knew and loved—but financial problems and the real world were way beyond him. He had never been a strong man emotionally, which was why she had never told him about her pregnancy and its tragic end.

'If you're sure, Immi. Well, you might put some clothes on, young man!'

With this last attempt at defiant challenge, Joe turned on his heel and left, the speed of his departure betraying how glad he was to be on his way.

It was that final retort that proved to be too much for Imogen. Suddenly, the appalling sense of tension that had been twisting in her stomach since the moment of Ciara's arrival snapped, shattering her composure and taking her sense of control with it.

'Put some clothes on!' she gasped, fighting the wave of near-hysterical laughter that overtook her. Her eyes closed, her head bent as she struggled with the giggles that swept through her. 'Y-young man!'

'It is some time since I was called that.'

Raoul's tone was wry. The tiny touch of humour, totally unexpected in his voice, was too much, too full of memories to cope with, breaking her in a very different way. Imogen stiffened and pulled back against his hold and away from the warmth and strength of his body. It was only when she put that space between them that she recognised how, weakly and dangerously, she had given in to the sense of comfort that being held had brought. A lying, deceptive sense of comfort, because Raoul's arms offered no safety. Instead, he was the real source of menace, the true threat to her peace of mind.

How could she have been weak enough to let herself even think of surrendering to that malign temptation? The shock must have rattled her brain more than she'd imagined.

'Dad was right—you should put some clothes on,' she said sharply. 'If you think I'm going to talk to you with you looking like that...'

'Why?' It was wickedly cool and smooth, curling round her like perfumed smoke. 'Am I distracting you?'

Totally. The sight of so much beautiful skin, the haze of black hair that shadowed the muscular chest tracing a path down towards the point where it disappeared under the immaculate white towelling that was fastened around his narrow waist, was too much of a reminder of the way it had felt to have his hard body, the heated thrust of his manhood, pressed against her. It sent the blood rushing through her body and thundering inside her head.

'Not at all,' she managed with a pretence of carelessness. 'But I think we've caused enough scandal for tonight. And if we're going to talk…'

'Are we?' Raoul pushed a lean hand through the crisp, damp strands of his hair as he raised one dark brow interrogatively. 'What do we need to talk about?'

'Well…'

She'd spoken without thinking. Stupidly, it seemed. Raoul had managed to turn her whole life upside down and inside out. He'd sent her fiancé away in a black rage, breaking their engagement. He'd ruined the prospect of the wedding that was supposed to be happening to-morrow—*today*, she realised as she remembered she'd heard the chime of midnight. The wedding that was supposed to have saved them all. It was only now she recognised that somewhere, naively, deep down inside, she'd allowed herself to think that perhaps he might do something to help.

What could have put such a crazy idea into her head? And yet where could she go now that her future lay in ruins at her feet? The idea of going back to her room, to the emptiness and darkness, to face the loneliness and destruction of what she'd done, was more than she could bear.

'I'm sorry. There's nothing, of course. I'll leave you.'

'Non!'

Somehow the command sounded much more emphatic in his native language. Imogen flinched inside as it reminded her of the time they had once spent together, the way she had tried to learn French to be able to talk to him and to understand the signs and the notices on the sun-warmed island where they'd met. She'd also hoped it would help her understand him. Fat chance of that!

'N-non?'

'Perhaps we do need to talk.'

He needed to get out of this towel and into some more concealing clothing. The effect she was still having on his body was so primal that if she came close again she would feel the evidence of how aroused she made him just by breathing. Hell, no, that was a mistake. Thinking of her breathing inevitably brought his gaze to the top of that flame-coloured nightgown, still exposed by the way the silken robe hung half off her shoulders. The smooth curves of pale skin and the deep cleft of her cleavage were tormenting temptation in themselves, and the way those curves rose and fell with the uneven, heightened pace of her breathing threatened to destroy his ability to think at all.

'And I will put some clothes on.'

Now, what was that look? Relief? Or annoyance? He wasn't arrogant enough to call it disappointment, no matter how tempting it had been to tease her over that a short time before.

'You too.'

As he moved past her he paused to lift the edges of the robe up and over her shoulders, tugging them together to remove the temptation of her breasts. The ragged way she was breathing brought those soft curves up to meet his hands, brushing against his fingers for a moment so that he had to complete the movement with an awkward jerk, letting the silk drop into place as he stepped back and away abruptly.

'Help yourself to a drink.'

He waved a hand in the direction of the rich red wine he'd left to breathe on the dressing table as, impatient to get out of the way of temptation, he snatched up the jeans and shirt that he'd left on the bed on his way into the bathroom.

There wasn't time to shower all over again, no matter how much he needed the pounding of icy water to suppress the hungry demand that was making his body ache with discomfort. For one thing, Imogen knew he'd just come out of the shower when she'd stumbled into the room.

His pulse rate skyrocketed at the memory of the way she had looked then, appearing like a fantasy in his dream just when he'd been imagining her, remembering that last night in Corsica, before she had turned into another woman, one so like the greedy gold-diggers he'd come up against too often already.

She'd even used the same words that Alice had spoken: 'I need to tell you something. I can't let you go…'

No, damn it, no! He forced his eyes away from the shower and instead contented himself with filling the sink with cold water and dunking his head and face deep into it. It did little to quell the throbbing pulse in his groin, but it did force him to clear his mind and try to think as coldly and rationally about things as he could. The memory of the way Alice had used him, taken his love and cast it aside, did the rest.

This was not how he had expected the evening to go. Though, if he were honest with himself, he hadn't really *expected* anything.

Certainly not the sudden appearance of Imogen in his room, bringing with her too many memories, too many hopes he had once cherished. Hopes he had once been young enough and fool enough to believe in.

The thought of those naïve dreams threatened to distract him from the path he had determined on. The path that had unexpectedly opened up so clearly and easily in the space of the last hour. When he had planned his revenge on Imogen O'Sullivan he had never really anticipated it being handed to him on a plate like this. But he intended to take full advantage of it.

CHAPTER FIVE

'HELP YOURSELF TO a drink.'

Imogen gritted her teeth against the irritation those words caused her. The casual invitation drifted over his shoulder as he walked away from her into the *en suite*. As if he was the host here and she a mere visitor.

Which she might well be soon, cold reality reminded her. The marriage of convenience to Adnan had been their last chance to save the stud, her father's reputation and her own future. Now those plans lay in ashes, the hope she'd had disappearing out of the door with Adnan in that black rage.

Who could blame him? When she thought of the scene that must have met her fiancé's eyes—her *former* fiancé's eyes—just minutes before, her skin burned, her eyes stinging with hot tears of shame. She had lost Adnan's friendship as well as everything else, she knew. His powerful male pride would never stand for seeing her in another man's bedroom, in his arms—and both of them half-dressed.

Shaking fingers moved over the rumpled silk of her robe, feeling how, even now, her insubstantial clothing was still not fully restored to any degree of order. The memory of the cold, indifferent way that Raoul had hauled her robe around her—the speed with which he had pulled his hands away as if, once their audience had gone, it disgusted him to touch her—made her feel as if something cold and slimy had slithered over her skin. Once, he hadn't been able to wait long enough to peel her clothes from her body, but had ripped them away in the heat of hunger. Several of her dresses had ended up as mere shreds of cotton, discarded on the floor.

This time, he had shown the same need to have her cover herself, had done the job for her with a rough coldness that brutally contradicted the desire she'd thought she'd felt when he was pressed up against her back. Obviously, that had been the primitive, basic response of a red-blooded man to any half-tolerable female. But then, when he had realised precisely which woman he had been dealing with, his whole mood had changed in the space of a heartbeat.

With an abrupt movement, Imogen yanked her robe up around her, belting it as tightly as she could, then made her way across to the table where the bottle of wine stood next to two glasses.

Two? Who had he been expecting? The question froze her hand, leaving it suspended in mid-air as she forced herself to consider the question. Had Raoul had an assignation here? But he didn't know anyone in Ireland. Or did he?

He'd said that he'd visited Ireland once before. Was it possible he had met some other woman? In a bar, maybe, as he had once met her, inviting her back to the house, to his room…

Having previously not dared to risk the effects of alcohol on her already jangled mood, Imogen now grabbed for the bottle and slopped an amount of the rich red liquid into a glass, not caring that some of it splashed over the side. The thought of arriving here in this room, having come along the secret passageway, to discover Raoul entertaining his female visitor, possibly even in bed with her... She needed the wine even more at the thought, gulping it down with foolish abandon.

That would be worse...

Shocked, she pulled herself up short, the closing of her throat making it impossible to swallow the last dregs of her wine. How could it have been worse if she'd come upon Raoul here, with another woman? How could that possibly be worse than *this*? Worse than the destruction of her hopes and dreams, her plans for the future?

For both herself and Adnan.

The sudden opening of the bathroom door behind her made her start, and she almost choked on the rich liquid.

'Don't kill yourself.' Raoul's tone was dry and darkly amused. 'You're supposed to sip the stuff, not swig it down.'

'I do know how to drink wine,' Imogen managed as she forced the liquid past the knot in her throat. 'I'm not the same person you met all those years ago.'

Then, she'd rarely drunk wine, or alcohol of any sort. She'd seen what it had done to her father in his dark days and she'd never wanted to go down that road herself. But Raoul had introduced her to the sensual experience of a really good wine, the enjoyment of sipping it slowly.

Not like she'd done just now.

'I can see you're not,' was Raoul's drawled response, the dark gleam of his eyes going to the drops of wine on the table, the level in the bottle that had dropped rather too far for comfort. 'But clearly your father is.'

It was a remark guaranteed to have her slamming the near-empty glass down on the nearest surface. She had forgotten that she'd confided in Raoul the reason why she was so hesitant to share the bottle of wine he'd brought over to her table on her first night in Corsica. He had taken it that she'd been accusing him of trying to get her tiddly, so she had flung the explanation at him in a nervous rush, anxious that this devastatingly handsome man should not think her naïve or, worse, that she was trying to repulse his approach.

Short of admitting she'd been watching him for some time across the bar, and begging him to stay because he'd just made all her dreams of the perfect holiday come true when he had strolled over to speak to her, she'd blurted out the truth. That her father had a drink problem and that watching him lose himself in a bottle had made her wary. That it was only because she had left him in the care of his determined sister that she had felt able to snatch a moment of freedom and enjoy this short holiday on the beautiful island.

She'd expected that he'd laugh at her, or walk away from someone so naïve and vulnerable. Instead he'd hooked a chair out with one foot and lowered himself to sit opposite her.

'Forget the wine, then,' he'd said. 'A fruit juice—or perhaps just water. It comes from the mountain springs.'

She'd been delighted, so flattered that she'd even stumbled over asking for an orange juice, but he still hadn't laughed. And he'd stayed. Stayed and talked to her all through the evening, and late into the night, sharing a meal with her and persuading her to try some of the local dishes. He'd even paid for everything—as a welcome to the island, he'd said.

It was only later as they'd met more often and as she had got to know him—or so she'd believed—that she'd been relaxed enough to try the delicious white Vermentino and the esteemed Patrimonio red made on the island. By then she'd no longer feared he might ply her with alcohol in order to get her defences down. She'd already been deeply intoxicated just on his company alone, on the devastating sexual pull he exerted without trying.

'How much had he drunk tonight?'

So he'd noticed. It hadn't been just the memory of her past admissions that had heightened his awareness of her father's weakness.

'I'm not sure—possibly just a nightcap with Adnan after you all returned home. He was planning on an early night before the big day tomorrow...' Her voice faltered. 'Today.'

'Adnan doesn't drink.'

He shocked her with how much he knew about her fiancé. Did he also know of the tragedy that lay behind Adnan's decision?

Raoul had picked up the bottle of wine, twisting it round in his hands and almost pouring himself a glass before he obviously reconsidered and replaced it on the table beside his empty glass.

Imogen wished she'd done the same. She was still so unused to the effects of alcohol that even the one glassful she'd swallowed was already starting to affect her.

Or was that Raoul himself? It was illogical, quite the opposite of what she'd have expected, but now that Raoul had emerged from the bathroom, towel discarded and replaced by more concealing clothing—a white linen shirt and dark denim jeans—she should have felt much safer, more at ease. But the sensations that were stinging along her nerves were not calm, nor the remotest bit relaxed. Instead they were like the fizzing of an electrical current of awareness. He'd obviously splashed water on his face; the sheen of moisture still glossed his cheekbones and spiked the impossibly thick dark lashes around his eyes. Tiny crystal drops sparkled like diamonds in the jet-black strands of his hair, and the brilliant white of his shirt had been left hanging open against his tanned skin, highlighting the scattering of crisp black hair.

Dressed, but not fully. Clothes just tossed on because of her demand, but the open defiance of what she had wanted was clear in the casual half-dressed style he had adopted. It had once delighted her and made her blood heat, her heart race so fast. But that had been when she was strolling on a sunlit beach, or sitting beside the pool at the hotel, bare feet dangling in the cool blue water. It was not here, not now, not in his bedroom.

Nervously she twitched the sides of her robe close together again, then wished she hadn't, as she saw his dark eyes flick sideways to follow the betraying movement. Besides, she had no need to fuss, did she? He had already made it plain that his thoughts were on covering her up rather than taking her clothes from her.

She could feel the hot blood slide under her skin, flooding her cheeks with warmth at the thought. She could only pray that Raoul might take her response as being the effects of the rushed gulp of wine which was marking her skin as fast as the alcohol went to her head.

'So what do we need to talk about?'

She took refuge in attack and saw those straight black brows draw together in displeasure at the sharpness of her tone.

'You told Adnan the truth.'

It was obvious that was the last thing he had expected.

'That we were…'

The word 'lovers' wouldn't come. It didn't accurately

describe what they had been. Sex buddies? Friends with benefits? No, not *friends*. Adnan was a friend—*had* been a friend, she adjusted painfully.

'That we'd slept together. Did you think I wouldn't?'

'I thought you might want to deny what we had.'

'What did we have? You were a holiday fling, that's all.'

The way that one black eyebrow drifted upwards, questioning her declaration, made her stumble over her words.

'So—so I wanted it to go on a bit longer towards the end—what was wrong with that?'

Crazy with love for him, she had ignored his declaration that it was only a holiday fling. She'd teased him and tried to seduce him into agreeing that she could stay. That they could stay together. Maybe even make a commitment. She hadn't been prepared for the dark storm cloud that had settled over his face; the way he had shaken off her hands.

'At the time, I *thought* I wanted it,' she flung at him. 'That didn't last long.'

Something dark slid across his face, throwing shadows into those golden eyes.

She'd more than 'wanted it to go on a bit longer', Raoul recalled. She'd been pushing to keep the relationship going when she went back to Ireland. She'd even tried to get him to ask her to stay in Corsica, to move in together. *This relationship could really be going somewhere*, she'd said.

For a brief time, he'd fallen for it. It was only when Rosalie, the daughter of family friends—and for a brief time a teenage fling—had seen that he was actually considering going along with what Imogen wanted that things had changed. She'd admitted that she'd let it drop that Raoul was not just the farmer he'd made himself out to be. Imogen's sudden change of position had come about, Rosalie had said, because she had discovered the wealth that was the reality behind the 'simple farmer' pretence. Imogen had known exactly who he was and obviously that was why she was suddenly not going to be content with the two-week time limit on their holiday affair.

That was when he'd realised he'd been taken for a fool once again. That, like other gold-diggers before her, Imogen wanted the man she'd found out he was, not the story he'd told her to act as a protective shield.

That had burned so badly that he hadn't even been able to see straight. Because he'd felt something different for her. He'd wanted—hoped—that she would be someone who wanted *him* and him alone. Not the fortune he'd hidden from her.

'I didn't know you were protecting yourself that way,' Rosalie had admitted. 'I really thought she already knew...'

Imogen knew now. Raoul could mark the change in her from the moment his friend had let slip the truth. The girl he had thought was quiet, shy, innocent, so unlike the women who threw themselves at him with an eagerness that did nothing to conceal the gleam of greed, the euro signs in their eyes, was nothing of the sort. It had burned like acid to realise that she had only been that way as a carefully calculated approach. Once she had learned the truth from Rosalie, she had set herself to entice him in a way that was such a change around from her original behaviour that it was like a harsh slap in the face.

'And I certainly wasn't prepared to lie to Adnan. Not now. When he'd promised me so much, surely he deserved to know the truth.'

Only when he had appeared so unexpectedly, Raoul reminded himself. When he had discovered his fiancée in another man's room, another man's arms. Acid curdled in his belly at the thought she had only felt obliged to reveal the truth to her groom-to-be when circumstances had forced her into it. She had obviously not told him the full story, though. The acid ate into him more violently at the thought that, if Imogen had never admitted that they had been lovers until now, then there was no way that the other man could know about the baby.

His baby. The one she had aborted without a second thought.

Suddenly, he couldn't bear to be so close to her. The scent of her skin that he had previously found so enticing now made bile rise into his throat. The bottle of wine sent out a tempting message, offering a promise of the obliteration he had enjoyed when he had first learned what Imogen had done, but he forced himself to turn away, pacing across the worn carpet to stare out of the window into the darkness of the night.

Above the wide expanse of countryside, and the paddocks where beautiful thoroughbred horses grazed during the day, the stars glittered against the black velvet of the sky. His grandmother had once told him that the stars were the souls of tiny babies who had left the world too soon, waiting for their parents to join them. Was his son or daughter there, looking down at him and the mother who hadn't wanted their child?

He had to swallow down hard against the nausea before he could speak again.

'I thought the time for truths of that sort would have been earlier—when he asked you to marry him.'

Perhaps, if he'd been looking at her, then Imogen might not have been able to reveal the full truth. She couldn't help but feel that it put her in a position of danger to let this man know any more about the way her marriage had been arranged. The bargain she had made with Adnan.

'He didn't.'

It had been a sort of mutually accepted fact that this was how they were going to proceed—a business deal, really, but one in which they cared about each other enough to make certain aspects of it work. The memory of how it had felt to be held close to Raoul—the heat that had seared through her, then and in the past, the acknowledgement of how easy it would have been to go along with the heir-making part of *that* relationship—made her bring her teeth down sharply on her tongue to stop herself from adding anything even more stupid to her last remark.

But it was too late. Raoul had clearly already noted it, spinning round to subject her to a frighteningly intent scrutiny.

'He *didn't ask*?'

'We didn't need things like that. It was…accepted that we would marry. Almost from the day we were born.'

That was the story they'd decided on if anyone challenged their commitment. She'd never expected to have to justify it to this man who'd stolen her heart so that, like Adnan, she didn't have one to give to anyone else.

'We both grew up here, and were both likely to inherit the two studs. So joining them together through a family union seemed inevitable.'

What had she said to draw those dark, straight brows together in an ominous frown?

'And this arrangement—was it in place when we were together?' It was a harsh demand.

'Er…no. We were…' She couldn't believe she was actually going to say this. 'We were on a break.'

They'd rebelled against the way that both their families had kept suggesting that the dynastic union was the best way to go. Adnan had lost the real love of his life when the girl he had wanted to marry had been killed in a vile hit-and-run accident, and Imogen had come to feel that she could never go through with a marriage without love and passion. That was why she had been holidaying in Corsica. She'd needed the freedom and relaxation to find herself. To find what she really wanted in life.

She'd believed that in Raoul she'd found what she wanted, only to discover that he didn't want her. And he wouldn't have wanted the tiny baby she had barely realised she had conceived before she'd lost it. When she'd come back to Ireland after the nightmare of her visit to Ciara in London, she'd understood so much more about the way Adnan had felt. At the same time, it seemed that he had sensed the deep wound in her, so that his consideration, his gentleness, had made it so much easier to accept the marriage of convenience that was all he had to offer. He had never asked for details about her private sense of loss, and for that she had been grateful, knowing that to tell anyone would rip open the barely healed scar and leave it raw and bleeding.

Somehow, by opening her eyes wide and staring straight ahead, Imogen managed to force back the burn of salt behind her lids. She needed to rebuild her defences, put something up between herself and Raoul. He was getting far too close.

'And, besides, we—you—were nothing but a holiday fling.'

He hadn't liked that. She saw the blink of his heavy lids, the way his head came up.

'A holiday fling—was that all?'

'Of course it was!' Did her claim sound too emphatic, too shrill? It seemed so in her ears. 'You don't think I wanted you to marry me, did you?'

His expression said everything she had thought she'd imagined back then, and she had been dreading that he might remember to throw it in her face.

'You did, didn't you!' she bluffed, grateful for the lingering effects of the wine that took the edge off the dark bruises of her memories. 'Oh, really, Raoul—sorry to disappoint you. You were fun, but you were just not that irresistible.'

He shrugged away her comment with a nonchalance that said the idea had never really troubled him, even if it had crossed his mind. Seeing that gesture, Imogen was taken right back to the beach at Rondinarra on the penultimate day of her holiday, and the way he had already been running the relationship from one step removed, distancing himself from her even before her time on Corsica was up.

'And now?' he questioned, not really sounding at all interested.

That made her determined to give it to him with both barrels. Two years ago, his indifference had almost broken her. She was not going to let him hurt her that way ever again.

'Now you've blundered in with both feet and ruined everything. There's a wedding service and reception prepared for tomorrow—today. I'm supposed to be getting married and obviously now I'm not—and that's all thanks to you. So what the hell am I supposed to do now?'

'You could always marry me.'

'Oh, now you're being ridiculous!'

She stopped, stared, unable to believe the seriousness in his face. The black humour had been bad enough. This pretence that he meant it was too much.

'You don't—' She stopped, confusion running across her features. 'Why would you want to marry me?'

A lift of those powerful shoulders dismissed her question. He obviously believed she should know exactly what was behind the crazy suggestion.

'For the same reason as Adnan would, I believe.'

'To get the stud? Believe me, it's not worth it.'

She'd blurted it out before she could think, and she realised it was a dangerous mistake as she watched his expression close up, golden eyes narrowing until they were just slits above his carved cheekbones.

'Is that why Adnan was marrying you?'

It was like the pounce of a hunting tiger, launching himself at his prey. Her stomach knotted to think of what she'd revealed. He'd accused her of being a gold-digger once and now she had obviously just confirmed his dark thoughts.

'I— Obviously, not! There was much more than that.'

Which was the truth, but only part of it.

At her side, Imogen's fingers clamped against her thigh as she fought for the control she needed. The warmth of her own skin against her hand was a stinging reminder of the way she was dressed—or, rather, undressed. Just the thought had her reaching again for the edges of her robe, jerking them together unnecessarily.

'There's no need to worry.' Raoul's lazy drawl froze her jittery fingers as they closed over the belt, wanting to tighten it as much as she could. 'Believe me, every inch of your body is hidden from prying eyes. Except perhaps your legs.'

That bronze gaze drifted down to where the red silk ended and her slender legs and feet were revealed. A carefully calculated moment of assessment and then his eyes came back up again fast, to clash with her own so fiercely she felt stars explode inside her thoughts.

'But then, I have a very good imagination—and an exceptionally long memory.'

Imogen felt as if the room had tilted wildly, and she longed to lift her hands, to bury her burning face behind her palms, but she refused to give him the satisfaction of seeing how accurately his pointed remark had hit home.

She had never felt this nervous, this vulnerable, with Raoul in the past, even when she had been totally naked with him. Then, she had found a new and glorious sense of self-esteem to know that this stunning, powerful man who could have had his pick of any of the female holiday makers staying in the hotel had wanted her. She had been his from the start, lost in the wild fires of her first adult sexual passion. She still felt that way, just to be in the same room as him. As he'd said, she was adequately clothed, far more modestly covered than on any of the days when she had worn a bikini at the swimming pool; and yet she felt totally naked, brutally exposed, and sizzling in response to the dark power of the man on the other side of the room.

Adnan had never made her feel like this, even for a moment, she realised with a terrible sense of shock. It didn't matter that he was a gorgeous man with the honed body of a professional sportsman from his days in competitive riding. She had always only felt the warmth and closeness of their friendship. Other women had felt very differently. She'd seen it in the green-eyed jealousy that she'd caught directed at her when their engagement had been announced. She'd also seen how her own sister's eyes had widened when she'd first introduced her to her fiancé.

But the shocking, heart-twisting truth was that, when Raoul was in a room, he was the only man she was aware of.

It had been one hell of a mistake letting himself remember what she looked like under that robe, Raoul told himself, knowing that now he had remembered there was no chance of him forgetting again. Hell, as if he had needed to *remember*. The image of her tall, sexy body had been imprinted on his brain ever since those long, hot days—and even hotter nights—of the Corsican summer they had shared. He had only to close his eyes to see her again, even when they had been miles apart.

Now that they were in the same room, with the scent of her skin coiling around him, the sound of her softly accented voice in his ears, the recollection of the way it had felt to hold her close and the thunderous pounding of his heart were scrambling his thoughts. He needed to think but his body was one raw pulse of hunger, the primitive need that he hadn't felt in so long.

Not since she had walked away from him without once ever looking back. Taking the child he hadn't known she carried with her.

How could he still want such a woman? And want her with a hunger that was threatening to destroy his mind? Because his mind was not involved or, *grâce à dieu*, anything that could be described as his *heart*. He had come here telling himself that he wanted revenge for what Imogen had done to his child but standing here like this, feeling the thunder of blood at his temples, knowing that his body ached with a hunger he could barely control, he was forced to admit that there had been more to it than that.

It was about a much more primal need than he had ever been able to acknowledge until now. He still wanted Imogen O'Sullivan and he wasn't going to leave until he had her in his bed again.

He could even cope with the way his mind seemed to split in two. Hating her for what she was, what she had done, and yet knowing he had never been able to forget her. He could never go back to Corsica until he had sated himself on that glorious body that still held him in thrall, no matter how much he might wish he could resist.

CHAPTER SIX

'I HAVE TO GO…'

Imogen was looking towards the door, slender bare feet moving restlessly on the floor. He couldn't let her go, not yet. For one thing, he knew that if she turned and walked away from him he might not be able to resist the primitive urge to go after her, grab her arm and haul her back against him. If his control shattered so badly then heaven knew what would happen as a result. Or did he mean hell?

'And that's it? You just go back to your room and—what?—go to bed?'

Her shrug seemed controlled, almost resigned. He wanted more from her, wanted to see her hurt as he'd been when Pierre had told him about the child. Apparently he'd learned of it from Ciara and Pierre had enjoyed telling his brother-in-law the black truth. Even knowing that his philandering brother-in-law had flung the vile story at him in an attempt to distract him from the fact that he had still been chasing after the younger O'Sullivan sister despite her leaving his employ, Raoul had felt as if his heart had been ripped from his chest and he'd wanted her—the woman who had caused that pain—to feel the same. But now that he was face to face with her in the moment of success, the triumph he had wanted to experience wasn't there.

He was on the verge of getting everything he'd wanted out of this and yet…he'd got nothing. This wouldn't bring back the child he'd lost. The triumph he'd thought he'd feel tasted like dust in his mouth.

'What else is there to do?'

'I thought you said we needed to talk.'

'We've talked!'

At last she was showing a spark of feeling, but not in the way he'd wanted. It did nothing to ease the cold, hard lump inside where his heart should be.

'Not enough.'

An autocratic wave of his hand dismissed her protest.

'What else is there?' Imogen demanded.

'Well, for one thing, you don't seem exactly broken-hearted about Adnan's defection.'

Did he really want to think she might have *loved* the other man? Or that he had loved her? Hell, no. He wouldn't put another man through what he'd endured when she'd left him. He was damned sure that Imogen was *not* in love with Adnan.

'Of course I never wanted to hurt him. I wouldn't have done that willingly but for you. What you did to-night, *you're* the one who hurt him.'

'Hurt his pride, more likely. I saw his face when he came into the room—and I watched him last night with you. I've never seen anyone less in love.'

'You think so?' Defiance rang in her tone, and he saw the way her neat chin lifted high.

'I know so.' It was arrogant and hard. Totally assured.

She had to acknowledge that Raoul was right, Imogen admitted unwillingly. Though she was shocked at how easily he had seen through the act that she and

Adnan had put on so that everyone would believe their marriage was real. Even Ciara had been convinced. She had to have been, because Imogen knew that her sister would have tried to dissuade her from going through with the marriage if she'd thought it was fake. And she'd promised Adnan that this arrangement would look like a marriage that meant something, so she had had to keep to that promise, even if it meant pretending to her new-found sister.

It was bad enough knowing that Raoul had seen through Adnan's behaviour, but the thought that he might also have seen the truth of her own emotions made her feel as if the robe she had tightened round her so desperately only moments before was now as constricting as a corset, making it almost impossible to breathe.

'You won't exactly come out of this smelling of roses!' she flung at him, needing to attack him to hide the tsunami of feeling that was raging inside her. 'That stupid deal you came here for will all be for nothing. You don't think Adnan will want to go through with it after this!'

'Do you really think that was what I came here for?'

The challenge made her head go back, her face tensing.

'Well, it sure as hell wasn't for me.'

Again, there was that flicker of an expression across his face, changing the set of his muscles, the burn of his eyes. It made her shift uncomfortably from one foot to the other on the shabbily carpeted floor, her eyes going unwillingly to the bottle of wine and the two glasses. Surely another drink would ease this dragging, draining tension between them? But she didn't want to go that way, the way her father went when anything went wrong, the path that had contributed so much to the perilous state they were in. Would her mother have left if Joe hadn't already been too keen to turn to alcohol when times got rough? Could she and Ciara actually have shared a childhood, grown up together, if alcohol hadn't been Joe's answer to everything?

'Two…' she said unexpectedly, and saw that dark frown appear again in puzzlement at her words.

'Two?'

'Two glasses. You have that bottle of wine and two glasses.'

A sharp, silent nod was his only answer, acknowledging her awareness, but waiting for her to take the puzzle further.

So how much of this had he planned? Had he been expecting someone else here tonight? She knew he was a devastatingly good-looking man, but would he have been able to pick up another woman, met in the village only this afternoon? He'd done that with her in Corsica, so she guessed he was capable of doing exactly the same here.

'Who were you expecting?'

The devilish smile that curled up the corners of that wide, sensual mouth was warning enough. But it was a warning she knew it was too late to heed.

'I was waiting for you,' Raoul drawled, letting that smile grow, widen fiendishly.

'You…'

Just the thought knocked the air from her lungs, leaving it hard to breathe.

'You thought I would come to you!'

'Not thought.' It was a flat, dark statement. 'I knew.'

'No way.'

That she might be so easy to read was something from her nightmares. If he had guessed—known—that she would come to find him, then what else might he know simply from looking into her face; reading the truth there?

Oh, dear heaven, how much of the truth could he see?

'You couldn't know!'

'Well, you're here, aren't you?' Raoul tossed at her, soft and dangerously low. 'You're here, drinking my wine.'

Imogen felt as if a noose had been thrown around her throat, inexorably tightening with every word that Raoul let fall. He had known. He had prepared for just this, ready for her to fall into his trap.

But how could he have known? How had she given herself away? A dark thread of fear ran through her veins, making her shiver. When she thought of the devastation the evening had brought, her legs weakened, threatening to give way beneath her. How much of this had he planned?

How much of this had been just bad luck and how much had Raoul acted as the master manipulator, pulling the strings of the puppets he had under his control, making them dance to his tune when they didn't even know the name of the song?

'How could you know?'

'I know you.'

'Oh, come on, how can you claim that?' she scoffed, wincing inwardly at the high pitch that turned her defiance into a squeak of fear. He was watching so intently that she couldn't hide a thing from him. 'You knew me once, for what—two weeks, if that? We were just ships that passed in the night, a holiday fling—a lot of fun but…but…'

'But what, Imogen?' Raoul challenged with that singular, individual pronunciation of her name that only he used. The one that brought back the memories, the long, warm days of Corsica, the hot passion of the nights in his bed.

'But nothing more…'

She broke off in shock and disbelief as he shook his head so fiercely that the tiny diamond-like water droplets still lingering on his hair from his rapid face-wash scattered over her, sprinkling her face with moisture.

'How can you say nothing more? How dare you say there was nothing else between us?'

'Oh, yes, there was sex!'

High and tight, she flung the word in his shuttered face, knowing a sense of despair as she saw that there was no flicker of reaction, not even a blink of those basilisk eyes.

'And that was all.'

'All?' To her horror, it was almost laughter, the word shaking on the edge of dark amusement. 'You call that all?'

She wished she could convince herself that there had been nothing more but, watching the way his mouth moved on the words, scorched by his smile, she knew that even to describe them as old flames wouldn't come anywhere near it.

Old flames still burned and she could feel the heat searing the room, recognised the smouldering embers in Raoul's deep-set eyes.

'All…' she tried but the word was just a croak in her throat.

Raoul smiled that dark smile. Lifting one hand, he crooked a long finger, beckoning her towards him.

'Come here,' he said, unexpectedly softly.

'No.'

She wanted to shake her head in rough denial of the

command but her neck seemed to have stiffened so that all she could manage was a slight tilt backwards, her chin coming up in defiance. That smile grew worryingly.

'Scared?' It was even softer, tightening the knot in her stomach.

'Scared? Never!'

Oh, but she was. And not of him. It was herself she was scared of. The fizz of electricity along her nerves, the burn of fire in her veins, made her feel as if her body was not her own. Once again the puppet master was pulling her strings and she had no choice but to dance to his tune.

He was going to kiss her, no matter what. She saw it in the darkness of his eyes, the way the black pupils had almost obliterated any trace of colour. She could see the curve at the corner of those sensual lips, the way they were slightly parted over his white teeth. She could almost taste him on her own mouth already, the memory of years ago so vivid that she expected to feel the warmth of the sun on her back, the shift of soft sand between her toes.

He was going to kiss her and she could read the thought in his face. He believed that all he had to do was move forward, take her face in his hands, lift her mouth towards his…and she would either melt into his embrace—or twist away from him and run for the door. Either one of those reactions would show him just too much of what she was feeling, however hard she tried to hide it.

That was what he expected. But there was one way she could take the initiative, knock him off-balance. He wasn't getting all his own way on this; and, right now, that one way fitted so much with what she wanted anyway.

'Not *scared*!' she declared and, high on the excitement of wrong-footing him, dodging the hand that was reaching for her, she almost danced towards him, taking him by surprise as she came close enough to drop a fleeting butterfly kiss on that warm, sensual mouth.

There, and away again…or at least that was how it was supposed to be. That was the way she'd seen it in her mind before she'd embarked on this. The kiss she'd wanted since the first moment she'd seen him again in the church, and she was allowing herself to take just this one kiss—and then she would be gone… Everything going her way, at last, nothing his.

But in the moment her lips touched his—when the taste she had recalled became real, the warmth of his skin brushing against hers, his breath mingling with her own uncontrolled gasp—she knew that she'd overplayed her hand. That she'd lost. All thought of holding back vanished in a heartbeat. One kiss was not enough, would never be enough. She couldn't just sip from that glass. Once she had tasted, she needed to drink deeply.

'Raoul…'

The sigh escaped her in the same moment that his mouth formed her own name. Then he had moved, taken her arms, held her just where he wanted her. His dark head bent, his mouth closing over hers.

It was the gentleness that shocked her. There was no lust or demand in his kiss, nor was he holding back. Oh, dear Lord, but he was *not* holding back. His mouth took hers with a caress that seemed to draw out her soul and place it right in his hands. She had lost all sense of herself except where she ended and he began. It was as if they were just one person, two combined into one, perfectly aligned, perfectly absorbed.

Her bones seemed to melt as she leaned into him,

feeling the warmth and the scent of his flesh enclose her, her breasts pressed close against his skin, which was exposed where his shirt hung open. It was like coming home, and yet it was the slow burn of a dormant ember, one that was being fanned back into life with every breath she took, every caress, every new pressure of his mouth. The slow, seductive slide of his tongue along the seam of her lips enticed her to open to him, taking in that taste, the warmth that was more intoxicating than any potent spirit sending her blood racing.

Had she kissed other men in the time they had been apart? She had to have done—there had been other guys who had tried to win her round from the pit of loneliness and darkness she'd fallen into when she had finally come home from London. There had even been Adnan...

But right now, Adnan was just a name to her. She couldn't even conjure up the image of his face, his presence. Least of all, his kisses. It was as if he had been a dream and this—this was reality. The only reality she knew. The only reality she wanted.

'Imogen...'

It was a murmur against her mouth as he adjusted his position slightly, just enough to ensure that every inch of her was pressed against him. There was still no pressure; he was so careful, so measured. That restraint was already fretting at her own control, fraying it at the edges, making her struggle with impatience, with the need for more.

His hands had curved over her shoulders, the heat of his palms burning through the fine scarlet silk and seeming to brand her skin, to mark her out as his. As they slid slowly down her back, smoothing along her spine, she couldn't hold back the murmur of response that slipped from her as she lost all sense of control. With a little shimmy of her hips she moved closer still, feeling the hard heat of him pressed against her pelvis, noting the way his breath caught in his throat as he reacted to her enticement.

'Want…'

It was all she could manage, all she could think. She was so far gone that she didn't recognise the danger she had put herself into until she heard the faint sound of his soft laughter, felt him nod his head in dark agreement.

'I know, *ma belle. Je sais…* And this will make it so much better—easier.'

Easier? The word exploded in Imogen's thoughts. How could this be easier? Suddenly, the rush of realisation became a sense of shock and horror, despair flooding through her as she realised what she was doing, the depth of the trap into which she had fallen all over again.

She thought she'd come to terms with the gentle friendship she had for Adnan. Had told herself she could live with that and be happy. It was safer, kinder, than what she had known before with Raoul. But now there was no Adnan, there was only Raoul, and he had opened the door she had thought so firmly locked against her memories. Those memories were dragging her in and down into the same danger that she had known before.

This was how he had made her feel all those years ago, in Corsica. This was how he had swept her up into a heated world of fantasy and sensuality that had stopped her from thinking, destroyed her ability to reason. She had fallen head over heels, believing that what she felt was love—a love that he shared. Now she knew so much better. She knew all he had felt for her was the burn of lust, the stab of the most basic, primitive hunger a man feels for a woman.

It had flamed hard and hot and hungry—but only for a short time before it had burned itself out. She had still been riding high on the waves of her first encounter, with the passionate feelings that a grown woman could know, when he had tired of the whole thing and had let her drop from a very great height. She had landed so hard and so violently she had never fully recovered.

Now he had stirred up all those unwanted and unwelcome feelings all over again, making a mockery of her belief—her hope—that she was over them for good.

'Easier!'

How could this ever make anything easier between them? It just twisted things, making them infinitely more complicated than they had been in the moments before their lips had met.

That kiss had opened up her long-locked, hidden Pandora's box of sensuality and feelings and there was no way she was ever going to be able to close it again. But if Raoul thought that that made her *easy*…

She wrenched her mouth from his. She pulled away so she could stare into his face, seeing the burn of sensuality under the heavy lids, the moisture that glistened on his mouth from her foolish, unthinking kisses.

'If that's what you think then you had better start thinking again! There's no way that anything between you and me could be any sort of easy. I wish I'd never seen you in the first place—and I *so* wish that you'd never turned up here again. If I never see you again in my life, it will be way too soon.'

The laughter that shook his powerful form had little real amusement in it. Instead it was filled with a hateful triumph that scalded her mind just to hear it.

'Forgive me if I don't believe you, *ma belle*,' he

drawled softly. 'You can claim the words—but that's not what your kisses say.'

'My kisses?'

Imogen laid her hands flat against his shoulders, pushed with all the strength she could gather up and was happy to find that she must have caught him off-balance, or so sure of himself that he hadn't braced against any possible response she might make. With one sharp push she had him taking an unwary step backwards, and then another, freeing her to twist away from his grip and move partway across the room.

'You believe in my kisses Raoul?' she tossed at him, enjoying seeing the momentary blink of confusion that flittered across his face before he caught it back and froze into immobility.

'Well, more fool you. Because kisses can deceive every bit as much as words, in fact. And I should know.'

She was almost at the door now, fingers on the handle. She couldn't get out of there fast enough, but she had one last riposte to fling at him, tossing the words into his now dark, shuttered face.

'You see, I learned how to lie with a kiss from the very best. I learned it from you.'

And that was as good an exit line as she was going to get, she told herself as she pulled the door open and dodged through it as fast as she could. She didn't dare look into the black, opaque sheen of his eyes. The way every muscle in his face tightened in anger was more than enough warning that she'd stretched what little patience he had left to its absolute limit.

'You're a great teacher, Raoul,' she tossed over her shoulder as the door began to close behind her. 'You must be if I convinced you!'

CHAPTER SEVEN

THE CHURCH LOOKED every bit as beautiful as she had hoped. But the lovely arrangements of flowers, the huge, beeswax candles, were all destined to go to waste. The wooden pews would remain empty, the candles unlit, the aisle silent throughout a day that should have been filled with the bustle and murmur of invited guests, family and friends.

No one was coming to the wedding. Not even the groom, it seemed, though she'd hoped and prayed for a reprieve. Adnan was determined to stay away and have nothing to do with what was supposed to have been their wedding day, and who could blame him? As a result, she was here alone, at this time when she should have been preparing for the big event, getting ready to put on the beautiful, elegant wedding dress that had been hanging in her wardrobe for the past few days.

She would never wear that dress now. Not even for the sort of marriage of convenience that she and Adnan had agreed on, eyes wide open, knowing that what they planned would suit them both—and help everyone else involved.

Now she couldn't even get in touch with her ex-fiancé. She didn't know where he was or what he was doing. She had tried to ring him again and again through the night and had only ever got voicemail.

'Leave a message and I'll get back to you.'

He hadn't, of course. Her own phone had remained stubbornly silent, except the one time when it had rung and it had been a call from Ciara.

Imogen shook her head as she recalled the stilted, difficult conversation with her sister. It had been like going back a couple of years to the time of their very first conversation, when her sister hadn't been too sure she wanted to meet up, to reconnect with the family she knew so little about. Imogen had thought—hoped—that they'd got past that and were on their way to creating a real family relationship. But last night had changed everything. Ciara wouldn't be here to support her through the misery of cancelling everything involved with the day. Wherever Adnan was, her sister was there with him, but the younger girl had refused to tell her where they could be found.

'He doesn't want to talk to you,' she'd said, her voice sounding strange and alien, the unusual echoes around it making it almost eerie, and totally unlike her sister's usual warm tones.

'But I have to explain to him. I'll come to the manor.'

A long pause. She could hear Ciara's breath at the other end of the line, and the silence had worried her.

'We—he's not at the manor and he won't be for some time. He's not coming back, Immi—and really, after what happened, you shouldn't expect him to.'

And then the phone had been switched off, confusing her even more. She'd assumed that Ciara had gone after Adnan last night to try to make him see reason and obviously that had failed. But…

Just what did that 'we' mean? Why was Ciara still with Adnan? And where were they?

The truth was that that last comment had had a clear note of reproof in it. A note that made Imogen realise that, even though they'd made great strides in getting to know each other after the distance their parents' split had put between them, there were still areas of her sister's life where she didn't really know Ciara at all.

'I knew I'd find you here.'

It could only be one person's voice. Only one man had those deep, slightly husky tones, that sexy, lilting accent. Immediately her spine stiffened, tension taking over every muscle.

'I came here because I wanted to be alone,' she managed from between lips that felt like wood.

'And I knew you'd say that,' he added, the tiny hint of amusement setting her teeth on edge.

'Then will you please do me a favour and leave me alone?'

'No.'

It was almost pleasant, but it was still the most determined, adamant refusal she had ever heard.

'Raoul!'

She turned to scowl at him, adopting the most determined look she could manage. But somehow it didn't work, that glare bouncing off his expressionless face with no effect. It was impossible not to think that she had hoped to face him today looking her very best, with her hair and make-up done, wearing that beautiful silk dress and her grandmother's Brussels lace veil. Instead, her worn jeans and a plain blue tee-shirt had been the only things she could think to pull on this morning, knowing most of the day was going to have to be spent cancelling things, apologising…

'*Ma belle.*'

'Don't!' Her hands came up in front of her face. 'I'm not your—your anything. Certainly not your...'

'Ah, but there you are wrong. You are beautiful—I've always thought that.'

Beautiful on the outside at least. Raoul had to fight with himself to keep his face from showing how the memories of the day he'd found out about her visit to the London clinic still burned in his mind. He'd been on a wild seesaw ride ever since he'd been told about it, even more since he had seen her again for the first time in years.

Here, in this little village church, where she had been supposed to marry Adnan today. That was why, when he hadn't been able to find her back at the house, and everyone had told him that she was nowhere to be found, he had known exactly where to come. Exactly where he'd find her.

'Spare me the flattery!' Imogen protested now and he couldn't help but smile at her vehemence.

But what was hiding behind that determination? It could be the effect of the shadows in the church, the pitiful light of the hazy sun shining through the stained glass windows, but she looked pale and drawn, as if she hadn't slept at all well. That was inevitable, he would have thought, after the way they had parted last night, the way her life had exploded in her face in the midnight confrontation in his room.

It was what he had aimed for; the reason he had come here in the first place—so why did it leave him with a raw sense of dissatisfaction rather than the ultimate triumph he had looked for?

'No flattery—honestly,' he reassured her. 'I never speak anything less than the truth.'

'The truth, huh?' Her chin had come up, her luscious mouth tightening in defiance. 'Then tell me the truth about why you've followed me here today. What part of "if I never see you again in my life, it will be way too soon" did you not understand? Why are you still in Ireland and not on your way back to Corsica?'

It was a question he'd been asking himself ever since he'd woken—after probably as bad a night's sleep as she'd had.

He'd intended to go. He'd planned on packing his bag as soon as he'd woken and clear out of the house, out of her life. But it was as he'd headed for the bathroom that the second and third thoughts had started to hit him.

The first was the result of seeing the belt lying on the floor on the far side of the room, close to the door. A long, thin strip of scarlet silk, it was the belt from the robe that she had tugged so tightly round her. It had obviously slipped free as she had stalked out of the door, tossing what she had clearly intended to be the last words she'd ever speak to him over her shoulder as she went.

When he had picked it up it had slithered in his hands, like a satiny snake, reminding him of how it had felt to have that silk underneath his fingertips, and the warmth of her skin beneath that. He'd resorted to the long, icy shower he'd needed earlier in the evening, but had found that it brought him no release from the intense pulse of unappeased desire that had tormented him. It had lingered all through the night, making him toss and turn until he'd woken in a tangle of sheets, his mind hazed with hunger, his body sheened in sweat. His last thought before falling into what had passed for sleep had been of Imogen, as had his first thought on waking.

'I never was very good at taking orders. And I came to see how you were doing.'

It was the truth. Well, at least it was part of it.

He knew he couldn't leave without seeing her again, without making a move to turn the hot dreams that had plagued his night into a reality. At least for as long as it took to get this burn of hunger out of his system. It was time to acknowledge that he hadn't been able to forget Imogen in the time since he had walked away from her on the beach at Rondinarra. That had been part of why he'd come to Ireland the first time, filled with dark fury after seeing that revealing photo of her and her sister in the gossip columns. Then he'd learned that her father was looking for a partner in his stud, and that had stayed him when he'd been about to rush into turning on Imogen the bitter rage he had felt at her actions. It had become a much larger part of why he'd stayed, to watch and learn, and later he'd made the approach that should have brought him here as a potential business partner.

Whoever had said that revenge was a dish best served cold had no idea how it could feel when that cold revenge was mixed with the revival of a blazing, white-hot sexual need that it seemed only Imogen could create in him.

'Well, now you can see I'm still standing.'

Imogen made her way out of the church, refusing to allow herself even one regretful glance back.

'So you can go and pack your bags—'

She broke off in shock as he shook his head firmly, the raven-black strands of his hair falling forward over his forehead. How was it possible that, wearing almost exactly the same outfit as she was dressed in—except that he had on a crisp, short-sleeved linen shirt instead of the tee-shirt she wore—he managed to look cool and even elegant when she felt like something the cat had dragged in, her hair already beginning to frizz in the muggy heat of the day.

'I'm not leaving until I know you're all right.'

Whether he knew it or not, that was a stab at the weakest point in her mental armour. Never had she felt so alone as she had this morning, the time when she should have been facing, if not the happiest day of her life, then at least the moment when so many of her worries would start to be resolved. She should have been the centre of attention, surrounded by family and friends. Instead, she found herself isolated, with no one to support her. Her father had locked himself in his room—with a large bottle of some spirit, she assumed—and Ciara was heaven knew where, with Adnan.

So, it was a bitter irony that Raoul, of all people, was the only person here offering her a shoulder to lean on.

'I take it you haven't heard from Adnan?'

'What do you expect?'

She turned to make herself walk down the path that led to Blacklands and was shocked to find that Raoul followed her, silently and closely.

'I can make my own way home!' she flashed at him, but was disconcerted to be met with the sort of disarming smile that sizzled all the way from her head to her toes inside the well-worn sandals she'd slipped on with as little care as she'd chosen the rest of her outfit that morning.

'I know you can. But, as I have to go that way myself, we might as well walk together.'

Then, just as she was cursing him for taking away her defensive argument, he knocked the ground right from under her feet by adding, 'Have you managed to get in touch with all your guests? I know you've been on the phone almost all morning.'

'Not everyone,' Imogen admitted, shuddering faintly inside at the thought of him observing her as she went through the painful process of phoning everyone on the guest list. 'Some had already started out and couldn't be contacted. I'll have to explain when they arrive.'

'Then wouldn't it be easier to have someone with you when that happens?'

Easier to have someone, yes—but not the man who had caused all this!

She had to pull herself up with the realisation that she couldn't dump all the blame on Raoul. If she had not gone to Raoul's room to try to talk to him then this wouldn't be happening... But had he really come to Blacklands solely to discuss the stud deal with her father—a deal that her father couldn't possibly have gone along with? Or had he had other plans, as she'd feared? Was this whole situation just bad luck—or was she being manipulated all the way along by Raoul?

She was going to ignore him, she resolved. She would pretend he wasn't there and maybe he would pack his bags and disappear. It took only seconds to realise that, without seeming to make any extra effort, he was keeping up with her perfectly easily, his long stride covering the ground at twice the pace of her own.

'What are you going to tell them?' he enquired now.

'That the wedding's been called off. Is there anything else I could say?'

'And are you going to stick to that unexpected new habit of yours of telling the truth?'

'What's new about it?'

She caught his indifferent shrug as he came close again. In spite of the muggy heat of the day, she felt a sudden shiver, as if the sun had just gone behind a cloud as blue eyes clashed with bronze.

'You obviously hadn't told Adnan—or your father—about us before I turned up.'

'There was no "us", not when I got home, so it was totally irrelevant.'

'Not if you were getting married.'

'So have you told anyone about me?'

'No—no one except Rosalie, but then she knew at the time.'

It had been Rosalie who had revealed to her just how much Raoul had been keeping back from her.

Use your eyes, she'd said. *Look around you. Look in the shops—in the kitchens in almost every hotel on the island!*

And Imogen had looked, seeing the distinctive labels for Cardini Olive Oil that she had been blind to before. She'd believed his story that he was a farmer, that he had olive trees on his land. That had been all. She had never dreamed that that was only a part of his fortune—that the rest came from the breeding of the small, sturdy Corsican horses that had brought him to Ireland to destroy the sense of peace she had thought she was reaching.

'And I was not getting married.'

'Still loving and leaving 'em?' Imogen tossed at him, not wanting to acknowledge the flutter of something deep in her stomach at the thought that there had been no one special in his life in the years they had been apart. But then, she'd already known that Raoul was not the marrying kind.

'Not loving,' he returned, flat-voiced. 'I'd be a fool to look for any such thing. And I was never the marrying kind. I told you that.'

He certainly had. Was she actually weak enough to let her memories make tears burn at her eyes? She blinked hard to keep them back, telling herself they were there for the baby who had had no hope of survival, not for its cold-hearted father who had never even known his child had existed.

Would he have cared? If she had done as she had planned, and managed to go back to Corsica to tell Raoul that she was pregnant before the agonising pain that had seemed to tear her in two had struck, would he have cared? Would he have insisted they marry for the sake of the child? The thought of that was somehow more unbearable than the way he had rejected her, turning his back on her at the end of their time in Corsica.

There was a heavy stone in front of her on the path and, eyes blurred, caught unawares, she almost stumbled on it. But she didn't fall because Raoul's hand shot out, hard fingers clamping around her upper arm and hauling her back so she thumped against his chest, losing her breath in a totally different and much more disturbing way.

Weakly, foolishly, she welcomed the feeling of his strength against her. At a time when she felt so alone, so afraid of the future, she wouldn't dare to admit to herself how she longed to throw herself into that strength, feel it close around her.

He'd done that once before, in the sea off Bonifacio, when the tide had been unexpectedly rough. An uncertain swimmer at the best of times, she had been caught in a strong current and knocked off her feet. Going under the waves, with salt water stinging her eyes and water swamping her face, she had known a moment's panic. But only for a moment. Because then, strong, bronzed arms had closed around her, taking firm hold and hauling her up and out of the water. As she had soared out into the heat and brightness of the sun in the clear blue sky, she had known such a glorious sense of freedom and delight. It had been as if she was reborn, rediscovering the joy of living—and loving. It was in that moment that she had known she had fallen deeply, irrevocably in love with Raoul and that her heart would never truly be free ever again.

Not even when he had rejected her before the end of her holiday, tossing aside her weak, stumbling suggestions that maybe they could make this more than just a fling, that perhaps they could see each other again. That maybe she didn't have to go home...

Could he hear the thudding of her heart, see her uneven breathing? She could only pray that he would take it as being the result of coming close to falling. Though, from the dark gleam in those tiger eyes, she doubted it. He had looked that way when he had held her against him last night and he had made it plain that desire was all he felt. So she'd better get rid of the crazy idea that this time he might come to her rescue again.

'OK?' His voice was surprisingly low and husky on the question but she didn't dare to meet his eyes to try to read why that was so. Instead, she fixed her gaze on the spot where his white shirt was open at the neck, the pulse that beat at the base of his throat heavy and strong, and disturbingly in time with the hungry thunder of her own.

'I'm fine.'

She prayed it sounded convincing. She would have to be fine. No one was coming to her rescue like a knight on a white charger. Not Adnan and very definitely not Raoul.

'You can let me go now...'

It was even weaker to feel disappointment as he released her without hesitation, dropping her back down onto the path as if he was glad to be free of her.

But nothing could stop him following her all the way back to the stud. Because of course he had to go back there, didn't he? If he needed to pack his clothes, collect his belongings and get out of here?

The thought of him leaving was just the worst possible straw of misery to add to the list of wretchedness that had to be endured to get through the rest of the day.

CHAPTER EIGHT

IMOGEN SAGGED BACK wearily against the door frame, watching as the last car disappeared down the drive, heading for the main road and home. She let the hand she had raised to wave drop down against her side and closed her eyes for a moment against the sense of exhaustion that had almost overwhelmed her.

She couldn't give in yet; she still had more to do. Every guest had been spoken to personally, given an explanation—as close to the truth as possible—about the reasons why the wedding had been called off. Apologies—so many apologies—had been offered again and again, and now all the visitors to Blacklands had gone, the house empty except for the small army of catering staff who were packing away the food meant for the reception. The task was performed in a strange silence compared to the excited buzz of conversation that had first greeted her announcement.

After that there was only the floral arrangements, the decorations and—a bitter laugh nearly choked her—the dress to be taken from her wardrobe.

'If you let me know what you want doing with all this food, then I'll get on with it.'

The voice came from behind her, bringing her spinning round so fast she had to grab hold of the huge brass handle on the heavy oak door and keep herself upright with an effort.

'What does one do with enough food for three hundred people?' she sighed, despairing at the thought, and Raoul—because of course it was Raoul—shrugged his broad shoulders under the white shirt that was no longer quite so immaculate as it had been this morning.

He had been there with her all day. Every time she turned around, it had been to see his tall, lean figure moving silently and efficiently through the tasks that were needed to help sort out the confusion the cancelled wedding had created. She had never actually had to tell him anything; he had just seen what needed doing and got on with it, leaving her free to deal with the demands for explanations, the apologies, finding the parcels containing the wedding presents that would have to be returned.

'I should have thought to get a message to the caterers to stop them bringing it in the first place,' she sighed. But food had been the last thing on her mind. She'd been far more concerned with trying to get in touch with as many guests as possible to stop them arriving for the wedding that wasn't to be. It was only when she'd got back from the church and seen everything had been unloaded that she'd realised what a mistake she'd made.

And, once delivered, they'd adamantly refused to take it back.

'Freezer?'

'Only if you happen to have industrial-size freezers that actually work,' Imogen managed wryly. 'The ones in the kitchen have been there for the past fifteen years and they weren't the most modern or the best even then. We never got round to renewing them because...'

Because even then there hadn't been enough money to buy new ones, and the family finances had been leaking desperately ever since.

'Because no one cooked that much after my mother walked out and there was just Papa and me.'

'She took Ciara with her?'

Imogen could only nod silently. No point in denying it. Her mother's departure and her choice of daughter to take with her had been common knowledge at the time. She'd lived with the pitying looks, the swiftly hushed conversations whenever she appeared, her whole life. She was the daughter her mother hadn't wanted, and the whole village knew it.

'That knocked the stuffing out of my father and he hasn't been the same since. He'd always liked a drink before, but now…'

She thought she'd kept her voice even enough to avoid any further questioning, but as soon as she saw Raoul's black brows snap together in a dark frown she knew he was far too perceptive for that.

'Why not you?'

Only by digging her teeth down hard into the softness of her lower lip could Imogen hold back the bitterness that almost escaped her. The morning she'd woken to find that both her mother and her sister had gone, and no one could tell her where, was etched into her memory with the burn of acid. She knew why, of course, or at least she could explain it now. But how could anyone explain to a seven-year-old that her mother had wanted her younger sister—but not her?

Unable to get a word out without risking her precarious self-control, she waved a hand in a rather wild gesture that indicated the view from the door, the expanse of green fields, the stable buildings away to the side.

'The stud was not your mother's sort of thing?'

It was written all over her face so she didn't really need to answer, Raoul acknowledged inwardly. But still she nodded silently, those blue eyes cloudy and unfocused. She looked exhausted, worn out by the long day of explanations and rearrangements. Her delicate face was paler than ever, drawn tight over the fine bones, a touch of blue showing underneath where her pulse beat at her temples and the base of her neck.

It made him want to reach out and pull her towards him, to press his lips to the spot where the throb of her blood revealed the depth of her feelings. But, at the same moment, it disturbed him, and the fact that he'd even noticed it bothered him most of all.

Wasn't this why he had come here in the first place? To make sure this wedding didn't go ahead? To stop her from proving herself to be the gold-digger he had always believed her to be by marrying a wealthy man without love? The man she had chosen so soon after their relationship had fallen apart because he hadn't been prepared to be taken for a ride by any other woman.

And, into that toxic mix, he had to add the little sister who had seduced his brother-in-law and almost ruined his sister Marina's marriage, as well as the father who had tried to pull a fast one in the business deal they were supposed to have by claiming he had the stud rights to the magnificent stallion Blackjack, when in fact they would belong to Adnan and his family.

But nothing had worked quite as he'd planned since he'd arrived. So much had changed and complicated the revenge he'd determined on.

He'd never expected to find that Imogen was still as beautiful—if not more so—than he remembered. He hadn't thought the fiery pull of the sexual hunger he had felt for her would still be there, scrambling his thoughts and turning them into a molten pool of need. He hadn't expected to like Adnan Al Makthabi, or to find the sister to be so charming. And he certainly hadn't expected to feel the painful twist of an uncomfortable conscience to see Imogen now, when his plan was more than halfway to completion, with the grey marks of tiredness and strain around those shadowed eyes, etched along that gorgeous mouth.

He had certainly never anticipated that he would want to *help* the woman who had only come after him for his money, and who had cold-bloodedly got rid of his child before he had ever even known the baby existed.

'My mother was terrified of horses,' Imogen was saying now, her mouth twisting slightly on the low words. 'She never understood my father's fascination with them—or mine. So she didn't feel the connection with me that she obviously had with Ciara. Or that we thought she had. She wanted a girly girl—one who would enjoy clothes and make-up and perfumes as much as she did. And I'm sure she wanted to take her younger daughter because then she could pretend that she wasn't the age she was—knock a few years off the total. And of course she always thought Ciara was the prettier of her daughters.'

'She actually said that?'

A slow nod of her head was her silent answer.

'Then your mother was a blind fool,' Raoul growled, unable to hold back the disbelief he felt. 'Ciara is a little glamour puss, there's no doubt of that—that burnished hair, those emerald eyes, will be many men's fantasy.'

His brother-in-law's, for one thing, and look where that had led.

'But you are the real beauty in the family. You have a natural elegance and grace. Your hair—'

'Oh, don't!' Imogen broke in sharply, rawly, her voice cracking on the words. 'Please don't!'

'Why not?'

Looking into her eyes, he was astonished to see the pleading expression in their depths. It shook him rigid. Never before had he offered a woman a compliment— a heartfelt compliment like this one—only for her to react as if he had just thrown acid in her face.

'But you must know that's true,' he said, astounded. 'Your mirror must tell you it's so each time you look into it. And you must recall the way I— the way it used to be. I was knocked off-balance from the moment I saw you in that bar. I still am.'

'Oh, please, no!'

She shook her head so violently that the dark, silky strands of her hair flew out around her face, the soft essence of some shampoo she had used reaching his nostrils and tantalising them with the subtle fragrance.

'I don't want to think about that—I don't ever want to remember how you claim you felt back then.'

'Not claim—' he began, but her hand came up between them in a slicing gesture, cutting off what he had been about to say.

'No! The past is the past and I want it to stay there. We don't want to revive any of those unwanted memories.'

'Speak for yourself.'

He'd revive everything right this minute if he could. Nothing of the way he had felt about her had been buried. He still hungered; his body still burned for hers. The only thing that would be different was that this time...

He couldn't hold back the cynical laugh that escaped him at the thought that last time he had hated the fact that she had only wanted him for his money. This time that fact would be an advantage, a lever to get exactly what he wanted.

'What's so funny?'

'The idea of you claiming that all of that was buried when you know it's a lie. Remember…' he reproved when her pretty mouth opened, obviously about to frame a tart protest.

He found he actually liked the thought of her protesting. He didn't want too easy a conquest; a spirited woman was much more satisfying. He had enjoyed Imogen's spirit when they had been together before.

'Remember, I had you in my arms last night. I held you against me.'

The fluttering of those long, lush eyelashes told him he'd hit home with that and she was, even now, remembering just how it had felt to be that close.

'I kissed you. I felt your response—the instinctive response you couldn't hide.'

'I…'

Was she going to try to refute it? How could she even think of lying about that? He'd held her, kissed her, tasted her, felt her response. And he had known then that he could not walk away again without experiencing the heat of her embrace; the warm, welcoming moisture at the core of her; the pressure of her body against his; her slender, soft legs entwined around him, hips opening to him, breasts crushed against his chest.

Under the force of his reproving stare, she bit the words back. He could see the rapid adjustment of her thoughts, the change that flitted behind her eyes.

'You said that would make things easier,' she muttered, with a defiance that didn't match her expression. 'What did you mean by that? Make what easier?'

Now was not the time to go into that. That would come when they had time really to talk. When everything about this abandoned wedding had been cleared away. When she was left to face the future without it.

Then he would tell her what he had planned—and how she fitted into it. He would reveal most of his thoughts, but not all of them. The last truth would come when he knew he had her where he wanted her.

'Not now.'

He was already turning away, back into the big dining hall where the caterers had just about completed their packing away, and the fine food and elegant dishes were all waiting to be disposed of like so many guilty secrets.

'We have to get things sorted out. What do you want doing with all this?'

As he expected, drawing attention to all that needed to be done immediately distracted her. He actually felt a twist of sympathy when he saw the way her face paled, her eyes dulling as she surveyed the task before her. She looked very slender, almost delicate, and disturbingly vulnerable. The way she straightened her spine, squaring her shoulders, brought a new sensation of admiration for the way she was handling this. Alone.

'Where the hell is the rest of your family?' That sister—her father?

Her soft mouth actually twisted into a sort of wry amusement.

'My father will still be sleeping off his hangover or…'

A quick glance at the watch and another wry smile.

'Starting on a new one. And Ciara? You tell me.

Ciara is wherever Adnan can be found, but Adnan seems to have disappeared off the face of the earth. He's not answering his phone; no one at the Hall has seen him. Not even his mother.'

'She spoke to you?' Raoul let his surprise show.

'Not for long,' Imogen admitted. 'Just to say that she had seen or heard nothing of Adnan—then she took great delight in shutting the door in my face.' Her shrug was one of resigned acceptance. 'And who could blame her? She'd been looking forward to being mother of the groom at the perfect society wedding. Watching her son make a brilliant dynastic union...'

She couldn't finish the sentence. Couldn't add the other parts of the bargain she and Adnan had come up with between them. Geraldine Al Makthabi had also been hoping to become a grandmother—and her future father-in-law to achieving his dream of becoming a great-grandfather. Under the cover of the piles of food containers stacked up on the tables, she slipped a hand over her lower belly, remembering how it had felt to think that a new life was forming there, nestling deep inside...

A new life fathered by the man who now stood beside her, amongst the ashes of her hopes. The man who had sent her dreams toppling down into ruins.

'What am I going to do with all this?' she said again, sharper now, the fight against the bitterness of her memories making her tone harsher than she had planned.

Obviously Raoul thought so too because he shot her a quick, assessing glance from under hooded lids, then those golden eyes slid away from her and a frown creased the space between his brows as he considered the food problem thoughtfully.

'Do you have an old people's care home nearby? Disabled living? A children's home?'

Impossibly, now, when she had coped with everything else that had gone before—had coped without a single tear—the introduction of a very practical solution almost demolished the walls she had built around herself. The room blurred, her eyes stung and roughly she rubbed her hands against them to dash away any tears before they even had the chance to fall.

'Great idea,' she managed gruffly. 'Perfect.'

'Leave it to me,' Raoul said and helplessly she found that she was capable of nothing more than nodding as she handed the responsibility over to him.

CHAPTER NINE

'COME AND SIT DOWN. You've been on your feet all day.'

Raoul's voice caught Imogen by surprise as she wandered into the shabby, old-fashioned sitting room where the glow of the setting sun gilded the windows and made the cream-painted walls look as if they were blazing red and gold.

'I thought you'd gone.'

She hesitated on the threshold of the room as she tried to decide whether to go in or to make some hastily concocted excuse to take her away from there, away from him.

'Not yet,' Raoul said now. 'Only just got everything sorted and finished. I helped myself to a drink. I hope you don't mind.'

He lifted a glass of white wine, so much paler than the rich, red liquid from the previous night. But still, the memory of that time in his room, the way it had trapped her with him, destroying all her plans and hopes for the future, kept her frozen, not knowing which way to move. To turn and walk away seemed impossibly rude after he had spent so much of the day helping her sort out the results of the disaster that was supposed to have been her wedding day, but to walk into the golden shadows of the room where he sprawled comfortably in a huge armchair seemed to bring an intimacy that she shied away from nervously.

'Of course not,' she managed unevenly. 'A drink's the least I owe you after the help you've given me today.'

Whenever she had needed help, whatever had wanted doing, he'd been there, silent, strong and disturbingly reliable. So now, if it wasn't for the fact that the downstairs part of the house still looked like a display for the Chelsea flower show, one might almost believe that today had never been planned as anything special.

It hadn't been anything truly special, she couldn't help reflecting, remembering the way she had been thinking in the church when Raoul had suddenly reappeared in her life. Was it really just two days before? It felt as though she had lived through several different lifetimes since then—one of them as Adnan's fiancée, another as the bride jilted almost at the altar. Or wouldn't everyone really think that she had jilted Adnan when he had found her *in flagrante* with Raoul? And now...

What was she now? *Who* was she now? What sort of life was she to go forward into when everything she had hoped and dreamed of had been blasted apart, shattered into tiny, irreparable fragments? She had seen the hope of marriage to Adnan, the joining of their two families, the restoration of the Blacklands stud's fortunes, the hope of a child to ease the non-stop nag of loss ever since she'd miscarried Raoul's baby, as a way to give herself the prospect of a future. A future that would help heal the wounds that Raoul Cardini had inflicted on her vulnerable heart.

But now that future had been closed off to her, the darkness of the bleak tomorrow she faced closing in around her. Once again, it seemed that Raoul Cardini was the darkness at the centre of the storm surrounding her that had ruined every chance of happiness. Even knowing that, when she heard him speak with quiet consideration after a day of so much anger, disappointment and upset, it was almost more than she could take.

She couldn't let herself rely on him—on anything about him. Not just for today but for any sort of future. The weakness in her heart because he had been there for her during such a difficult day was just that—a weakness she couldn't afford to indulge. She'd been here before and had paid a terrible price for her naïve trust.

'Then share it with me.'

His smile was what did it. She needed that smile, needed some company—even *his* company.

No, Imogen admitted as she moved to sit opposite him on the other side of the huge inglenook fireplace: *especially* his company. He had only been back in her life for what? Three days? And once again she was back in the feeling that had overwhelmed her from the first day of their meeting two years before. The feeling that he was as vital to her as breathing, essential to life itself. He kept her heart beating. It couldn't be for long but she would take whatever she could and be grateful for that.

She was no longer the naïve young girl who had met him in a bar in Corsica. She had much more experience of life. She had known love and loss—too much loss. She had been a mother, if only for a few weeks. She'd lost the love of her life.

There, she could finally admit that to herself as she looked into his face, the burn of the setting sun casting deep shadows across his carved features. Did she need any more evidence of what she'd known already? The loss of the wedding she'd planned with Adnan, the hopes she'd had for a future, had all but knocked her flat. But with Raoul at her side, for today at least, she'd been able to cope. His quiet strength had seen her through the day, bringing her through the rough waters of shock and distress to this quiet mooring where at least she had a moment to breathe, to let her shoulders down and to think about which way to turn next.

The idea of any time, any space, with Raoul being considered quiet or calm was such a shock that Imogen found her hand shook as she held out her glass for him to pour the wine. Since the moment he had walked back into her life just days ago, she had been in turmoil. How could she feel peace when he was the cause of all the upheaval and destruction from the start?

But she'd take it, such as it was; it was what she needed right now. And if by midnight she found that, like Cinderella, all the magic of the moment vanished and her fantasy handsome prince had turned back into a rat, then at least she would have had tonight.

'Have you heard from Ciara?' he was asking now, and only someone as attuned to everything about him would have noticed the tiny hesitation before the name. The one that revealed he had actually meant to ask had she heard from Adnan, but had held back. Was that because, like her, he wanted to enjoy the moment of truce between them, even if it was temporary?

'Not a word.'

Her tone was low, regretful, and it made Raoul scowl darkly to hear it.

'What sort of a sister is she?'

'Oh, don't!'

Imogen's head came up sharply, the wine glass jerking in her hand. The raw note in her voice, an unexpected sheen on her eyes, caught on something uncomfortable deep inside him and stilled the cynical comment he had been about to make.

'Why not? She's your sister. Family matters. I know I would do anything for my sister.'

It was part of what had brought him here after all. The way Ciara had behaved with *his* sister's husband. And because…

For a moment his vision dimmed as he recalled the photograph he had seen in the newspaper. The way Imogen had been leaning on her sister's shoulder. The slightly glassy smiles they had shared.

The Scandalous O'Sullivan sisters.

'Not for very long,' Imogen said now. 'We barely know each other.'

Raoul froze with his glass halfway to his lips again and then lowered it slowly to rest on the wide arm of the chair.

'Why not? I know your mother took Ciara with her when she left, but surely… No?' he questioned as she shook her head slowly, black hair falling loose from the tie she had it fastened with at the back, tumbling around a face that he could now see was pale and shadowed with stress.

'If you're trying to say that surely we were still sisters—well, of course we were, but we never got to see each other.'

'Never?'

Raoul became aware of the way his grip had loosened on the stem of his wine glass so that it almost tipped over. Hastily he closed his fingers round it, pulling it back, but still a small spill of wine slipped over the edge and onto the furniture.

'*Pardon…*' He pulled a handkerchief from his pocket and dabbed it on the offending stain.

'Oh, don't worry.'

Imogen's smile was reassuring, though slightly weary, and to his consternation he found that caught on his over-tight nerves, leaving him feeling uncomfortable and unsettled.

'That chair—the whole suite—is so old it's practically vintage. In fact, I think it was the same sofa that was in this room when my mother took off with her lover. Papa could never bring himself to replace it. In fact…'

One long-fingered hand moved over the well-worn velvet, smoothing the nap one way and then stroking it back the other way.

'He used to say he could remember his two little girls playing together on it.'

'Two little girls,' Raoul echoed, crumpling the white cotton into his hands and clenching his fingers tight over it.

That gleam in her eye was stronger, brighter. Tears? Now? Why tears for this when she had been so strong through all the rest of the day? The shift from the admiration he'd felt to a disturbing twist of sympathy was not an easy one.

'How old were you when your mother walked out?'

'Seven.' And already crazy about the horses, lost in the world of the stud, the beautiful animals bred there. 'Ciara was not quite three.'

The memory of the day she had woken up to find that not only her mother but also her beloved little sister had disappeared into the night was almost more than she could take. As she had grown up, she had tried so hard to keep this home for herself and her father—and now that Ciara had returned to the family, that had been so much more important. But Ciara had vanished, allying herself with Adnan, and the house and stud would soon belong to someone else. So what had alienated her sister?

'I know what it's like to live without a mother,' Raoul stated now, and her startled glance into his face caught the burn of darkness in his hooded eyes. 'My mother died of cancer when I was nine.'

'That must have been so horrible for you. At least I had had the chance that my mother might come back one day. You had no such hope. How on earth did you cope?'

'My father was determined to help us through. He was always there for us—and my older sister took on the mothering role as well as she could.'

'I would have loved to do that for Ciara.'

The unevenness in her voice was put there by the thought of him as child of nine. Her own memories told her how he must have felt.

'Mother kept us apart,' she forced herself to continue, staring wide-eyed into the empty fireplace. 'We didn't even know where she was. She was determined that we wouldn't have any contact with each other—or Ciara with my father. It was her way of getting back at my father, of carrying on the civil war between them.'

'To keep sisters from knowing each other?' His disgust showed through the question, sharpening the bitterness of memory so that she had to swallow hard as she nodded her answer.

'We only found each other again a couple of years ago. We'd both been searching, but Mother had changed her name, and she gave Ciara no reference to the past—she only had the vaguest memories of a young child. It was just after we...'

The childhood memories had been bad enough but the way her reunion with her sister had coincided with the end of her time with Raoul threatened to destroy her. Lifting her head to look into his face, she saw the shadows of memory shift across his face, watched that sexy mouth tighten, as if to hold something back.

'I'd been trying to find Ciara for ages, but got nowhere.'

Focusing on that aspect of the time after she'd left Corsica gave her enough strength to tell the story without going back over more difficult memories. It had been as a reprieve from the worries of the situation at home, the frustration of finding nothing about her missing sister, that she had treated herself to the short holiday in Corsica. If only she had known she had been jumping out of the frying pan and deep into the heart of the fire when she'd done that.

'But when the financial settlement was finalised, there was no more war to fight, so my mother finally put us in contact with each other.'

She had barely been back home from Corsica before a wary Ciara had contacted her. She had barely realised she was pregnant before she had made that trip to London to meet with her long-lost sister; barely started to discover the new and wonderful experience of having a family before the tiny seed of what could have been her family for the future had been lost in the most horrific circumstances.

Recalling the shock and the pain, both emotional and physical, of those days, Imogen folded her arms around herself, cradling her lower abdomen where the minute beginnings of her baby—hers and Raoul's child—had once nestled, safe and secure. At least, it was supposed to have been safe, but fate had dealt them a brutal blow, dragging her baby from her womb and almost killing its mother in the process.

'Imogen...'

It was only when she heard Raoul's voice, the note of surprise and shock roughening its edges, that she realised that she hadn't been able to hold back the tears her memories had stirred. They were spilling down her cheeks in a silent declaration of the misery she couldn't even begin to voice aloud.

'Here.'

When had he moved? She hadn't heard a sound, or noticed any change in his position, but suddenly he was beside her, perched on the arm of the chair, reaching out to her. If he touched her then she would collapse. But no, he was holding something out to her. A blur of white through tear-strained eyes—the handkerchief with which he had wiped the wine from the chair.

'It's a little marked—not exactly the crisp white handkerchief of a regency novel.'

His voice had a surprising shake to it. Was that because he was laughing at the image—at himself?

'No problem,' she managed, breaking off as the soft cotton touched her face, pressing gently, mopping up the trails of tears down her cheeks. Her heart thudded once, hard and high up under her breastbone, making her catch her breath, and she could find no way to say anything more.

The white handkerchief smelled of his skin after it had been crushed in his hand, the traces of his personal scent still lingering. It was all she could do not to turn her face further into it, inhale that scent, take it deep into her. She wanted to lift her hand, press it against the fingers that held the cotton, crush them against her face so she could remember how it had felt to have him hold her, comfort her.

She could feel the warmth of his body next to hers,

the weight of his arm around her shoulder. She'd longed for him to hold her like this in the long, dark days after she'd lost their baby. She'd even thought about contacting him again, or perhaps daring to travel to Corsica to find him and tell him what had happened. Surely at least sharing the loss and the sorrow with him would have helped.

But of course she hadn't gone. She'd felt she could never return to him, never confront him with that terrible news. Never force him to comfort her when he hadn't wanted the baby, hadn't even thought it might exist. He had never even wanted her, so how could he have shown comfort for a loss that only she had known? If she'd told him then he would have made the effort, she had no doubt. He might have expressed a degree of sorrow but it would never have been truly meant and she would have seen the effort he was making in his face, hear it in his words. She would have been broken even further by the insincerity beneath his actions.

'Your mother must have been the worst kind of person to do that to her children. I can see how it meant so much to you to meet up with Ciara again. You'll have had a lot of catching up to do.'

There was an uneven delivery to his speech, and the pressure of his hand had altered. He now held the handkerchief still in one place, resting against her cheek, his thoughts seeming to be elsewhere.

'My sister and I are very close,' he said slowly. 'I would do anything for her.'

What had put that darker note into his words? Imogen couldn't even begin to guess. She could barely cope with the fact that he thought her sorrow was all about her family, her mother's behaviour and Ciara's. She couldn't let him in on the truth. On the fact that it had been at that special moment of reunion with Ciara that the deepest, harshest blow had hit her and it was only because her sister had been there that she had got through it.

She had even let Ciara persuade her to go out on the town way too soon, in a desperate attempt to put the sorrow behind her. Ciara too had been in an emotional state, because of the circumstances in which she'd lost her job, and they had both struggled to accept the way their mother had behaved. The glass of wine they had intended to share that night had turned into another— a bottle—and, totally unprepared for the effects of the alcohol on their systems, they had both staggered out to find a taxi before the evening disintegrated any further.

Now even Ciara had left her life, it seemed, alienated by something she didn't understand in her relationship with Adnan.

'Imogen...'

Raoul had moved, sliding down to the floor in front of her, kneeling to take her in his arms.

'Where is your father? Shall I fetch—?'

'Oh, no!'

She shook her head. The addition of her father into this emotional mix would be a move too far.

'He'd be no use at all—he's given up already and gone to bed.' With a bottle, she had no doubt. Perhaps, in a way, seeing Raoul's obvious impatience with her father's behaviour, she began to understand her mother's attitude just a little better, to see there might have been two sides to their disastrous marriage.

'Given up on what? He hasn't done a thing all day. Couldn't he have offered to help at least?'

'It's his idea of a nightmare, what happened here today.'

'And not yours?

She hadn't expected his anger, and that sceptical glance, the narrowing of those penetrating eyes, was too much, too close. Hastily she tried for a diversion in the hope of distracting him.

'He looked in once and saw you were there.'

She'd seen her father put his head round the door and back away at the sight of Raoul in full organising mode.

'I suppose he saw that I had some clothes on.' The twist to Raoul's mouth was wry. 'And that was enough.'

Laughter choked in Imogen's throat at the memory of her father's awkward command in the middle of the night.

'He also heard your nickname being bandied about,' she managed, recalling the way several of the village matrons brought in to serve at the wedding breakfast, and now entrusted with the clearing up, had looked as if their eyes were out on stalks at the sight of Raoul, sleeves rolled up to expose tanned forearms as he hefted bundles of starched linen tablecloths or the boxes packed with food to go to the hospice. His hair had tumbled forward over his wide brow and he had had the look of the untamed bandit the scandal papers had named him.

'The Corsican Bandit?' A lift of his broad shoulders dismissed the familiar title. 'I've heard worse. And considering the stories that have been spreading...'

'Stories?' Imogen sat forward sharply. 'What stories?'

Those gleaming eyes clashed with her uneasy ones for a moment, then again that inscrutable smile flickered across his mouth.

'That I'm here to break your father down—to steal the stud—and worse. I think you'd better be prepared for the fact that now I'm also supposed to be planning to steal away his daughter.'

'Oh, no, they can't think that?'

The way one black, straight brow drifted upwards, questioning her assertion, had her thinking backwards, remembering the knowing looks that she'd received as she'd struggled to explain that the wedding was off, that her prospective groom had left the area—maybe even the country for all she knew.

'Would it be so very bad?'

His voice had lowered, becoming richer and darker. The soft traces of his accent had deepened, turning his words into a husky purr. The warmth of his breath told her that he was closer, his face almost touching hers. If she blinked she felt her lashes brush across his cheek, and she inhaled his intensely personal scent with every indrawn breath. The handkerchief slipped to the floor and its pressure on her cheek was replaced by the burning touch of his hand, skin against skin. She had only to turn her head and...

'*Oui...*'

She heard the agreement forced from his lips, felt it against her cheek as her mouth found the skin of his palm. The scent of his body was like a drug reaching straight for what little was left of her functioning brain and blotting out rational thought.

'That's what I've wanted to do all day,' she murmured as she let her tongue slide out to taste him, taking that essence of him into her mouth.

'And I've wanted that for days too.'

His voice was thick and raw, the words struggling to be heard above the beat of his heart so close to hers, the heat of his breath dancing over her skin.

'Ever since I arrived in that church and saw you there.'

'Really?'

It was all she could manage as she tried to look into his face, to read the truth in his eyes. But she found that the heat and focus of his stare was too much, too strong for her to take without dissolving into a puddle of molten awareness. Her need for him was like a throbbing pulse all along her body, centring at the juncture of her thighs. The stinging hunger that pooled there made her shift uncomfortably on the chair, uncontrollable need making her reach for him, link her hands behind his head, pulling his face down towards her, holding it there while her lips explored his with the yearning she couldn't control.

'*Vraiment.*'

It sounded like the truth he'd declared it to be. It sounded like the words she'd heard him whisper in the darkness of the long, hot nights on the island in the days when she knew she'd been falling in love with him. In the time when she'd thought there was no reason not to fall in love with him.

'Me too…' There was no point in denying it, so why even try. 'That's the way I've felt too. From the moment I turned and saw you.'

No, before that. As soon as she'd heard his voice and known who was behind her. Wasn't the truth that in that single moment she had known the wedding could never go ahead? Wasn't that why she had gone to Raoul's room in the middle of the night? She'd gone about things the wrong way. She should have spoken to Adnan first. She should have told him that she could never love him as he deserved a wife to love him. She should have acknowledged to herself that she had always loved Raoul, falling for him in a heartbeat and never escaping again. She'd known she could never have a proper marriage with Adnan, but that had done nothing to destroy all the reasons why she *had* to marry him and live up to their agreement.

'W-what did you come back for?' She asked and felt his soft laughter against her ear. His warmth surrounded her, cutting out the rest of the world and enclosing her in a bubble of security, if only for these moments.

'Exactly as they said,' he murmured. 'I came to steal you away.'

She didn't believe him for a moment, but right now it was what she wanted to hear. What she wanted to feel. That someone thought she was special. That she was wanted for herself, not for what she could offer him or what she brought with her.

That she was *wanted*—for this one night at least.

'I hoped that was what you'd say.'

At least that was what she had meant to say, but she barely got the first sound out before her lips were taken in a fierce, demanding kiss. Her head fell back under the pressure of his mouth, her lips opening eagerly to his plundering tongue. His long body came up and over hers, crushing her back into the chair as his heavy, muscular legs slid between her denim-clad limbs. His hands seemed to be everywhere, holding her, hot fingers pushed into her hair, the hard weight of his palm against her thigh, her hip, sliding under the hem of her top, searing across her skin. Instinctively she writhed in delight, pressing herself further into his touch, her pelvis shifting against his, pressing up against the heat and hardness of his erection, dragging a moan from him that sounded right into her open mouth.

'Raoul…' She tasted him on the breath that had filled

her mouth, felt it burn all the way down to her soul. She wanted this. Oh, dear heaven, but she wanted it.

She was sliding down deeper into the chair, almost to the floor, the heat and the weight of his body against her. And it was all too much. Too hard, too hot, too heavy. And she was too hungry, too needy to take this—just this—and nothing more.

She wanted him on top of her, covering her, the hard weight of him pressing her down into the worn and shabby rug before the fire. But when he was there, sliding over her, long legs entangling with hers, it wasn't enough. He had too many clothes on and so did she. She didn't want to feel the linen of his shirt, the fine material of his trousers rubbing against her, making the denim scrape against the highly sensitised nerves under her skin.

Her hands were moving over him feverishly, tugging at the buttons in his shirt, fingers sliding in through the spaces she had made, electrical prickles of response buzzing along her nerves as she felt the crisp brush of hair against her fingertips, the heated satin of his skin.

'*Ma belle*... Imogen.'

There it was again, the sound of her name as only he could pronounce it, muttered against the arched lines of her neck, moving down, down towards where the curves of her breasts just showed above the deep vee neck of her shirt. The movement crushed the softness of her body against the hardness of his. So close—and yet far too far away. She wanted, *needed*, so much more.

But even as Raoul followed her down onto the floor, she felt the sudden tension in him, the slight drawing away from her, creating a gap between the burn of their bodies that let a disturbing drift of cooler air creep over her exposed skin.

'*Ton père*—your papa.'

Raoul could have cursed himself for the muttered words that seemed to jolt her out of the burning response she'd shown, freezing the hands that clutched at his shoulders, forcing open those beautiful eyes. Eyes that even in the dim light of the gathering dusk he could see were still glazed with passion. The last thing he wanted was to destroy the mood that had flared so fast and so hot in the moment she had turned her head to kiss his hand. But he had no desire at all to have their passion interrupted by the appearance of her father—drunk or sober. Once had been enough.

'Your room…'

It was on the other side of the house, up a separate flight of stairs. It would be silent and secret and would give them all the time in the world to give in to the sexual tension that had been burning between them since the first moment they had seen each other again, complete the connection that had never been destroyed by their separation. It had only ebbed temporarily, fading down to smouldering embers, needing the hint of a breath, a touch, a kiss, to coax it into an untamed fire that swept through them all over again, devouring every hesitation or doubt in its path.

This was what had always been between them, how he had always felt about this woman. And everything he had thought had destroyed it, the distance he had believed he had wanted to put between them, had only been a lie. This was why he had never been able to forget Imogen, why he had never been able to replace her in his thoughts, in his dreams, with any other woman. No matter how he'd tried.

And he'd tried, damn it! Tried and failed completely. So tonight was what he had been dreaming of for all the empty years since he'd walked away from her. It was all he had wanted in the time they'd been apart. And nothing—*nothing*—was going to stop it now.

Imogen was of the same mind, it seemed. He had barely whispered his warning before she was scrambling to her feet, reaching out for his hand to curl her fingers tight around his, tugging him towards the door.

'My room,' she agreed, and the thickness of her voice, the unevenness of her breathing, told him she would have as much trouble as he would to get up the stairs without ripping clothes off and discarding them along the way.

CHAPTER TEN

THEY MADE IT to the bedroom, but only just. Imogen's tee-shirt was already ripped at the seams, coming apart in Raoul's urgent hands. His belt had been tugged free, the button on his jeans snapped open in a struggle that was then abandoned in place of an assault on the fastenings of his shirt which Imogen found easier to wrench out of the way.

Small white buttons flew across the room, to land with a faint sound against the wall. The sight and scent of his skin, the temptation of the bronzed satin before her, was almost too much and she pressed her mouth against the wall of his chest, tasting and tantalising without restraint.

'Imogen…' Raoul growled, hard hands clenching in her hair, seemingly undecided whether to hold her there or to pull her head up and away so he could crush his own kisses on her hungry mouth.

The kisses he needed to give her won the battle and she found her head was pulled up, lips crushed beneath his marauding mouth, his invading tongue plunging into the moist softness, setting up a sensual dance as he tasted her intimately.

His hands were urgent at her waist, lifting the torn tee-shirt and wrenching it over her head, pausing only for the time it took to remove it before he claimed her lips again. Imogen had the easier task and with Raoul's help his shirt was soon shrugged off and tossed to one side on the floor. The white cotton bra shared the same fate, discarded without a second thought, and Imogen could only sigh out her relief and satisfaction as she felt her skin press against his, the whirl of black hair tantalising and teasing her already sensitive nipples.

'*Mon Dieu*, but I want you!' Raoul muttered roughly, pushing his hands up between them to capture and cup the curves of her breasts, teasing the sensitive nipples until she was swooning with desire, swaying against him, only supported by the hands she had flung up around his neck, fingers clenching over his shoulders, digging in to the corded muscle there.

'Me too.'

It was all she could manage, because to say anything more would require her to separate her lips from his demanding mouth and that was more than she could stand. Stinging pulses of desire were shooting through her, all the way from her nipples down to where the hot moisture of need gathered between her thighs. She was blind, deaf and dumb to anything but Raoul and the needs he was waking in her, the pleasures she knew were waiting for her, if she could just…

'These have to go.'

Sensing her needs, Raoul had already unzipped her jeans, tossing her down on the bed with an impatience that spoke of the hunger that was building up inside him too, threatening to break through the dam of restraint he had tried to impose on his actions.

And that was fine with Imogen. Patience and restraint were not what she wanted from him. Not here. Not now. Almost frantically she wriggled herself free of the clinging clothing, knowing a hot rush of relief and anticipation as Raoul's demanding hands exposed her to his hungry gaze, the faint wash of cooler air an almost unbearable addition to the rush of sensations.

'You too.'

Their hands met and clashed as both of them tried to rid him of what little was left of his clothing, and a moment later they were back down on the bed together. Imogen's arms went up around his neck as she pulled him down to cover her, giving herself up to the delicious sensation of having his hard body over hers. His hot skin scorched her, his hair-roughened legs came between hers, nudging her limbs apart, exposing her to him. All the time his mouth was at her breasts, licking, suckling, nipping sharply, until she arched high against him, letting out a high, keening cry of delight and need.

Drifting, lost on a heated sea of sensation, she felt his fingers at her moist core, brushing aside the damp curls, stroking just where she needed him most. It was too much, though, and she caught his hands in hers, demanding more.

'You,' she said roughly. 'I want you. All of you.'

His faint groan told her that he was as close to losing himself as she was, and she let her legs part even further to encourage him, inviting him in. The blunt heat of him was nudging at her; his mouth was fixed on one breast, tugging sharply on the aroused nipple as she gave herself up to his intimate invasion. Abandoning all control, she raised her hips from the bed, pushing herself against him, and felt the hard force of his possession surging into her, taking her out of herself and into a mindless, needy hunger that could only be satisfied by joining together harder and faster.

'Ma belle...'

His voice was a rough, hoarse gasp as he pushed in, deeper, further, then drew back, again and again and again. Each time he took her higher, further, the storm of pleasure building, swirling, growing until there was nowhere else to go but over the edge and into the oblivion of ecstasy that splintered all around her.

A thudding heartbeat later, she heard Raoul's cry as he abandoned himself to his own release and followed her into the raging darkness.

It was a long, long time before her breathing slowed, her heart stopped racing and she slowly, dazedly came back to reality and awareness of the room she was in, the man who lay beside her, long body slick with sweat and the aftershocks of reaction.

'And you wondered why there are the rumours that I'm here to steal you away.'

His broad chest was still heaving, his words coming roughly and unevenly.

'I think it's a little late to try and deny that now.'

'But I can't have people thinking that—it would ruin everything.' The words escaped in an unthinking rush.

'Ruin?'

Raoul heaved himself up onto the pillow, propping it behind his back as he leaned against the bedhead.

'That seems to be a word that's been used a lot today. If I'm supposed to have ruined everything, at least you could have the courtesy to tell me exactly how I've done that.'

The way he looked down at her, the laser probe of those bronze eyes, made her shiver inside. She wanted to reach for the sheet, to pull it up to cover herself from that searching stare.

'It doesn't matter,' she hedged. 'Nothing matters now—everything's…'

'Ruined?' he supplied sardonically when she let the sentence trail off unfinished. It was unfinishable. There was nothing left to say. 'Explain!'

'Nothing to explain.'

She couldn't meet his eyes, so instead stared down at her own fingers where they lay on the bedspread, watching them trace out the pattern of the golden flowers as if they could wipe away the design and everything that had happened in the past few days. She couldn't explain anything, least of all how she had ended what had been supposed to be her wedding day here, in bed, with a man who was not the bridegroom. She had just made hot, passionate…

No; her mind flinched desperately away from the word 'love' in that sentence. She had just had hot, passionate *sex* with the man who was responsible for breaking up the marriage she had thought she would be consummating tonight.

'You can't expect me to believe that.'

'Can't expect you to believe that, because of the way you broke up my marriage plans, I am probably—no, definitely—currently spending one of my last nights ever in Blacklands?'

The full horror of the truth broke over her like a cold wave, and even the way Raoul's black brows snapped together in a fierce frown couldn't stop her.

'Can't expect you to believe that as soon as the news about the cancelled wedding gets out—which I expect it already has—there will be a line of creditors queuing up outside that door?'

A wild gesture with her arm indicated the window and the drive up to the house that lay beyond it, yet Raoul's eyes didn't follow it, but instead stayed, unblinking and fixed on her face.

'And why would they do that?'

'Because we owe them. We owe them more than we can ever pay. Even our famed stud horse isn't ours! And as soon as they see our last chance of redemption has gone then...'

'Al Makthabi was your last chance?'

He fired the question at her like a bullet and she winced as she felt it hit home.

'Yes.' Her voice was low and despondent, the slow nod of her head a sign of surrender.

'Your father has let the stud go to rack and ruin.'

His mouth twisted on the repetition of that emotive word.

'He's never been able to resist a bet—and when he had the knowledge and the brain power to pick a winner that wasn't always a bad thing. But then he started pickling what brain cells he had in whisky and any trace of expertise he had went out the window.'

It was like hearing the words inside her own thoughts being spoken aloud, but in Raoul's deep, accented voice they sounded so much worse, so much more appalling that way.

But she hadn't spoken those words. Raoul himself had supplied them to fill the silence. There had been no surprise in his voice; he'd just listed every detail. He had known without being told. He had known everything before he had even arrived here.

So was that why he had come? He'd said there was a scheme that he'd agreed on with her father—to breed horses from his precious stallion. But to do that he would have had to co-operate with Adnan who after their marriage would have been the owner of Blacklands as well as his own grandfather's stud. And who would have owned the magnificent Blackjack.

If the marriage had taken place.

Was that what Raoul had planned? To make sure Adnan didn't marry her and then take over Blacklands?

Shifting awkwardly on the bed, she turned so she could look into the room. The beautiful white lace dress she was supposed to have worn today still hung from the edge of the wardrobe. In the gathering dusk of the evening it looked like a long white shroud, a ghost of what might have been.

'So Adnan was going to come to your rescue— financially?'

She'd heard that cruel note in his voice before. When he'd turned on her, accusing her of being nothing but a gold-digger, only wanting him for his money. That was why she knew what was going through his head now. He was seeing her following the same path with Adnan, marrying the other man only for what he brought to her. In a way it was true, and the only thing she could do was to nod in silent agreement.

She couldn't see Raoul's face but she heard the swift, roughly indrawn breath that revealed his response to her answer. Disgust? Or dark fury? Or just the fact that, deep down, he had always believed this would be the case? To one side, she could see the way his long, powerful fingers clenched over the bedcovers, his bronzed tan dark against the gold and white cotton. The way the material crumpled and bunched damagingly made her stomach clench in instinctive response.

'What I don't understand was what Al Makthabi got out of this.'

Adnan had come to her rescue, put forward the plan of the marriage of convenience, but she had known there had been nothing of the heart in their arrangement. He had promised his grandfather two things—a Derby winner and an heir, and she would help him provide both. The big, black stallion that was the one thing the stud had left of any value was to have been her wedding gift to her new husband, and the heir...

'What did you offer him?' Raoul flung the question at her, cold and sharp.

He was going to hate her answer; hate *her*. Flinching inside at the thought, Imogen pulled the sheets up around her.

'A marriage.'

'Hell, yes, I know there was to be a marriage but— did you sleep with Adnan before you were to take your vows?'

The question burned on his tongue. Of course she had been to bed with Adnan. How could any man have a relationship—an *engagement*—with Imogen and not want—need—to take her to bed?

He couldn't imagine it could be any other way. But, after the heat and passion they had just shared, he could barely control the internal fury and disbelief that raged through him at the thought of her with another man.

'None of your business.'

She was absolutely right. It was none of his business. Or, rather, it had been none of his business. It shouldn't have mattered. But right now it mattered like hell.

'And if you want to know what I...what Adnan was going to get out of this bargain...'

Her voice sounded weird. It was going up and down, swinging all over the place. Was she crying? Or angry? Her face was still turned away from him, her eyes fixed on the opposite side of the room. On that damned wedding dress that was hanging on the wardrobe.

The sight of that damned dress now seemed to have developed the power to stab at him, right in the heart, twisting dangerously in his already uncomfortable conscience.

He had come here to stop the wedding. He had planned to tell Al Makthabi what she was really like. That she was only after him for his money. But when he had met her husband-to-be, he had soon realised that Adnan was nobody's sort of a fool. And that the other man knew exactly what he was getting in Imogen O'Sullivan. The neighbours, the locals who lived in the village, regarded the two families—the O'Sullivans and the Al Makthabis—as the modern day equivalent of lords of the manor. They might believe in the fairy-tale love story of the two big houses joined together, but he knew more about them than that.

He'd told himself that if he'd seen one trace of love in Imogen's face, one hint of that fairy-tale being true, then he would have turned and walked away. But he'd been all sorts of a fool to imagine he might see such a thing. He'd read the signs in her face, the look that said this wasn't a wedding of love, with a bride so happy it shone out of her eyes. And what he had seen in Adnan's face had not been love either.

But even before that had really sunk in, he'd known that whatever happened he couldn't turn and walk away. Couldn't leave Imogen behind and go back to the disturbing emptiness of the past few years when nothing and no woman had satisfied him.

After tonight he knew why. After tonight he knew that no one could ever make him feel as this woman did. No other woman could make him burn and hunger, the heat of need sizzling up every nerve and leaving him just a husk of a man.

'He got to make his grandfather happy.'

'*Quoi?*'

He had to drag his thoughts back from the burning paths they'd followed, forcing his mind to focus on what she'd said.

She'd shifted on the bed now, turning back towards him. Although she still held the sheet tucked tight around her, it did nothing at all to hide the sexy enticement of her body. If anything, it made matters worse, with the fine cotton stretched tight over the curves of her breasts. He could clearly see the darker pink of her nipples, the lift of the peaked tips pressed against their covering, and at her hips the fall of the delicate fabric was not enough to hide the shadow of dark hair at the juncture of her thighs. Even just to think of the way he had been buried in her body at exactly that point, with the warmth and moisture of her welcome enclosing him, had his penis stiffening in such a rush that he had to grab the sheets himself and pull them up over the heated evidence of the way he was incapable of controlling himself where she was concerned.

'No need to be embarrassed.' Imogen had seen his reaction and her soft voice, her faint smile, had even more of a damning effect on him.

'Je n'ais pas honte,' he growled, glaring a fierce rejection of her words straight into her face.

He wasn't in the least bit embarrassed by the force of his reaction. It was what had brought them into this bed tonight after all. And it was a response that she shared totally. He'd felt her reaction to his touch, known the way her body melted under his, her spine arching up to press her softness against his chest, his thighs, his pelvis. He'd heard her soft cries of delight and the way they'd morphed into moans of hungry demand as their bodies moved faster and faster, coming together in one mind-blowing, overwhelming rush of release that had

had them both collapsing back exhausted on the pillows, their breath coming in great heaving gasps.

He knew what he wanted from this woman and she knew what she wanted from him. But that was not enough.

Hell, no! He was not going down that path again. Not until he had some things sorted out. He had no doubt about his physical reaction to Imogen—and hers to him—but he'd been that way before and had burned with regret as a result.

'Hell!'

It escaped him at the realisation that the hungry passion he'd felt for Imogen had had him in bed with her— *inside* her—without a pause for thought or even the idea of protection. He had brought condoms with him, damn it; he should have used them.

He'd made this mistake once before, in the out-of-control early days of their relationship. One mistake when desire had overwhelmed him in the warm darkness of the night, on the cliffs above Porto, when he'd had no protection with him, no thought of being able to hold back. Every other time he'd been scrupulous about using contraception but stupidly, irresponsibly, he'd made that one mistake. And one mistake had been all it had taken…

The thought that he might have impregnated Imogen with *another* child of his when she hadn't even cared enough to keep the first one sent black waves of horror crashing through his mind. How had he let the overpowering lust he felt for this woman scramble what little was left of his rational brain cells? He had been thinking only with his.

He hadn't been *thinking* at all!

The realisation pushed him out of bed as if he had

been stung. His clothing was still scattered about the floor, evidence if he needed it of how uncontrolled his thoughts had been as they'd made their way up here, tumbled onto that bed…

'What is it?'

Imogen had swivelled round, the sheets twisting even tighter about her. Her face had lost the flush that orgasm had left on her cheeks but there was still that wide-eyed, unfocused look she had turned on him, revealing that, like him, she still hadn't fully collected her thoughts.

'I asked, did you sleep with Adnan?'

He was dragging on his trousers as he spoke.

'You asked me that,' Imogen acknowledged, her thoughts reeling, remembering the way he had declared he was not ashamed of his growing erection. Not concerned to show that he wanted her again even after so short a time. And she had seen no reason for shame either. In fact, the truth was she had found it a thrill to know that the burning connection between them was still there. That, like the way it had been on those passionate nights in Corsica, he had not been satisfied easily, or quickly, but wanted her again straight afterwards.

So how had they got from there to this in what seemed the blink of an eye?

'And I said it was none of your business.'

'It is my business, seeing as we've just come together—without protection.'

Oh, hell.

She felt as if the whole room had suddenly started to close in on her, growing darker with every breath she sucked in. Raoul's face was shaded and hidden, the brilliant bronze eyes just glittering cold pools above the slash of high carved cheekbones, his mouth nothing but a thin, hard line. What had happened to those softly sensual lips, the hotly demanding mouth that had taken hers so passionately, forcing her own lips open, tongue plunging into her mouth, tasting her, taking her?

Realisation had happened. She could read the thoughts that were going through his mind as clearly as if they were transmitted on to the bleak, withdrawn face.

He had realised what they'd just done; how foolishly they'd behaved. And now, because he so obviously had second thoughts, the horrifying truth dawned on her too.

'You don't need to worry!'

'No?' One black eyebrow lifted sharply, cynically questioning. 'And why not?'

She felt the truth bubbling up like lava in her mouth, but she didn't dare to let it out. Not now, not ever, possibly, as she was sure there was no way he'd ever have wanted to know the truth about the tiny legacy their past relationship had left with her. The heavy sensation of tears clogging the back of her throat told her there was no way she was going to be capable of revealing that truth to him.

So she stuck to the one fact she was sure of, the simple, irrefutable declaration she could make.

'Adnan and I…we haven't, we never, slept together.'

'You've not been intimate?'

It was such a strange, old-fashioned way of expressing it—coming from the man who looked like a bandit, standing there before her with his bare feet splayed out on the shabby bedside rug, dark jeans pulled on roughly so that they were up around his waist but not fully fastened, the belt undone and hanging loose at his narrow hips. His bronzed, broad chest was still exposed, almost shockingly dark against the white and gold décor of her room.

'No—never.' It was vital that he believe her. 'I—I haven't been with anyone at all, not since you.'

'No one?'

His breath hissed in between his teeth and he seemed to come back to himself as if from a long way away.

'But we should have used contraception. And we were damned stupid not to.'

If there was any reason why she could never, ever risk telling him about the child they'd created, the baby she'd lost, then it was there, stamped on his face, dark, brutal and like a mask. The thought that they might have created a child appalled him, horrified him. He would do anything to avoid the possibility.

She couldn't tell him, and she had to reassure him now. She also had to protect herself. It would destroy her to let him express so openly how much he hated the idea of fathering a child with her.

'That…that…will be fine.'

'No repercussions?' It was a lash of a demand, making her skin shiver where the words seemed to land.

'None.'

'Dieu, merci.'

If Imogen had had any tiny trace of hope left then it evaporated at that fervent murmur. The whole atmosphere of passion and hunger that had filled the room only moments before dissolved and vanished, leaving her feeling as flat and limp as the remnant of the sheet that was hanging from her bed. Unable to speak another word, she dragged herself towards her clothing lying on the floor, stooping to pick it up, and then just stood there, tee-shirt and jeans in her hands, unable to do anything more. She couldn't do as he had done and pull on clothes, as if declaring this time was finished. Over and done with.

She knew that was how it should be. There was nothing left between them. The inferno of passion that had consumed them had burned itself out, and what was there to put in its place?

Nothing, Imogen admitted as she watched Raoul's hands go to his shirt to tuck it in at his waist, bringing the belt tight and buckling it with firm, decisive movements. What she might have thought of—dreamed of— as being a new beginning was in fact the end. One final, last sensual fling. A moment of self-indulgence on his part, a wish for oblivion on hers.

But the bill always came in the end.

She had hoped for that insensibility until the morning, one night at least with Raoul by her side, his arms around her, keeping everything that assailed her at bay for just these few hours. Instead, the brief, bittersweet moments of passion were all she'd had; and the reality she woke up to now was worse than ever before. She had loved Raoul, but he had tossed her aside and walked away from her. She had fought hard to win herself a sort of peace, an acceptance, even after the loss of her baby, and she had thought she'd reached it. She had even let herself think of marriage to Adnan, imagining the brutal wounds Raoul had inflicted had started to heal.

But in just a few days—not even a week—his reappearance and all that followed from it had ripped away the flimsy sticking plaster that she had put over those wounds, opening up the barely closed scars. She was right back where she had started—but this time it was worse. This time she knew the rescue package she and Adnan had offered each other had been blasted to smithereens with no hope of repair. She'd ruined Adnan's life and her own in one blow. Her father's future held only bankruptcy, repossession of the stud, and he would probably now face the bottom of far too many bottles to count.

It would mean she would lose the only home she'd ever known, her dream of having her family live here, with Ciara finding a base here too, in ashes. All the beautiful horses would be taken in payment of their debts and sent heaven alone knew where. But, worst of all, she would have to face that bleak and empty future knowing she had never truly managed to recover from the love she had felt for Raoul. She still loved him, would probably love him until the day she died, while he had only wanted her to sate the sexual passion he had felt, and she had been weak enough to give into it.

Now it seemed he had had what he'd wanted and, thankful that there would be no possible consequences from this night of passion, he was dressing and on his way. Somehow, she had to find the strength to stand and watch him walk away from her once again.

'Imogen.' Raoul's tone was rough and hard, no sign of any of the softening she might hope for in it. 'This was a mistake.'

'I know,' she managed, waving a hand dismissively in front of her face so she didn't have to look into his. 'But it's fine. No consequences, no ties. We both had…' her voice hiccupped on the word '…fun, and that was that. Now, if you'll excuse me, I need a shower. And you…'

She didn't need to finish the sentence. She was sure the pointed way she glanced towards the door did that for her.

On her way to the bathroom, still with the sheet trailing behind her, she passed the case with the clothes she had packed for her honeymoon. Unable to bear the thought of putting back on the clothes that Raoul had torn from her so ardently, she dropped them on to the floor and snatched up the first items from the top of the case to take them with her into the *en suite*. Turning on the shower with a force that had the water pouring down, she didn't even wait for it to warm up before she stood underneath the torrent, letting it pound down on top of her head. The force of it deafened her ears and numbed her thoughts, bringing on a much-needed state of oblivion.

CHAPTER ELEVEN

SHE WANTED A SHOWER.

Raoul could only stand and stare at the door that Imogen had so forcefully shut behind her. The sound of the shower running seemed like a physical barrier she'd erected between them, cutting her off from him as effectively as the solid wood of the door. Whatever else he'd expected, it had not been that. She wanted to wash away every trace of his touch, his kiss, his possession. It made him feel terrible, vile and *dirty*. As if he had tainted her, when all the time he had...

He had what? It slapped him hard in the face, shaking up his thought processes, leaving him blinking in confusion and shock.

He had wanted to comfort her.

Comfort? How could he feel that towards the woman who had destroyed his child? And how could he be fool enough to have made love to her without any form of protection—no matter how much she assured him that all would be well? How could he risk fathering another child with her when he had no confidence that it wouldn't meet the same fate?

No. That was never going to happen, and there was one way he could make sure of it. The memory of the way she had looked walking across the room, the sheet trailing behind her like the train of a wedding dress, was all the confirmation he needed.

He was standing beside the window, watching the first faint glimmers of the dawn touch the sky, when the sound of the shower ceased. A few minutes later the bathroom door opened and Imogen came back into the room. Her dark hair was wrapped up in a towel turban-style on the top of her head, her feet were bare and she wore a turquoise and white dress that reminded him of the one she had been wearing on that first day on Corsica where he had glimpsed her across the bar and had never been able to look away again.

'You're still here!'

It was obvious that didn't please her. Her voice was tart and her brows drew together in a frown.

'I told you I was never very good at taking orders.'

'I didn't order…'

'You think not? So what was that deliberate stare, the nod of the head towards the door?'

She plonked herself down on the bed, tugging the towel loose and rubbing at her wet hair.

'I thought you'd want to go—you got what you wanted. And, as you said, it was fun.'

'You were the one who said that,' he pointed out. 'I didn't even agree with you.'

The hands that were rubbing at her hair stilled, and he could see she was looking up at him, peering through the black strands.

'Don't lie to me, Raoul!'

'Why should it be a lie? I can assure you that, for me, it wasn't fun.'

So how did she take that? Imogen asked herself, thankful for the concealing curtain of hair that hid the confusion and pain she knew must show in her face. He sounded so serious, her heart twisted in apprehension.

'Just a one-night stand…' she tried and felt the constriction in her chest tighten as she saw that proud dark head move in adamant denial.

Turning, he gestured to where the beautiful lace dress hung from the top of the wardrobe, shrouded in its cotton covering.

'You would have looked beautiful in that.'

'Oh, don't!'

She didn't even want to think about it.

'You still could,' he went on, keeping up that casual, conversational tone. The one that contradicted so starkly the words he was actually saying.

'We should give you another chance to wear it.'

That hit home so hard it knocked her flat, falling back against the pillows, her eyes closing in shock. She had to be dreaming or hallucinating; this couldn't be happening! But when she opened them he was still there, still looking down at her with that skin-scouring stare that seemed to have scraped away a much-needed protective layer, leaving herself raw and vulnerable.

'Better not let it go to waste.'

'Why?' She could barely form the word and it came out in a raw croak. *'How?'*

He couldn't mean what it sounded like, and yet there was no hint of any amusement or anything that might indicate he was anything but deadly serious. With the emphasis on deadly.

'You could always marry me.'

He'd said that before, in the middle of the night, but she'd taken it as a joke. A black, sick sort of joke that she hadn't even let register in her mind. But now he was saying it again and the dark emphasis left her in no doubt that he meant what he was saying.

'But why?'

'Let me see…'

He lifted a hand, ticking off the points he made one by one.

'You need someone to get you out of the financial mess you're in—I can manage that and more. I want the stud. I like what I've seen of it so far—though it needs huge investment and modernisation. I want that stallion Blackjack.'

Didn't he hear what he was saying? Didn't he realise that what he was offering was the reason why he had originally turned away from her so callously?

'But this is what you accused me of before—of wanting you for your money. Like the others, no?' she questioned as he shook his head almost savagely.

'Alice—the others—played a role. They claimed they wanted me for myself.'

'Which is why you pretended you were just a farmer?'

'Until Rosalie told you the truth.'

'That you actually owned the farm and the business. Yes, she pointed out the olive oil in the shops…' Her words dried as she saw the quick frown, the disbelieving look, he had turned on her.

'What else?' he demanded.

'Nothing else! Are you telling me your friend embroidered the truth a little—more than a little—when she reported to you? Did she claim she told me about the worldwide market for your oil?'

Rosalie hadn't needed to add any such thing, Imogen admitted to herself. Because the truth was that she hadn't actually listened—or cared. If Raoul was just a farmer, or something more, it didn't matter. What mattered was that she had fallen crazily in love with him and all she wanted was for the magical island interlude to carry on into a much longer future. So she hadn't even thought of it, and instead had blundered in with her naïve and over-enthusiastic attempt to persuade him to let their relationship become something so much more than a holiday fling.

'And perhaps she added in the details of the horse breeding programme you were working on? The beautiful stallions I might want to use in the Blacklands stud, just to make sure I bit?'

The answer was written on his face and she almost laughed as she put a hand up to touch his cheek, trace the line of the wry twist to his mouth.

'Believe me, that was more likely to make me want to turn and run, rather than fight my way through your obvious defences. Oh, Raoul, don't you think that perhaps your "friend" was a little interested in you herself? I feel sorry for you,' she added as she saw his eyes change, darkening as realisation set in. 'No—really, truly, I do. If you can't trust anyone.'

'I did once.'

It was a low, muttered growl and the fact that his eyes slid away from hers as he said it told her this was something important. Something he found it hard to speak of.

'I was young, foolish, barely twenty. I met a girl and fell—hard. I thought she had too.'

'What happened?'

'She believed I had money—but it was my father who held the purse strings then. When she found out, she made a play for him instead.'

'She dumped you for your own father?' Imogen

couldn't disguise the shock she felt—and her horror—
at his story.

'After that I developed a sort of sixth sense where
women were concerned. If they wanted money, there
were plenty of other places they could find it.'

He made it sound as if it didn't matter, as if he had
just tossed those feelings aside. But there was so much
control in his voice, in his expression, that Imogen knew
he was concealing the full truth.

'I only ever came close to making that mistake one
other time.'

'And then?'

His smile was hard, cold, a flash on and off, and then
it was gone again, leaving his eyes like polished stone.

'I don't put my head in the noose a second time.'

Imogen flinched away from the cold darkness of the
declaration. It echoed back through the years, taking
her to a Corsican beach, the slow wash of the waves
against the shore in her ears, the warmth of the sun
on her back.

'But—isn't that what you're doing now?'

She cursed herself for actually saying it. But she had
to. After the way he'd opened up to her, she couldn't
just leave things as they were.

'It will be. You're giving me money—paying my
family's debts—that's the inducement you're using to
get me to marry you.'

She was looking up into his eyes as she spoke and
she saw the tiny movement as his head went back, the
long, slow blink as he accepted what she had said.

'But this time you're not asking for it. I'm offering it
to you. If it means I get you in my bed, then that's a deal
I'm prepared to agree to. And I want you, Imogen. More
than I've ever wanted any other woman in my life.'

'I don't want…'

A blazing flash from those molten bronze eyes shrivelled the rest of the sentence on her tongue and made it die there unspoken.

'Surely we're past the time for lies? At least we know we're compatible in bed, if nowhere else.'

His words threatened to choke off her breathing. If only he knew how much she wanted to be with him anywhere and everywhere—in bed, out of it; at home or away; *in her life*!

'There's more to marriage than sex.'

Raoul nodded slowly, though his eyes refuted her claim.

'But it's a good place to start—a very good place in our case.'

Unable to stay on the bed any longer, Imogen pushed herself upwards onto her feet so she could face him, eye to eye.

'You think that because you're hot in bed… Yes, I'm acknowledging that!' she admitted as she saw the quirk of his arched brow. 'I'd be a fool to deny it. But if you think I'd do that—for you…'

'No.' Another shrug. 'Not for me. For your family, your father, the stud, the horses. You could even make sure that Adnan can save face.'

'Oh, come on!'

How could she ever make it up to Adnan? How could he ever forgive her, or at the very least still tolerate her presence in his life? She might as well have renounced him to his face in public. Or turned and walked away from him at the altar.

'How on earth could I do that?'

Raoul looked totally unmoved by her vehemence. Reaching out, he took her hand, lifted it between them, and the smile that slowly curved his beautiful mouth made a trickle of ice slither down her spine.

'We were lovers,' he said smoothly. So smoothly that she couldn't interrupt him, no matter how she might want to refute his words. He had never been her lover, except in the physical sense. 'Long lost lovers who had never forgotten each other, still cared for each other. Still lov—'

'No!' That was too much. How could he even use the word 'love' after all that had gone on?

'Yes!'

He tightened his grip on her hand when she would have jerked away.

'That is the only way it will work—for Adnan's sake. Damn it, woman, you were prepared to marry him; you would have taken everything he was offering—surely you can do this for him now.'

Imogen wanted to deny what Raoul was saying. But she knew she couldn't do any such thing. She couldn't even refute what he was accusing her of doing, though not in the way he meant it. He made her pact with Adnan sound dark and materialistic. A greedy contract based on money and profit only. He knew nothing about the way her ex-fiancé had felt about his grandfather, the way she had wanted to help him fulfil the old man's dreams.

Nor did he know anything about the broken heart that had driven her into that agreement with the man who had once been her best friend. And he never would.

'This way, he'll be a man of honour, doing what was right. He'll be seen as standing aside to let two soul mates—'

'*Soul mates!*' The words choked her, burning in her throat. 'Never! We're whatever the opposite is…'

She couldn't finish the sentence in the face of his slow nod, the sardonic twist to his mouth.

'*You* might know that—*we* might know that—but for this to work the world has to believe in those soul mates. And so does Adnan. For the devil's sake, Imogen—give the man back his honour.'

So he acknowledged that Adnan had gone into this for honourable reasons—but not her? Of course not; he believed that all she was after was the money—just as he'd decided that had been her motive with him. But at least this way she could give something back to her friend, for what he had been prepared to do to help her. She owed him that at least.

And maybe that way Ciara too would no longer be so angry at what she obviously now saw as a dark lie she found so hard to forgive. Something tugged at her brain, a thought of Ciara meeting Adnan. Worried about the story she had had to spin to her sister, was it possible that she had failed to interpret their feelings for each other properly? But now, if Adnan was free...

'All right. If that's the way you want to spin it.'

It wasn't so terribly far from the truth, was it? She had fallen madly in love with Raoul when she had first met him. She'd been carrying a torch for that love for years. She might have thought her love for him had been lost when their baby had died, but the truth was that she had never truly let go of it. She had always had the tiny, secret hope that if she had gone back to Corsica and found him, if she had told him about the baby they had created between them, then he would at least have given her a hearing. She'd even allowed herself to dream that one day he might realise she had not been after his money but had loved him with all her heart. She still did, she acknowledged miserably, while all the time the dark, sombre sound of the death knell for her hopes and dreams rang inside her heart.

'You call it a spin?' Raoul had the nerve to look surprised, even a trifle shocked. The man could lie through his teeth and not turn a hair, it seemed. 'It's a win-win situation—surely you can see that?'

Win-win for everyone but her. She could marry Raoul and give him what he wanted, give everyone what they needed—rescue her father, the stud, Adnan, even Ciara. At the very least, her sister would have the family home to stay in—and perhaps a chance with the man her sister had once admitted she'd fallen for since she'd come to Ireland, even if she was determined to keep his name a secret. But she couldn't do a thing for herself.

Except to admit to the weakness of dreading watching Raoul walk away from her again as he had done years ago. She didn't know how she'd survived that separation then, and he had only to reappear in her life for her to realise she couldn't go through it again. If she agreed to his proposal—such as it was—then she could at least give herself the double-edged pleasure of knowing she could live as Raoul's wife, loving him with all her heart. But at the same time, she would have to know that he did not love her and had only married her for the business deal he had cold-bloodedly offered her.

But what other choice did she have? He could ruin everyone, destroy them completely, and still walk away from her. Or she could take the little he was offering and pray that one day she might find a way to make him see how she felt—perhaps even bring him to care for her just a little.

Perhaps one day she could end up loving his child, as she had so longed to do years before.

He admitted that he wanted her more than any other woman in the world. Was that enough for her to face the future that lay before her?

It would have to be.

'OK, then.' She forced herself to say it. 'That's the way it will be.'

Raoul's smile was fast and hard, a mere curl of his lips, bringing no light to his eyes at all.

'I knew you'd see sense.'

He was drawing her towards him as he spoke. No force, but he didn't need force—just a gentle, persistent pull that seemed to make her feet move without her volition, her eyes fill with him, her face lift to his for the kiss she knew was coming. The kiss she wanted. So much. If this was all he had to offer her of himself, then she would take it.

The alternative was nothing at all.

'And what would you get out of it?'

Why couldn't she keep her mouth shut? Why did she have to ask the sort of question that could only land her in even more trouble? She knew what he wanted—*all* he wanted—from her. Why did she have to push him to state it bluntly?

'I told you—I get you. In my bed.'

His head had bent and his mouth was trailing hot kisses all over her face, down the side of her cheek, heading for her mouth. Immediately, all the blood rushed to the surface of her skin, waking every nerve, making her shiver and ache deep inside for the heat of his touch, the demand of his possession. She was swimming on a hot sea of need, finding thought impossible, knowing only the hunger he aroused in her simply by existing.

'Is—is that enough?'

His response was a raw, shaken laughter against the side of her throat, hot breath feathering across the hollow where her pulse beat hard and rapid in response.

'Oh, *ma belle*, what do you think?'

His hands skimmed her body, lingering at the curves of her breasts and hips. His teeth took hold of one of the narrow straps of her sundress, tugging it to the side, away and down her arm.

'But it…'

Was she questioning him or herself? This was what he was offering her. *All* he was offering. But was it enough for a lifetime?

'Damn it, Imogen, stop arguing.' It was a rough mutter against her skin. 'If I say it's enough, then it's enough. After all, Adnan was prepared to go ahead for no more.'

'Adnan…'

Could he feel her tension, the shock that ricocheted through her? Could he read her panic, the way her mind reeled away from letting him know the truth?

'He…'

'He what? What the hell else were you offering Adnan as your husband?'

Raoul's tongue slid over the skin he had exposed, tracing an erotic path over the exposed tops of her breasts, making her sigh in swooning response. She didn't want to talk, she just wanted to give in to the molten sensations that were flooding her body, swamping her brain.

'Adnan wanted an heir…' It escaped without thought, without rational control. 'I promised him an heir.'

The shockwave of his reaction was like an atomic explosion close at hand, rocking her sense of reality. He froze, not even breathing against her neck. His very stillness was so terrifying that she was sent scrabbling through her thoughts, trying to work out what she had said.

It burst on her like an ice shower, cascading over her heated skin and taking all the warmth from it in the space between one heartbeat and the next.

'You promised…?'

Raoul's voice wouldn't work. His throat seemed to have been scratched raw so that words would have to force their way past the scars that filled it. He couldn't swallow, couldn't breathe, couldn't think. All that was inside his head was a white-hot roar of fury, one that was slowly turning to ice as it slid through his veins, freezing his heart.

'An heir.'

At least, that was the way it was supposed to sound. But the way he had to force it out tangled the words up, his accent turning them into something that even he couldn't quite make out. The way Imogen turned, as if to question him, was like a bullet right between the eyes. He couldn't repeat the words; couldn't believe what he was hearing. And yet, deep down, he realised he had known all along. Wasn't this what had brought him here in the first place? An instinctive, unconscious awareness of the only reason why Adnan Al Makthabi would marry at all?

He had wanted to stop the wedding, but he had told himself it was because he couldn't stand by and watch as Imogen got her gold-digging claws into another man. But Adnan was no fool. So why would he have wanted to do it? What could Imogen have promised him in order to win his support?

An heir.

A child.

What else could be worth all that Al Makthabi would have to pay out?

'Raoul...?'

The distance in his withdrawal had communicated itself to Imogen. She knew the reason for it too, if the dawning horror in her eyes was anything to go by.

'Raoul...' she began, her voice in the same condition as his had been.

This was where it began. This was how she was preparing to tell him the truth. She was going to admit what had happened to the child she hadn't even given him a chance to know.

He didn't want to hear it. He didn't want her actually to speak the words.

'No!'

It was sharp, brutal, meant to cut off this topic before it had time to form. He didn't want her to confirm the one thing that could come between them. He wanted to stop this right now, freeze the moment so it couldn't go any further. Before he said something he totally regretted.

'Raoul—we have to talk.'

Imogen felt like she was fighting her way through frozen fog, so thick she couldn't even see Raoul's face, in spite of the fact he was so close. But the ice she took in with each breath told her that he was there and that he had changed from the second she had said that one word.

An *heir*.

'Nothing to talk about.'

Something of the mist had thinned so she could see his expression, and deep down she wished that she'd stayed frozen and blind. There was nothing to help her in the opaque blankness of his eyes, the way his mouth was clamped tight into a thin, hard line.

'Of course there is.'

The shake of his head was adamant, but far worse was the way that he had turned from her, snatching up the shoes that had been discarded on the floor—a lifetime ago, it seemed—and pulling them on with brutal efficiency, his silence shocking after all that had been between them.

What had happened to the ardent, passionate lover? The man who had taken her to the stars and held her as she splintered into a thousand tiny pieces under him? Where was the man who, however unemotionally, had said they should marry?

Did that 'proposal' still hold now? Was she a fool to fear that what she'd said changed everything? That Raoul had no intention of marrying her, even in the businesslike way he had suggested?

He was fully dressed now, shirt buttoned up with frightening precision, belt tightened around his narrow waist. But it was not the clothing or the move away from her that emphasised the distance between them. That was stamped onto his face, etched around his nose and eyes.

'I understand,' she managed. 'If…if you don't want a child.'

Now what had she done to bring his head up like that, the blaze of his eyes threatening to shrivel her where she stood?

'Not want a child?' It hissed in between clenched teeth. 'Of course I want a child.'

Was it relief or lack of understanding that made her head swim? Or was it the unravelling of bitter memories twisting out from under the mental rocks she had tried to pile on top of them, demanding to be heard?

'I want *my* child.'

It was the tiniest emphasis on that word that told her all she needed to know.

Raoul knew. Somehow he had found out what had happened and he knew all about the secret she had tried to keep hidden. He knew about the baby. Dark tendrils of grief were tangling round her heart, making it impossible to think straight, to find any way to answer him.

'*Our* child,' she hedged.

It did nothing to lighten the glazed darkness in those stunning eyes. There was no easing of the tension in any muscle.

'You can't just demand—'

'Why not?' Dark, brutal, savage. 'You were prepared to have one with Adnan.'

But that had been so much easier. She had cared about Adnan and she would have loved the child. Adnan's child wouldn't have come trailing such memories, complications, such unhappiness and loss. She had known that baby would have been wanted and Adnan would have loved his son or daughter.

'Adnan—Adnan is a friend.'

'We were more than friends.'

'We were not! I fancied you like hell—couldn't keep away from you—but how could we even be friends? I didn't even like you—I still don't!'

Not now. Not when he was this aggressive, this dangerous. How could she like him like this? This was the man who had turned away from her. Who had told her to get out of his life. Who had left her alone with the baby that had never had a chance.

'You would have given Adnan a child. So you would have kept *his* baby if you'd conceived it?'

He was throwing words at her, tossing them at her with such ferocity and speed that they didn't make sense. But there was something else in his voice, a ragged edge to the words that shocked her rigid.

'Would you have kept it for him, or would you have got rid of it like you did mine?'

Got rid? He couldn't think…

'Adnan had promised his grandfather.'

'Don't talk to me about Adnan! This isn't about him—it's about us. About you and me and our child. I wanted that child. I still want it. Our baby. You *owe* me a child!'

CHAPTER TWELVE

How long had the silence dragged on? Was it just minutes since Raoul had thrown those words at her or was it hours?

There was something wrong with her heart. Something wrong with her brain. She couldn't quite absorb the meaning of those hateful words. And yet there was only one possible meaning. Wasn't there?

'You want—' The word swelled up inside her, blocking her throat and choking her.

'The child we should have had.' He sounded no better than she did. 'And when we're married—'

'When we're married? You think I will marry you now—after this?'

Somehow, from deep inside, she'd found a new strength. She didn't know if it came from pain or anger or loss—but she welcomed it as it gave her the courage to speak the truth at last.

'You want me to agree to your terms? You want the stud—and the horses—and a child… Why? You want an heir? Is that it? Why with me?'

'The only person I would ever have wanted a child with was you.'

'Well, that's a pity for you.'

Strength was growing inside her, giving a force to

her words that he clearly wasn't expecting. But no, of course he wasn't expecting her to defend herself, to fight back against his accusations. He'd thought she was this callous, careless, selfish creature—for how long? For the two years they'd been apart?

But what did it matter how long? What mattered was what he believed and how wrong he was. And she was going to throw it right in his face and see the truth hit home.

'Because I can't actually guarantee you that child you claim you want. The one you've planned all this payback to bring about. Because, you see, it could be tricky. Adnan knew that but he understood.'

'Understood what?' Raoul demanded when she had paused to gather her strength.

'He understood that it could be a problem because… because it can be difficult to conceive again if you've had…had…'

She lost the words. She could feel the burn of hot tears cascading down her face, taste the salt on them as she had to force her mouth wide open, gasping for the breath that eluded her. Her arms were clasped tight around her middle, holding herself together because she could not afford to fall apart now.

'What? Say the word!'

'Had an ectopic pregnancy.' He looked as if he'd been slapped hard, right across his face. She could almost see the bruise forming as he blinked, tried to speak, stopped, tried again.

'Ectopic…' was all he managed.

At last she succumbed to the sorrow she had tried to hold back for two long years. The fragile, desperate wall she had built around her memories had crumbled at last and she was lost, head bent, face hidden. She'd held out so long, but she couldn't manage any more. Her legs sagged at the knees, refusing to support her. She was going to fall.

But then arms came around her, warm and powerful. She was supported, held against the hard strength of a masculine chest. She could feel his raw, ragged breathing under her cheek, hear the uneven thunder of a pulse that was as out of control as her own.

'It's all right.'

Raoul's whisper was right next to her ear, the hard pressure of his cheek, the weight of his head on her hair. One hand cupped her face, the other stroked over her skull, soothing her tears.

'It's all right.'

But it would never be all right ever again. Her baby was gone and the fact that Raoul had believed she had got rid of it just made the tears flow faster. She had lost her child—and obviously she had lost its father at the same time. She'd lost him, lost everything.

'It's all right, I've got you. I've got you, Imogen. I'll not let you fall.'

If he said anything else then she couldn't hear it as she abandoned herself to a fury of weeping, unable to hold back any longer. Two years' worth of stored up tears soaked into his shirt, plastering the linen against his skin as she clung onto his arms, feeling the powerful muscles bunch and clench under her fingertips. She swayed against him, felt his long body adjust to take her weight, strong in support.

Then it was as if the world had given way as Raoul's long legs seemed to buckle beneath him. He sank to the floor, taking her with him. Still blinded by tears, by having her face pressed into his shirt, she found herself sitting curled onto his lap, held until the storm of misery gradually slowed, eased, came to a raw, hic-cupping stop. Sniffing inelegantly, she managed to lift her head, staring in shock at the mess of black mascara and tear stains marking the white linen.

'I'm sorry,' she said.

'No.' His low, husky assurance sounded worse than she felt. '*I'm* sorry. More sorry than I can ever tell you. I should have known…never have believed…'

But he did believe *her*. That was the one thing that registered. He had never doubted or questioned her dec-laration that she had lost the baby because it had been an ectopic pregnancy. This couldn't heal the bitter memo-ries—ease the terrible pain, both physical and mental, that she had endured—but it smoothed a balm over the wounds and gave her a new strength. The sort she hadn't known for years.

'I should have trusted… But then I saw that photo-graph.'

That brought Imogen's head up sharply. She had known the picture of herself and Ciara after their long-awaited reunion had been published in some of the gos-sip pages, but she had never thought that any of it would be read by Raoul in Corsica.

'It was after… Ciara was helping me.'

'I know.'

If his mouth had been any further from her ear then she would never have caught that low whisper, but it was enough to have her lifting her moisture-smeared face, finding the courage to look into his eyes.

The dampness from her own tears marked his cheeks, running into his rough stubble. Or was it? Blinking to bring him into focus, she could see the moisture that glis-tened on his thick, black eyelashes, spiking them against eyes that had a suspiciously bright sheen across them.

'Raoul…' At last she had found her voice as she lifted a shaking hand to touch his cheek, his eyes, her heart clenching as her fingers came away wet. 'You believe me?'

'Of course I believe you. You would never lie about something like this. I should have known. And yet when I came—'

He caught, snapping off the sentence as he shook his head. But Imogen needed no further explanation.

'That was when you first came to Ireland?'

A slow, sombre nod of his dark head was his answer.

'I saw you with Adnan.'

Admit it, Raoul told himself, *the jealousy that had burned at the sight of her with the other man—laughing, smiling up into his face—had bitten hard. So hard it had stopped him thinking rationally.*

'I was wrong. So badly wrong. I let the past embitter me. You are no Alice. Or any of the others…'

For a moment, he closed his eyes against the memories. The time he had learned how Alice, tiring of his father's more mature interests, had turned her back on both of them, later aborting the child she had conceived with her new lover in order to live the carefree life with the much younger man.

'I understand.'

'Then you are wrong to.' His voice was rough-edged, dark. 'I don't deserve your understanding.'

With a gentleness that was so much at odds with the grimness of his words, he reached out and wiped the back of his fingers across her cheeks, taking the traces of her tears with them. For one long moment he looked deep into her eyes and a tiny suggestion of a smile played at the corners of his mouth.

'I believed the stories I was told—not once but twice.

I believed the worst when I should have believed the best. I came here to ruin your wedding.'

'But that wasn't actually your fault. If Adnan hadn't come back with Ciara and my father, that scene in your bedroom would never have happened,' Imogen hastened to assure him, but the words had exactly the opposite effect.

'Not the way it happened,' Raoul forced himself to admit. 'But it would have happened. I would have made it happen. I was wrong.'

It was only when he felt Imogen's hand reach up again, one finger outstretched to touch against the corner of his eye and come away with a drop of water resting on its tip, that he knew he had not been able to hide his reactions. But he didn't care. It was what he owed Imogen for the way he'd betrayed her, what he owed the memory of their child that had never had a chance to live. And had almost taken Imogen's life with it.

'But if I can forgive you?' Her voice was soft and so were her eyes, her hand still resting against his cheek, delicate and gentle.

If only she knew what it cost him not to turn his head, to press his lips against her hand. She was warm and soft in his arms, pure temptation, the scent of her skin coiling round him, making his head spin in desire. But that had led him astray before. He could not go down that path again. Not if he wanted to try to appease his conscience and give back to this woman everything he owed her.

'Forgive? *Oh, ma belle...*'

Reluctantly he eased himself into a more comfortable position, pushing his arms underneath her, between their bodies, lifting her from his lap. He felt the cold rush of air like a loss as he moved away from her, taking her upwards, adjusting his stance until he was fully upright, holding her above the bed. He hesitated a long moment, fighting the urge to let his grip tighten round her and draw her close up against his yearning body.

Then at last, unwillingly, he lowered her to the surface of the bed, depositing her softly on the rumpled covers. For a moment, she lay down, her arms still holding him, coming dangerously close to drawing him down alongside her, but he could not let that happen. Putting all the determination he possessed into resisting the demand of his hungry senses, he pulled back and away from her. But he couldn't fight the impulse to drop one last lingering kiss on her upturned face.

'You might be able to forgive, but I cannot. I can never forgive myself for this. For the damage I have done.'

'But, Raoul!'

Imogen couldn't bear the way that the atmosphere had changed. The moments of empathy, the tears they had shared over the loss of their baby, were evaporating all around them. He was moving further and further away from her with every breath she took and the glaze of sorrow in his eyes was like a warning not to try to bridge the chasm that had opened up between them.

'Non, chérie,' he told her, holding up his hands like a barrier between them as each step backwards took him further away. But the real desperation was what she could read in his face, and that was what kept her frozen in her place, unable to move or to speak. 'I betrayed you.'

'You…'

She wanted to say it but no sound would come. And even if it had she knew he wouldn't listen. So she tried a shake of her head, and saw his slow, dejected smile.

'Oh, yes—not so much here, perhaps.'

One long-fingered hand touched his brow, pressing just for a moment as if he could wipe away a memory.

'But here.'

That hand flattened hard against his chest, where his heart was. It was the way the pressure of the gesture turned his knuckles white that told her she had lost. She could fight so many things, but not the way Raoul's own conscience was turned against her.

'Let me do this, Imogen,' he said, almost at the door. 'Your future is secure—I promise you that. Whatever you would have gained from our marriage of convenience, it is yours. No strings, no conditions—my gift to you. But let me go. Let me set you free.'

'I…'

Once more she tried to speak, closing her eyes as she forced the words from her numb and unresponsive lips.

'I don't want my freedom—not from you!'

But as she flung the words out, opening her eyes to see the effect they had had, she found she was speaking to the empty air. Raoul had already gone and she was alone.

In an urgent scramble, she pushed herself from the bed and dashed to the door, stumbling over a ragged edge of the carpet as she made her way out into the corridor. The trip and the time needed to recover from it was enough to hold her back for a moment too long. She had barely recovered when she heard the slam of a car door, the roar of an engine.

By the time she got to the front door, all that was visible were the tail lights on Raoul's car disappearing down the drive and out of sight.

CHAPTER THIRTEEN

SO *THIS* WAS where Raoul really lived!

Imogen got out of her car and leaned against the bonnet, staring in total amazement at the wonderful building before her. If she had needed any evidence of the fact that the real Raoul was light years away from the olive farmer she'd thought him, then this was it. Nothing could be further from the simple hotel where they'd shared those passionate nights; the plain inns and restaurants where they'd eaten; the clear blue bays in which they'd swum.

One of those bays, the Gulf of Liscia, stretched out now on the other side of the road, below the steep drop of the cliffs, while behind villa San Francescu the acres of olive trees stretched away into the distance. The villa itself was a fusion of ancient and modern, with the original stonework blended with contemporary touches, like big glass doors to let the sun flood in from all sides.

Over to one side of the sprawling building was a large paddock where several horses, the sturdy bay Corsicans that Raoul bred, contentedly cropped the grass. But Imogen spared the animals only the briefest of glimpses as she made her way across the stone path to rap at the main door.

She had thought she would have some warning of

Raoul's approach; that she would see him through the glass in the door or at least catch the sound of his footsteps approaching. But her attention was fixed on the interior of the villa so she missed the silent man who appeared around the corner of the house until he was only inches away from her.

'Imogen.'

The sound of her name spoken in that special way brought her spinning round, her hair flying about her head and catching across her face so she had to tug it away to be able to see properly.

At first he was just a dark silhouette against the brilliant sky, a tall, powerful frame with narrow hips and long, long legs. In a worn black tee-shirt and ragged, cut-off jeans, he appeared much the farmer she had first taken him for, the man she had given her heart to all those years ago. Only the luxury and expanse of his surroundings gave any clue to the power and the wealth that were so much a part of the real Raoul Cardini she now knew. But it was the way her heart leapt and twisted, all in one moment, that left her in no doubt that, whoever he was, whatever his circumstances, Raoul was the man she loved. Totally, without reservation or hesitation.

'Hello, Raoul.'

It was inane, but it was all she could manage. She had spent the length of the journey here thinking and planning, trying to work out just what she would say to him in the moment she saw him; how she would persuade him to listen to why she was here. And how she would convince him that the message she brought was the truth and nothing else.

But one look into his beloved face, one moment of recognition, and every thought fled her mind. All she could manage was, 'Hello, Raoul…' and the hastily swallowed declaration that she was here because she loved him. Because she couldn't be anywhere else and be happy.

'I've missed you.'

Understatement of the year. Was it really only five days since he had walked out of the house at Blacklands, driving away into the cool, pink dawn, heading for the airport and this beautiful villa that was his island home?

Only five days, but he looked as if he had aged in that time. Strain or tiredness…or would she be a fool to hope that the same sort of sorrow and sense of loss that had plagued her had also stolen his sleep at night? He had dark shadows under those spectacular eyes and his hard jaw was shadowed with a growth of stubble that indicated he hadn't taken the time and trouble to shave for a day or more.

'I would have been here earlier but there was an accident.'

'Not you? Your sister?'

The sharpness of his voice gave her room to hope.

'No, not me. And not Ciara either. I still don't know where she is—or Adnan. She rang me again, just once. Said she and Adnan were fine—but they wanted to be by themselves for a while. I had to promise not to try and find them—or let anyone else do it. No, my father had a fall from Blackjack, and we had to get him to hospital. He broke his leg—but he's doing well now.'

'So why aren't you there with him?'

'He told me to come, and I had to talk to you anyway. We can't go on as things are.'

'We can't? I thought things were exactly as you wanted them.'

There was no warmth in his response, no light in

those beautiful eyes. Had she got this all wrong? Had she misread him? The memory of that gesture of his hand from his head to his heart had been playing on a loop inside her thoughts over and over again, ever since the morning he'd declared he couldn't forgive himself.

'It's not how I want things. Look—do we have to do this out here? Couldn't we go inside and talk?'

'Of course.'

Stiff-backed, stiff-faced, he strode past her towards the door, pushing it open and holding it so she could precede him. Was she imagining things or was he holding himself just that little bit too far away, making sure no part of her body touched him as she stepped into the cool, tiled hallway? After the sun outside, the interior seemed dark and she had to stand, blinking, as her eyes adjusted to the change in light. Behind her she heard Raoul come inside too and stand so close that she could feel the warmth of his breath on her neck.

'I've missed you too,' he said, low, rough and totally unexpected.

'What?'

Imogen spun round, her hair swinging out again, catching on the rough stubble on his chin. It was the look in his eyes that caught and held her as his hand went up to free the shiny black strands. It was only when she had to take in a long, deep breath, and then another, that Imogen realised he was taking far too long about it, his fingers lingering, reluctant to let go.

'Raoul…'

His head snapped up, the mouth that had softened, lips parting, clamping tightly shut again.

'I'm forgetting my manners. Would you like a drink? Some coffee—or perhaps water?'

'To hell with your manners!'

She couldn't hold it back and knew from the stunned blink that the force of her response had shocked him.

'That isn't what I came here for!'

'Then why are you here?'

He'd made a mistake with that admission of missing her, Raoul acknowledged to himself. It was stupid and totally inappropriate after the efforts he'd made to free her from the relationship that he'd made such a mess of. But he hadn't been able to hold it back. In the moment that she'd walked past him and he'd caught the soft scent of her skin, mixed with a delicate floral perfume that the warmth of the sun had brought to the surface, he had felt every cell in his body awaken to the intoxication of her presence and the revival of the memories he'd been struggling to put aside. They were the images that had haunted his thoughts, tormented his body, every night as he'd tried to settle to sleep. In the end, he had given in and gone out to the stables, saddled one of the horses and ridden through the darkness of the night until both he and the stallion were slow with tiredness and his eyes were closing even as he headed home.

But, once back inside the house in his bed, even the exhaustion had failed to claim him. He'd lain, staring up at the darkness of the sky, fighting an ugly battle with the images of Imogen as he had last seen her playing across his mind, tormenting his body into further restlessness.

The Imogen who had turned up so unexpectedly at his door could have been the girl he had met two years before. The loose waves of her dark hair gleamed in the sunlight, and the soft cotton of her simple blue dress was so much like the sundresses she had worn before that just for a moment he'd actually let himself think that he was back in that time. Back in the days when their relationship had been new and fresh, and he'd had hopes of a future.

'Imogen, tell me what's brought you here.'

'I came here to bring you this.'

As their words clashed in the air, slowly Raoul realised that Imogen was holding up a briefcase, pushing it towards him as if she wanted him to take it.

'What is it?'

'There's no need to look at it as if it's a snake about to bite you!'

There was a shaken edge of laughter in Imogen's voice.

'It's just paper.'

'Paper?'

He didn't understand or believe that, Imogen knew. It was stamped all over his face. And the way he eyed the briefcase tugged on something in her heart, so she couldn't drag this out any further.

'These came on Monday.'

Snapping open the briefcase, she pulled out the sheaf of papers it contained and waved it in front of him.

'From you.'

Could his eyes look any more blank or his face show any less expression? That was what gave him away to her, telling her without words just how hard he was fighting not to reveal anything.

'Yes. I wanted you to have them.'

Then when she caught her breath in an effort not to break down, to tell him what she really felt, his eyes flashed to her face and she saw the burn of intense emotion flaring in their golden depths.

'I told you I would make everything all right. I promised,' he said.

'You promised.' Slow and careful, it revealed the

battle she was having for control of herself. 'You promised—but you didn't ask if it was what I wanted.'

'Imogen, it was what I owed you. What you would have had if you'd married Adnan—what I took from you.'

'No.'

She saw the swift dark frown, the burn of anxiety on his face, and it almost destroyed her. But she'd started on this now; there was no going back. And this was the only way to show him the truth. To show him how she felt.

'No, Raoul, you took nothing from me.'

'I did.' It was raw and ragged, his hand coming up in a gesture of surrender. 'Everything I did was wrong. I ruined your wedding plans, I behaved like a monster and I destroyed the future of the stud—your father's freedom. If you'd married Adnan...'

'But the truth is that I could never—*would* never—have married him,' Imogen admitted, knowing there was no way forward but the truth. 'Even if you hadn't turned up, I could never have gone through with it. I knew that. I was thinking it already in the church, that day you found me. And then when I saw you there—well, nothing was the same after that. I don't know what I would have done, what I could have done, but, once I remembered that you were in the world, how could I ever marry another man?'

'But...' It was just a croak of sound, of disbelief.

'Yes, I know. There was everything Adnan had promised me—and everything I'd promised him. But how could I go through with that? How could I marry him, have his baby, when the only child I ever wanted was the one we made between us? The one that...'

'*Oh, mon Dieu!*'

Raoul was moving forward, enfolding her in his arms, holding her tightly. The briefcase fell to the floor and the papers she still held were crushed between them.

'Imogen—I wish I'd known.' The thickness of his tone told her of the emotion that clogged his throat, and the rough, unsteady pulse of his heart underneath her cheek revealed the struggle he was having for any degree of composure.

'I wish I had known. I wish I could have done something.'

'There was nothing anyone could have done.' It was barely a whisper, buried in the protective cave of his arms, but she knew he had heard it when she felt the heavy, raw intake of his breath and the sorrowful nod of his head in acknowledgement.

'But I could at least have been there.'

'And how I wish you had been. We both lost so much that day.'

'Because I listened to the wrong person,' Raoul admitted, the words rasping desperately.

'You'd been hurt—badly. I never realised quite how badly until I came here and saw…'

From under his arms her hand waved unsteadily, taking in the luxurious surroundings, the huge estate beyond the glass doors. 'It must be so hard to know whether someone wants you for you—or for…' Her voice sank even lower. 'Or for this.'

Slowly, carefully, she eased from his grasp, lifting her head so she could look into his eyes and meet that questioning gaze head-on.

'That's why I had to bring this back to you.'

Raoul's burning eyes went down to the documents she held. The legal forms that sorted out the whole sorry mess that she and her father had been. Financial provision for the stud, the stallion Blackjack and the small fortune needed to pay her father's debts, and keep them solvent for many years to come.

'I can't take it, Raoul—I don't want it.'

'But how will you manage if you don't? I *wanted* to give it to you. I wanted you to have it. I wanted to try to repay all the wrong that I'd done you. The way I rejected you. It will never be enough...'

'No,' Imogen agreed and she saw the way that shock landed like a blow on his face, bringing his head up high and sharp. 'No, this is not enough, Raoul.' She smiled sadly. 'And it will never be.'

'Then what else do you need? How can I make sure that you're happy going forward? How can I give you everything you need?'

'You can't.'

'But I will. I'll try. Just ask and—' he began, but she reached up a hand to lay it across his mouth, closing his lips, silencing him.

'There isn't enough money in the world to give me everything I need,' she told him, turning her hands so she was holding onto his arms, feeling the warmth of his skin, the strength of powerful muscle even through the papers she still held. 'Because money won't do it. Money can never do that.'

She knew her words had hit home when she felt his total stillness, the tension that held his muscles taut, his long body pressed against hers.

'You don't want...'

It was as if he was exploring his thoughts, and trying to discover hers, finding his way slowly through a mass of confusions; travelling blind, as if he was afraid to find that the truth he'd thought he was aiming for was in fact something entirely different. And it was that hesitancy that made her heart swell with the thought that she'd judged him right and he really understood.

'I don't want anything that money can buy,' she assured him. 'How can that give me everything I need when what I need…'

At this last moment her nerve almost failed her and she had to snatch in a hard, strengthening breath in order to be able to continue.

But when she looked into his face, and saw the beginning of hope start to flare in the depths of his eyes, she knew she'd made the right move, staked all her future on the right hope. The answer to what she needed was right here in front of her.

'You said you wanted to make sure that I'm happy going forward. And the truth is that the only way I can be happy going forward is if you go forward with me.'

'You want me?' It was just a breath.

'I want you.' His faintness made her strong and the declaration was brave and bold, joy spreading along every vein, every nerve, bringing a brilliant, assured smile to her face.

'I want you. And only you. I love you, Raoul. You are my future—the only life I want is with you.'

'And me with you.'

Raoul rubbed a hand across his eyes, blinking hard as he focused on her uplifted, intent face.

'Is it possible? Can we really try again? Begin afresh? Can we have a future?'

Imogen felt her lips curve into the smile that was growing inside her heart.

'Why not try?'

She hadn't even finished speaking before he was down on one knee before her, holding her hand tight, looking up into her face with an expression that spoke of a near-desperate hope, a longing to get this right.

'Imogen, will you do me the real honour of being my beloved wife? For today, tomorrow, our future? Our life?'

'I will. Oh, Raoul, yes, I will—but...'

She'd shocked him now and she saw the hope leave his eyes and darken his face, so she had to hurry to reassure him.

'But I can't promise a baby.'

'Sweetheart...'

He was on his feet in a moment, holding her close.

'My darling—you are the only person I ever want a child with, and if it happens, then I will be the happiest man in the world. But, if it's not to be, then you are still the only woman I want to have as my wife, to go into the future with.'

His lips came down on hers, crushing back all the fears, erasing all the doubts and replacing them with hope and happiness.

'You are my love, my life,' he said when at last he had to lift his head to snatch in a much-needed breath. 'And together we can create a world worth living in.'

'Our world,' Imogen echoed, soft and sure. 'Our world—together.'

* * * * *

MILLS & BOON

Coming soon

BOUND TO THE
SICILIAN'S BED
Sharon Kendrick

Rocco was going to kiss her and after everything she'd just said, Nicole knew she needed to stop him. But suddenly she found herself governed by a much deeper need than preserving her sanity, or her pride. A need and a hunger which swept over her with the speed of a bush fire. As Rocco's shadowed face lowered towards her she found past and present fusing, so that for a disconcerting moment she forgot everything except the urgent hunger in her body. Because hadn't her Sicilian husband always been able to do this—to captivate her with the lightest touch and to tantalise her with that smouldering look of promise? And hadn't there been many nights since they'd separated when she'd woken up, still half fuddled with sleep, and found herself yearning for the taste of his lips on hers just one more time? And now she had it.

One more time.

She opened her mouth—though afterwards she would try to convince herself she'd been intending to resist him— but Rocco used the opportunity to fasten his mouth over hers in the most perfects of fits. And Nicole felt instantly helpless—caught up in the powerful snare of a sexual mastery which wiped out everything else. She gave a gasp of pleasure because it had been so long since she had done this.

Since they'd been apart Nicole had felt like a living statue—as if she were made from marble—as if the flesh and blood part of her were some kind of half-forgotten dream. Slowly but surely she had withdrawn from the sensual side of her nature, until she'd convinced herself she was dead and unfeeling inside. But here came Rocco to wake her dormant sexuality with nothing more than a single kiss. It was like some stupid fairy story. It was scary and powerful. She didn't *want* to want him, and yet . . .

She wanted him.

Her lips opened wider as his tongue slid inside her mouth—eagerly granting him that intimacy as if preparing the way for another. She began to shiver as his hands started to explore her—rediscovering her body with an impatient hunger, as if it were the first time he'd ever touched her.

'Nicole,' he said unevenly and she'd never heard him say her name like that before.

Her arms were locked behind his neck as again he circled his hips in unmistakable invitation and, somewhere in the back of her mind, Nicole could hear the small voice of reason imploring her to take control of the situation. It was urging her to pull back from him and call a halt to what they were doing. But once again she ignored it. Against the powerful tide of passion, that little voice was drowned out and she allowed pleasure to shimmer over her skin.

Continue reading
BOUND TO THE SICILIAN'S BED
Sharon Kendrick

Available next month
www.millsandboon.co.uk

LET'S TALK

Romance

For exclusive extracts, competitions
and special offers, find us online:

 facebook.com/millsandboon

:camera: @millsandboonuk

:bird: @millsandboon

Or get in touch on 0844 844 1351*

For all the latest titles coming soon, visit
millsandboon.co.uk/nextmonth

*Calls cost 7p per minute plus your phone company's price per minute access charge